DEVICES & DESIRES

The Lyons Pride~Book One

PAMELA SHERWOOD

BCP
BLUE CASTLE
PUBLISHING

Published by Blue Castle Publishing

Trade paperback edition/February 2016

Mass-market edition/November 2019

Cover design by Kim Killion

Photograph © Nata Sdobnikova | Shutterstock.com | Image ID: 98187404

ISBN: 978-1-945112-03-4

*To James Goldman, Peter O'Toole, Katharine Hepburn,
Anthony Hopkins, John Castle, Nigel Terry, Timothy Dalton,
and Jane Merrow—*

BECAUSE

Love doth approach disguis'd,
Armed in arguments...
—WILLIAM SHAKESPEARE, *LOVE'S
LABOUR'S LOST*

Prologue

Heap on more wood!—the wind is chill;
But let it whistle as it will,
We'll keep our Christmas merry still.
—Sir Walter Scott, *Marmion*

Yorkshire, December 1880

"Good God, are your brothers *still* arguing?" Sir Anthony Stirling demanded of his godson. "That billiards match was more than two hours ago!"

"That makes no difference, unfortunately," Lord Gervase Lyons replied. "You've heard of fellows who don't know when they're beaten? Well, that's Hal. And then there's Reg, who never knows when he's won. They'll be arguing every stroke until the Last Trump has sounded—or until my lady mother has found other employment for them."

"The latter appears a distinct possibility. I believe she intends to have them oversee the raising and decoration of the Christmas tree."

"On which they will no doubt argue the placement of every ornament and strand of tinsel," Gervase said dryly. "Having no desire to subject myself to that, I thought it best to retire to the library with you before Mother enlisted my services as well."

"Very politic of you," Sir Anthony remarked. "And it will give us some time to discuss your future in private, will it not?"

Gervase smiled. "I knew I liked you best of all my godfathers, sir."

Sir Anthony raised an eyebrow. "As I am your *only* godfather, that compliment holds rather less water than it might, my boy!"

Gervase's smile broadened into a grin. They understood each other very well, he and Sir Anthony, and always had. "But enough, I hope, to grant me a full hearing?"

For answer, his godfather sank down upon one of the padded leather armchairs by the fire, gesturing to Gervase to take the one opposite. "So, how old are you now —twenty?"

"Twenty in September, sir."

"And flourishing at Oxford?"

"My tutor believes so, yes." Indeed, Gervase's tutor cherished hopes that he'd earn a First next year, when Final Schools were held. Gervase himself did rather more than hope: First-class honors were firmly in his sights, and barring an unforeseen disaster, he meant to have them.

"And your father is no closer to making a clergyman of you than he was two years ago?"

Gervase shuddered. "God forbid, sir—if you'll pardon the expression!"

"Consider it pardoned." Sir Anthony's shrewd grey eyes regarded him appraisingly. "Well, then, I assume you have another plan for your future?" *You wouldn't be your parents' son if you didn't* was the unspoken implication.

"Yes, I mean to study law, actually."

"The law, is it? Well, there's no disgrace in such a career. Indeed, I think you would make a very creditable barrister—and perhaps, in due course, a Queen's Counsel."

"Thank you, sir, but you see—I don't wish to be a *barrister*." Gervase took a breath. "I intend to become a solicitor instead."

"A solicitor?" Sir Anthony's brows rose. "A barrister would be far more prestigious—"

"I'm the son of a duke," Gervase pointed out. "I should think that sufficiently prestigious for anyone. You see, sir, I've thought this through quite thoroughly," he continued in his most persuasive tone. "There may be more... cachet in being a barrister, but a solicitor wields just as much influence—and possibly more power. A barrister, however skilled, must still depend upon a solicitor for employment, especially during the early stages of his career. A barrister must depend upon a solicitor for *payment*—and that, I think, I should find intolerable." He paused, searching Sir Anthony's face. "I trust I need not explain why—to *you,* of all people."

"Indeed." His godfather eyed him intently. "Does your father know of your plans?"

"Not just yet, sir." Gervase's mouth crooked. "I am fortifying myself for just such an event. I expect it to be quite... cataclysmic."

"Very prudent. He's had his plans for you rather set in stone these last five or six years."

"I'm well aware of that." *And if he'd taken as much time to get to know me as he did hatching his precious scheme, perhaps he would have understood why it could never work.* "But I wish to be my own man—not spend my life as the Duke of Whitborough's."

The very thought chilled him. A tame cleric dwelling in his father's living, beneath his father's eye—and thumb—for the rest of his life. It didn't bear thinking of. As the heir, Hal might have to remain close, but Gervase would be damned if he'd follow his brother's example.

"Hmm." Sir Anthony drummed his fingers on the chair's armrest. "If you'll permit me to play devil's advocate for a moment, your father might not be *altogether* displeased to learn of your plans. Especially if you plead your case as articulately as you have for me."

Gervase stifled a sigh. "With respect, sir, unless His Grace can convince himself that this was all *his* idea, I expect him to be very displeased indeed."

"And your mother? Have you apprised her of what you intend?"

"Mother has known since last summer that I won't enter the Church. She is surprisingly calm about it."

"Sensible woman," Sir Anthony approved. "She knows a true vocation when she sees one—or, in your case, *doesn't* see one."

"That could be." It was likewise true, Gervase reflected, that the Duchess of Whitborough tended to be less overbearing than her husband—at least when it came to her younger children. Reg, the heir to her French properties, was her favorite, and she guarded *his* rights jealously.

But that was an old grievance, with which he'd come to terms years ago. It would suffice, for now, that his mother would not oppose his plans. Indeed, she might even support them, if only because she thought it salutary for his father *not* to have his own way all the time!

"You'll need someone to take you on as an apprentice," his godfather mused aloud. "Even with a university degree, you'll have to put in several years as an articled clerk."

Gervase did his best to quell his rising excitement. "I'm not afraid of hard work, sir."

Sir Anthony nodded acknowledgment. "Which is why I hold out every hope of your succeeding in this endeavor. I'll tell you what, my boy—once the New Year begins, I shall ask among my acquaintances if they know of any solicitors who'd be willing to take you on, once you're finished at Oxford."

"Thank you, sir!" Gervase said fervently.

"And when the time comes to speak to your father, I will support you then as well."

Gervase exhaled, almost giddy with relief. "Thank you," he said again. "Truly, sir, I could hardly ask for anything more."

Sir Anthony gave him one of the rare smiles that transformed his rather saturnine face. "You're a likely young man, Gervase. The cleverest in a clever family, I shouldn't wonder. Are you *sure* you don't wish to be a barrister? You argue most eloquently on your own behalf."

Gervase smiled. "Quite certain, sir. But I am flattered that you think me eloquent."

"You should go far, with that tongue and those wits," Sir Anthony predicted, leaning back in his armchair and stifling a yawn. "Pardon me, dear boy! When one gets to be my age, a nap in the afternoon becomes less of an indulgence than a necessity."

"Then I'll leave you to your rest." Gervase rose from his chair. "And thank you again for your support, and for —well, for listening, I suppose."

His godfather smiled, his eyes already closing. "I find it refreshing to talk to someone who knows exactly what he wants. So many young people *don't*, nowadays." He yawned again, sinking deeper into the cushions. "Very far indeed," he murmured, not even stirring as Gervase solicitously draped an afghan over him before stealing from the library.

Easing the door closed behind him, Gervase made his way along the passage, his spirits considerably lighter than before. No doubt there'd be a reckoning when he finally revealed his future plans to his father—the Duke of Whitborough was nothing if not autocratic—but with Sir Anthony's support and his mother's lack of opposition, he stood a good chance of prevailing.

A burst of laughter issued from the Great Hall, further down the passage. Laughter, followed by a snatch of song: "*A-wassail, a-wassail, all over the town—*"

His younger sisters, Elaine and Juliana, the most musical of the family. In spite of his earlier reluctance, Gervase found himself drifting towards the source of that sound. Denforth Castle, *en fête* for the Christmas holidays. For all his cynicism, that was still a sight worth seeing.

The carol broke off amidst more laughter, as his sisters debated the next lines. And Gervase could hear the hum of other conversations now, a medley of different voices, including his mother's rich, throaty contralto and his father's deep, authoritative baritone. Their Graces of Whitborough, presiding over their considerable brood.

Pausing outside the doorway, Gervase peered into the room. From this distance, he could study his family more objectively... like the outsider and observer he so often felt himself to be.

His gaze rested first upon his mother, who never ceased to command with her very presence: Helene de Sevigny-Lyons, regal and still beautiful, in spite of or perhaps even because of the silver threading her black hair like tinsel. Swathed in a crimson velvet cloak—his mother loved rich colors—she stood in the center of the Hall supervising the decoration of their Christmas tree, fully seven feet high this year.

And where Her Grace was, His Grace could not be far away—at least, not at Christmas. The duke and duchess fought as fiercely as they loved, but somehow, that ceased to matter once the snows began to fall. And there was Father, Gervase observed, casual as a country squire in tweeds and riding boots, his tawny hair rumpled and standing on end, striding about to examine the tree from every angle and occasionally countermand his wife's orders. The servants, long accustomed to such dissension, worked stolidly on.

And speaking of dissension, there were his two older brothers, ostentatiously ignoring each other on opposite sides of the tree... though Gervase would have wagered the contents of his library that they were darting hissing asides criticizing each other's handiwork when they thought their parents weren't listening. Young Harold, called "Hal"—his father's heir and namesake—must have got off a particularly stinging rejoinder, to judge from his smug expression... and Reg's fulminating one. But then Hal was one of fortune's darlings, supremely confident of his charms and secure in his position as firstborn.

Insufferably complacent, Reg would have said, jutting out that masterful chin of his. And Gervase might have agreed, had he not found Reg equally insufferable in his way. Aggressive, competitive, determined to prove himself the best at every masculine endeavor... the army should provide sufficient outlet for *his* energies, Gervase mused. Reg would be joining a cavalry regiment in the New Year—a natural choice, as he rode like a centaur.

With something like relief, Gervase sought out his sisters and found them more peaceably engaged at the other end of the Hall, sorting through baskets overflowing with holly, ivy, and mistletoe. Madeline, Hal's twin but dark-haired like their mother, her slim form just beginning to ripen with her impending motherhood, was directing the placement of greenery, while her husband, Hugo, Viscount Saxby, hovered protectively. And there was Elaine, golden and cheerful as a sunbeam, starting up another carol, accompanied by vivacious, flame-haired Juliana, still in the schoolroom but promising to equal her sisters in beauty and charm.

A small dark shadow wandered disconsolately between his elders. Jason, the youngest at almost eleven—and probably feeling his lack of importance very much at this moment. The changeling, Gervase had heard his little brother called, which he privately thought was unfair as the boy's coloring was actually quite similar to their mother's, and as for his height... well, Jason had some growing yet to do, and not everyone could be as tall as Hal or Reg. Gervase was a good two to three inches shorter than they, with grey eyes rather than blue and hair more bronze than gold. Given the choice, he'd have preferred to be dramatically dark like Jason.

There'd be whining in a moment, Gervase suspected, watching the frown developing between the boy's brows, the pout forming on his lips. Or at the very least, a complaint of how bored he was. But before either could take place, the duke strode over to rumple his youngest son's hair, then swept him up—all smiles now—into his arms with easy affection.

He spoiled that boy shamelessly, Gervase thought. But it was Christmas, and what was the harm with a bit of spoiling then? And the duchess had always found dealing with her youngest child difficult—for reasons that none of the family ever openly discussed.

Family... for better and for worse, these people defined him, Gervase realized. Not in his entirety, perhaps, but he would not be the person he was without them. And if he wanted, he could walk right into the room now, and become a part of the scene. Instantly recognized and accepted, as a son of the house should be. And his parents would smile at him, his sisters would invite him to help sort greenery, and his brothers might even take a moment from their ongoing competition to ask his opinion on some Christmas tree-related matter.

He took a step toward that laughing family group— and then stopped dead in his tracks.

She passed before the doorway, her hands full of ivy, their glossy leaves the same color as the dress that clung so delightfully to her newly mature figure: just eighteen and set to make her debut in spring. Richly waving hair the color of ripe chestnuts, velvety brown eyes like a doe's... eyes doubtless fixed on handsome, golden Hal— as was only right, fitting, and proper.

And Gervase found his feet moving, seemingly of their own volition, carrying him past the Hall and towards the staircase leading up to his chamber—and some much-needed privacy. He'd come back later, he told himself. When he felt more confident of his ability to conceal these highly inconvenient and inappropriate yearnings.

Someone who knows what he wants, his godfather had called him. But what good did *that* do, he wondered bleakly, when you had no hope of ever getting it? He mounted the stairs, doing his best to block out the sounds of laughter and song behind him. And *her* voice most of all.

Everyone in the family knew, to some extent, how much Reg coveted the dukedom and Hal's place as firstborn.

No one knew—no one would ever know, if Gervase had anything to say about it—how much *he* coveted Hal's fiancée.

Chapter One

... A man whose blood
Is very snow-broth; one who never feels
The wanton stings and motions of the sense,
But doth rebate and blunt his natural edge
With profits of the mind, study, and fast.
—WILLIAM SHAKESPEARE, *Measure for*
    Measure, I, iv

London, December 1888

THE ATMOSPHERE WAS CONVIVIAL, the food excellent, and the cellar superb—as was only to be expected in a club of the Sherburne's caliber. The perfect place to celebrate a hard-won victory, Gervase reflected with satisfaction. The *Roscoe vs. Armitage* libel case had been particularly challenging, not least because the plaintiff and defendant were bitter former spouses.

He glanced at his companions, his partner John Addison and Peter Townsend, the barrister they'd engaged to represent Miss Armitage, animatedly rehashing the day's proceedings in court. Hearing the name "Stoddard," Gervase permitted himself a thin smile. *He'd* engaged the opposing counsel in the past, until the man's lack of effort had cost the firm an important case last year. Hiring the barrister who'd defeated him then had seemed like poetic justice, especially since Townsend had again routed Stoddard—horse, foot, and artillery. If looks could kill, Gervase suspected that he, Addison, and Townsend would have perished the moment the verdict was returned in their favor.

A good day's work—and another feather in the cap of Lyons and Addison, now one of the top solicitors' firms in London. Well-pleased, Gervase reached for the decanter at his elbow. "More port, gentlemen?"

Townsend shook his head. "No, thank you, my lord. I have an early morning tomorrow, and it's best not to overindulge. But thank you for this excellent dinner."

"Thank *you* for your no less excellent closing argument," Gervase countered. "I am certain it made a significant difference to the outcome."

"More than significant," Addison asserted. "And we hope to work with you again in future, Mr. Townsend."

Flushed with pleasure, the barrister thanked them again and departed, leaving the partners to their port and each other's company.

"A well-spoken young fellow, Townsend," Gervase observed. "He should have a bright future before him."

"Yes, and he had a pleasing manner as well. Sociable." Addison studied Gervase over the rim of his glass. "Do you know, after working with him these past few weeks, I feel I know him better than I know *you*—even after two years' partnership?"

Gervase raised his brows. "You know me well enough to do business with me, surely?"

"You mean, I know you as well as you *allow* me to know you," his partner retorted, his usually mild blue eyes narrowing. "Which is precious little, come to that. You're one of the most self-contained men I've ever met, Lyons. Oysters are forthcoming by comparison."

Gervase shrugged, trying to conceal his discomfort at this unexpected conversational turn. "Perhaps, like an oyster, I would prefer not to disclose any information unless I'm certain of its value?"

"Not every utterance has to be a pearl," Addison countered. "I'm simply saying that you could be more... open with those you consider your intimates. Unless," he added with a faint edge to his tone, "you don't consider that anyone of your acquaintance even *qualifies* as such?"

Gervase's hand tightened about his glass, but he kept his tone level, even allowing a slightly conciliatory note to slip into it. "On the contrary, I regard a number of my acquaintances quite highly—yourself included. I am... simply in the habit of keeping my own counsel, a habit that, you must admit, has benefited our practice. Everyone should play to his own strengths, and as you are the more outgoing of us, I am content to leave the more social aspects of our business to you." A change of subject appeared to be in order, so he resumed smoothly, "So, today marks our last day of business until the New Year. Any special plans for the holidays?"

Addison continued to regard him with that challenging air. "Visiting my family in Cambridgeshire. Just as I've done ever since you've known me."

Gervase winced inwardly. What was wrong with him tonight? He was dropping bricks right, left, and center. Quickly, he adjusted his course. "Naturally—what could be more fitting than spending Christmas in the bosom of one's family? I had just wondered, in light of your recent engagement, if you might be visiting your intended's relations instead."

Addison's expression softened, as it usually did at the mention of the charming Miss Godwin. "Lilias and her parents will be coming to us." He cocked an eyebrow at Gervase. "And I suppose you're off to the south of France, as per usual?"

Gervase inclined his head. "You'd suppose correctly."

"Regular as clockwork. Very fitting." Addison swirled the port remaining in his glass. "You know what they call you, don't you?"

"The Spider? Yes, I'm aware of that." And was secretly amused by it, if truth be told. Spiders were clever, adaptable, persistent, and had a knack for survival, after all.

"No, not that one. They also call you the Clockwork Solicitor."

"Clockwork?" The term surprised him, but he wasn't about to betray that. Instead he favored his partner with a cool stare. "How extraordinary."

"A legal automaton," Addison went on, with an air of deliberate provocation. "The perfect lawyerly device. Hardly requiring food, rest, or companionship. It walks, it talks, it settles estates, it meets with clients, it makes wills—"

"It acquires briefs," Gervase retorted, unexpectedly

stung. "Without which we wouldn't have done nearly as well these last two years!"

He could not see his own expression, but he could hear the snap in his voice—an echo of the snap he'd heard in his father's more times than he could count. Addison recoiled, as though realizing he might have gone too far. "Of course, Lyons, I—I didn't mean to make light of your efforts!" he said hurriedly. "I'm aware we owe much of our success as a firm to them! I merely —that is, I only wished to..." His voice trailed off uncertainly.

To see how far you could go with me, Gervase finished for him. He took a breath, reminding himself that Addison had drunk a bit more than usual tonight. As Sir Anthony had often observed about men in their cups, the wine flowed in and the wit flowed out. And they *were* partners and on amicable terms most of the time. He steered the conversation back to safer waters. "I think we may share equal credit for our success. Now, shall we drink to another year as profitable as this one?"

Relief spread across his partner's face at the reprieve. "Indeed, we shall!" He hastily clinked his glass against Gervase's. "To another banner year at Lyons and Addison!"

Amity restored, they drank the toast.

ALTHOUGH HACKNEYS and hansoms trundled along the thoroughfare, Gervase set off briskly on foot. After all, it wasn't that far from the Sherborne Club to his house— formerly Sir Anthony's—in Half Moon Street. And perhaps the walk would settle his temper.

It rattled him more than he would ever admit—that his temper *needed* settling. He'd learned long ago to cultivate a façade of cool composure, while turning whatever anger he might feel to a more constructive purpose. Tonight the façade had slipped, and he'd found himself perilously close to lashing out—like the duke in one of his rages.

Clockwork. The word had taken him by surprise, but it galled him far more than he'd expected. Was that really how the rest of the world saw him? As a machine?

Wheels, gears, and perhaps a key in his back, to be wound once a day to set him through his lawyerly routine?

A ridiculous conceit! Just because his feelings were well-defended did not mean they did not exist. And he'd reason for maintaining his defenses, did he not?

Arguing with himself, as if he were the barrister he'd refused to be eight years ago... which was even more ridiculous. Impatient, he exhaled, his breath forming a frosty cloud on the air. The sight of it sobered him, reminding him that ice, not fire, had become his ally over the years. And his current surroundings were providing plenty of that, he mused as he turned up the collar of his overcoat. While no snow was falling at present, London in December was invariably grey and chill, with a wind that cut to the bone.

Yorkshire would be still colder at this time of year. So cold it almost hurt to breathe there, so cold that one's face felt frozen after mere moments out of doors. He'd said as much when Addison, making one last attempt to draw him out, had asked if he'd ever considered spending the Christmas holidays with his family instead.

Gervase had regarded him with the polite concern of a doctor confronted with a raving lunatic. "My dear Addison, given the choice between the south of France and Yorkshire in December, which would *you* prefer?"

And as for family, his mother would be in France, where she'd spent the last four Christmases. Her Grace had always complained that Yorkshire was utterly barbarous in winter... although Gervase was well aware that the weather was not the reason she now absented herself from what had been the annual Christmas gathering.

Hal wouldn't be there. Would never be there again. And the thought was startlingly painful, even after five years. Handsome, golden, fortunate Hal, whose luck and life had run out at a fence his horse had failed to clear...

Nothing had been the same after that. How could it have been?

His parents, at the funeral. For the first time Gervase could remember, his mother had actually *looked* older than her husband. And his father's vitality had drained away, leaving him an empty husk, staring hollow-eyed at his son and heir's magnificent coffin. Worst of all, the old constraint had arisen between the duke and duchess again. Each blamed the other—in part, at least —for Hal's tragedy, and they'd been unable to comfort each other as fully as they might.

His sisters had wept openly during the service, and Gervase had found his own eyes stinging. They'd never been close, he and Hal—they were too different for that —but a world without his charming, confident, life-loving eldest brother had been impossible to imagine. Jason had been silent and red-eyed, though at more than twice his age, Hal had been almost a stranger to him. Even Reg had looked pale and stunned, as though lost without his lifelong rival to contend against.

Who could blame any of them for shunning Denforth at Christmas?

They had all tried that first year, barely six months later. Seeking comfort from the familiar rituals, and from each other. And if in the end, the ghosts had proved too powerful to overcome, they'd made the effort all the same.

And now Madeline and Elaine had families, Reg—recently promoted to major—still followed the regiment, and Gervase had his own life in London. Only Juliana and Jason called Denforth Castle home these days, and both were away at university much of the time. While His Grace, Gervase supposed, divided his time among his various properties, doing what best suited him... as he'd always done. If he felt the lack of either wife or children at Christmas, he'd never *said* as much.

Not openly. Not *directly*. Not until last week.

Unbidden, Gervase's thoughts turned to the letter he'd received—written not by his father but by Juliana, who'd become mistress of the household in their mother's protracted absence. A charming letter, all the more so for its sincerity, in which she'd expressed the hope that the family might come together again, perhaps at Christmas? *Remember how lovely things used to be then, Gerry? If only we could recapture that somehow! It might do us all some good, especially Papa and Maman. Would you come, if it could be arranged?*

He'd held off on writing back, letting work serve as an excuse. But he knew his real reason for not responding was his reluctance to disappoint Juliana—a reluctance that *all* the men in their family shared, including His Grace. The youngest Lyons daughter had a brightness to her, an unquenchable spirit that endeared her even to casual acquaintances. Gervase no more wished to shatter her illusions about their family than he'd wished to tell her, years ago, that Father Christmas didn't *really* exist—not as a flesh-and-blood entity!

Except that he could hardly avoid disappointing her in this regard. He hadn't yet booked his passage to France, but he'd already written his mother in anticipation of his visit. And tomorrow, he concluded with an inner sigh, he would have to write to Juliana as well.

Resolved, if regretful, he turned onto Half Moon Street, and felt his spirits lift as his house came into view. Terraced and Georgian, Sir Anthony's former dwelling had a mellow dignity, a bit staid, perhaps, but entirely suitable for a serious man of business. Not for the first time, Gervase silently thanked his late godfather for the generosity that had made his life in London so much easier than it might have been. With a handsome bequest *and* a roof over his head, Gervase could concentrate wholly on his career.

Lengthening his stride, he hurried up the walk, eager to get out of the cold. Farnsworth, his manservant, would have had a fire lit in the library, and while the townhouse had central heating, Gervase had to admit that a fire blazing in the grate was a cheerful sight on a cold December evening. The only thing missing, he mused, would be a cat dozing on the hearth, but Ozymandias—the imperious grey tom he'd inherited along with the house—had succumbed to old age several months ago. Gervase found that he rather missed the tyrannical beast; a house did seem somewhat more... homelike, with a cat in residence. Perhaps he should acquire another one, or even a pair of them, to keep one another company while he was at work.

He let himself in, and Farnsworth was there at once, divesting Gervase of his hat and overcoat with effortless ease.

"A bitter night, my lord. Shall I fetch you a whiskey and soda, to take away the chill?"

Gervase shook his head, pulling off his gloves and relishing the warmth now enveloping him. "No, thank you, Farnsworth. I dined quite well at my club. All I want now are my slippers, a book, and a chair by the fire."

"Ah." Farnsworth paused, a faint frown creasing his forehead. "As to that, my lord, you have a visitor—waiting in the library."

Gervase stifled an oath: there went his quiet evening. "On a night like this? Who?"

"Lady Bellamy, my lord. She said it was a matter of some importance."

His heart stuttered in his chest at the name. "I see." To his relief, his voice betrayed nothing. "I'll go in to her at once."

He strode along the passage toward the leather-furnished, book-lined room that had been Sir Anthony's sanctuary and was now his. But not tonight. Pausing just outside the door, he took a moment and a breath before going in.

The reason he knew he was flesh and not clockwork turned from the fire at his entrance, and smiled a welcome, the lamplight turning her chestnut hair to copper and flame.

Gervase raised his chin and greeted his late brother's former fiancée with what he hoped was perfect composure. "Good evening, Margaret. What a pleasant surprise."

MARGARET'S first thought was that he looked prosperous, his charcoal-grey suit impeccably cut, his linen immaculate. Her second was that he looked... just a little tired, which surprised her. One did not associate ambitious, driven, confident Lord Gervase Lyons with fatigue. He must be working too hard, she thought with a flash of concern that she quickly masked, sensing that it would only irritate him. She smiled instead, and held out her hands to him.

"Good evening, Gervase. I hope you don't mind my stopping by."

He did not return her smile, not exactly—but she thought his eyes warmed at her greeting. "Not at all—it's always a pleasure to see you. I'm merely astonished that anyone with sense would venture out on an evening like this."

"And do you include yourself in that assessment?" she teased.

Now he did smile, the faint, sardonic curve of the lips she remembered vividly from their childhood. "But of course. However, I have the excuse of my profession. The libel case at the Old Bailey was decided today—in our favor."

He'd just begun work on that when she departed London, Margaret remembered. "Congratulations," she said warmly; as hard as Gervase worked and as fiercely as he'd fought to become what he was, he deserved every success that came his way. "I take it you were celebrating, afterwards?"

"Indeed. Addison and I took Mr. Townsend—the barrister—to dinner at our club." He made his way toward her now, taking her still-outstretched hands in a light, brief clasp. "A most convivial evening."

"Gracious, how cold your hands are!" Margaret exclaimed, releasing them almost at once. "Haven't you any gloves? Here—come closer to the fire, before you take a chill."

He arched an eyebrow at her, but complied, holding his hands out to the blaze. "Thank you for your concern, but have you ever known me to be ill?"

"Not seriously, no," she conceded. "But it *is* bitterly cold, outside." And his clothes smelled of winter, holding the sharp, almost metallic tang she associated with the onset of snow. "London is always miserable in December."

"Much nicer in—Somerset, was it? I trust the wedding went off well?"

"Beautifully," she assured him. "Not a cloud in the sky that day! And Cordelia made a lovely bride. I know Mr. Norwood will be a good husband to her. As good as—"

"As Bellamy was to you," Gervase finished levelly.

The memory of Alex brought a twinge of pain, a bittersweet ache about her heart. But it was no longer the stabbing agony of nearly two years ago. "Yes," she said on a sigh. "As he was to me. And I know he'd have wanted his sister to know the same kind of happiness that we did."

Resting one arm upon the mantel, Gervase stared into the fire. "Miss Bellamy was fortunate indeed to have had such an example before her."

He spoke without his usual light irony, sounding almost... wistful, and she glanced at him more closely. Wistfulness was not something one associated with Gervase Lyons either. As usual, his expression gave nothing away. Gervase the enigma, as inscrutable as a cat. He'd always been so hard to read—except during those times in their childhood when he'd deliberately set out to infuriate her. To needle and provoke her about those things that were her particular passion, like women's suffrage and Richard the Third's innocence. And yet, Margaret could now admit that their exchanges had been as stimulating as they were maddening. One felt engaged—*alive* —during an argument with Gervase, even when one wanted to wring his neck!

And he could also be kind. She knew that too; he'd been the first of his family to write to her after her bereavement, to offer his sympathies. And from that tentative exchange of letters, something like the old childhood intimacy had gradually grown between them once more. Their correspondence had continued throughout her year of mourning, and when she'd finally relocated to London this past spring to take up her life again, he'd come to call on her, with Juliana *and* Elaine— once her closest friend—in tow.

Why had *Gervase* not married yet? Margaret wondered suddenly. He was twenty-eight now—an age at which many men contemplated settling down with a wife and family. Surely he could afford to marry, if he'd the inclination. And surely any lady would welcome an offer from Lord Gervase Lyons: successful, well-born, well-connected, and—she realized with a sudden shock —quite startlingly handsome.

She couldn't have said why the discovery surprised her. The Duke and Duchess of Whitborough were a striking pair who'd produced a brood of hardy, handsome children: *all* the Lyons boys were good-looking. At the height of her girlish passion for Hal, she'd believed no other man could match him for looks, with the possible exception of Reg, who'd run him a close second. Gervase might not catch the eye as quickly as his older brothers, but he was well worth looking at, built on lighter, leaner lines than they, and moving with an almost catlike grace that was all his own.

Just now, he stood gazing down into the fire, the leaping flames reflected in his eyes. And like one mesmerized, Margaret gazed at *him*: watching the play of firelight upon a face that was familiar and strange at once. Sharp cheekbones and firm jaw; a strong, straight nose; a high forehead, partly obscured by the thick fall of his hair, brown by daylight, shot through now with glints of red and gold. Even his eyes... a changeable blue-grey that reminded her of woodsmoke or the sea on a misty morning.

He glanced up then, his eyes meeting hers, and a surge of heat pulsed through her that had nothing to do with her proximity to the fire. Standing just a few feet away from Gervase, she was conscious as never before of his body and its lean, supple strength.

Alex had been tall and—not fat, but solid: a comforting, reassuring wall of a man. Someone she could lean on, in every sense of the word. A bear, rather than a lion —or a Lyons. Different from Hal in almost every particular... and hadn't that been one of the things that drew her to him? There would be nothing in Alex's embrace to remind her of her late fiancé.

What might it be like to feel *Gervase's* body against hers? He wasn't as tall as Hal or Alex, but he topped her by a good five or six inches. And his superbly tailored clothes defined a form that was spare but well-proportioned, not lanky or ungainly in any way. He kept fit, she knew, riding in Hyde Park when the weather and his schedule permitted, and taking regular fencing lessons. *Mens sana in corpore sano*, he'd quoted at her once, with that crooked half-smile of his.

In corpore sano. The heat settled low in her loins now, smoldering like a barely banked fire, and Margaret sternly told herself not to be a fool. She was a grown woman, not some silly schoolgirl with no experience of men. And this was *Gervase*, whom she'd known since they were practically in leading strings. Gervase, who'd nearly been her *brother-in-law*...

"Margaret?" His resonant baritone sent a hum through her very bones. "Are you feeling quite well? You seem a bit distracted."

Flushing, Margaret made herself glance away. "No, no—I'm perfectly well, thank you. My goodness, it's warm in here," she added, taking a small step away from the fire—and him.

His brow rose again, but much to her relief, he made no comment on that. "So, what brings you here tonight?" he asked instead. "Farnsworth informed me it was important?"

"Er..." For just a moment, she could not recall why she had come, then, mercifully, memory, along with sanity, returned. "I—I came to ask about Christmas. You're going up to Yorkshire, aren't you?"

Both brows rose this time. "Yorkshire? Good God, why would you think that?"

"Because I just received an invitation to spend Christmas at Denforth!" she confessed in a rush. "Haven't you?"

CHRISTMAS AT DENFORTH.

The words seemed to belong to another life, but their utterance proved as powerful as any spell. In his mind's eye, Gervase saw the Great Hall rise up before him, bright with candles and holiday greenery—Advent wreaths and Christmas garlands. Delicious scents wafting from the kitchen and dining room. Mulled wine steaming in a silver bowl, the Yule Log blazing in the fireplace, and the tallest Christmas tree that could be found towering over them all. His brothers arguing, his sisters singing, his parents trading gibes in their unique form of love-play. And Margaret, always Margaret: sensible and serene, adding another voice to the singing, another hand to the placement of holly and ivy, and something more that was all her own...

He forced himself to return to the present. Margaret—Lady Bellamy, not the girl of Christmases past—was gazing up at him, her velvety brown eyes intent on his face. "Gervase—"

"An invitation to Denforth," he repeated carefully, to ensure that he hadn't heard wrong.

She nodded confirmation. "Addressed by Juliana. I have it here, in my reticule."

"When did it arrive?"

"Just today. Have you seen your post?"

"Not yet. The mail hadn't arrived by the time I left the house this morning."

"Well, check it now. It's inexplicable that your family would invite *me* and not you."

He refrained—heroically—from pointing out that his family was capable of any number of inexplicable things and went over to his desk, where Farnsworth usually placed the post in his absence. A neat stack of envelopes awaited him: he rifled through them expertly, setting aside the bills... and paused at the sight of Juliana's familiar handwriting. Keeping his face impassive, he broke the seal and extricated the contents: the invitation Margaret had mentioned, on heavy cream-colored stationery.

"You did get one, then." The relief in Margaret's voice was palpable.

"So it would appear." He opened the invitation. Below the formal printed phrases was a short note, also in Juliana's handwriting: *I've invited Reg and our sisters too, so it will be like old times, Gerry! Do say you'll come. All my love, J.*

Like old times. If it were anyone but his little sister, Gervase would have suspected sarcasm of the highest order. As it was, he wondered if nostalgia and grief over Hal had blurred her memories of just how... *trying* those old times could be.

He glanced at Margaret, who was holding up her own invitation. "I was surprised to receive it," she confessed. "I never expected to."

"Why not? Your family spent any number of Christmases at Denforth," he reminded her. His parents and hers were friends as well as neighbors, and Denforth had effortlessly absorbed the Duke and Duchess of Langdale and their three children on any number of social occasions.

Margaret colored. "That was—that was *before*."

Before Hal's death, Gervase translated without difficulty. And everything that had come after that.

"If the truth be told," she went on, "I've never known exactly how your parents feel about me—since they lost Hal."

"They loved you. They thought of you as another daughter." *One of the family...*

"For a time. But when I married Alex..." She looked away, her flush deepening, and Gervase knew that her thoughts, like his, had gone back to that Christmas at Denforth five years ago. The first Christmas since Hal's death: everyone subdued, still in mourning, but trying to carry on. Margaret and her siblings had come, as had the recently widowed Duke of Langdale, and all had seemed, if not merry, then at least tranquil.

But within a day of the gathering, Margaret had stolen away in the night, with no word beyond a reassuring but unrevealing note to her father. At the time, Gervase had thought he'd known why, and silently cursed his father's well-intentioned meddling. So he'd been as shocked as anyone—more so—when the announcement of her marriage to Earl Bellamy had appeared in the society pages less than a fortnight later.

He could no longer recall which of his family had read the news aloud, but every detail of how it had *felt* was permanently etched on his memory: the roaring in his ears, the pain like a dagger thrust between the ribs. He'd got up and left the breakfast table at the first opportunity, hoping that no one had noticed.

No one had—except Elaine, and he could count on her secrecy.

What followed had been almost as unpleasant. Ugly gossip had circulated in the wake of that runaway match: Lady Margaret Carlisle, denied her place as future Duchess of Whitborough by Hal's untimely death, had snatched at an earl, rather than risk being left on the shelf. An earl more than fifteen years her senior, with two young sons—a sure sign of her desperation.

Which was all spiteful nonsense, as far as Gervase was concerned. As a duke's daughter, Margaret could still have made a brilliant match, once she was out of mourning for Hal. Beautiful, intelligent, well-dowered... any man of sense would have leapt at such a prize. If she'd chosen Bellamy, then she must have wanted him, as much as Bellamy had wanted her.

Because he *had* wanted her. More than once, Gervase had caught the man gazing at Margaret wistfully but quite without hope at London parties, the year she came out. Nor were they strangers. On more than one occasion, she'd danced with Bellamy and gone in to supper on his arm. Indeed, why should she not, seeing as Hal could scarcely be bothered to pay attention to his fiancée?

No, if anyone had done the "snatching," it had been Bellamy. And by all reports, the earl had adored his new young countess, and they'd settled comfortably at Bellamy's estate in Gloucestershire, rarely coming to London. On hearing that they'd been happy, Gervase had done his best to be happy for them—or to put up a suitably convincing façade to that effect.

"Time heals all wounds." He did not realize at first that he'd spoken aloud, and he wanted to kick himself once the words were uttered. *Really, how banal could one get?*

But Margaret looked up again, her expression lightening. "Do you really think so?"

He offered her a wry smile. "I suppose even the hoariest of platitudes contains a grain of truth. And I can't imagine that my parents would hold a grudge against you. They certainly didn't expect you to mourn forever, after Hal died."

"They might have expected a longer mourning period all the same," she pointed out.

Gervase shook his head. "There are no ironclad rules for a bereaved fiancée as there are for a widow. You'd come of age, *and* your father was still living then. If *he* approved of your marriage to Bellamy, then I can't see how it was anyone else's concern." He studied her face, still so lovely despite the shadows lingering about her eyes, and asked gently, "Do you even *want* to go to Yorkshire, Margaret? No one is forcing you to do so, and I thought you usually spent Christmas with your stepsons." Bellamy's brother was the official guardian of the boys—both away at school now—but Margaret remained close to them.

"I do, usually. But this year Crispin and his wife want

to take them to visit *her* family in Wales. There will be other children there, some the same age as the boys," Margaret explained. "Sandy and Charles are so excited about going—it would be selfish to deprive them of their treat, just to bear me company at Christmas. Crispin invited me as well, but I'd feel as if I were imposing on his in-laws' hospitality. So I told him I might spend the holidays with my brother, in Yorkshire. Except," she took a breath, "Augustus cabled today to inform me that he and Alicia have also been invited to Denforth. *And* he's accepted, for both of them!"

Gervase frowned. "I thought your sister was staying in Paris, with friends."

"She is, but according to Augustus, she's already booked her return passage to England." Margaret's faint frown mirrored his own. "Gervase, what do you think is going on?"

"I couldn't begin to guess." He stared down at his own invitation. *Like old times*, his sister had written. "Juliana's mentioned wanting to gather everyone together for Christmas—it *could* be nothing more than that."

The skeptical look she gave him would have done credit to a born Lyons. "Do you think it might have something to do with Alicia or Reg? Trying to get them to—to set a date for the wedding?"

"Possibly. Reg doesn't confide in *me*, but he's dragged his feet about this match long enough in all conscience. Much to Father's displeasure—he thinks it's high time Reg left the army and started setting up his nursery." And ensured the succession, as Hal had failed to do. Having witnessed a few of those arguments, Gervase had felt almost sorry for his older brother.

"He may have his reasons for doing so," Margaret said, her voice oddly colorless.

Gervase glanced at her sharply, but her face, usually so reflective of her feelings, was as unrevealing as her tone. "You think he might not want to marry her?"

"I... couldn't say, really." She paused, worrying her lower lip. "But, if truth be told, I never thought Reg and Alicia had much in common, to begin with. I was quite surprised to learn they'd become engaged that spring. Alicia wasn't even out yet!"

"There *is* a considerable age difference," he conceded. "But nine years is not an unbridgeable distance. Many married couples are further apart in age and happy in spite of it. Perhaps even because of it."

He carefully did not mention Bellamy, but Margaret flushed up to her hairline all the same. "*Touché*, my friend. Nonetheless," her candid brown eyes met his squarely, "you know as well as I that an early betrothal does not guarantee happiness—especially if it's not to the right man. After my experience, I'd hoped my sister could make her own choice when the time came."

"They've been engaged for nearly five years. *Has* Alicia met someone else?"

"Not that I know of. At least no one to compete with her image of Reg," she added with a sigh. "She idolizes him, you know—much as I once idolized Hal."

"Might not matters end more happily between them?" Gervase suggested. "I have not seen Reg for nearly two years, and your sister for longer still. Perhaps he might be more receptive now to the thought of an adoring wife and children prattling at his knee."

She rolled her eyes. "Oh, Gervase—pray do not ask me to believe *that*! Not of Reg!"

"Perhaps not. *I've* often thought Reg was married to the army myself," he admitted. "However, I should think that whatever exists or does not exist between your sister and my brother is *their* business to sort out. Would you not agree?"

Margaret worried her lip again, her eyes still troubled. "Ordinarily, I would, but—"

"No buts," he interrupted firmly. "Now, do you intend to go to Yorkshire?"

"Do *you*?" she countered.

"I—haven't yet decided." He set the invitation on the desk. "Juliana informs me that Reg and our sisters have also been invited, and God only knows how *they'll* respond. But if they all decide to go to Denforth, I think someone should spend Christmas with Mother in France."

"France?" Margaret echoed, her eyes widening. "Gervase, hasn't Juliana told you? The duchess is coming to Yorkshire too."

Chapter Two

Love, unrequited, robs me of my rest,
Love, hopeless love, my ardent soul encumbers...
—W. S. GILBERT, *Iolanthe*

London, 21 December 1888

KING'S CROSS STATION teemed with travelers, which was only to be expected with Christmas just days away, Margaret concluded philosophically. Even so, the sheer volume of people was staggering: men enveloped in mufflers and shapeless overcoats, women swathed in shawls or sporting modish fur-trimmed jackets, and families of various sizes with children shrieking underfoot, beside themselves with excitement.

Margaret stifled a wistful pang at the sight. She would miss the boys this Christmas, but she hoped with all her heart that they'd enjoy Wales and make new friends there. They were growing up so quickly: Sandy was more like his father every time she saw him. It wouldn't be long before he could assume Alex's responsibilities as Earl Bellamy in more than name. The prospect filled her with a mixture of pride and sadness. If only Alex could have lived to see his sons grow to manhood...

A train's whistle jolted her from her reverie, and she scanned the crowd milling about the platform, hoping to catch sight of her traveling companion. No easy task, given not only the press of humanity but the fog and steam that hung like a pall over the station.

Then she saw him approach, immediately recognizable by his smooth, loose-limbed stride—at least to her, and just when, she wondered distractedly, had *that* happened? She raised a gloved hand, waved, and saw those cool grey eyes sharpen as they caught sight of her. He quickened his pace, cleaving effortlessly through the crowd, reaching her within moments.

"Hullo," Margaret said a bit breathlessly, when they were face to face.

"Good morning." His tone, like his expression, held its customary trace of sardonic amusement. "Farnsworth's gone off with a porter and the luggage."

"My maid, as well." Margaret studied him thoughtfully. As always, he was impeccably turned out, from the tweed Chesterfield overcoat that flattered his lean figure to the grey Homburg that sat perfectly straight upon his head.

On impulse, she reached out to tip the hat just slightly askew, at a jauntier angle. "There—you look much more human that way."

His eyes narrowed. "My dear Margaret, what else would I be but human?"

"I mean, not so *controlled*," she explained, surprised by the faint edge in his voice. "Not so rigidly *perfect*. Spontaneity isn't a sin, you know. Besides, you look more dashing this way."

"Do I indeed?" Gervase relaxed, the amusement creeping back into his eyes. "Shall I perform a similar sartorial adjustment on you? One good turn deserves another, they say."

"Thank you, but that won't be necessary," Margaret said hastily. She'd chosen her most becoming traveling ensemble—a dress and cape of dark green velvet, edged with golden-brown marten fur. It always helped, knowing that one looked one's best.

"No? Well, perhaps not." He tilted his head to regard her appraisingly. "Very smart, Lady Bellamy. I am hard-pressed even to think of an improvement."

Margaret felt herself flush with pleasure, even as part of her wondered when it had come to matter what Gervase thought of her appearance. "Thank you."

"Although that hat..." His voice trailed off critically.

"What's wrong with it?" She'd thought the peaked

bonnet, with its aigrette of pheasant quills, was a perfect match for the rest of her costume.

"Too plain," he told her, straight-faced. "To be truly fashionable, you should have purchased a hat trimmed with the entire bird, instead of merely a handful of feathers."

Margaret's befuddlement lasted no longer than a few seconds—once she saw the betraying glint in his eyes. "You," she declared, around an exasperated huff of laughter, "are the most *maddening* of men!"

He inclined his head, his lips quirking in their familiar half-smile. "Why, thank you. As you know, I aspire to uphold the Lyons legacy in all things."

"In that regard, you've succeeded beyond all expectations. Now, shall we go inside?"

Not waiting for a response, she led the way to the Bellamys' private rail coach, which had been commissioned by Alex's cousin and immediate predecessor as earl. Not even Margaret's father—or Gervase's, for that matter—owned one, and Alex himself had been initially dubious of retaining such an extravagance, but Margaret had managed to convince him of its usefulness. In her opinion, the opportunity to travel in privacy and comfort was worth every penny, and her husband had come around to her way of thinking after making a few trips in the coach.

He'd even grown accustomed to the décor, which was just this side of opulent: burgundy, with touches of dull gold. Now Margaret watched Gervase's expression as he took in their surroundings, from the mahogany paneling, gleaming in the light from the car's numerous oil lamps, to the padded leather armchairs and sofa to the Turkish carpet on the floor.

"Impressive," was all he said, but the single raised eyebrow was eloquent.

"I know it *looks* a trifle overdone," she said hastily, "but I assure you, everything in here is perfectly sound and of the best quality."

"I don't doubt that." He glanced about the car. "Well, it's impeccably maintained: spotless as a dowager's sitting room."

"I thought it looked more like a gentleman's study myself—at least *this* part does." Margaret removed her bonnet and traveling cape, draping the latter over the back of an armchair.

Gervase continued to study the coach, clearly intrigued despite himself. "Dare I ask what the rest of it resembles?"

"Nothing scandalous, if that's what you're thinking," Margaret tried to sound severe, and received a rare flash of a dimpled smile from him that did strange things to her insides. It always surprised her that Gervase *had* dimples, mainly because he so seldom displayed them—on purpose, she suspected. "But beyond those curtains," she gestured toward the luxurious burgundy drapes. "Is a dining room that can seat at least four people. And beyond *that* is a little washroom, should you wish to tidy yourself."

She had the satisfaction of seeing his eyes widen. "Good Lord, all the comforts of home," he murmured, with a bemused headshake.

"Actually, this car is quite modest, for its kind," Margaret informed him. "Alex knew a rich American who has *his* coach fitted with a stateroom, a kitchen, and servants' quarters!"

"That doesn't surprise me. I've heard Americans relish their creature comforts even more than we do." Gervase shrugged off his overcoat and laid it on the sofa, along with his hat. "Well, we shall be making the journey in some style. Thank you for inviting me to share your coach."

Margaret smiled. "You're quite welcome. It seemed the least I could do, when you agreed to accompany me to Yorkshire." Not to mention that she would find the coach far less empty—and lonely with a fellow traveler along. And for all his acerbity, Gervase could be a pleasant enough companion when it suited him.

Another whistle sounded, and they felt the first lurch of motion as the train began to pull out of the station. Margaret quickly seated herself on the nearest armchair, while Gervase settled into the one just opposite her.

"The stationmaster said it would take about four hours or so to get there," she mused aloud, gazing out the window at the overcast grey sky. "Likely more, if it snows."

"We're heading north," Gervase pointed out. "Of course there will be snow."

"Always a white Christmas in Yorkshire." In spite of her apprehension, Margaret felt a twinge of pleasure at the thought. "Or *almost* always. I've told Sandy and Charles about what it was like to grow up there—and how definite the seasons are. Especially winter: the sharpness, the clarity, the whiteness of the snow..."

"The chilblains, the catarrh, the impassibility of the roads..."

Margaret rolled her eyes. "You *could* still have gone to France, you know."

He raised a brow. "And miss out on what promises to be the most... exciting Christmas in years? Heaven forbid."

"To be honest, I wasn't entirely sure you'd show up this morning," she confessed.

"I gave my word, did I not? That I wouldn't abandon you to the tender mercies of my family? You caught me in a weak moment. Besides," he added, "I confess to a singular curiosity about what could have led Her Grace to leave France for England at this time of year."

"Perhaps she misses her children?"

Gervase regarded her with polite incredulity. "That would argue a sentimentality my mother has never possessed. Except perhaps where Reg is concerned."

"That is harsh!" Margaret protested. "You must know, in your heart, that Her Grace loves *all* of you."

"Not equally." His voice had gone almost as expressionless as his face. "Although to be fair, it's a rare mother—or father—who does. Most parents have favorites among their children. Some are just better at hiding it than others."

Margaret winced inwardly, unable to deny the truth in what he'd said. And that had been one of the things that baffled her most about the family into which she'd almost married. *Her* parents had always sworn they loved her and her siblings equally; she'd never felt second-best to Alicia, the golden-haired baby of the family, or Augustus, the all-important son and heir. But it was hard to overlook the favoritism in the Lyons clan—especially when it came to the boys.

Predictably, Whitborough had preferred Hal, his

heir and the son he kept the closest, whom he was grooming for his future position. And after that, he was quite indulgent towards his youngest child, Jason. Meanwhile, Reg was the unquestioned apple of the duchess's eye, the heir to her French properties, and save for his fair coloring, the image of her own adored father.

That Gervase, with his brilliant mind and wry humor, had been no one's particular favorite struck Margaret as deeply unfair. How long had it taken him to discover that, she wondered, and was that one of the reasons he was so guarded? Because he knew himself to be the forgotten, overlooked son?

Margaret chided herself for her obtuseness. Of course it was—or, at the very least, it had to be *one* of the reasons for Gervase's extraordinary self-containment. Showing that he resented or even minded his parents' unequal affections would be to make himself vulnerable in ways he could not afford, not in a family as contentious and competitive as his.

She studied him covertly as he stared out the window, but his expression was as unreadable as ever, his eyes partly veiled by lowered lashes. No *visible* sign of tension that she could discern, but she felt a pang of conscience nonetheless. Had it been terribly selfish of her to cajole him into coming with her to Yorkshire? To a place that was probably as much a source of pain as of pleasure for him?

You caught me in a weak moment, he'd said, and Margaret could not deny the truth of that either. She *had* played upon Gervase's emotions, appealed to his well-hidden but by no means nonexistent sense of chivalry, and in the end he'd capitulated—even if he now claimed that he was motivated as much by curiosity as friendship. Even the knowledge that she'd manipulated him in what she believed to be a good cause did not wholly assuage her guilt. *Forgive me, dear friend, but if what I suspect is true, I may sorely need your guidance.*

As if he felt her gaze on him, he turned his head, smiled wryly. "So—any word on who else is coming? Juliana seems to keep you rather better informed than she does me."

Margaret shook her head. "I haven't heard anything

further, about who's accepted or who's declined. Who do *you* think will attend?"

"If the word's got out that Mother's coming, I suspect everyone will be there—even Reg, now that his regiment's back in England." Gervase shuddered eloquently. "A Lyons family Christmas. God help us, every one."

"Perhaps it won't be so bad." Margaret did her best to sound bracing. "After all, it's been years since all of you have seen each other—"

"There's a *reason* for that."

"I wasn't referring to your brothers," she continued, as if he hadn't spoken. "Do you not wish to see your sisters again? Juliana, and Elaine, and Madeline—I haven't even met Madeline's new baby yet, much less remember whether it was a girl or a boy."

"A boy—Oliver. She has a daughter and two sons now. And Elaine has one of each."

"Well, there you are. Young children are the perfect reason to come together in peace—or what passes for it, in your family," she added dryly, and was rewarded by another fleeting glimpse of a dimple.

"I'll admit, the presence of my nieces and nephews might have a salutary effect on the gathering," he conceded. "At least temporarily."

"It's a start," Margaret reminded him, then glanced out the window in turn. London was behind them now, and the track before them seemed to stretch towards eternity, as it always did at the start of a journey. "We've a good four hours until York. Why not a game to pass the time? Are you up for a round of Quotations?" It had been a favorite parlor game of both their families. And one she'd rather missed, as Alex had never shown much interest in such diversions; poetry had not been something at which he'd excelled.

"Words or first letters?"

"Words," she said firmly. "Much more flexible that way."

His eyes gleamed. "Shakespeare?"

"Of course." Good thing they were both well-versed in the Bard, or he'd trounce her within five minutes. "Shall I begin?"

Gervase held out a hand, palm-up. "Ladies first."

Margaret cleared her throat. "*When shall we three meet*

again? In thunder, lightning, or in rain? When the hurly-burly's done, When the battle's lost and won..."

His brows drew together but only for a fraction of a second. "*Was ever woman in this manner wooed? Was ever woman in this manner* won?"

Richard III, unsurprisingly. Margaret made a face at him, which he met with his blandest expression, but managed a quick riposte. "*Sweet, do you not know I am a* woman? *When I think, I must speak.*"

"*Oh,* speak *again, bright angel*," Gervase fired back.

"*Noble or not I for an* angel," Margaret countered.

"*O, what a* noble *mind is here o'erthrown!*"

The game lasted more than an hour, with Margaret finally conceding defeat after his contribution of "*Quail, crush, conclude, and quell!*"

By then, the train had traveled deep into the Midlands, and necessity impelled them both to get off at the train's next stop. The snow Gervase had predicted was blowing in the wind, a flurry of white flakes that stung and then numbed exposed skin. Shivering, Margaret attended to her needs, then hurried back to the coach, more grateful than ever for its comfort—and for the stove that Alex's cousin had had installed at the back, which kept the car tolerably warm even on a day like this!

Gervase reentered the car some minutes later, his hat and Chesterfield well-dusted with snow, and a copy of *The Times* under his arm.

"Oh, good," she hailed him with relief. "I was beginning to wonder if you'd got lost on the way back—or simply froze to death waiting in the queue for the convenience. *I* nearly did!"

His lips twitched. "My sympathies. I suspect the queue for the men's convenience moved considerably faster than the one for the ladies'—anatomy being what it is."

"Still another reminder of the injustices of Nature," Margaret grumbled, and received a full, if fleeting, smile in response. "I'm surprised Alex's cousin didn't include a convenience in the coach, but perhaps it was beyond his means at the time. Ugh, I can't believe how cold it is today—even for December!"

"December *and* the winter solstice," Gervase pointed

out, removing his hat and running a quick hand through his bronze-brown hair. A few strands strayed across his forehead, she noticed, giving him an appealingly tousled, almost boyish look. "And the last few winters have been quite harsh. Scientists think it has something to do with that volcanic eruption back in '83." He cast off his overcoat, resumed his seat opposite her, and reached for the newspaper. "I might as well discover what's going on in the world, since I'm to be effectively isolated from it for the next fortnight. May I?"

"By all means. I brought along a novel to keep myself entertained." Margaret reached for her reticule and extracted *Lady Audley's Secret*.

Both of his brows rose when he saw the title. "Good Lord, when did you take to reading sensation novels?"

"In the schoolroom," she retorted. "Just like your sisters, I might add!"

"You astonish me. I'd thought you subsisted on a literary diet of Shakespeare, Jane Austen, and any history book even slightly favorable towards Richard the Third."

Margaret resisted a childish urge to poke her tongue out at him. "I'll have you know, Lord Gervase, I am full of surprises," she informed him loftily.

"That is not news to me... Lady Margaret."

Not Lady Bellamy, but the courtesy title by which he'd known her since they were children, running wild with their siblings over Denforth's vast grounds or exploring the castle from top to bottom. Suddenly flustered, she glanced down, wondering if she were imagining the warmth in his eyes, the gentler note in his voice when he spoke?

But when she plucked up the nerve to look again, Gervase had unfolded his newspaper and disappeared behind it.

Typical male evasion. Stifling a sigh, Margaret opened her own book. If truth be told, she *did* find sensation novels a bit too lurid for her present taste, but they beguiled the time most effectively. Within a few pages, she was caught up in the story, oblivious to all else. For a time she and Gervase read in companionable silence, broken only by the rustle of a page.

She did not know when the quiet of the coach penetrated her consciousness. But glancing up from *Lady Au-*

dley's Secret, she saw that Gervase had fallen asleep. Without a sound, without a warning, just closed eyes, even breathing, and the stilling of that restless, incisive intellect. *Out, out, brief candle...*

Amused and oddly touched, Margaret laid her book aside and studied her companion. He looked more approachable in sleep, the severe line of his mouth relaxed, his sardonic gaze hidden behind his closed eyelids. Unguarded, almost vulnerable... a strange way to think of a man whose mental acuity made razors seem dull. To say nothing of his well-filed tongue, which she remembered all too clearly from some of their childhood arguments!

And yet... she knew he had a softer side. She'd seen it herself, when he was a boy. And so had his sisters—especially Juliana, who could wind all her brothers round her little finger, whether it came to telling her stories, letting her ride on their shoulders, or, in Gervase's case, rescuing her favorite kitten from a tree.

Margaret smiled at the memory. How many years ago had it been? Ten? No, eleven. She'd been fourteen, Gervase sixteen, and Juliana eight, exactly half his age. A lazy summer afternoon at Denforth, a picnic lunch, after which everyone had scattered to pursue his or her own amusements. Returning from a solitary ramble, she'd spied a tear-stained Juliana running up to Gervase, who was stretched out beside a stream, reading a book...

"Mr. Scorton's horrid mastiff chased Xerxes up a tree, and he won't come down! Please, Gerry, you've got to help—he could be stuck up there forever!"

Gervase closed his book with a martyred air, accompanied by a put-upon sigh. "Ju, didn't Mother tell you to leave the little beast at home? He hasn't the sense to fend for himself out here."

"I—I forgot," Juliana faltered, flushing.

"How convenient," Gervase observed dryly. Then he looked at his sister, gazing up at him with tear-drenched blue eyes... and relented. "Oh, very well, brat. I'll see what I can do. But I'm not risking my new jacket for that wretched bit of fleabait. Which tree was it?"

Juliana, to her credit, did not so much as bristle at this slur on her beloved pet. "One of the trees we picnicked under," she sniffed, swiping at her eyes.

Margaret surprised herself by coming forward. "Can I help?" she asked.

"How are you at climbing trees?" Gervase inquired.

"Not so good," she admitted. "At least, not while I'm wearing a dress. But if you need an extra pair of hands..."

"All right" he conceded. "Come on, Ju—take us to the tree."

Minutes later, they stood at the foot of an ash tree, looking up into the leaves. A scrap of ginger fur clung to one of the higher branches, mewing pitifully.

Gervase considered the kitten for a moment, then turned towards the blanket still spread out upon the grass. Shrugging off his jacket, he rummaged through the picnic hamper, emerging with one of the finger sandwiches. "Fish paste," he explained, and returned to the tree.

"You'll need both hands for climbing," Margaret warned him.

"I'm aware of that." He glanced at the sandwich, gave another forbearing sigh, and gingerly tucked it into the cuff of his left sleeve before starting his ascent.

"Will the branches bear your weight?" Margaret called anxiously as he shinned up the trunk. Agile and lightly built as he was, he should climb more easily than Hal or Reg, but still...

Gervase glanced down, his expression slightly pained. "I'll find out soon enough, won't I?" he remarked, and reached for the nearest bough.

Strangely breathless, Margaret and Juliana watched him climb, a slim figure moving from branch to branch, a fish paste sandwich peeking incongruously over his left shirt cuff. Up he went, balancing carefully. Once his foot slipped, and Margaret thought she heard him mutter a curse as he strove to regain his balance, then adjusted his position, set his foot on a different branch and resumed his climb.

Finally, boy and cat were face to face, with barely a foot of distance between them.

Gervase clicked his tongue, and held out the sandwich just within reach. "Come along, then."

The words were brisk rather than coaxing, but his tone was low and gentle enough. Margaret could just imagine the kitten's whiskers twitching at the smell of the fish paste. He gave another plaintive mew, scarcely more than a squeak, stretching out an imperious little paw.

Gervase leaned in, extending the sandwich further, and Xerxes inched closer. And closer... until he was just within reach. Quick as a flash, Gervase tugged the kitten free of the branch, and pulled him close to his shirtfront as he began to climb down.

He moved cautiously, not rushing his descent, but Margaret wasn't sure she breathed until he was on the ground again.

"Here you are, brat." Gervase held out the kitten and the by now half-eaten sandwich to his sister. "Now for pity's sake, take him home, and don't let him out until he's bigger and has more sense than a dandelion puff!"

Juliana, eyes shining, kissed her brother on the cheek and ran off, the kitten still clutched in her embrace.

"Little pest," Gervase observed.

Margaret couldn't tell whether he meant Juliana or the kitten. But when he reached up to push back his hair, she caught sight of something more alarming, "Gervase, you're bleeding!"

"Ah." He pulled his hand back, glanced at the drops of red welling on his forefinger and thumb. "Little beast managed to get a claw into me, after all."

"Here." Margaret fished out her handkerchief—clean, thankfully—and wrapped it carefully around the affected digits. "Juliana will be everlastingly grateful."

"Well, she'd better be," he retorted. "It's not every brother who'll risk life, limb, and wardrobe retrieving some dim-witted cat. I must have looked a proper fool trying to coax him down." He pulled a face. "And my shirt now reeks of fish paste, though it had to be laundered in any case, so no harm done, I suppose."

"I thought... I thought you were rather splendid, actually," Margaret confessed.

He stilled, his grey eyes flaring wide. "Good Lord, was that a compliment? From you?"

Margaret felt herself flush. "I pay them—now and then," she said, a touch primly. "When someone deserves it."

His mouth quirked up and she caught the unexpected flicker of a dimple. "Lady, I shall study deserving," he misquoted, and swept her a mock bow.

The train's whistle shrilled, jarring Margaret back to the present. And opposite her, Gervase started awake, his eyes flashing open, more blue than grey in the lamplight. For a moment, he glanced almost wildly about the car as though he couldn't remember where he was or how he'd got there, then his gaze alighted on her and he smiled—a softer, more unguarded smile than perhaps any she'd ever seen from him.

Margaret smiled back, surprised by the answering softness welling up inside of her, and thought again of a boy, a sandwich, and a treed kitten. "Sleep well?"

He slumped back in his seat and passed a hand over his face, still looking disarmingly young and unfocused. "My apologies—I must have been more tired than I thought."

"Given how hard you've been working, that doesn't surprise me. You'll be the better for something to eat," she told him, pushing down that unsettling softness and doing her best to sound brisk and practical. "Shall we have luncheon now? I had my cook pack a hamper for us —unless you'd prefer to chance the dining car."

He shook his head. "Whatever's in the hamper will be fine, thank you. Besides," he added, the amused glint back in his eyes, "you can show me the rest of the coach as well."

COMING from a family in which everyone tended to guard jealously what was his—or hers, Gervase had long ago developed a deep appreciation for Margaret's willingness to share whatever treat or good fortune came her way. Indeed, her open-handed generosity was one of her most endearing traits.

Now she swept aside the burgundy drapes, and led the way into the coach's dining area with the enthusiasm of a society hostess showing off her newly decorated townhouse. And on seeing it for himself, he had to admit that it was as impressive as the rest of the car. A mahogany sideboard stood along one wall, its drawers containing all the necessary plates, utensils, and glassware, Margaret informed him proudly. In addition, a pair of well-upholstered armchairs had been drawn up before a table draped in white damask, set with silver and fine china.

"I thought it best to be prepared," Margaret explained at his raised eyebrow. "And Alex and I preferred to dine like this—privately—whenever *we* traveled."

Only someone who'd known Margaret as long as he had would have caught the slight change in the timbre of her voice when she spoke of her late husband. But Gervase needed no reminder of how deeply she had cared for Bellamy and he for her.

"A fine idea," he said lightly. "I know *I'd* just as soon forego the walk to the dining car in this weather."

"As long as you don't mind serving yourself," Margaret warned, producing the hamper from under the table and lifting the lid.

"Not in the least," he assured her, coming to lend a hand with the unpacking.

"There's bread and cheese, to start," Margaret explained, as they lifted out the contents and began setting them on the table. "That always travels well. A wedge of pâté, hothouse grapes, and apples. Ginger cakes. One of my cook's famous meat pies, still warm," she reported triumphantly. "Pigeon or veal-and-ham, I would guess— both are equally good."

Gervase unpacked a corked pottery jar, which, when opened, proved to contain a creamy, pale liquid. "Soup?" he guessed, inhaling the savory steam.

"Potato and leek," Margaret confirmed, after sniffing in turn. "With a dash of rosemary. Another of her specialties."

He shook his head. "My dear, I'm impressed. Not even Fortnum and Mason could have improved on the menu. I'd thought for certain we'd be dining out of tins."

"Oh, ye of little faith!" she retorted. "Not that there's anything wrong with eating out of tins. But I'd thought we might have something a little better today. Shall we begin with the soup, while it's still hot?"

With everything now unpacked, they sat down to an excellent meal, accompanied by a fine selection of wines, also from the sideboard.

"Alex's cousin was an ardent connoisseur," Margaret explained. "So he and his wine collection went *everywhere* together. Alex's tastes were more modest, but he saw the practicality of keeping some liquor aboard, if we were dining in the coach."

"I gather you helped Bellamy amass a fine collection of his own?"

"Well, I tried. It's not a very extensive collection, but I'd say we've enough here to accompany most dishes. Although I don't know that Alex's palate was quite the equal of his cousin's," she added, a touch anxiously.

Gervase swirled the contents of his glass, a white wine chosen to complement the soup, inhaled the aroma, and took a sip, tasting judiciously. "You needn't worry—this is quite a decent Chardonnay. Even my mother would find it satisfactory."

Margaret relaxed, smiling. "High praise indeed! I know how particular the duchess is about wine."

"Oh, God—yes." Gervase shook his head reminiscently. "She made sure to educate us all—well, my brothers and myself at least—about it. According to her, Father's palate was no more than serviceable." Which had never particularly bothered the duke—he was content to claim superiority in other matters.

"All of you together?" Margaret asked, resting her chin on her hand in a way that reminded him sharply of the girl he'd first known. The lamplight shone on her hair, turning it the same rich mahogany as the paneling and making her fair skin appear almost translucent by comparison. Just to look at her sorely tested Gervase's powers of concentration, to say nothing of his self-restraint, but he forced himself to reply.

"Not Jason—he was still too young," he amended. "But the rest of us, yes—from about the time Hal was twenty. Mother thought as young men due to enter Society within a few years, we should cultivate our knowledge of good food and good wine. Especially the latter, given that winemaking was part of our heritage on her side of the family.

"So, on summer afternoons, she'd have the three of us meet her in the conservatory, sample the contents of our cellar, and learn how to tell one wine from another. Usually at a rate of a dozen or so bottles at a time."

"How did you all keep from getting as drunk as lords?" she marveled.

Gervase's mouth twitched. "I could point out that we *are* lords, at least by courtesy, so drunkenness might be considered our prerogative. However," he resumed when Margaret rolled her eyes at him, "Mother only let us have a swallow at a time, and once we'd got a full impression on the taste, we were to spit it out. Hal always hated that part," he added. "In fact, he managed several times to swallow what he was tasting when Mother wasn't paying attention. He'd get tipsy, of course, but he always claimed it was worth it. And Reg took to following his example, though I think that was mostly to prove he had a much harder head than Hal's."

"And what did *you* do?" she inquired, her eyes alight with amusement.

Gervase sighed. "I was revoltingly obedient, and obeyed Mother's directives to the letter. Until we got to the last two or three wines of the day's lesson—I felt I deserved *some* sort of reward for my forbearance."

She laughed, the sound clear and bright in the carriage. He'd not heard her laugh like that since Bellamy's death... perhaps not even since Hal's. And laughter became her well, he remembered, animating her somewhat serious face and warming her velvety dark eyes. Sometimes, when they were children, he'd been especially provoking just to see her laugh once she'd realized he was doing it deliberately.

"I don't know if she ever put the girls through that," he began.

"She did," Margaret revealed, smiling mischievously. "Perhaps not as intensively, but according to Elaine, she and Madeline were taught enough to recognize good from inferior wine. I suppose she kept their instruction separate from yours to make it easier. Dealing with tiddly sons and daughters at the same time might tax even Her Grace's powers."

"I'd say Mother was equal to just about anything."

Except the loss of a child. He saw the thought flash through Margaret's mind a fraction of a second after it flashed through his. And there was suddenly a ghost in the carriage with them, a laughing, carefree fair-haired ghost who had never grown up—and would never now grow old.

He said, perhaps a shade too heartily, "Enough about *my* family! We'll be seeing plenty of them for the next fortnight. What about yours? Have your stepsons left for Wales yet?"

"I saw them off at the station two days ago," Margaret confirmed, seizing upon the question with alacrity. "They've promised to write, though I shan't mind if they're enjoying themselves too much to do so..."

Warming to her subject, she went on to speak of the boys' progress at school while Gervase finished his soup and listened, focusing as much on the affection in her voice as on what she said. Her fondness for her stepsons might be more sisterly than motherly, given the age difference between her and their father, but it was also clearly mutual. A pity that she and Bellamy hadn't had children of their own.

"And I heard from Cordelia just yesterday," Margaret was saying now. "She and Mr. Weston have gone to Penzance for their honeymoon, as Cornish winters are so mild."

The bride, Gervase remembered belatedly. "I trust she finds married life to her liking?"

"Very much so. And I couldn't be happier for her, even though I wish—" Margaret broke off, a shadow crossing her face.

"Wish what?" he prompted.

She flushed, and toyed with her own soup, not looking at him. "I must admit, that's the one thing I *didn't* enjoy about the wedding. All these people—my in-laws, mostly—asking if I intended to remarry, now that I'm out of mourning. 'You're still a young woman, my dear,'" she mimicked in a quavering contralto. "'And Dear Bellamy would want you to be happy again.'"

Gervase took a careful breath, trying to conceal his reaction. "Well... wouldn't he?"

She raised troubled eyes to his. "I—suppose. But it's not as simple as that. I know Alex wouldn't want me to mourn him forever. But I can't imagine myself married to anyone else. Not yet. Perhaps not ever."

He'd prided himself on his air of cool composure. He donned it now like a mask, like armor—protection against a blow to the heart. "I see. Still, it's early days yet." The platitude emerged sounding unruffled, as he'd intended. "And you've just taken up your own life again."

"Yes," she agreed, with obvious relief. "I knew you'd understand. You're so perceptive, dear friend."

He managed a thin smile. "So I've been told."

"A woman should be able to lead her own life, if she chooses," Margaret went on. "Without having well-meaning friends and relations *pushing* her towards the altar again. Even Cordelia suggested it in her letter. *Men* don't have that problem, do they?"

Her question was rhetorical, but he replied anyway. "I can't speak for my entire sex, but personally, *I* do not."

"No, I shouldn't think you would!" she exclaimed, almost approvingly. "And if you did, I'm sure you'd find a way to discourage the matchmakers. You're so self-sufficient, Gervase—so independent. You don't seem to need or even want anyone."

God. Gervase's hand tightened about the stem of his wine glass. "I don't... know that I'd go that far. No man is an island, after all."

"*I* wouldn't mind being an island," Margaret said pensively. "Just for a little while, until I've sorted out my life."

"And after that—book your passage back to the mainland?" He kept his tone light, almost teasing. The raillery she expected from an old friend, a childhood chum.

She smiled, responding to it. "Something like that."

"A commendable plan, if one could manage it." He sipped his wine, more to conceal the emotions roiling inside of him at her latest disclosure than from actual thirst. Which was just as well, since the wine had mysteriously lost its flavor.

You don't seem to need or even want anyone.

He could have told her how wrong she was. About what he needed, what he wanted. Had wanted since he was nineteen—and known he could never have. Not then... and apparently, not now either. Instead, he drained his glass and changed the direction of their conversation once more. "Well, since we're on the subject of islands, which one would you visit, given the opportunity? I've always thought Tahiti sounded particularly appealing."

AFTER LUNCHEON, they returned to the passenger area of the coach, where they talked desultorily of this and that. A play he'd seen in London, a history lecture she'd attended at Oxford, books they'd read or wanted to read, Gilbert and Sullivan's most recent opera—which Margaret had found too sad, saying she'd been nearly moved to tears by Jack Point's fate. Gervase had expressed his own preference for *The Mikado* and *Trial by Jury*, with its amusing send-up of the legal system. All topics upon which old friends could comfortably converse.

The train wound its way northward, slowed but not hopelessly impeded by the weather. They were due in York by late afternoon, and carriages would be waiting at the station, to take them to Denforth. All the same, Gervase mused as he consulted his watch, their arrival was at least an hour away.

Across from him, Margaret dozed, nestled in the folds of her velvet cape, breathing evenly, her lashes like dark fans upon her cheeks. She'd made a valiant attempt to resume reading *Lady Audley's Secret*, but had soon set it aside, yawning prodigiously and apologizing profusely. Sleep had overcome her bare minutes after she'd closed her eyes.

He studied her, a dull ache in his non-clockwork heart. She looked the merest slip of a girl, disheveled chestnut hair framing her sleep-flushed face, her lips curved in a faint smile, as though she were dreaming of something pleasant. So lovely, warm, and generous... and so utterly oblivious. Not that he could blame her entirely for that—he'd concealed his feelings from the start, knowing how hopeless they were. There'd always been talk between his parents and hers about a match between their children, and what could be more suitable than a duke's eldest son—the all-important heir—marrying a duke's eldest daughter, and uniting their families and fortunes? A lowly third son would surely never be considered a fit mate for such a prize. Even if Gervase had had the audacity to try his luck back then, the adoration in Margaret's eyes whenever she beheld her splendid betrothed would have stopped him in his tracks.

Not even Hal's untimely death had changed the situation, especially once Alex Bellamy entered the picture. Between golden, charismatic Hal and solid, estimable Bellamy, what chance had Gervase ever stood? And while the gilt might have rubbed off Hal's gingerbread, largely thanks to his brother's own carelessness, the earl's sterling worth remained untarnished in his widow's eyes. Even Gervase could admit that Bellamy had been worth Margaret's devotion.

So that left friendship, with which Gervase had told

himself long ago that he would learn to be content. After all, it had sufficed before, hadn't it? In time, he'd rallied from the shock of her marriage to Bellamy and lived his life, becoming one of the top solicitors in London. He'd even contemplated marriage a time or two, only to reconsider and withdraw before any expectations were raised. The woman he wanted might be forever out of his reach, but it would not be fair to wed one for whom he could not feel anything like the same affection. Instead, when the inclination arose, he'd sought *other* forms of female companionship.

He thought back to the elegant widow with whom he'd had a most civilized arrangement for the last year or so. An amusing, sophisticated woman who had understood how matters were conducted among their set and made no pressing demands on him, any more than he'd made on her. And from whom he'd parted amicably last summer, when she'd actually met a man she wanted to marry. The end of their affair had roused only mild regret in him—and a secret relief, especially since Margaret had recently taken up residence in London.

Dear God, had *that* been at the back of his mind, all this time?

Apparently so. A hope he'd suppressed for years, ever since her elopement with Lord Bellamy, had reignited, almost without conscious volition. He did not know whether to laugh, weep, or curse at its revival.

But was it truly such an impossible dream? Gervase argued with himself. There was nothing to prohibit a deeper relationship between him and Margaret now. Family expectations were to be satisfied by a match between Reg and Alicia. Gervase was now successfully established in his career, and a man of independent means as well. Margaret had been married and then widowed. No bar, no impediment, nothing to stand in their way...

Except for Margaret's own reluctance to remarry, whether from loyalty to Bellamy's memory, a desire for independence, or a combination of the two.

He had a fortnight to change her mind—if he had the courage to try.

If he succeeded in winning her heart and hand, he would strive to make her the happiest of women. And he would surely be the happiest of men.

But if he failed... would he lose even her friendship?

Gervase shifted in his chair, his discomfort growing as he forced himself to consider that possibility. Margaret's kindness would preclude any cruelty in her rejection. Even in the midst of an argument, she hated to give pain, to wound needlessly. But he could imagine her becoming uneasy, even uncomfortable, afterwards, if his suit were unwelcome. Withdrawing, putting distance between them, letting their friendship cool until they were mere acquaintances...

Was it worth the gamble: to risk losing what he already had—and cherished, to reach for what he wanted but which had always been beyond his grasp?

A conundrum. And like all conundrums, it required further reflection. He stared out the window at an overcast grey world, random quotations flitting through his mind in rapid succession: *Faint heart never won fair lady. Better is half a loaf than no bread. Out of this nettle, danger, we pluck this flower, safety. Discretion is the better part of valor...*

Gervase sighed, resting his forehead against the cool windowpane. No point in consulting the ancients, when they offered such conflicting advice—even his revered Shakespeare!

He must have dozed finally, lulled by the train's motion and the rhythmic clacking of the tracks, because a shrill whistle jarred him back to consciousness as it had before.

Margaret started awake as well, blinking owlishly as she glanced out the window. "Oh, we're here!" she announced, in obvious thankfulness.

Gervase looked out his own window and experienced a jolt of recognition when he saw the familiar walls of the station sliding by. York, at last. *Home*, a small voice in his head insisted, though he did his best to ignore it.

"Indeed," he acknowledged, letting the mask of trusted friend and companion slip back into place. "I'd recognize this station anywhere."

Margaret threw him a quick smile, even as she smoothed her hair, fastened her bonnet under her chin, and began to gather her cape around her. Gervase rose a bit stiffly and stretched, before donning his overcoat again and reaching for his own hat.

Margaret had just got to her feet, when the slowing

train gave a sudden lurch. Already off-balance, she stumbled forward with an exclamation of dismay, and Gervase caught her, taking the full force of her momentum upon his chest. They staggered under the impact like a pair of drunkards, but somehow managed to remain standing.

Are you all right? That was what he meant to say, but the words dried on his tongue as she looked up, all wide eyes and parted lips. In his arms, as he'd so often imagined her being, her warmth and softness pressed against him, so close he could breathe in the spicy-sweet fragrance of carnations—her favorite scent.

Speechless herself, Margaret continued to stare at him, her eyes as wide as a startled doe's. And in their dark depths, he saw awareness of him as a *man*... for the first time he could recall.

You don't seem to need or even want anyone.

But I do.

Quickly, not letting himself think, he bent his head and kissed her.

Chapter Three

I'll take that winter from your lips, fair lady.
—WILLIAM SHAKESPEARE, *Troilus and Cressida, IV, v*

BOTHER! was Margaret's unspoken thought as the train's convulsive jerk flung her forward. Futilely, she thrust out her hands to arrest her fall, only to find herself caught and securely held against a solid masculine chest. The collision jarred the breath from her all the same, and she grasped Gervase's upper arms, trying to steady them both. He regained his footing almost at once—not for nothing did he have reflexes like a cat—and glanced down at her.

Still too winded to speak, Margaret looked up at him, into the face she'd known since childhood... and saw someone who was almost a stranger looking back at her. The grey eyes had lost their habitual coolness, were alive with concern—and something that would have taken her breath away if she hadn't already lost it. At that same moment, she became conscious of the strength of him, the hard contours of the torso against which her own body was pressed. And the scent of him, fresh linen, clean male skin, overlaid with a hint of some crisp cologne. Lemon—or perhaps, bergamot? Different from the bay rum Alex had used, but just as pleasant in its way. She found herself breathing it in, breathing *him* in, as they stood locked together in their unexpected embrace.

Afterwards, she could not have said who moved first, but between one breath and the next, his lips were warm on hers, their touch light and seeking. Closing her eyes, she leaned into the kiss, seeking something as well... though she could not have said what. Something was stirring deep inside of her, something she hadn't felt in almost two years.

He pulled back, his eyes staring dazedly into hers, and then the curtain descended, leaving them cool and opaque once again. "For luck," he explained, and was she imagining the trace of huskiness in his voice? "We're about to spend Christmas with my family, after all."

Margaret moistened her lips. "Gervase..." Her own voice was a mere thread.

A corner of that sardonic mouth hooked up. "Didn't you tell me that spontaneity was not a sin?" he inquired lightly. "*Bon courage, ma belle amie*. The Lyons den awaits."

She pulled a face and managed to rally. If, after all, he meant to make light of what had just happened, she could do no less. "*Two* puns in one utterance? For shame, sir!"

"Blame it on the circumstances, which are dire enough to warrant puns," he retorted. "Now, as this infernal train appears to have stopped moving, shall we descend?"

The train might have stopped, but Margaret's legs felt as unsteady as though it were still hurtling along the tracks at top speed. She took a breath and an extra moment to compose herself before replying. "Yes. Time we were off."

Gervase dropped his arms, and she experienced a feeling almost of loss as he moved away from her and turned to tackle the carriage door. Surreptitiously, she moistened her lips again, recalling the taste and feel of that kiss. Not casual, more than friendly. Too affectionate to be resented, but too... intimate to be ignored —or dismissed. Or was she reading too much into it? All she knew for certain was that the kiss had shaken her to the core—and possibly Gervase as well.

The door opened, and the wind gusted in, cutting through the coach's warmth like a blade of ice. Grimacing, Gervase stepped back. "*The air bites shrewdly. It is very cold...*"

"Nothing like stating the obvious," Margaret observed tartly, shivering as she drew her cape around her. "Let's go—before we both change our minds and run off to holiday in France or sunny Spain!"

"Too late," he reported, peering out onto the platform. "Unless I'm much mistaken, there's a man in Whitborough livery, waiting for us."

GERVASE'S EYES had not deceived him. No sooner had they left the train and reunited with their servants than a sturdy, middle-aged man wearing the dark-blue Whitborough livery strode up to them.

"Lord Gervase, Lady Bellamy." His Yorkshire brogue sounded like home to Margaret's ears. "If you'll come this way, the carriage is waiting. And a wagon for your luggage."

"Excellent," Gervase said in that crisp, no-nonsense tone she remembered from London. "A large wagon, I hope? I've brought Christmas gifts for the family."

The coachman assured him of the wagon's size and escorted them to the carriage—a *closed* carriage, Margaret noted with relief. But she didn't know whether to be relieved or disappointed when Gervase insisted that she and her maid, Tilda, take the forward-facing seat, while he and Farnsworth occupied the back-facing one.

Margaret draped a thick woolen lap robe over her knees and Tilda's, trying not to imagine *Gervase* sitting beside her and sharing the robe instead. Memories of his kiss, and how his body had felt against hers kept flooding her mind, warming her more than any blanket.

She stole a glance at him, but he was gazing out the window as the carriage ventured further into the Yorkshire countryside. In the dim, wintry light, his profile looked austere, almost unapproachable, and she could *almost* convince herself that the kiss had never happened.

Lowering her gaze, she idly pleated a fold of the lap robe between her fingers. *Belle amie*. A pun on her married name, of course, but, literally, the phrase meant "beautiful friend." Had he ever called her that before? And how—exactly—did he mean it? Easy to dismiss it as affectionate teasing, a light-hearted play on words... if it hadn't been for the heat in his eyes.

She swallowed, feeling an answering heat coiling low in her belly. For a moment, her thoughts sped back to that encounter by the fire, just a few evenings ago. When he'd been too near—and far too attractive.

On the other hand... as far too many people had reminded her at Cordelia's wedding, she *was* still a young woman—just turned twenty-six—and a young widow who'd enjoyed all the pleasures of the marriage bed to which Alex had introduced her. Perhaps it was the wedding itself that had her thoughts turning in this direction, remembering what she'd once had.

But did she want that again? She'd told Gervase she couldn't imagine being married to anyone but Alex. However, that did not necessarily mean she had to live like a nun for the rest of her days. There were *other* possibilities, especially for a widow.

Like taking a lover. Unbidden, the thought flashed into her mind, and she could just *feel* herself turning scarlet. Wishing that the brim of her bonnet provided more concealment, she sank a little lower in her seat. Much to her relief, her companions did not appear to notice her discomfiture. Tilda was dozing, lulled by the motion of the coach, while both men were studying the scenery through their respective windows.

Gradually, Margaret felt her flush subside. Really, the idea shouldn't shock her *that* much—one couldn't grow up in Society, as she had, and not know how the game was played, especially among couples who married for reasons other than affection. Except that her parents hadn't had such a marriage, and neither had she and Alex. She'd found it no hardship to be a faithful and devoted wife, and Alex had been a fond and no less faithful husband—to her *and* to his first wife, who'd died when Charles was still an infant. There'd been no distractions, no temptations—and no mistresses, as there almost certainly would have been with Hal.

Hal. Her first love. Hers—because she had most decidedly never been *his*.

The thought had ceased to rankle years ago, but she

could remember how his indifference had stung during the earliest years of their betrothal. At seventeen, she'd have given her hope of heaven for the slightest sign of affection—even interest—from her handsome, golden fiancé. Oh, he'd been fond of her in a careless sort of way, as one was of somebody who'd always been there, and he'd assured her that he'd be more than willing to do his duty when the time came.

Which should have told her something right there, Margaret reflected with a rueful shake of her head. But like most young girls, she'd hungered for passion and romance—perhaps because she'd been the practical, sensible child for so long. It had taken her two years to lose most of her illusions and face what her life with Hal was likely to hold. Their marriage would have been... perhaps not a disaster, but she doubted it would have been a great success either. Nonetheless, she'd been prepared to do her duty, just as he was—until the accident that had changed everything.

Golden girls and lads all must, / As chimney sweepers, come to dust.

She'd grieved for him, the handsome, feckless boy she'd known all her life, but in the midst of her sorrow... she'd felt a secret relief—of which she was almost ashamed—that she was no longer bound to him. And then there'd been Alex, with whom she had found—unexpectedly—some of the romance for which she'd longed. Alex, whose loss had devastated her and whom she still missed, even as she settled into life without him.

I have loved two men in my life—and they both died before their time.

Which left *her* somewhere she could never have predicted: in a carriage bound for the estate that housed so many of her childhood memories. And in the company of a man whose history with the place was even deeper and more complicated than hers.

She risked another glance at Gervase, wondering at the thoughts behind that composed countenance. Remorse rippled through her: how selfish she was being, to think only of *her* qualms and misgivings! He must have plenty of his own, and perhaps that stolen kiss—uncharacteristic as it had seemed—had indeed been for luck, as he'd claimed. Luck certainly wouldn't come amiss, she conceded, and as for her reaction to that kiss... well, that concerned no one but herself.

Gervase turned his head then, and their eyes met. "It won't be long now. We've almost reached the bridge."

His voice was carefully neutral, but Margaret thought she heard an undercurrent of tension—and his posture was almost too perfect, his spine too straight for relaxation.

She looked out her own window, seeing a white-blanketed countryside under an overcast grey sky. Gervase could only mean Stamford Bridge, where King Harold had defeated the Vikings before falling to the Normans just a few weeks later. The Duke of Whitborough had been named for that ill-starred monarch, though he was considered to be far more fortunate—in most respects, anyway.

And once across the bridge and a little deeper into East Riding, within sight of the snow-topped Wolds rising in the distance. Denforth Castle formed something of a triangle with Castle Howard and Burton Agnes Hall, Harrowfield lying further west and to the north, closer to the actual Dales.

Margaret's hands clenched in her lap, while her stomach attempted to tie itself in knots. Despite Gervase's assurances that she'd been loved like a daughter by his parents, she could hardly help being nervous. She'd severed that tie through her own actions, and who knew how Their Graces had truly felt about her marriage, which some might have considered overhasty? Hal had been a great favorite in Society, as gregarious as he was charming, and generous to a fault. By contrast, Margaret had never achieved her fiancé's level of popularity. She knew of the unkind rumors that had circulated about her and Alex. Perhaps Hal's parents had wondered along with the rest of the world how she could have moved on so quickly from their glorious golden heir to a man so different from him in many ways.

No sense in borrowing trouble, Margaret told herself sternly. She'd been invited to Denforth, after all—why assume she would be treated coldly by a family that had known her almost since birth? And if there were any lingering awkwardness, a touch of mutual good will would surely dispel it.

Yes, *that* was the path to take. If her suspicions were correct, she had no other choice but to be pleasant and congenial for the entire fortnight: the perfect Christmas guest. Alicia's future might depend on it. Her sweet, golden-haired little sister deserved a chance at true happiness, and Margaret was determined to see that she got one.

Despite her resolve, her pulse quickened and her mouth dried when the arched stone gateway came into sight. How many times had she passed beneath it? Denforth Castle—the estate she might have been mistress of.

Earlier in the century, a previous Duke of Whitborough had enlisted the services of Nash to restore his crumbling home to its former glory. The architect had designed the estate's façade to resemble a Norman castle —not inappropriate, as in its earliest incarnation, Denforth had actually *been* a Norman castle. Its present form boasted round stone towers, crenellated walls, a broad courtyard with an outer and inner ward... one could easily imagine one had stepped back into the Middle Ages on entering its gates. Only a drawbridge and a moat were missing.

As a romantic schoolgirl, Margaret had sometimes envied the Lyons girls. What fun to live on an estate like this, to imagine oneself a princess or even a queen in a tower! To look down from the battlements upon the lands stretching away on all sides. Harrowfield, her own family seat, was a handsome Jacobean estate, mellow and gracious, but for sheer atmosphere it simply could not compete with Denforth—at least not on the outside.

Of course, every castle had a prince, and that had been Hal. She'd woven as many fantasies about him as she had about his home. And had been brought sharply down to earth on learning that her prince was all too human.

Now she saw Denforth through new eyes as well. Still impressive, still brimming with atmosphere... but not the home she'd hoped to find, not the home she *had* found—with Alex and the boys in Gloucestershire. Had she sensed that much, even when her girlish dreams about Hal and Denforth had seemed closest to fruition? Because she'd never been able to picture herself as the next Duchess of Whitborough. That title belonged to one woman alone—and it wasn't her.

Troubled, Margaret looked away. Did Alicia cherish the same dreams she'd once had, only centered on Reg rather than Hal? If so, her little sister might be in for the same rude awakening.

The carriage slowed, stopped, and suddenly, footmen appeared, opening the carriage doors and helping them descend. More footmen began to unload the luggage from the wagon, while another led Tilda and Farnsworth off towards the servants' entrance. Standing in the court-yard, its cobblestones dusted with snow, Margaret gazed up at the massive façade of Denforth and again felt her stomach descend into her neat ankle boots. No turning back now.

Then Gervase's hand was on her arm, steady and re-assuring. Yes, he could be kind...

"*Screw your courage to the sticking place*," he quoted, one corner of his mouth crooking up in that familiar half-smile.

"*Once more unto the breach, dear friend*," Margaret re-turned, managing to smile back. And together, they started towards the steps that led up to the front door.

SHE WAS NERVOUS. Although Gervase thought she had little to fear. Less than *he* did, at any rate. He could tell himself that his life was in London now, that Denforth Castle hadn't truly been his home since he left Oxford, but those assurances dissolved at the first sight of the place.

Easy to lose himself in memories, to let them over-whelm him... but Margaret needed his support—and his *sang-froid*. So he took her arm and guided her towards the front door. She leaned into him, perhaps uncon-sciously, as they walked, her earlier apprehension for-gotten—or suspended. He was the childhood friend she trusted, not the man who'd unsettled her with a kiss.

It afforded him some comfort—to know that he'd unsettled her but she hadn't pulled away. Indeed, for those brief moments he'd held her in his arms, she'd even seemed to return the kiss. It had been his own nerve that had faltered, he acknowledged ruefully. Faltered, but not failed... he would make another assay, when the time seemed right.

But for now, there was family to be dealt with: his *and* hers.

The front door opened, as if in answer to his thoughts, and a young woman emerged, her hair glowing even in the wintry light.

"Gerry!" And there was practically no one else from whom he'd tolerate that diminutive.

Memory struck him like a blow to the solar plexus—and rendered him almost as breathless as his youngest sister's embrace, as she flung herself into his arms.

"Good Lord, brat, is that you?" He spun her around in a little circle before setting her on her feet to look at her more closely. "You've become quite presentable since I saw you last."

Juliana wrinkled her nose at him. "Only a brother could say such a thing! And hope to get away with it!"

"Older brothers are privileged beings." Gervase regarded her with the air of a connoisseur. "Very well—perhaps slightly better than presentable," he conceded. Privately, he thought Juliana *might* just be the loveliest of his three lovely sisters, with her rose-gold hair and bright blue eyes. And that hint of fire and sparkle that was hers alone.

"High praise indeed." Juliana kissed him on both cheeks in the French fashion, but her manner was direct and wholly English. "I am so glad you've come! And Margaret," she went on, smiling as she welcomed her other guest. "It's lovely to see you here again."

"Thank you for inviting me," Margaret said, returning Juliana's embrace.

"It's to be like old times," Juliana told her. "The very *best* of old times," she qualified as Gervase raised a sardonic eyebrow. "You two are almost the last ones here."

"Whom else are we waiting for?" Gervase asked.

"Reg is supposed to arrive soon. He's spent the last week at Melton Mowbray, hunting with the Quorn. And Mother made the crossing two days ago, but she decided to break her journey at East Anglia so she can check on her property there. Still, her telegram said she'd be here this afternoon. We're not expecting Augustus until this evening," Juliana added to Margaret. "And Alicia's not due until tomorrow. How was *your* journey, by the way?"

"Fairly comfortable, until the end." Margaret drew her cape close around her with a shiver. "I'd forgotten how cold Yorkshire winters could be!"

Juliana slipped a companionable arm about her waist. "I tend to forget too, especially when I'm down at Oxford. Then, once I'm back here, I wonder how I ever *could* have forgotten! Let's all go inside. We've a *beautiful* fire going, and there's tea, coffee, and mulled cider if you'd like some."

"Mulled cider sounds wonderful," Margaret declared fervently.

They had just started for the door when Gervase heard an excited voice calling his name. Turning, he saw a boy—no, a young man—on horseback, riding towards them at a rapid clip, his mount's hooves clip-clopping over the cobblestones.

"Why don't you two go on ahead?" Gervase suggested to the women. "It's been a while since I've seen Jason."

Juliana nodded and swept Margaret inside with her, as Gervase watched his youngest brother approach. Less than ten feet away, Jason dismounted, tossing the reins to a groom, and strode up, grinning, to clap him on the shoulder. "Ger! I hoped *you'd* be the next to arrive!"

As opposed to his *other* older brother, Gervase translated without difficulty. Or the duchess—relations were still uneasy between her and her youngest child. "Pleased not to disappoint you," he said diplomatically, returning Jason's welcome. "Good God, whelp, you've grown! You must be two inches taller than the last time I saw you."

"Two and a half," Jason corrected proudly. "I'm to be measured for all new clothes before I go back to Oxford —Father says so."

Gervase made a noncommittal sound, studying his brother more closely. Jason had indeed grown taller, though he hadn't yet attained Hal's or Reg's height—or even Gervase's. But the family features were beginning to pare their way through the puppyish softness, and his coloring was as striking as ever: the sable hair and bright hazel eyes of their mother, though the expression in them was entirely his. All in all, his younger brother was a good-looking boy with the potential to become a handsome man, even with the streak of dirt marring one cheek.

"I see Father's letting you ride Kingmaker," Gervase observed, glancing over at the bay gelding who'd been the duke's mount for years, now being led off towards the stables. "He must be pleased with your progress as a horseman."

"Oh, Kingmaker's well enough," Jason said, with a dismissive shrug. "But he's getting old. Father's promised me a *real* hunter for my birthday. *And* a proper celebration—not some paltry thing tacked on to the Christmas hols!"

"Heaven forbid the Savior's birth should be permitted to overshadow yours," Gervase said dryly, thinking with some regret that his little brother appeared to be as spoiled as ever. He supposed it was only to be expected—and the blame didn't lie entirely with Jason himself. Between the duchess's restraint and the duke's overindulgence, it was little wonder that the boy had turned out this way; only a saint could have emerged unaffected.

His brother glanced at him sharply as though sensing the mockery, then stiffened, his eyes narrowing as he caught sight of something that seemed to vex him even more. Following the direction of Jason's gaze, Gervase identified the source of his displeasure at once.

Major Lord Reginald Lyons was cantering through the gate, some distance ahead of the baggage wagon. All the Lyons children rode well, having been introduced to the saddle at an early age, but Reg's expertise was particularly noticeable, his movements almost impossible to separate from those of his horse. And such a horse... even at a distance, Gervase could tell that his older brother's mount was of a superior quality, his conformation faultless, his coal-black hide glossy with health and good grooming. Jason was staring at that horse, his envy along with his hostility naked on his face.

Reg himself looked almost as robust, Gervase noted, as his older brother swung down from the saddle with easy grace, handing the reins to a groom before striding up to join them. He'd had a bad brush with fever during the regiment's last tour of duty in India, but appeared to have made a full recovery since then. As always, he was the very model of a soldier: tall and broad-shouldered, with a neat blond mustache and piercing blue eyes. The military life fit him like a glove, and Gervase understood his reluctance to give it up. The duke might rage and thunder—he'd done both in Gervase's hearing—but Reg's commitment to the army remained unshaken, despite the recent threat to his health. He was only just thirty, after all, and considered a likely commander of the regiment one day.

"An eye like Mars, to threaten and command," Gervase murmured. As often as Reg irritated him, he couldn't deny his older brother's presence or his military prowess. A grudging respect had developed between them as adults—possibly because they'd been the sons most determined to follow their chosen callings. As the ducal heir, Reg could have used Hal's courtesy title of Earl of Denforth; instead, he'd opted to ignore it in favor of the rank he'd *earned* in the army. *That* merited respect, Gervase thought—far more than an ability to pound one's opponent into the dust during a billiards game or a wrestling match.

"Good afternoon, brother." Reg's greeting sounded almost cordial, and his handshake was firm without being bruising. It was also—rather obviously—directed at Gervase rather than the still-glowering Jason. "Have you just got here, then?"

"Within the last five minutes," Gervase confirmed. "I traveled up from London with Lady Bellamy—she's gone inside with Juliana."

Reg's expression softened, just a fraction. "It will be good to see Margaret again."

"And Alicia." Gervase eyed his brother closely, trying to gauge his response.

"Just so." Reg's tone remained pleasant, but Gervase thought he sounded a touch guarded as well.

"Quite the family reunion Juliana has planned," Gervase went on. "And *she's* expected any minute now, or so I've heard."

Reg raised inquiring brows. "Mother?"

"Who else?" Gervase folded his arms and cocked a brow at his older brother. "The whole family gathered under one roof for the holidays. Think we'll survive it?"

Reg grunted. "Even odds if we do."

"I don't see why there's such a fuss being made over *her*," Jason remarked loudly, jutting out a truculent chin. "Anyone would think the Queen was coming for Christmas!"

Reg's expression tautened, but he did not spare his youngest brother so much as a glance. "Unseasonable weather we're having," he remarked, examining his gloves instead. "I thought the frost had killed all the gnats, but I seem to hear them still buzzing."

Jason flushed, his scowl deepening. Before he could say anything even ruder, Gervase fixed him with a stern gaze. "Mind your manners, whelp—unless you want coal in your stocking instead of a new hunter in your stable!"

"Stop treating me like a child!"

"Behave like one, and you'll be treated like one."

"And your face is dirty," Reg observed, his voice coolly dispassionate.

"Oh, the devil take *both* of you!" Jason burst out, and flung away from them, stalking up the walk with outraged dignity. The front door banged shut behind him.

"Like old times indeed," Gervase remarked with a wry smile. "Father's favorite resenting Mother's favorite. And vice versa."

Reg stiffened, his bearing more military than ever, if possible. "I don't resent Jason. I barely take any notice of him. You're the one who calls him whelp."

"And *you're* the one who did everything but tell him to run up and see his nurse."

Reg flushed in his turn. "Very well, then. It... irks me to see Father making so much of so very little. A scrubby schoolboy who has yet to prove himself in any way that counts."

Gervase raised a brow. "And I suppose you were never a scrubby schoolboy yourself?"

"He didn't make much of *me* then," Reg said shortly. "Or any of us. Except Hal."

And there it was. The shadow of a rivalry that had outlived his eldest brother—and now appeared to have transferred itself to his youngest. Not for the first time, Gervase reflected that there was a certain measure of peace in not being anyone's favorite, despite its having galled him as a boy. "I suspect all of us may be reverting to the nursery stage before this fortnight is over. Shall we go inside?"

Reg gave a curt nod, and they went in together. Lydgate, the Whitborough butler, met them in the foyer and bade them both an austere welcome, as he relieved them of their overcoats and hats. The rest of the family, they were told, was assembled in the Great Hall.

The brothers set off down the passage, almost side by side, easily matching strides despite Reg's greater height. The sounds of laughter and mingled conversation drifted out to them as they neared the doorway—so familiar that Gervase found himself *almost* smiling.

A covert glance at Reg revealed a similarly nostalgic expression on his brother's face. So even the major wasn't immune to the charms of home and family at Christmas. *All yet seems well...* so one might as well enjoy it while it lasted, Gervase mused as he stepped across the threshold—and into a scene that might have come straight from his childhood.

As always, the Great Hall was bright with lamplight, but today, a fire—a wood fire, no less, though there was coal aplenty—burned merrily in the fireplace. Baskets brimming with holly and ivy rested on a trestle table, as though waiting to be strewn about the place by knowledgeable hands. The Christmas tree, as yet unadorned, stood in its usual corner, towering over even Reg and perfuming the air with its evergreen sharpness. Other scents mingled with it: oranges, cloves, apples, and mulling spices. For a moment, Gervase felt as though no time at all had passed, and he was a boy again, back at Denforth for the holidays.

Not surprisingly, almost everyone was grouped about the fireplace. Even from a distance Gervase could see Margaret, a steaming cup cradled between her hands, sitting between Juliana and Elaine. As he and Reg approached, several faces turned in their direction, some breaking into smiles of welcome. Jason's, Gervase noted, was not among them: the boy, his face now shining with cleanliness, regarded his brothers from beneath lowered brows and turned his back rather pointedly, stretching his hands towards the fire and making a show of warming himself.

But Juliana rose and came forward at once, her face

radiant. "There you are! I was wondering when you'd join us! And Reg," she flung her arms around him as she had around Gervase, "so glad you're here! Did you have good hunting with the Quorn?"

"Passable, infant." Reg returned her embrace, then held her a little away from him. "*You*, however, look decidedly better than passable."

"'Better than passable'?" Juliana echoed, her blue eyes widening with deceptive innocence. "Gervase told me I'm 'quite presentable.' *Ma foi*, between the two of you, my head will be *hopelessly* turned!"

Reg unbent enough to smile fondly at her. "We're your older brothers. We have reputations to uphold."

"Besides, it wouldn't do to play favorites," Gervase added. "Especially as *all* of you are a most welcome sight."

"Very tactful," Juliana approved as she took his arm and Reg's, smiling impartially up at them both. "Come closer to the fire, and let's have a proper reunion."

So they did. Their other sisters had come with their husbands: Madeline with Hugo, Elaine with Alasdair. Gervase exchanged embraces with the women and handshakes with the men, and inquired after his various nieces and nephews, who were comfortably ensconced with their respective nannies up in the Denforth nursery.

Sipping mulled cider, Gervase let his gaze travel about the intimate family circle. Whether it was the softening effects of cider or sentiment, he found himself genuinely pleased to be where he was, with whom he was—at least for the moment. Surrounded by the warmth of his sisters, the camaraderie of his brothers— even Jason, beginning to emerge from his sullens to take part in the conversations going on around him. And Margaret, her face aglow in the firelight, fitting in with them as effortlessly as she had when they were all children together.

Then a familiar step was heard in the passage, and the Duke of Whitborough strode into the Hall. And everyone lounging about the fireplace immediately straightened up, as though galvanized by an electric current—even Reg.

When he was a boy, Gervase had thought his father

"bestrode the world like a Colossus"—and even now, with nearly thirty years of living under his belt, he could not deny the sheer presence of the Duke of Whitborough. His Grace wore his usual country tweeds, and his strongly handsome face was flushed with cold. There were more creases about his eyes and Gervase thought he saw more glints of grey in the thick head of tawny hair, but at fifty-six, his father still cut an impressive figure. And knew it.

"The Golden Duke"—the sun around which they all revolved, willy-nilly—surveyed them with a smile Gervase knew well... and had long ago learned to distrust.

"My boys," he greeted his two elder sons with a gleam of paternal pride—or was it calculation?—in his still-keen blue eyes. "It's good to see you here."

"Father," Gervase intoned, while Reg merely inclined his head.

"And my girls," the duke went on, his expression lightening further, but then he'd often found dealing with his daughters a good deal easier than dealing with his sons. "A bouquet of beauty on a cold winter's day! And Lady Bellamy," he greeted Margaret. "Delightful to have you with us again."

Margaret colored slightly, but smiled back. "Thank you for inviting me, Duke."

"My pleasure," His Grace replied, and turned to welcome his daughters' husbands.

Gervase bit back a sharp exhale, wondering how he could have been so obtuse. Until this moment, he'd believed the family gathering was Juliana's idea, indulged by a doting father. He couldn't have been more mistaken; whatever Juliana's desires, she'd never have been permitted to carry out this scheme... unless it tallied with the duke's own plans, whatever they were. Darting a sidelong glance at Reg, he saw by his older brother's rigid expression that he'd come to the same conclusion.

The whole family gathered under one roof. Think we'll survive it? His earlier words echoed mockingly in his ears. Reg had given them even odds. Fortifying himself with a swallow of cider, Gervase hoped grimly that his brother hadn't been overstating the case.

"Your Grace," Lydgate spoke from the doorway. "The

duchess's carriage is approaching the gates. She should be here momentarily."

Now it was the duke's turn to pause, his expression arrested... before disappearing under a mask of pleasant imperturbability. "Thank you, Lydgate," he said, after a moment. "Please go and see that Her Grace is properly attended on her arrival."

The tension in the Great Hall had thickened to a level commensurate with a London pea-souper, Gervase reflected. He glanced down at Margaret, who was fretting her lower lip, looking even more anxious than she had on seeing his father.

"You could plead fatigue from the journey and ask to be taken upstairs, you know," he said, stooping to murmur the words into her ear.

Her chin tilted up at that in the challenging way he'd always loved, and her velvety eyes sparked. "And miss your mother's grand entrance? *Not for thy fairy kingdom!* Only," she ran a nervous hand over her skirt, "do I look fit to meet her?"

"More than fit," Gervase assured her. She'd removed her cape and hat, but her dress looked mostly uncreased, and her hair—women always worried about their hair— was in order.

Margaret wasn't the only woman concerned about her appearance, Gervase noted. His sisters were surreptitiously patting their own hair and smoothing wrinkles, real or imagined, from their skirts as well. Only the knowledge of how ridiculous he'd look prevented him from taking a similar inventory of himself. As far as he knew, his face and clothes were clean—Margaret would have informed him otherwise—and that would have to suffice.

It couldn't have been more than five minutes before Lydgate officially announced the duchess's arrival at Denforth. Remembering Jason's earlier gibe about the Queen coming for Christmas, Gervase couldn't help thinking that not even Her Majesty could have received a more ceremonious welcome than Her Grace of Whitborough, standing framed in the doorway like a particularly splendid portrait, with her family gathered in the Great Hall to welcome her. There might be more silver in her dark hair, more fine lines about her eyes and mouth when one looked more closely, but his mother's bones would keep her beautiful until the day she died. And the rich burgundy cloak she wore only heightened that beauty.

The duke strode across the room to greet his wife. "Welcome, madam. Had you a peaceful crossing?"

She extended her hand, smiling. "I found nothing to complain of, Duke. The Channel appeared to be on its best behavior." Her voice was the same as Gervase remembered: deep-toned and throaty, her pronunciation flawless. Helene de Sevigny-Lyons spoke perfect French and English, her accent pure in both languages.

The duke bowed over that elegant hand. "I'd expect nothing less for your passage, my lady. Come over to the fire—our children await."

"So I see." She took in all of them at a glance; the duchess never missed much. "What a welcome this is," she remarked to her husband. "I'm amazed you didn't have the whole staff gathered in the courtyard just for my arrival."

"Say the word, madam, and it shall be done at once."

The duchess shook her head. "In this barbarous winter, they'd freeze solid within minutes. I'd far rather dispense with the ceremony than the servants." She turned to survey her children... and then swept up to them in a whirl of velvet and expensive, ineffable scent.

"Jason, is that *you*?" she greeted her youngest son first. "It seems only yesterday you were the merest schoolboy. My word, how you've grown! And you look so tidy too," she added with evident approval. "Quite the young gentleman!"

Jason flushed, suddenly looking the schoolboy Her Grace had called him. His expression was half-sulky, half-wistful—almost as it had been when he'd seen Reg's horse. Relations between him and their mother had never been easy, Gervase reflected, feeling a reluctant tug of sympathy. Then she was before *him*, her hazel-green eyes gazing up at him speculatively. He had a moment of being glad that he had, in fact, grown tall enough to look down upon her.

"Gervase." One slender gloved hand reached up to touch his cheek, and he had to resist an unexpected urge to lean into that touch, however briefly. "You're looking very prosperous. I hope you aren't burning the midnight oil too intensely. No success is worth one's health.

"And Reg," the duchess continued, moving along. "Your new rank becomes you, Major, to say nothing of that uniform! And I trust the English climate has restored you as well." Her brow creased in a faint frown as she regarded her favorite son. "Have you lost weight? We shall have to make sure you regain some of it during your leave."

Reg was—almost—smiling. "Fattening me up like the Christmas goose, Mother?"

She laughed, a delicious rippling sound, and took his hands in a light clasp. "Never as corpulent as that, *mon fils*! Merely enough to fill out those splendid regimentals of yours."

Her gaze alighted upon her daughters. "Darlings! How lovely you are, every one of you. Madeline, *chérie*," she kissed her eldest daughter on both cheeks, "you look tired—you *must* make Hugo take you away for a holiday in the New Year," she added, nodding towards her first son-in-law. "And Elaine—you're positively glowing! Are you and Alasdair expecting again?"

Gervase shot a glance at his second sister, whose flush gave her away at once. And her husband, the Duke of Castlebrooke, looked almost as flummoxed.

"We—we hadn't intended to announce it just yet, *Maman*," Elaine faltered. "It's still early, you see..."

"A mother can always tell, sweeting," the duchess assured her before moving on to embrace her youngest daughter. "Juliana, I see *you're* in looks as well! University life must agree with you, though you are doubtless leading your tutors a merry dance."

Coming to Margaret, she smiled warmly. "How like your mother you've grown, my dear! And what a pleasure to see you here again, at Christmas."

Margaret relaxed visibly. "Thank you, Duchess. It's a pleasure to see you here as well."

Her Grace laughed again. "'Here,' being the operative word, of course! My visits to Yorkshire have become as rare as a rose in winter—and for much the same reason," she added, with a theatrical shudder. "To judge from my experience today, the climate is as ghastly as ever."

"Then you should be pleased by the new steam radiators I've had installed in the bedchambers," Whitborough said, coming to her side.

Her brows rose. "Improvements at Denforth? You astonish me, Duke."

"Says the woman who insisted upon central heating in the main wing more than seven years ago," he retorted. "But even that thin French blood of yours may find Denforth sufficiently warm this Christmas, my lady."

The duchess lowered her eyes, her expression uncharacteristically demure. "I am all amazement... my lord. What other surprises do you have in store for us?"

What, indeed? Gervase wondered, watching his parents watch each other: a pair of fencers trying to anticipate their opponent's next move.

Whitborough gave his wife a slow, almost lazy smile and took her hand in his. "You have more than a fortnight to find out, *ma belle Helene.*"

A long, searching look—the duke's deceptively guileless blue eyes gazing into the tip-tilted hazel eyes of his duchess. He lifted their twined hands to his mouth, brushed his lips against her fingers, before turning to face the rest of his family. "My lady. My children. I promise all of you—a Christmas to remember."

Grasping his cup more tightly at the words, Gervase wondered if it was too early for something much stiffer than cider.

Chapter Four

OVERALL, the arrival had gone off well, much to Margaret's relief. Whatever her own qualms, the duke and duchess had shown no hint of awkwardness or constraint when they welcomed her to Denforth. So the first hurdle had been cleared successfully, and others lay ahead. Well, she would do her best to take them in stride.

As for Their Graces themselves, they remained as fascinating... and unfathomable as ever. They'd baffled her as a girl; their often-contentious interaction couldn't have been more different from the comfortable rapport between her own parents. Little wonder then, she mused, that several of their children—most notably, their sons—had grown up to be rather complicated people. Hal had actually been one of the simpler Lyons boys, though he'd had his share of problems, most notably his dependence on the duke's favor—and purse strings. Margaret suspected he'd been more than a little envious of the freedom Reg and Gervase enjoyed, as younger sons, though he never would have admitted as much to either of them.

"Margaret?" Juliana's voice broke in to her thoughts, and she looked up to find the younger woman smiling at her. "I remember how fond you were of the South Tower chamber, so I've put you in there. I hope that's all right."

The same room she'd had five years ago, Margaret thought with a *frisson*. The Christmas she'd taken her future in her own hands... but Juliana had been only fifteen at the time, and so not likely to recall its significance. "That will be lovely, thank you," she said quickly, rising from her chair. The family was vacating the Great Hall in twos and threes, retiring to their rooms to rest before dinner. She caught Gervase's eye, and he sent her a brief smile that was almost without irony as he and Reg filed out of the room.

Juliana beckoned to a footman. "Albert here will take you to your chamber now. And I've already had hot water sent, so you can have a bath. The dressing bell will be rung at six."

About an hour and a half from now, Margaret estimated. Thanking Juliana again, she followed her escort upstairs, and was soon enjoying the hot bath her hostess had promised. Afterwards, she wrapped herself in a thick woolen dressing gown and brushed her hair out before the blazing fire. Tilda was now unpacking Margaret's clothes, hanging the gowns in the wardrobe, folding the rest away in the huge chest-of-drawers.

Margaret glanced about the tower room, which, apart from the new steam radiator the duke had mentioned, appeared scarcely changed since her last visit: still furnished in robin's egg blue, with touches of cream and rose for warmth. The bed with its embroidered canopy and curtains looked as lofty and queenly as ever, the mahogany secretary and bookcases shone with polish, and the panes of the arched casement window sparkled in the wintry light.

How she'd loved the view from the tower window! Smiling nostalgically, Margaret rose and drifted over to the window, looking out over the south lawn. Now it lay beneath a blanket of snow, but in the spring and summer, that had been one of their favorite places to picnic —possibly because of the slight hollow in the earth wide enough to encompass all of them. In more fanciful moments, Margaret had imagined that it was like lying in the palm of a giant hand. When carpeted with velvety green grass, starred with buttercups and clover, the hollow became a delightful place for children to loll, daydream, exchange confidences—and the occasional difference of opinion.

Margaret's lips twitched as she recalled one vivid example of the latter. She'd been fifteen at the time, and in the grip of her first passion—not for Hal or any other boy, but for a Plantagenet king, slain in battle nearly four hundred years before. A king from whom her father's side of the family liked to claim descent on the distaff side, and whose reputation she'd burned to salvage from the ravages of Tudor historians...

"King Richard, late mercifully reigning over us, was through great treason, piteously slain and murdered, to the great heaviness of our city," *she quoted dramatically to her audience on a sultry August afternoon that marked the anniversary of Bosworth Field.*

Reg shrugged as he whittled away at a twig. "A Yorkist epitaph for a Yorkist king. Nothing unusual in that."

"But don't you see?" Margaret appealed. "If the city of York had the courage to speak that way—in their public records, no less!—about Richard, after Bosworth Field, then he can't *have been as black as he was painted! Maybe he didn't kill the Princes in the Tower! And maybe all of England* wasn't *flocking to Henry Tudor's banner, or hailing him as some great savior!"*

"Unfortunately, the Stanleys *flocked to Tudor's banner," Gervase observed, without looking up from his book. "And thereby hangs the tale."*

"Turncoats and traitors, the lot of them!" Margaret snapped.

"Perhaps, but they played their game more shrewdly than the king," he pointed out.

"And so we should let the likes of them *have the last word on history?" she challenged.*

"What does it matter who has the last word?" Hal asked in genuine bewilderment. "The man's been dead for centuries, so it can hardly make any difference to him."

"But he's still being talked about," *Margaret persisted. "Still* slandered. *And with every Tudor account, one gets further and further from the* truth. *There must be more to the story than Shakespeare—or any of his sources—ever knew!"*

"That's practically a given," Elaine agreed, looking up from the daisy chain she was making with Juliana. "Shakespeare was

a playwright, not a historian. And he wouldn't have dared to write anything too critical of the Tudors, in any case."

"Except that people generally prefer an exciting legend, accurate or inaccurate, to dry-as-dust facts and figures," Gervase pointed out, setting aside his book to enter the fray. "Drama trumps history almost every time, in popular opinion."

"Then we need more compelling accounts of the truth!" Margaret declared. "Real histories that will make people believe —or at least rethink the matter."

"Preferably written by someone who didn't end in Bedlam," Gervase drawled.

Margaret flushed. "Sir George Buck wasn't insane when he made the case for Richard's innocence! And Sir Horace Walpole believed in it too, and he was perfectly sound of mind."

"Between the Bard and Buck, my money's on the Bard," Gervase retorted. "As for Walpole, I doubt his best could compete even with Shakespeare's worst. Theater audiences want to see Crouchback, not some long-suffering, misunderstood martyr." His voice dropped to a deeper register, his features twisting into a cynical sneer as he quoted, maddeningly: "And therefore, since I cannot prove a lover, / To entertain these fair well-spoken days, / I am determined to prove a villain. / And hate the idle pleasures of these days."

Margaret just managed not to grind her teeth. "Theater audiences are welcome to 'Crouchback,' as long as serious scholars may have the real Richard the Third!"

Gervase raised his brows. "Would you not consider Sir Thomas More and Polydore Virgil to be serious scholars?"

"More and Virgil were—" Margaret broke off, trying to find words sufficiently scathing to convey her opinion of those two as reliable authorities on Richard III.

"Don't listen to Ger, Margaret!" Elaine advised, laughing. "He'll take the opposing side in an argument just to be perverse. And to get a rise out of you!"

Margaret glared at Gervase, who merely shrugged. "Temper becomes you," he observed with that crooked smile that made her want to lob her bottle of lemonade at his head.

"You are the most odious boy in the world," she told him darkly.

He bowed. "Thank you. I appreciate knowing that I excel at something."

Margaret shook her head, still smiling at the memory. That had been the first time she and Gervase had clashed over the matter of King Richard's innocence, but certainly not the last! Other skirmishes had followed, with both of them presenting their respective arguments thoroughly—and, in Margaret's case, sometimes heatedly. She'd been so determined not to let Gervase get the better of her on this! Not for some months had she realized how much her debating skills had improved as a result—and that her confidence had grown as well. More than that, she'd found herself almost enjoying their ongoing war of words. And she rather suspected Gervase had enjoyed it as well, if only because he'd never been able to resist a good argument. Besides, it wasn't as if anyone else in her family or his shared her interest. How strange that the boy who'd so often been a thorn in her side growing up should have become such a good friend to her...

The clang of the dressing bell roused her from her thoughts, and she turned from the window to find Tilda opening the wardrobe again.

"What gown will you be wearing tonight, my lady?"

"Hmmm." Margaret went over to survey her choices for the evening. She'd emerged from her year of mourning back in February, but even then, she'd dressed quietly for several months in dove-grey and lavender. Only in summer had she got up the nerve to order some gowns in the brighter colors she'd used to favor, colors that Alex had liked to see her wear. It still sent a pang through her to know he'd never see her in these, but she knew he wouldn't have wanted her to mourn forever. Or spend the rest of her life in widow's weeds, like the Queen bereft of her consort.

Which eliminated the black satin, right away—she'd packed that one more out of habit, remembering her mother's dictate that every woman should own one good black evening gown, but tonight it would remind her too much of her losses. Not just Alex, but Hal as well—and it would almost certainly evoke the same memory for her hosts, Margaret realized. Sobered, she chose the amber brocade instead: the rich hue would flatter her fair complexion and chestnut hair, while the heavy silk would provide additional warmth. Denforth Castle might have central heating now, but she remembered how cold the dining room could be. The bustle would be rather a bore—the size had increased over the last few years, though Alicia had written from Paris that it was to become smaller in the spring—but it was still one of her most fashionable dresses.

Tilda helped her into the gown and matching slippers, then dressed her hair high with gold filigree combs, and applied discreet touches of powder and rouge to her face. Finally, from her jewel box, Margaret selected a necklace of heavy amber beads—a gift from her father on her eighteenth birthday, and a more judicious choice than the diamonds Alex had given her as a wedding gift or the pearls she'd received from the Whitboroughs on her betrothal to Hal. There were amber earrings too: pretty drops dangling from twists of gilt wire.

Surveying the finished result in the mirror, she felt a cautious satisfaction. Coming to Denforth might have revived childhood memories, but at least she *looked* the grown woman—and countess—she had become since her last visit: elegant, even sophisticated. Unexpectedly, she caught herself wondering if Gervase would like her evening gown as much he'd liked her traveling ensemble, then sternly told herself not to be absurd. She did not dress for him any more than he dressed for her, though his approval certainly would be welcome. The women in his family were never less than exquisitely dressed themselves, all possessing the matchless French instinct for style.

Margaret swallowed, unsure whether the sudden hollowness in her stomach was due to nerves or merely hunger. Stifling her lingering qualms, she donned her evening gloves, draped a light shawl about her shoulders, and hurried for the door, her silk skirts rustling about her.

MUCH TO HER RELIEF, she was neither the first nor the last to arrive in the Great Hall. Over by the Christmas tree, Juliana, a vision in cornflower blue, was deep in conversation with her eldest sister, wearing her favorite shade of dusky rose and looking—as always—startlingly like the duchess. Mother and daughter had similar natures too, Margaret reflected: both strong-willed and determined to have their own way, but Madeline appeared to have mellowed over the years—possibly due to her husband's influence. Lord Saxby was famously even-tempered and more easygoing than the duke, at least in domestic matters.

Margaret made her way to the sisters, who greeted her warmly and regarded her gown with approval.

"You look splendid," Juliana told her, taking her hands in a light clasp. "It's good to see you wearing bright colors again."

"Thank you. It *feels* good to wear them again," Margaret confessed. "In spite of—" she changed course, not wanting to cast a pall over the evening. "You look wonderful yourself, Juliana. Is that gown from Paris?"

"Well, my dressmaker is, which is just as good," Juliana replied, giving her hands a reassuring squeeze. "There's no better time than Christmas for looking one's best, is there? Even the men," she added, nodding towards the fireplace.

Following her gaze, Margaret saw Reg, Gervase, and Lord Saxby gathered before the hearth: the former in regimentals, the other two in immaculate evening dress. No sign thus far of the duke—or her brother, for that matter.

She turned to Juliana. "Has Augustus arrived yet?"

"He has," Juliana confirmed. "About an hour ago, so he should be down soon." She paused, a delicate blush creeping into her cheeks. "He's grown quite handsome, by the way."

"A veritable Adonis," Madeline spoke for the first time. "Quite a transformation from his days as an undergraduate!"

"He's filled out quite a bit since leaving Oxford," Margaret agreed. "And his coloring is so much like Papa's." Although she had to admit, if only to herself, that Augustus's manner was entirely different. Papa had been a gentle soul, wholly lacking in arrogance, perhaps because he'd never expected to inherit the dukedom. Until his older brother's death, he'd been destined for the Church—or perhaps for a scholar's life. By contrast, Augustus had known from an early age that he would hold one of the highest titles in England someday. And fond as she was of her brother, Margaret couldn't help thinking he'd have been the better for just a touch of their father's humility. Even Hal, a duke's heir himself, had found Augustus's airs a touch absurd.

"Is it difficult, calling *him* Langdale now?" Juliana asked.

"A little," Margaret admitted. Papa had died two years after her marriage, and she still missed him sorely, especially since becoming widowed. He'd liked and respected Alex, while Augustus, so much younger, had barely known him. "I still expect to see Papa whenever I hear someone address Augustus by his title."

"I can't imagine anyone but Father as Duke of Whitborough," Juliana confessed. "Not even my brothers."

"Better not let Reg hear you say that—or Jason for that matter. Not if you want this Christmas peace to hold."

Margaret just managed not to jump when Gervase spoke from directly behind her. Those cat-feet of his... she'd never heard him approach. She slid him a covert glance, noticing how well the stark black and white of his evening kit became him. His expression was nearly as austere, his grey gaze fixed on his sister.

Juliana pulled a face. "Point taken, Gerry! Though I can't see why Jason should care. He's the youngest, after all, and unlikely to inherit."

"He's also Father's favorite, as he never ceases to remind us," Gervase retorted. "If primogeniture wasn't the law of the land, he'd be doing his level best to cut Reg out."

"And *you* wouldn't?" Madeline challenged. "I remember how you and Reg *both* acted when Hal was still alive." Her voice was not quite steady when she spoke her twin's name.

Margaret tensed as Gervase matched his older sister stare for stare. "On the contrary, Madeline, I think I've wasted enough time tilting at that particular windmill," he replied evenly. "Which is a realization I came to *before* we lost Hal."

Madeline's gaze dropped, and Margaret suppressed a faint shiver. She'd almost forgotten—perhaps had chosen to forget—how... fraught even casual interactions between the Lyons siblings could get. And Madeline and Gervase were usually on *good* terms.

Juliana said with determined cheer, "And we're all so proud of your success, Gerry! Margaret mentioned that your firm won its last case."

Gervase looked at her then, and Margaret felt herself flush at the warmth in his eyes.

"It seemed a victory worth acknowledging," she said, trying to sound casual.

"I am delighted that you think so." And despite his light tone, Margaret thought he meant what he said.

"And doesn't she look wonderful tonight?" Juliana asked. "That shade of amber is just glorious with her coloring."

"Enchanting." Gervase lifted Margaret's hand to his lips in a courtly gesture that nonetheless quickened her pulse and made her skin tingle beneath her glove. "*Here comes the Countess; now heaven walks on earth.*"

Sensing that Juliana and Madeline were watching with increased interest, Margaret strove to match his tone. "Never at a loss for a quotation, are you?"

He smiled with only a trace of irony. "I thought that one particularly apt."

"*I can no other offer make but thanks*," she retorted, from the same play, and saw his appreciative smile deepen until those blasted dimples made an appearance.

"Good heavens, are you two *still* at it?" Another voice, light and merry, inquired from behind them. "Between the pair of you, you must know the entire First Folio by heart!"

"Elaine!" Half-relieved, half-regretful at the interruption, Margaret turned to greet her friend, the most serene—outwardly, at least—of the Lyons sisters. "What can I say? Your exasperating brother has a way of bringing out the competitor in me."

"Tell me something I don't know," Elaine retorted, throwing Gervase a teasing look. "But competition appears to agree with you, my dear," she added to Margaret. "You look absolutely *ravissante*, tonight."

"So do you." Elaine wore a jade-green gown that did remarkable things for her hazel eyes, but Margaret suspected that impending motherhood was responsible for that special glow to which the duchess had referred earlier. And Elaine's husband, Alasdair, was gazing at her as though she was the most precious thing on earth. Margaret felt a wistful pang, not unmixed with envy. Fond as she was of her stepsons, she could not help regretting the child she and Alex had been denied in their short time together. But that was an old grief, which would *not* prevent her from rejoicing for her friend. "I'm so happy for you, by the way."

"Indeed. Congratulations to you both." Gervase smiled at his sister and reached over to clasp his brother-in-law's hand. "Are you hoping for a son or a daughter this time?"

"As we've been blessed with one of each, we'd be happy with either," Alasdair replied.

"As long as he or she is healthy," Elaine added. "Although," her expression grew pensive, "it might be more *practical* to have another boy. A spare to follow the heir."

"It might be more *peaceful* to have another girl," Gervase observed dryly.

Madeline gave him a quelling look, then asked solicitously, "Have you been well, my dear? No faintness or nausea? I'd the most dreadful morning sickness myself this last time."

Elaine shook her head. "Oh, no, I've been in excellent health throughout, save for a touch of queasiness in the first weeks. But that's passed off, and I find myself utterly ravenous this evening."

"Then I hope you approve of tonight's dinner!" Juliana laughed. "Among other things, I've asked Mrs. Hill to prepare one of her famous roasts. With Yorkshire pudding and an apple tart to follow."

"*The roast beef of England.*" Elaine closed her eyes and gave a blissful sigh. "Sounds just perfect for a cold winter's night."

"Talking of things that look good enough to eat..." Madeline murmured, not quite *sotto voce*, nudging Juliana and nodding towards the doorway.

Inevitably, everyone else followed the direction of her gaze. And despite knowing how much her brother's looks had improved, Margaret experienced a jolt of surprise akin to what the other women must have felt on first seeing him again. Even Gervase looked slightly startled by Augustus's metamorphosis from cygnet to swan.

A veritable Adonis, Madeline had called him, and she hadn't been exaggerating by much. From a weedy adolescent, Augustus had grown into an undeniably handsome young man, broad-shouldered but trim, his hair a true golden-blond, a shade or two lighter than Hal's or Reg's. His eyes were a pale, almost icy blue, but still arresting, and thickly lashed, and the somber hues of evening dress provided a perfect foil for his fair coloring. He looked so like their father for a moment that Margaret's heart ached, then he caught sight of her and smiled—the rather practiced smile he'd cultivated to conceal a few crooked teeth—and the resemblance vanished.

"Margaret." He strode over to greet her, bestowing a light, decorous kiss on her cheek. "I am delighted to see you here, and looking so well."

As a countess and a duke's daughter should, Margaret translated without difficulty. Still, Augustus's concern with appearance did not mean his greeting was insincere. She returned his salute, taking care not to muss his clothes. "Likewise, my dear. Have you heard from Alicia?"

"I received a telegram from her today," he replied. "You'll be pleased to know that she's safely arrived in England and will be staying with Bourne and his family tonight, then join us here at Denforth tomorrow."

"Oh, good," Margaret hailed the news with satisfaction. Earl Bourne—their distant cousin Ernest—owned a pleasant manor house in Oxfordshire, just a few hours away by train. "I'm looking forward to seeing her."

"As we all are," Juliana said brightly. "Langdale, you remember my sister Elaine. And her husband, the Duke of Castlebrooke, and my brother, Lord Gervase."

"Of course." Augustus bowed over Elaine's hand, then nodded at Alasdair and Gervase. "While Alicia and I were among the youngest of our little band, I do recall our adventures fondly. And I am happy to be here among such old family friends."

A pretty speech, Margaret thought, if a bit pompous for someone only twenty-three. But Augustus had always been precocious—and the Lyons sisters looked wholly charmed.

It was perhaps unfortunate that Jason entered the Hall at that moment. While the youngest Lyons boy wasn't bad-looking, his unfinished features and gawky limbs marked him as an adolescent: no longer a charming child, not yet a confident young man. Nor did he appear to be comfortable in his evening clothes—most likely because he was in the process of growing out of them. Margaret could glimpse nearly an inch of bare wrist showing beyond his sleeve, and from the way he was running a finger around the inside of his collar, he appeared to find his necktie too tight as well. A more striking contrast than the one between him and polished, self-assured Augustus could scarcely be imagined.

Margaret experienced a flash of sympathy. She knew Jason the least well of all the Lyons brood; Hal had had little use for his youngest brother, and Reg even less. And it hadn't escaped her notice that Jason was more than a bit spoiled and willful. On the other hand, it couldn't have been easy for him being born at the tail end of a large, contentious, competitive family. Not as handsome or athletic as Hal and Reg, not as clever as Gervase... little wonder that Jason clung to his father's favoritism as a way to feel important.

"He looks about as comfortable as a tied dog," Gervase murmured, from just behind her.

Margaret looked up and saw the same reluctant sympathy she was feeling reflected on his face as he regarded his brother. Jason was glancing from one end of the Hall to the other, clearly unsure whether to join Reg and Saxby by the fire or everyone else beside the Christmas tree.

Gervase huffed a faint sigh, and beckoned the next time Jason looked in their direction. The boy's sulky expression lightened—which improved his appearance remarkably, in Margaret's opinion—and he began to make his way towards them.

"That was kind," Margaret said in a low voice.

Gervase shrugged a shoulder. "He might as well go where he's less likely to be snubbed."

"True enough," she conceded, smiling ruefully. Keeping Reg and Jason apart as much as possible was also more likely to result in a happy outcome.

And so it proved. Jason's sisters welcomed him affectionately and introduced him to Augustus, who greeted him with appropriate formality but without any of the condescension that might have rankled the younger man. A few minutes later, Reg and Saxby broke off whatever conversation they were having by the fire and came over to greet Augustus too. Much to Margaret's relief, no snubbing took place, but then, it was easier to avoid potential altercations in a crowd. They were all conversing amicably enough, when the dinner bell sounded—and the last two members of the house party swept into the room together.

Margaret had always considered the phrase "time stood still" to be an exaggeration. But seeing the Duke and Duchess of Whitborough enter, arm in arm, as they had so many times in the past, she experienced the sense of the years rolling back. Once again, she was a child, a schoolgirl, a newly betrothed debutante, watching the most striking couple of her acquaintance make a royal progress through their kingdom. Tonight the duchess was resplendent in oyster satin, trimmed with narrow bands of sable. Diamonds glittered about her still-smooth throat, and a diamond crescent gleamed in her piled dark hair. As a peeress of the realm, she could have worn a tiara as well, but she looked quite regal enough without one.

Tonight the duke matched her in elegance. For all his professed disdain of formal dress, full evening kit suited His Grace just as well as the country tweeds he favored. Lamplight cast a halo upon his tawny hair, concealing any hint of grey, and his gaze, blue and piercing, swept the Hall, encompassing everything and everyone in a single look.

Margaret slid a covert glance at Gervase, surprising an almost wistful expression on his face before he resumed the cool impassivity he usually displayed in the presence of his family.

His siblings were no less affected, though they showed their feelings more openly. Juliana was positively aglow with happiness, her eyes—blue as her father's— shining like twin sapphires. Elaine and Madeline too were smiling, almost mistily. Jason, by contrast, was biting his lip, his expression wavering between awed and sullen. How clearly did *he* remember his parents, in happier days? Margaret wondered. The family almost never spoke of how and when the estrangement between the Whitboroughs had first arisen, but Margaret thought the rift had occurred around the time of Jason's birth.

Over the years it had appeared to narrow—but Hal's death had widened it to a seemingly unbridgeable chasm... until this Christmas, at least.

They paused now, almost in the middle of the Hall, and the duke's searching gaze alighted upon Augustus.

"Langdale." Still arm in arm with his wife, he approached the younger man and extended his hand. "Welcome to Denforth. Glad that you could join us for the holidays."

Augustus clasped the proffered hand briefly. "Thank you for inviting me, Whitborough. Duchess." He bowed over her hand. "You are as exquisite as ever."

She smiled. "And you are the image of your father as a young man. I hope you are finding everything to your satisfaction at Denforth?"

"Indeed. I was just telling Lady Juliana how comfortable my chamber is, especially with the new steam radiator," Augustus replied.

"I put Langdale in the Red Room, Mama," Juliana said, a slightly questioning lift to her voice. "It was one of the first bedchambers to be renovated."

"A fine choice, *petite*," the duchess approved, bringing a flush of pleasure to her youngest daughter's cheeks.

Just then Lydgate appeared in the doorway. "Dinner is served, Your Grace."

"Excellent," the duchess said. "I find myself absolutely famished. Juliana, *chérie*, I trust that you have the seating in hand as well?"

Juliana assured her that she did, and immediately began to assign partners for the formal procession in to dinner. Inevitably, the duchess was matched with Augustus, but Margaret was startled to find the Duke of Whitborough offering her his arm.

"Lady Bellamy, if I may have the pleasure of escorting you?" he inquired, smiling down at her with the fondness she remembered from her days as Hal's betrothed.

Margaret returned the smile, stifling an unexpected pang of regret that she wasn't to be paired with Gervase. "I should be delighted, Duke. Thank you." And taking her arm of her former almost-father-in-law, she allowed him to lead her in to dinner.

❄

In retrospect, Gervase supposed he shouldn't have been surprised that the peace did not last the entire evening. As it was, they all probably should have been grateful that it lasted through dinner.

Things had begun well, for the most part. He'd been disappointed but not surprised that his father was chosen as Margaret's escort. With the exception of his mother and Elaine, she was the highest-ranking lady present—and had the added advantage of not being a blood relation. Perhaps wisely, Juliana had assigned partners with more concern for harmony than hierarchy. She'd exercised similar prudence with the seating, placing Reg and Jason at opposite ends of the table, and closer to the parent with whom each was on better terms. Meanwhile, Gervase had the consolation of finding himself seated next to Margaret, with Juliana on his other side.

And while he did not claim to be an expert on such things, he thought his sister had done a creditable job with the cavernous space that was the dining room, making it look almost cozy with the artful placement of some Chinese screens and a potted palm or two. The linen tablecloth shone white as a new snowfall, the china and crystal gleamed, and an exquisite arrangement of camellias and ivy in a silver epergne graced the center of the table. Gervase noticed the slight nod his mother bestowed upon his sister, who colored again at this unspoken accolade. The duchess was nothing if not exacting when it came to entertaining, and while Juliana might be performing some duties as hostess tonight, there was no question as to who was mistress here. And only a matter of time before Her Grace took over the reins for this gathering from her daughter, Gervase estimated—not that Juliana was likely to resist.

Dinner itself was everything it should have been, in such a house, at such a season: elegant but hearty, and accompanied by the best wines Denforth's cellar could offer. A selection of the French dishes his mother loved were on hand, as well as the wholly English roast with all the trimmings of gravy, Yorkshire pudding, and roast potatoes.

"Better than Simpson's on the Strand," Margaret said, blissfully inhaling the savory steam that rose from her laden plate. "And that club of yours too, I'll wager."

"Perhaps," Gervase conceded, as he cut his portion into bite-sized morsels. But he suspected—no, knew—that she was right. No one knew her way about a roast better than Mrs. Hill, and his first mouthful confirmed that she hadn't lost her touch. To judge from the expressions all around the table, everyone else was equally impressed. Even his mother, usually so critical of English food, had no fault to find, and conversation languished for a time as everyone paid tribute to the cook's skill. A good thing, in Gervase's view, as it prevented people from dining on each other instead—an all too frequent occurrence when his family got together.

Only one thing was lacking... and Gervase wouldn't have mentioned it for worlds. But it seemed *wrong* somehow that Hal wasn't here, vying with Reg for any remaining Yorkshire puddings, praising Mrs. Hill extravagantly. His older brother had always loved Christmas, and in mellower moments, the rest of his family had been carried along on the wave of his enthusiasm.

Looking across the table, he saw Madeline, a pensive, almost melancholy expression on her face. He caught her eye and sent her a faint smile, an olive branch for their sharp exchange earlier, and saw her lips curve in response. Surely of them all, she missed Hal the most, though they'd been as different as twins could possibly be. Family wisdom held that Madeline had got all the sense, Hal all the spontaneity, but their bond had never been in question. Gervase hoped that Hugo and her children filled some of the void left by Hal's death.

He glanced at his parents, stately and self-possessed at their respective ends of the table. No outward sign that they were thinking of the son they'd lost, although he knew they must be, no less than he and Madeline were. Time might blunt the edges of grief, but the loss remained. And yet, here they were, making the effort to be cordial, even festive tonight. What might come of that—a Christmas truce or something more lasting— was anybody's guess.

Apropos of which... he turned to Margaret, finding her deep in conversation with his father. No sign of constraint that Gervase could perceive: good to see that her fears about meeting his parents again had been unfounded. Indeed, the duke appeared to be going out of his way to be charming and affable, and few men could be better company than he when he'd the inclination. And Margaret was smiling, opening up like a flower to the sun's warmth.

Relieved for her, Gervase relaxed in his chair to enjoy the rest of the meal. Conversations around him were light-hearted and desultory, consisting mostly of reminiscences of past Christmases and projected plans for the present holiday. Juliana thought they should decorate the Christmas tree and the Great Hall the following day, while the duke mentioned that he'd managed to engage a touring repertory company to perform at Denforth on Christmas Eve, a prospect all his guests greeted with pleased anticipation. A fondness for the theater was one of the more peaceful things that bound his family together, Gervase reflected.

"What will they be performing?" the duchess inquired of the duke. "A Nativity play?"

"Seasonably appropriate, but I had something a trifle more ambitious in mind."

Her brows rose in an elegant, questioning arch. "*East Lynne*, perhaps?"

The duke's eyes glinted. "You malign me, my dear. And just for that, I shall abandon you to the toils of your curiosity until the night in question." Ignoring the daggers she was now staring at him, he applied himself diligently to the last course, a spectacular array of desserts that included a chocolate gâteau that was one of the duchess's favorites, an apple tart, and several beautifully molded jellies.

Gervase traded an amused look with Margaret. "She did rather ask for it with that comment," he murmured, for her ears alone.

She gave a soft spurt of laughter, which she smothered in her wine glass. "My thoughts as well. But I do wonder what play will be put on."

"Something classical or Shakespearean," Gervase speculated, helping himself to apple tart with cream. "Father doesn't care much for modern plays."

"Especially not *East Lynne*," they said, almost in unison, and exchanged a smile. The duke's distaste for that popular, oft-performed melodrama was something of a family joke.

Once the last course had been thoroughly savored and the dishes cleared away, his mother and Juliana rose together and led the other ladies from the dining room, leaving the men to their age-old ritual of port and cigars.

No sooner had the door closed behind the last trailing silken skirt than Whitborough motioned for the port decanter to be handed around the table. "One of my finest, gentlemen—a Graham's Vintage '70, only recently acquired. I am certain you will approve of it."

Gervase just managed to conceal his surprise. His father's palate was merely serviceable, especially in comparison with his mother's, but he knew from his wine-tasting lessons the quality of such a port. Definitely a feather in the duke's cap... even Reg looked impressed.

A slight scratch at the door arrested the progress of the decanter as they all looked towards the direction of the sound. The footman obligingly opened it to admit the duke's current mastiff, who paced majestically to his master's chair and lay down beside it.

Gervase hid a smile. Some things never changed. His mother, while tolerant of the various forms of livestock at Denforth, drew the line at having her husband's dogs in the dining room, while dinner was served. His Grace had found a way around that, by having them enter *after* the ladies had departed. "So, what's this one called, Father?" he inquired; the previous mastiff, who'd died several years ago, had been Galahad.

"Bors," Whitborough replied, casting an affectionate glance at the dog. "After one of King Arthur's knights," he explained to Augustus, who appeared somewhat taken aback by the canine addition to their company.

The younger man recovered admirably. "One who achieved the Holy Grail, was he not?"

"Very good," Whitborough approved. "Yes, along with Galahad and Percival. A tireless seeker after the eternal mysteries," he proclaimed with a flourish.

Gervase glanced down at the mastiff, who yawned prodigiously before settling his huge black-masked head back on his paws. Hard to imagine this indolent beast pursuing a rabbit, much less a sacred chalice, but he sup-posed even a dog needed something to live up to.

The decanter had reached him by now, and he poured himself a liberal measure of port, but declined the cigars being offered as well. Reg accepted one, though, as did Hugo and Augustus. Jason regarded the box of Cubans speculatively, but, at a stern look from the duke, drew back his hand and contented himself with a glass of port instead.

It wasn't easy making the transition from boy to man, Gervase thought, swirling the dark wine in his glass and breathing in the bouquet. Five Christmases ago, Jason had been thirteen, old enough to dine with the family but still regarded as a child. Being accepted as an adult at last could be an intoxicating experience, so to speak... he made a mental note to ensure that his younger brother did not drink to excess. Overindulgence in liquor might be another masculine rite of passage, but he doubted Jason would enjoy it much, especially the next morning.

Once everyone's glass was filled, the duke lifted his. "As you no doubt remember, the first toast goes to our sovereign, and at my age, I see no reason to dispense with a fine old tradition," he remarked jovially. "Gentle-men, to the Queen!"

"To the Queen!" they echoed, and drank Her Majesty's health.

The port was every bit as good as its reputation had promised, and Gervase savored the taste, the mingled flavors of plum and blackberry, the smooth, almost syrupy finish. Gazing around the table, he saw similarly satisfied expressions on the faces of his companions. Reg was almost smiling, his eyelids at half-mast as he first lit, then drew upon his cigar.

"An excellent vintage, Whitborough." Augustus raised his own glass to his host. "I applaud your discrimi-nation—and your palate."

"Not at all, Langdale," the duke returned. "The duchess is the true connoisseur of the family. However, I believe I have picked up some useful tricks from her over the years."

And not just in wine. The words hung unspoken in the air. Gervase slanted a glance at Reg, catching the lift of his brother's eyebrow that usually presaged a less than tactful remark.

Fortunately, Hugo saw it too. "So, Reg, I hear you spent last week with the Quorn," he said heartily. "Good hunting there?"

"Oh, yes—excellent country. Of course the Shires can't be matched for hunting. Took a fox two out of those three mornings we rode out."

"Alas, poor Renard," Gervase murmured into his glass.

Reg and Hugo both ignored this remark, but Alasdair, who preferred fishing, grinned.

"Duke, is there to be a meet on St. Stephen's Day this year?" Hugo asked his father-in-law. "I'd hoped to put my newest hunter through his paces."

"There should be," the duke replied, sounding somewhat less enthusiastic than his wont, Gervase noticed. Puzzling, since his father had enjoying riding to hounds for years. "And possibly one just before New Year's, if the weather permits."

"Good." Reg nodded his approval. "*My* new hunter should have arrived by then."

Hugo leaned forward, all interest. "You've bought another horse too?"

"Well, I've made a handsome offer," Reg qualified. "The owner's a Melton man himself, and I've given him until Christmas Eve to respond."

Hugo, a keen sportsman, pressed for further details about the horse, which Reg was more than willing to share. His brother had a reputation for choosing only the best, Gervase mused, whether it was horses, hunting hounds, or guns. There was hardly any masculine pastime at which Reg did not naturally excel. And if that skill did not come naturally, he would drill relentlessly until he attained proficiency. Several years ago, he'd bought himself a trim little yacht and learned to sail it, ignoring all the naysayers who'd scoffed at the idea of his mastering the sea comparatively late in life. Even now Reg could never admit defeat or rest in too-easy consciousness of his victory—a trait as admirable as it was annoying. And one that Gervase had to admit that he and Reg might actually share. Useless to deny that he was every bit as driven to succeed in *his* chosen areas of expertise. Indeed, how could he and his brothers have been otherwise, given who had sired them?

Watching Reg and Hugo now, Gervase was struck by a sense of familiarity so powerful it stole his breath for a moment. It could so easily have been Hal sitting among them, discussing—or more likely, disputing—the finer points of horseflesh with Reg. Both had insisted on the best quality in their mounts, though Hal had also been easily attracted by what was showy. In the end, Gervase recalled with an inner chill, that preference, along with his reckless riding, had cost him his life. And that of the unfortunate horse as well.

He glanced towards his father, and saw that the duke was also watching Reg and Hugo through half-lidded eyes, like a somnolent lion. Someone who didn't know him so well might think he was almost dozing, mellowed as they all were by food and wine. But Gervase would have wagered money that the mind behind those eyes was sharply awake. Impossible to gauge what his father was thinking—or feeling. Nostalgia, for his own younger days in the field, when he'd ridden as tirelessly, even recklessly as Reg? Melancholy, over the lost son who'd also loved such sport? Or something else, something more... unpredictable. And therefore dangerous.

He was watching his father so closely that the sound of Augustus's voice took him—and perhaps everyone else—by surprise.

"And I imagine, Major, that you intend to repeat your exploits at Melton here?" The young duke's voice was as smooth as the port they were drinking, but some undercurrent to it made the back of Gervase's neck prickle uneasily.

Reg regarded him through narrowed eyes and a cloud of cigar smoke. "Is there any earthly reason I should not, Langdale?"

"None at all, Major," Augustus returned. "I applaud your zeal in pursuing English foxes. I am merely curious as to why you have chosen *not* to pursue a far more attractive quarry. And one much less inclined to flee your advances."

"I mean to have a new hunter too," Jason announced loudly into the charged silence that followed. "And one that's every bit as fine. For my birthday—Father said so."

His elders ignored him to a man. Gervase looked from his brother to Augustus, his uneasiness growing. He'd never known Margaret's brother well, could not yet fathom just how he fit into this scheme of things, but it would be a mistake to discount him. Here was no overgrown boy like Jason, but a young man growing into his authority—and liking it.

"Are you referring to Lady Alicia?" Reg inquired with somewhat forced lightness. "I shouldn't have thought a fond brother would describe his own sister as quarry."

"I shouldn't have thought a fond betrothed would leave his intended withering on the vine," Augustus countered, his tone almost eerily level.

Reg's lips thinned. "I have no intention of putting Lady Alicia in such a position, Langdale."

Augustus raised skeptical brows. "Might I inquire exactly what position you *do* intend to place her in, Major? Your betrothal was formalized almost five years ago, and you are no closer to the altar than you were then."

"I must confess, Reginald, that a similar question has crossed *my* mind as well," the duke remarked, his own voice deceptively pleasant. "Any number of times."

Oh, God—here it came. Another bout in the ongoing strife between Whitborough and his heir. Gervase braced himself, wondering just how acrimonious this latest round was going to get. With the unpredictable element of Augustus now in the mix, anything was possible—including imminent cataclysm. He felt a flicker of sympathy for Reg that surprised him, probably because two against one was still unsporting any way you looked at it.

Reg's expression went stony as he addressed his father. "When the arrangement was first made, my betrothed was still in the schoolroom. I cannot think that a child of barely seventeen is ready for marriage, certainly not to a serving officer in Her Majesty's Army. Would you have had one of my sisters marry under such conditions, sir?"

"Probably not," the duke conceded grudgingly, after a moment. "But Lady Alicia is no longer in the schoolroom. She has made her debut in Society, and recently come of age. The reason for your reluctance to wed no longer exists."

"I am still a serving officer, however," Reg retorted, his face still unyielding. "And a life following the regiment might not be to Lady Alicia's liking. It is, after all, far removed from the life to which she is accustomed."

"A life in which you have displayed little interest thus far," Augustus observed. "Which leads me to question this so-touching concern for my sister's welfare, especially since you apparently cannot exert yourself to write to her more than twice yearly."

Twice-yearly? Gervase just managed to conceal his astonishment on hearing that tidbit. While he'd always known that Alicia's interest in Reg far exceeded his interest in her, a letter every six months—after returning to England no less—seemed particularly blatant proof of his indifference. Even Hal, as careless as he'd been with Margaret's affections, had been more attentive—at least in public.

"I fail to see how the frequency of correspondence between your sister and myself is your concern, Langdale." Reg's tone was as stiff as his posture. Stiff—and defensive, Gervase thought, eyeing his brother more closely.

"Anything that touches upon my family's honor is my concern, Major," Augustus retorted. "As the daughter and sister of a duke, Lady Alicia Carlisle is not to be trifled with, or taken for granted. And this Christmas," he paused, his pale blue eyes taking on an icy cast, "I mean to see her confirmed as the next Duchess of Whitborough. Or formally released from this engagement, along with every penny—and acre of her dowry."

The duke leaned forward at this, his gaze probing. "You are referring to Moorhaven?"

Augustus met his gaze squarely. "Indeed I am. According to the arrangement my father made with you, Moorhaven was to serve as a home for her and your son. If the betrothal is terminated, then I wish the property to revert to *my* possession, as part of the Langdale holdings."

Whitborough steepled his fingers. "As I recall, Moorhaven is an unentailed estate, which your father was free to bestow upon whomever he chose."

"I am aware of that," Augustus began, but the duke continued as if he hadn't spoken, "The estate was first designated as part of your sister Margaret's dowry, when she and my eldest son were betrothed—at which time I agreed to undertake most of the costs for its maintenance. That provision was retained after Moorhaven was settled upon Alicia, following her betrothal to Reg. For the last nine years, the estate has been largely supported by Whitborough resources."

"I was aware of that as well," Augustus replied. "Do you require recompense? I am certain something can be arranged, if necessary."

"Magnanimous of you." The duke raised his glass in an ironic toast. "However, I merely wished to point out that, for all intents and purposes, Moorhaven now belongs to Whitborough."

Augustus's eyes hardened, though his well-cut lips remained curved in the semblance of a pleasant smile. "I have a deed of property that says otherwise. Unless my sister marries your son, you have no legal claim on the estate."

"And unless the betrothal is officially dissolved, neither do you," the duke countered. He lifted his glass again. "I believe we have reached a stalemate, Langdale."

Gervase glanced from one to the other. Something was afoot here, something he couldn't quite put his finger on. He'd never known the terms of Margaret's betrothal to Hal, nor seen the property over which his father and Augustus appeared to be contending. And that in itself was enough to rouse suspicion. Landed estates—indeed, land in general—were worth far less than they had once been. So why were two wealthy dukes vying for the possession of this one? A display of dominance, he wondered, or something more?

"In any case," his father resumed, "the matter cannot be decided upon in Lady Alicia's absence. So I propose we set it aside, for now."

Augustus looked none too pleased, but after a moment he inclined his head. "Very well, Whitborough. I concede that you have a point. My sister will no doubt wish to have her say."

"One ignores landed women at one's peril," the duke agreed. "Or so I have learned."

Out of the corner of his eye, Gervase saw Reg curl a derisive upper lip at that remark. Unfortunately, Whitborough appeared to have seen it as well, for he now turned his attention back to his heir.

"Leaving aside the matter of your marriage, Reginald, I find I have another equally pressing question for you," he remarked. "When do you intend to resign your commission?"

"When. I. Am. Ready." Reg bit off each word with chill precision.

"Any notion of when that will be?" his father inquired, still in that falsely pleasant tone. "At the next blue moon? Or had you another date in mind—the Second Coming, perhaps?"

Reg's mouth tightened, a muscle twitching at the corner of his jaw. "The army has been my life for nearly ten years. And will remain so a while longer."

"In other words, you prefer to play soldier rather than take up your responsibilities here."

The tension in the room thickened, as choking and impenetrable as smoke. Gervase was aware of Hugo and Alasdair exchanging uneasy glances; his brothers-in-law had long since learned to keep their heads down during Lyons family disputes. Jason, he observed with some distaste, was watching avidly, far too pleased by this turn of events. By their father and Reg being on the outs yet again.

"Being a soldier has never been a game to me." Reg's eyes were flint-hard, his bearing more military than ever. "And I have a duty—to the regiment and my men."

"What of your duty to Whitborough, Reginald?" the duke persisted. "What of your duty to this family?"

"And to my sister?" Augustus chimed in, but intent on each other, neither the duke nor Reg spared him a glance this time.

"This family prospers," Reg reminded him. "Only Juliana is unmarried among my sisters, and only the pup is left to establish creditably, a task better left to you... or to God," he added, flicking a disdainful glance at Jason. "As some tasks are clearly beyond human capability."

Jason flushed hotly, mouth opening to respond in kind. Gervase kicked him under the table, and when the boy turned to glare at him, shook his head meaningfully. His brother subsided, still scowling.

"What of your duty to *me*, then?" the duke inquired, his tone sharper now.

"What of it? You are the Duke of Whitborough." Reg swept him a mocking obeisance. "Lord of all he surveys. A man in the prime of life, with years still before him. You don't need another lackey about the place."

The duke shook his head. "At my age, I cannot afford the luxury of assuming that time is on my side. It may not even be on *yours*, if your commanding officer's report is accurate."

Reg went still. "Spying on me now, Father?"

"Merely attempting to stay informed about the health of my heir."

"In your usual overbearing fashion." Reg smiled without humor. "And yet you fail to understand why I will not return to life under your thumb. Time and again I have witnessed your reluctance to yield or even to delegate *real* authority over the years—not even to your future successor." He crossed his arms, his jaw taking on its customary uncompromising jut. "Well, I won't be your lapdog, Father. I won't sit tamely at your feet like Bors there. And above all, I won't sacrifice my career or my independence to you—like Hal!"

The name was out, and Gervase saw the shaft strike home, his father's face tightening across the strong cheekbones, his eyes going stark and bleak. It lasted no longer than a second or two before the duke's mask of imperturbability slipped into place... a mask that Gervase recognized with a shock as being strikingly similar to his own.

What would have happened next he would never know because Alasdair's voice—sounding perhaps just a shade too hearty—broke the strained silence.

"Gentlemen, why don't we go and join the ladies now?" he suggested. "I don't like to leave Elaine alone too long, in her present condition."

Alasdair the peacemaker, something he had in common with his wife. But given the circumstances, Gervase thought his brother-in-law deserved all the support he could get. "An excellent idea," he said, pushing back his chair and getting to his feet. "Perhaps we might have music too, as befits the season."

Music to soothe a savage breast... of which there were far too many in this room alone.

Much to his relief, no one offered any resistance to Alasdair's proposal, but quickly drained their glasses and stubbed out their cigars before leaving the dining room, in a silence more like an armed truce than a lasting peace.

Chapter Five

❧

DISASTER AVERTED, at least for now. Climbing the stairs to his chamber, Gervase silently thanked Providence that the rest of the evening had passed without incident. Once reunited with the ladies, the men had been on their best behavior—more or less. Still, he wouldn't have been surprised if his mother suspected something might have happened, if only because Reg and the duke had rather ostentatiously avoided speaking to each other. And Jason hadn't exactly concealed his satisfaction over the renewed hostility between his father and older brother.

Someone needed to take that boy in hand before he was completely ruined, Gervase mused. "Spoiled till salt won't save him," their old nurse had used to say. However much the duke might favor Jason, Reg, Gervase, and any legitimate sons they might produce would have to die before his baby brother could inherit. Which was possible but unlikely, and the sooner Jason woke up and started making a future for *himself*, instead of depending on their father to smooth his pathway in life, the better off he'd be.

He'd reached his room now—the same one he'd had as a boy, and wasn't *that* guaranteed to revive old memories?—and was just about to enter when he noticed the door was slightly ajar. Strange… he thought he'd heard it snick shut behind him when he'd gone down to dinner. Well, perhaps Farnsworth had inadvertently left the door open when he himself had gone below stairs after helping Gervase dress.

Shrugging, he pushed the door open and went inside —only to stop short when he saw that his bed was already occupied.

"Madam," Gervase sternly addressed his uninvited guest, "I do not recall expressing a desire for your presence here."

For answer, the occupant stretched with sinuous grace, then rolled over, exposing her stomach while regarding him coyly through tilted eyes the color of peridots. Gervase sighed, perched on the edge of his bed, and began to perform the necessary offices.

"You are fortunate to have made your move when I am in a relatively amiable humor," he informed her, stroking away. "And when you yourself are *not* in expectation of a happy event. Otherwise, I would have no qualms about removing you at once from *my* place of repose."

She batted playfully at his hand, then uttered a soft trill and butted her head against his fingers, wanting more.

"Never satisfied, are you?" Gervase observed, chucking her under the chin. "I know your kind all too well."

"Who on earth are you talking to, Ger?"

He looked up to see Elaine standing in the doorway. She came further into the room, then shook her head with an indulgent smile when she saw his visitor. "Ah, of course. They always do seem to like you best."

"It is not a sentiment that is necessarily reciprocated." Gervase ran a hand down the tortoiseshell cat's smooth flank, and was rewarded with a throaty purr. "What's this one called?"

"Messalina. And according to Juliana, she's a cat of easy virtue. Her kittens are just weaned, and she's already eyeing the toms with interest." Elaine reached out to scratch Messalina between the ears. "She certainly has a fondness for male companionship, to judge from the way she's making up to you."

"I suppose that ginger monster of Juliana's continues to rule the roost?"

"Xerxes?" Her smile broadened. "Who do you think sired Messalina's last litter?"

"Why am I not surprised?" Gervase moved aside so Elaine could sit on the bed as well. "So, what brings you to my door—apart from curiosity about my companion?"

"Curiosity about certain other things as well," she replied frankly. "Such as what happened between Papa and Reg before you joined us after dinner."

So someone besides his mother had noticed. "Why don't you ask one of them?"

"Because I'm far more likely to receive an honest answer from *you*."

Gervase regarded her thoughtfully. Of all his sisters, Elaine was the sunniest and seemingly the most uncomplicated. She had their father's tawny hair, perhaps a shade lighter than his, and their mother's tip-tilted hazel eyes, though in Elaine's smooth oval face, they looked almost innocent. He had learned years ago, however, not to underestimate his next youngest sister.

"Just the old argument again, Lainey," he said, using her pet name. "Father wants Reg to leave the army, marry Alicia, and take up his duties here. Reg refuses, Jason gloats, Augustus bridles over this perceived slight to his own family, and Alasdair and Hugo do their best to stay out of it."

"While you analyze the entire situation, and wonder if there's any advantage to *you* in getting involved," Elaine finished, without censure.

"Yes to the former, not necessarily to the latter," Gervase corrected. "Of late, I've been following the example set by my brothers-in-law."

"You amaze me," she teased. "Truly?"

He shrugged. "Having a profession and an independent income tends to alter one's perspective. I can understand why Reg doesn't want to give them up, especially after watching Hal chafe under Father's restraints for so long."

"But it's been five years," she pointed out. "I know

Papa can be overbearing, and that he doesn't like handing over the reins to anyone, but how can Reg change that if he stays away?"

"So you're on Father's side about this, then."

"I'm on this family's side," she corrected. "Reg *is* the next duke. Sooner or later, everything will be his. I can't understand why he hasn't sold out yet—he was always telling Hal how much better *he'd* do as heir."

While Hal would smugly point out that Reg would never get the chance to prove it, Gervase remembered with an inner chill. *Pride goeth before a fall*... "Perhaps he finally realized how difficult life in Father's shadow— under Father's *control*—could be. I wouldn't fancy the prospect myself, dukedom or not."

"Perhaps," she conceded, sighing and drawing her knees up to her chest the way she had as a young girl, heedless of her satin skirts. "But Ger, Papa's *not* going to live forever. Wouldn't it be better to come home and try to work with him and learn from him, while there's still time?" She wrapped her arms about her knees, her eyes taking on a distant look. "Because time goes so *quickly*. I don't think I realized that until I married Alasdair. One day you're in the schoolroom, being taught your numbers and letters, then suddenly you're a wife, then a mother, and your children are growing like weeds, learning to walk and talk..." She broke off with a self-conscious little laugh. "I suppose this all sounds foolish to you—"

"Not at all. But I'm not the one you need to convince."

"No?" Elaine tilted her head, regarding him with bright, inquisitive hazel eyes. "What about your own life, Ger? All the things *you* intend to do, all the chances you have yet to take?"

He bent over the still-purring cat again, avoiding his sister's gaze. "Such as?"

"Such as telling Margaret that you're in love with her. And have been for years."

Gervase paused just long enough to pique her curiosity, then rose, walked to the door and opened it pointedly. "Goodnight, dear sister."

"Goodnight, dear brother," Elaine returned, not at all offended. She got up, patted his cheek affectionately, and made her unhurried way to the door. "Sweet dreams."

Sweet dreams, forsooth.

Hands shoved in the pockets of his dressing gown, Gervase stalked down the passage to the library, built on a grand scale like everything else at Denforth. Somewhere in that massive collection must be some impenetrable, dry-as-dust tome on law or history to help induce the slumber that had eluded him for the last hour... thanks to Elaine, whose challenge about Margaret had essentially murdered sleep for the time being.

He bared his teeth in a silent snarl at the memory. All very well for his sister to talk—she and Alasdair had more or less picked each other out when they were twelve and fourteen, respectively. Quite the touching romance too: the lonely young Duke of Castlebrooke— who'd acceded to his title at the tender age of three— and Lady Elaine Lyons, who'd spied him watching her at play with her siblings and invited him to join them. Nothing had impeded their eventual march down the aisle—like an engagement or, worse, a *marriage* to someone else.

Still, Lainey had been right about one thing, he conceded grudgingly: time *did* fly. *Tempus fugit.* And moments had a way of slipping through one's fingers, unless one had the perception... and the courage to grasp them. As *he* meant to—and would, when he deemed the moment was right.

Fortunately for his mood, the library was deserted, though the lamps were lit and a fire crackled on the hearth, still bright although its flames were beginning to subside. Gervase surveyed his surroundings from under lowered brows, absorbing the familiarity of it all. Contrary to what Elaine had said, he could almost believe that time had stood still since his last visit. Here were bookcases that reached nearly to the ceiling, their shelves accessible only by ladder. And the gallery— housing some of the rarer, more esoteric volumes— which one could reach by a short flight of stairs in the far corner of the room; he remembered spending hours there on rainy afternoons. An antique globe occupied another corner, and a marquetry table, on which reposed an elaborately carved ivory chess set, stood between a pair of padded leather armchairs to one side of the fireplace.

At first glance, a masculine sanctuary, like Sir Anthony's library. Until one looked more closely and saw the feminine touches. The leather sofa ornamented with bright cushions. The soft afghan blankets that lay folded on the window seat. The vase of fresh flowers—white and bronze chrysanthemums, this time—on the alcove table. The bowl of floral potpourri on the mantel—which his mother must have started long ago. Closing his eyes, Gervase breathed in the mingled scents of roses, orris root, cinnamon, and bay... and felt the past catch him in its undertow.

Summer of 1882, the night of Elaine and Alasdair's betrothal ball, and Denforth was crowded to the rafters with people—family, friends, and well-wishers—all eager to congratulate the young couple and celebrate with them. Gervase's ears fairly rang from the chorus of benedictions, to say nothing of the noise from the ballroom. In tribute to the groom-to-be's Scottish ancestry, a piper had been engaged for the occasion, and for much of the evening, the man had plied his trade with deafening enthusiasm, skirling tirelessly through countless jigs and reels. Withdrawing discreetly from the clamor, Gervase vowed never again to take the relative tranquility of a waltz for granted.

No one else was in the passage, so he made his way unimpeded towards the library. Pushing open the library door, he paused on the threshold when he saw it was already occupied... and by whom.

Margaret sat on the sofa, her ivory silk skirts crumpled around her, staring into the fire; Yorkshire nights could be chilly, even in the spring and summer. A cluster of white Roses of York in her hair, shining like stars against the heavy, chestnut waves that Gervase had so often imagined running his fingers through.

He regarded her somberly now, knowing how difficult the past year had been for her. The Duchess of Langdale had succumbed to a sudden illness just after Margaret's first Season had ended. Tonight had marked her emergence from mourning, but grief had its own schedule, and he knew how much she still missed her mother. As did everyone who had known her. Gervase remembered the late duchess as unfailingly gracious and warm-hearted. Hers had been the soft glow of candlelight, not the fierce blaze of a bonfire, and her husband appeared to be lost without her. He'd attended the ball tonight, but an air of melancholy had hung about him—and about Margaret as well.

Perhaps he should leave. If she'd come here because she desired solitude...

Just then she looked up and saw him. "Gervase." To his relief, her lips turned up in a smile—a small one, to be sure, but real enough.

"Am I disturbing you?" he asked. "I can go, if you'd prefer to be alone."

She shook her head. "That's all right. I don't mind a bit of company. Human company, that is," she added, nodding towards a nearby armchair on which one of Denforth's many cats was sleeping soundly.

Gervase smiled back and came further into the room. "I felt the need for a little peace and quiet," he explained. "Especially once the piping started."

This time her smile seemed more spontaneous, even amused. "Nothing if not vigorous, was he?"

"That's one word for it," he agreed with a mock shudder. "I know Alasdair's Scottish, but I hope a piper doesn't become a permanent fixture at Denforth. I'm not sure my eardrums could survive it!"

"Oh, I don't think you need worry on that score," she assured him. "To judge from her expression, your mother's love of music doesn't appear to extend to bagpipes!"

"She did look a touch strained," Gervase remarked. "Especially during that—what was it called?—that raucous piece at the beginning?"

"A pibroch," Margaret told him. "Elaine says this one is traditionally played to rally the clans to war. I can't say I cared for it much myself, but I didn't mind the pipes once the dancing started. They do add a certain something to the reels!"

He'd seen her dancing a reel with Reg, the pair of them moving with admirable grace and speed through the set. His own dance with her—a Lancers—had been much more sedate, even a little staid. He would have preferred a waltz or even a polka, but those were reserved for other men—like her fiancé. Apropos of which...

"So, is Hal anywhere about?" he inquired, trying to sound casual. He had seen them together earlier, partnered in the quadrille that opened the ball.

Her slim shoulders rose and fell in a light shrug. "I suppose. He's probably gone off to the card room with some of his friends."

Gervase opened his mouth, then closed it without speaking. Typical Hal, abandoning his fiancée in the middle of a party. And Margaret had sounded cool, almost indifferent—which, he supposed, was preferable to sounding heartbroken or humiliated. Nonetheless, it was strange to hear her speak so dispassionately about Hal, when he remembered how starry-eyed she'd been on the night of their betrothal.

"She looked lovely, didn't she?" Margaret went on, her expression turning oddly wistful. "Elaine. And Alasdair couldn't take his eyes off her."

"That's nothing new. He's wanted her from the moment she put her hair up and left the schoolroom. Possibly before then, when she coaxed him down from that tree seven years ago."

"No one's ever looked at me *like that." Her lips crimped. "Especially not Hal. I imagine he saves such attentions for his mistress."*

Damn it to hell. "Margaret—"

She shook her head. "Please, Gervase, don't pretend you don't know."

He blew out a breath. "I didn't. At least, not entirely," he qualified at her skeptical glance. "One hears a good many things, and it's not as if I'm in Hal's confidence."

She sighed, an infinitely weary sound. "Even if you were, it could hardly count as a betrayal when I already know the answer. I've heard that she's a dancer at Covent Garden—could anything be more banal? Or obvious?"

"Hal's not exactly known for originality."

"True," she agreed with a dreary little laugh that caught at his heart. Not as indifferent as she'd sounded, after all.

"Look, Margaret," he began, feeling more awkward than he had since his schooldays, "It may mean nothing—"

"Perhaps. But I mean even less to him than that."

"Then he's an idiot."

Her eyes widened, whether at the epithet or the harsh note that had crept into his voice.

Gervase amended hastily, "Most young men about town are idiots. Trying to prove something, always. But he'll tire of her soon enough, you'll see."

"And find someone else, I suppose. That's usually how it works, isn't it? And women are expected to turn a blind eye to everything, and carry on as if nothing were wrong. After all,"

she continued, with saccharine sweetness, "we're 'ladies.' We don't make scenes. Or demands. We should be ever so grateful just to have a man's ring on our finger." She stretched out her left hand, ornamented with the Whitborough betrothal diamond, with a vicious simper, which dissolved a moment later into sadness and disillusionment. "No matter how many others there are... whom we're not supposed to know about."

Gervase swallowed, wanting nothing so much as to take her in his arms and comfort her. Or to knock some sense, literally, into his eldest brother. "Margaret—"

She gave a sharp sigh, spearing her hands through her hair and knocking the cluster of roses slightly askew. "I'll be twenty this autumn, Gervase. Twenty! And Hal is no closer to naming a wedding date than he was at our betrothal. And that was nearly three years ago!"

"I know." The memory was burned into him. The one and only time he'd drunk himself sick, though fortunately for his dignity, no one had witnessed that particular humiliation. And it had supposedly been an occasion for merriment: the betrothal of a duke's eldest son and heir to another duke's eldest daughter. So no one would have thought twice of someone overindulging— especially a younger son of the house, who might not be accustomed to strong drink.

Ha. As if his mother's son didn't know exactly how much he'd imbibed... and why. And wretched though he'd felt the next morning, he hadn't completely regretted his debauch. It had been far easier to endure the occasion drunk than sober.

On impulse, he crossed over to the liquor cabinet, took out the port decanter, and poured them each a glass.

"Here." He strode over to the sofa and offered Margaret one of the glasses. "This might put some heart in you."

Too surprised to refuse, she accepted it, staring nonplussed into the deep red wine. "This isn't sherry, is it? I've never been that fond of sherry."

"It's port," he informed her, before tasting it and nodding his approval. "And one of our better ones. Try it."

She gave him a dubious glance, but took a sip—properly, he noticed. Perhaps one of his sisters had taught her. Her face cleared as she took in the mingled flavors. "This is good," she observed with pardonable surprise. "Thank you."

"You're welcome." Gervase weighed the possibility of sitting down on the sofa beside her, and decided the arm was a more discreet choice. He perched there, studying her disconsolate face.

Disconsolate, but not despairing. And perhaps more receptive to what he might say, the ideas taking shape in his mind.

They drank their wine in companionable silence for some minutes, then Gervase began, "You know... there's no rule that says you have *to sit tamely by, waiting for Hal to finish sowing his wild oats. Sauce for the goose, after all."*

Margaret glanced at him over her shoulder, her eyes widening in something like alarm. "Are you suggesting that I sow some wild oats? Because I don't know if I—"

"I wasn't suggesting that you take up with a tenor, or your dancing master, or some such fellow," he broke in. "You've more sense than that." And the cost of such an indiscretion was too high for a lady, as they both knew. Which was unfair, but the way of the world in which they'd grown up. "I'd something else in mind. Something that might be more to your liking."

She gave a small nod, inviting him to continue.

"We both know that Hal takes you for granted," he resumed. "Because he thinks you'll always be there, waiting for him. So stop waiting for him."

"Stop waiting?" A tiny frown etched itself between her brows. "How do you mean?"

"Live your life, make it an interesting one—and I'll wager anything you like that Hal will start to find you more *interesting too. Like a cat," he added, warming to his theme. "You can't coax or cajole it, but ignore it, and it suddenly decides you're fascinating, and that it wants to be your most intimate friend."*

She smiled then, a tentative but genuine thing. "Do you truly think that would work on your brother?"

"It stands as much chance as anything else does," Gervase pointed out. "And whether it does or not, at least you'd have something to show for your time. You could travel, now that you're out of mourning. Go to Paris or Italy..."

She looked tempted for a moment, then shook her head regretfully. "I couldn't leave England, not while Papa's still so lost without Mama."

"Well, then, stay in England and go to university instead."

She stared at him as though he'd just suggested that she run naked over the moors in the dead of winter. "Me, at university?"

"Why not? History's your passion. Go to university, and study it. Girton would admit you in a trice. Or there's Oxford now. A college practically made for you," he added provocatively. "Lady Margaret of Lady Margaret Hall."

She made a little face at him. "Just for that, I'll apply to Somerville."

"Just as long as you do apply," he countered. "Act quickly, and you could get in by Michaelmas. And you'd be close enough to come visit your father between terms. He was a scholar himself, so I should think he'd be pleased to have you follow in his footsteps."

Margaret fretted her lip, visibly caught between the familiar existence that was all she'd known and the lure of one she'd never imagined for herself. "You liked being at Oxford, didn't you?"

"Enormously," he confessed with a smile. "I've seldom worked or studied harder in my life, but it was worth every minute. And I met some remarkable people, encountered some brilliant minds, even made a few lifelong friends. Above all, I felt challenged there... fulfilled. And I think you will too, if you decide to go."

She exhaled, a flush mounting to the crest of her cheeks. "Papa once said something similar. That he felt as though he'd found his truest self at Oxford, among all the knowledge of the ages."

Gervase spread his hands. "Well, then, what better testimonial could you have? And why not permit yourself the same opportunity, now that they're admitting women?"

She put her hands up to her cheeks. "But Gervase, what could I say—or do, to contribute to all that? What should I study? I haven't written an essay since leaving the schoolroom!"

"I suspect it'll all come back to you once you've started. And as for what you study, I'd say that was obvious. Convince me and the rest of the world of Crouchback's innocence." He used the epithet deliberately, knowing it would galvanize her. And sure enough, her velvety eyes took on a familiar, almost militant spark, her chin a defiant tilt.

"I believe I will. I will," she repeated with new resolve. Unexpectedly, a mischievous smile played about her lips. "And if I manage to convince you, then the rest of the world should be child's play!"

"That's the spirit!" Gervase lifted his glass of port. "To your brilliant Oxford career, Lady Margaret!"

"To my brilliant career!" she echoed, reaching up to touch her glass to his.

They downed the last of the port and set their glasses aside. And in the silence, the mantel clock chimed midnight.

Always midnight... the hour when enchantment was destined to end.

Margaret gave a guilty start. "I really should go back to the ballroom. I hadn't meant to stay away so long." She rose from the sofa, shaking out her skirts and smoothing her hair. "Are you coming?"

"Presently," he said, watching as she attempted to set herself to rights. "I thought I'd take a few more minutes, let my ears stop ringing..."

That earned him a light laugh. "I'll see you by and by, then. And Gervase?" She paused unexpectedly, within inches of him, her eyes intent on his.

He raised a questioning brow.

"Thank you. For listening, and for... everything else." She studied him with that sweet gravity that always set an ache just below where his heart was supposed to be. Then she stooped, and brushed her lips against his cheek. A fleeting kiss, as light as the brush of a butterfly's wings, that he felt all the way down to his bones.

Ah, Margaret...

Then she was gone, the heavy silk of her gown sighing in her wake, the door closing behind her almost soundlessly.

The library felt cold without her, although the fire was still burning. And almost unnaturally quiet. The ticking of the clock, the crackling of the flames, even the faint snoring of the still-slumbering cat had never sounded louder by contrast.

One of the roses had fallen from her hair, and he picked it up, mindful of its delicate petals. The fragrance wafted up to him, like the ghost of summers past, and he breathed it in, as he'd longed to breathe her *in.*

My Rose of York.

Except she wasn't. And never could be. Someday, she'd wear roses again—probably when she walked down the aisle to his undeserving ass of a brother.

Mouth twisting, he walked over to the mantel and dropped the petals one by one into his mother's potpourri bowl.

Waste not, want not...

"Gervase."

The sound of his name pulled him back into the present, and he surfaced with a start. His father was standing in the doorway, the lamplight bright upon his tawny hair, his expression quizzical. "Good God, boy, I thought for a moment that you'd gone deaf!" he remarked. "I must have called you at least three times. Nothing wrong, I trust?"

"Not at all." Gervase wondered fleetingly just what sort of response he'd have received if he *had* actually confessed his current thoughts. But he and the duke had seldom shared such confidences. "I just came down for a book—to help me sleep."

"Ah." Hands in his trousers pockets, Whitborough rocked back and forth on his heels, which usually indicated some abstraction on his part. "Well, as it happens, I'm glad that you did. Would you believe me if I told you that you were the very man I wanted to see?"

Gervase hesitated, then inquired with a faint smile, "Would you prefer a tactful answer, sir, or an honest one?"

The duke stared at him with those bright blue eyes, and then broke into a huge grin. "Very clever, my boy— though you were always that! But I'll have you know, I speak nothing less than the truth," he insisted. "There are some things I wish to discuss with you—over a nightcap, and perhaps a game of chess as well?"

Chess—and strategy. Gervase knew his father well enough to read between the lines. Nonetheless, the invitation piqued his curiosity; he could not recall the last time the duke had singled him out like this. When he'd come down from Oxford—and the predicted row over his chosen profession had materialized? In any event, something was clearly afoot, and he could not deny wanting to know what it was, especially after that scene he'd witnessed in the dining room.

"Very well," he agreed. "As I haven't yet found a suitable book, perhaps a drink and a game will relax me." Matches against his father tended to end in a stalemate, if they were both playing at the top of their form.

Entering the library, the duke made a beeline for the liquor cabinet. "Well, then, I've an excellent cognac on hand—a Courvoisier that even your mother would approve of—unless you'd prefer whiskey?"

"Cognac will be fine." Gervase had always found whiskey too raw for a nightcap.

"I'll have the same." Taking out the crystal decanter, Whitborough poured a small measure of brandy into two snifters and handed one to Gervase, then led the way towards the two armchairs with the chessboard set between them.

"Black or white?" he inquired, gesturing at the pieces.

"Black, thank you." White supposedly had the first move advantage, but when dealing with his father, Gervase felt he needed all the advance warning he could get.

They seated themselves behind their chosen chessmen and contemplated the board. Gervase cradled the bowl of his snifter, letting the warmth of his hand warm the aromatic liquor within, and watched his father intently. But the duke seemed in no hurry to commence play; instead, he swirled the brandy about in his own glass, took a leisurely sip.

"So," he remarked at last, "I understand your career is going well."

"Yes, very." Gervase sipped at his own cognac, letting himself taste it fully. Yes, the duchess would definitely have approved.

"No regrets or second thoughts?" Whitborough's tone sounded just a little too casual.

"None at all." Studying his father over the rim of his glass, Gervase ventured a small smile. "I would have made a terrible clergyman, sir."

"Well... you may be right," Whitborough said, after a moment, with the air of one making a major concession. "And I did find a worthy man to occupy that living —eventually."

"Then, all's well that ends well, wouldn't you say?"

"Perhaps." The duke picked up a pawn, turning it over and over in his long fingers. "In any event, I can't deny that your chosen calling may prove fortuitous."

Gervase raised an inquiring brow. "Sir?"

His father leaned forward in his chair, still idly toying with the pawn. "I have a proposition for you, my boy. I find myself in urgent need of a solicitor."

"A solicitor?" Gervase echoed, nonplussed. "Why not use Adeney and Briggs, as you've always done?"

"Adeney and Briggs have served this family faithfully for years," Whitborough agreed. "I have no fault to find with their efforts, when it comes to the usual matters. But for what I have in mind this time, I require someone a bit more—audacious. Someone who's tenacious, brilliant... and ruthless. Which I rather think fits *you* to a T."

Only in *his* family would being described as "ruthless" count as praise, Gervase reflected. "*Merci du compliment, mon pere*," he said lightly, raising his glass in an ironic toast. "What is it, precisely, that you have in mind?"

The duke leaned back, glanced at the chessboard, and set his pawn down two squares ahead of its previous location. "I wish to know what is involved in breaking the entail."

"The entail?" Gervase paused with his hand poised over his own chessmen, unsure whether he'd heard correctly. "On Denforth?"

"Denforth and the other properties attached to the dukedom," his father confirmed.

Gervase exhaled and reached for his snifter, distantly relieved to see that his hand was still steady. "Has this family fallen into debt, sir? A failed business enterprise, perhaps?"

"Good Lord, no—nothing like that!" The duke sounded genuinely surprised. "No, no, we're doing quite well financially. I'd another reason for asking." He paused, then resumed with a nonchalance Gervase could not fail to find suspect, "You're no doubt aware that the Lyons wealth stems from many sources, most of which were bound over the years by my grandfather, my father, and myself into the maintenance of Denforth and other landed properties. A veritable Gordian knot, as it were. I wish to learn what it would take to sever that knot, to separate the monetary wealth from the land, the land from the title, and how it might be accomplished."

"I can tell you straight off that it would take a great deal—in time, effort, and money," Gervase retorted, advancing one of his own pawns in turn. "And there would be no guarantee of success. For one thing you would need the cooperation of your heir in order to change the terms of the entail. Should you undertake to strip all the wealth and all the property from the title—"

"Then I would essentially make a cardboard duke of my successor," his father returned smoothly, capturing Gervase's pawn on the diagonal.

Reg, a figurehead... with none of the resources to

support his new position, Gervase realized. His brother wouldn't stand for that—and neither would their mother. There was no need to say as much; instead, he lifted an eyebrow and waited. "And then?"

"I am not an unreasonable man," Whitborough continued, steepling his fingers and stretching his legs out in an assumption of ease that belied the tension Gervase could sense in him. "And if certain conditions are met, matters need not come to such a pass. Should my heir accept his responsibilities and fulfill his duty to the family, I see no reason why the estate and its wealth should not remain intact for the next two generations at least. However," steel crept into his voice now, "I require some assurance that there will actually *be* generations to inherit what I have striven to preserve."

"In a nutshell, you want Reg to marry Alicia, give up the regiment, and stay in England to breed up the next litter of Lyons cubs," Gervase summed up. As Hal, in his prolonged and frivolous bachelorhood, had neglected to do.

"Rather baldly put, but not inaccurate."

"Might I remind you that you have other sons who might inherit or provide future heirs, should Reg not fulfill his dynastic duty?" Gervase asked in his dryest, most lawyerly tone.

The duke's brows lanced together in a dissatisfied frown. "It will be years before Jason is ready to marry and start a family."

Jason. Of course. Overlooked, once again. Good thing he was used to it, Gervase reflected mordantly, but he couldn't deny that it still stung... if less than it might have, ten years ago. He dropped his gaze to the chessboard and moved his queen's pawn, forcing back the unwelcome and all too familiar emotions.

"And *you're* not engaged either," Whitborough added a little too quickly, as if just realizing his *faux pas*. "Unless there's something you haven't told us—"

"No," Gervase broke in. He wasn't about to confide his hopes about Margaret to his father—or anyone else, for that matter. "I am, as you see, presently unattached."

"So, then, you understand why I have pinned my hopes on Reg—and Alicia." The duke continued his diagonal advance up the board, taking Gervase's second pawn. "I understand that I won't live forever. But before my time comes, I mean to dandle at least one Lyons grandson on my knee and know that the future is assured."

"How very affecting." Gervase savored the last of his cognac, then moved his bishop, experiencing an admittedly childish sense of satisfaction at capturing his father's encroaching pawn. "And you believe *I* can supply you with the means to force Reg's hand."

His father's eyes held a limpid innocence that would have fooled anyone except another Lyons. "Well, can you?"

"A more pertinent question to ask might be 'will you?' or even 'would you?'" Gervase retorted. "Reg said at dinner that he wasn't going to be your lapdog. I have some sympathy with that point of view. And by that same token, I should like to add that *I* am not one of those pieces of ivory you're moving about the board."

"Are you not?" His Grace inquired provocatively.

Gervase met his gaze full on. "I consider myself a player in the game, sir. Would you not be disappointed in me otherwise?"

"Hmm." The duke's eyes narrowed in thought. "You have, I suspect, the best brain among my sons. Perhaps I have not appreciated that quality as fully as I might have, but I am prepared to recognize that now."

Gervase widened his eyes. "Praise from *you*, Father—after almost thirty years? Good Lord, what next—pigs sprouting wings and taking to the sky? I'll be sure to look for them in the treetops tomorrow morning."

"You may have your little joke, boy. I'll concede you might even be entitled to it. But that doesn't answer my question." Whitborough's gaze, searing in its intensity, bored into his. "I need you to find examples, find *precedents,* of entails being successfully broken, and present to me a detailed report of the results."

Gervase steepled his own fingers in deliberate mimicry of his father's position. "And what would my incentive to do this be, Father?" He kept his tone level, almost pleasant. "Reg *will* be the next duke, whether the entail stands or not. And I need not remind you that he would fight you tooth and nail to keep his inheritance intact. Meanwhile, Jason appears to have succeeded Hal as your particular favorite, and it's clear that you mean to provide lavishly for him. Recognizing those realities, I have elected to lead my own life and make my own fortune—a course that has afforded me considerable satisfaction and even more considerable freedom."

"I can add to that fortune, Gervase," Whitborough promised. "You would be handsomely recompensed for your efforts. Consider it employment, if you like. And I may have something else you'd find to your liking."

Gervase raised his brows and waited. *This should be good.*

"I recently acquired a property in Warwickshire," the duke continued. "Quite a nice one, and in good order. No bad drains, no crumbling walls, and the roof has been repaired recently and is guaranteed not to leak. You could have your own country home, and the rents would surely be a welcome addition to your assets."

"Land isn't worth as much as it used to be," Gervase reminded him. "Owing to the agricultural depression." Of which his father was well aware; indeed, that was among the reasons he had his finger in so many pies. The duke was nothing if not long-sighted. "And the dukedom notwithstanding, I can't say I seriously entertained fantasies of being lord of the manor. My life is in London."

"Very well. You could let it, if you choose not to live in it—perhaps to a rich American. As Langdale claims *he* wishes to do—with a certain property."

"So that's his plan for Moorhaven?"

"So he would have me think. Unfortunately for him, I happen not to believe him." A touch absently, the duke moved his rook pawn up a square. "Moorhaven happens to have... a great deal more to offer than meets the eye. And I'd be willing to share what it has to offer."

"Buried treasure on the grounds, perhaps?" Gervase suggested with a sardonic lift of an eyebrow. "No... a diamond mine!"

"Lead, actually," the duke corrected. "Possibly silver as well, as the two are often found together. Moorhaven is located near the Wharfedale Valley. You may recall that there were a number of Roman workings in that area. A few months ago, I received information suggesting that one such mine is located on Moorhaven land. Langdale has apparently been apprised of the same possibility, which is why he's so eager to retain possession of the property. And why," again his voice hardened, his blue eyes sharpening, "after nearly ten years of maintaining it at Whitborough's expense, I am not about to hand it over to him without a fight."

Gervase digested this in stunned silence. "My God, you're serious."

"Never more so," his father assured him. "I imagine I'll have to share ownership of the mine with Langdale—unless I succeed in buying him out. But in any case, I'm prepared to offer you half of my own half of what we find."

"You're offering me shares in a hole in the ground. A *hypothetical* hole in the ground."

"There won't be anything hypothetical about the profits," the duke pointed out. "Half of half is a good twenty-five percent. Plus the Warwickshire property I mentioned, as well as your commission. You will not find me ungenerous, I think."

"It has never been your generosity that I questioned, sir." Merely the strings his father invariably attached to his promised largesse.

"So, will you take it on?"

"I would like to take some time to think about it, before giving you my answer." Gervase surveyed the chessboard for a moment, looked again more closely to confirm what he was seeing, then made his move. "Checkmate."

Whitborough's eyes flared wide as he stared down at the unimpeded path between Gervase's bishop and his king. "How did you—?"

"It helps to avoid distraction—and not lose sight of one's main objective," Gervase advised, assuming an expression of bland benevolence. He pushed back his chair and rose—steadily, he was pleased to note, despite the cognac. "Goodnight, Father."

Chapter Six

Oh that my words were now written! oh that they were printed in a book!
> —JOB 19:23

MARGARET AWOKE to the sound of Tilda bringing her morning tea—or rather, morning chocolate, which she preferred on icy winter mornings like these.

She stretched luxuriously, relishing the lavender-scented linens and thick woolen blankets. And the steam radiator had done its job: the tower felt wonderfully warm, despite the fire having burned itself down to ashes by the time she retired last night. It was burning again now, however, the flames dancing brightly in the grate. She must have slept right through the housemaid coming in to relight it. Ordinarily, she might have been a little embarrassed at being still abed at this hour, but after yesterday's journey, it had been delicious to sleep as long as she wished. Besides, breakfast at Denforth was usually served later in the morning, a casual meal to which she need not come down before nine or even ten o'clock.

Tilda, setting the tray down on a table before the fireplace, glanced towards the bed and smiled. "Good morning, my lady. Will you be taking your chocolate in bed, or here, by the fire?"

Margaret pulled herself into a sitting position and

resolutely tossed aside the blankets. "Oh, by the fire, please—otherwise, I shall succumb to sloth and never get out of bed at all!"

Clad in dressing-gown and slippers, she poured out a cup of frothy hot chocolate from an exquisite Sévres china pot. There was a plate of hot buttered toast, as well, kept warm beneath a covered silver salver. Margaret sipped her chocolate—rich, creamy, and just sweet enough—and nibbled a triangle of toast. The only thing missing from this delightfully self-indulgent interlude was something to read, she mused, glancing towards the nearest bookcase.

No harm in letting her still-steaming chocolate cool for a few minutes, while she went in search of some decent reading material. Replacing the cover on her toast, she rose and drifted over to the bookcase. Tilda, accustomed to her mistress's early-morning vagaries, paid no heed but continued to set out Margaret's clothes for the day.

Head tipped to one side, Margaret peered at the spines, many of them worn with years and use. Novels, poems, essays... she could recall reading some of these during previous stays at Denforth. Once or twice she paused in her search, her hand poised over a spine, only to move on. Difficult to make a selection when one wasn't completely sure *what* one wanted to read!

She was weighing the possibility of choosing several titles, when she caught sight of a familiar name—in surprisingly bright letters—on the spine of a book shelved just below eye level. Unable, as always, to resist looking at *anything* bearing that name, she eagerly reached down and pulled the book out for a closer inspection.

A slim, but not skimpy, volume, handsomely bound in burgundy leather, with the *Arguments On The Innocence Of King Richard III* etched in gilt lettering on the spine. Margaret stared at it, seized by a growing sense of familiarity. She'd seen this book before, even *held* it before... but when?

Almost hesitantly, she opened the front cover—and heard the faint creak of newness, breathed in the mingled scents of leather and fresh paper. This hadn't been opened before, she realized—this was, in fact, a brand-new book. A suspicion took root in her mind, and she turned over the flyleaf with a slightly unsteady hand.

Shock rippled through her when she saw the inscription, penned in a sharp, slanting hand that was as distinctive as its author.

To the king's most faithful—and fervent—defender,

Happy Christmas!
G.

Margaret swallowed, unsure whether to laugh, burst into tears, or beat herself about the head with the heaviest book she could find.

Memory flooded through her, along with a hot rush of what might have been shame. Dear heaven, how could she ever have forgotten? The last time she'd seen this book had been five years ago, almost to the very day, in this very room...

The tower chamber had all the atmosphere Margaret remembered... but an air of melancholy pervaded it now, heavy and oppressive as the scent of tuberoses. Or perhaps it was her own melancholy that made it seem so.

The first Christmas without Hal. The accident had been six months ago, long enough perhaps for the wound to start healing over, but oh so easy to make it bleed once again!

Especially for his family. She saw it not just in the mourning they all still wore, but in the subdued mien of his sisters, especially Madeline. In the lines on his father's face, in his mother's shadowed eyes and periodic silences. Even in his brothers. Gervase seemed more self-contained than ever. Reg too appeared subdued, less bellicose than was his former wont. And Jason moved uncertainly through a world in which he'd suddenly risen to prominence: from a fourth son to a third son, in the most tragic way possible.

Margaret wasn't sure how she felt herself. Her girlish passion for Hal had waned long before his death, to the point where she'd almost come to dread the prospect of their marriage. What sort of future could they have together, where there was neither great love nor mutual respect? And yet she genuinely grieved for the charming boy she'd known since childhood, and would have gladly seen him restored to life in an instant—for his family's sake, if not for hers.

She blinked back a sudden rush of tears, and forced herself to concentrate on the present moment. One day at a time, one minute at a time... that was how one got through a tragedy. She remembered that from losing her mother more than two years ago.

Think about pleasant things... like Christmas. No sorrow could completely dim the joy of the season: the music, the lights, the comforting little rituals, the effort most people made to be just a bit kinder and more charitable towards each other.

Like Lord Bellamy, surely one of the kindest men she knew. He'd written her family such a warm, sympathetic letter after learning of Hal's death, expressing regret over the loss of "such a charming and spirited young man." And just last week, he'd called on them in London, where they'd gone for a few days of Christmas shopping, and brought a bottle of fine brandy for her father, flowers and hothouse grapes for her and Alicia—from his estate in Gloucestershire, where he'd be spending the holidays with his two young sons. A quiet family Christmas, he'd said— and Margaret had felt a pang of something almost like envy at his words. Christmas at Denforth might be many things, but quiet wasn't one of them, and these days she found herself desperately in need of quiet—and peace.

In an unguarded moment, she'd confided as much to Lord Bellamy as they took a sedate turn about the garden at Langdale House, and seen understanding dawn in his warm dark eyes.

"Perhaps, someday, if you and your family happen to visit Gloucestershire," he'd said, with such significance that Margaret had felt herself flushing and quickly dropped her gaze to the ground. Tactful as ever, Lord Bellamy had steered the conversation onto other subjects, but the memory of what had passed between them lingered for her long after he'd taken his leave.

Was it too soon, she wondered, to be having feelings for another man—and one who was so different from her late betrothed? Hal hadn't been gone a year yet. How would his family, so close to her own, react if she and Lord Bellamy...

A knock on her half-open door pulled her back to the present, and she turned and saw Gervase standing in the doorway.

"Hullo," he greeted her casually. "I heard you'd arrived. Settling in all right?"

"Fine," she assured him, thinking how much more grown-up he looked since the last time she'd seen him—at the funeral. Granted, Gervase had always seemed intellectually older than his years, but any lingering traces of boyishness appeared to have

vanished in the last six months, revealing the strong, angular planes of his face. Still slender, though—Margaret wondered fleetingly if he were getting enough to eat, now that he was working as an articled clerk in London, but it seemed impertinent to ask. "You look well," she added hastily. "City life must be agreeing with you."

"London has its charms," he told her, leaning easily against the doorjamb. "Although I'm usually too busy to take advantage of its myriad dissipations."

"Is Mr. Allingham pleased with your work?" Margaret asked, smiling.

"He appears to be. I try to give satisfaction." Grey eyes that never missed much scanned her from head to toe. "And what of you, Margaret? How have you been these last few months?"

"Oh, well enough," she replied with determined lightness. "Life has been very quiet, of course. But I have my books—and I've been doing my best to keep up with my studies."

"Do you think you'll go back to Oxford—once you're...?" He gestured at her black afternoon dress. Of fine merino, rather than crepe, but still recognizable as mourning; Gervase himself still wore a black armband, Margaret noticed.

"Once I'm out of mourning?" she finished for him. "I haven't decided, actually. You were right, you know," she added, more lightly. "I was very happy at Oxford—I could probably be so again. But if I did go back, it wouldn't be before spring."

"Well, then, perhaps this will help you decide one way or the other." From behind his back, he produced a slim parcel wrapped in plain brown paper, handing it to her with a flourish.

Margaret ran her hands over the parcel. "It feels... like a book! What did you—?"

"A copy of Thomas More's History of Richard III, *of course." His expression was as bland as milk.*

"If it is, I'll have no compunction about hurling it straight at your head!" she warned.

"Ah, but will you hit your target?" he mused, sidling out of reach. "Perhaps I should make myself scarce while you unwrap it. Happy Christmas, Margaret."

She sighed. "Happy Christmas, you aggravating boy."

He gave her that maddening dimpled smile and sauntered off down the passage...

Margaret stared at the book in her hand. She *could* recall unwrapping it—and the mingled interest and amusement she'd felt on seeing the title—but she'd never got round to reading it. Other events had crowded that detail from her mind... particularly the one that had led to her departure from Denforth the following night. She'd packed in haste, hoping to avoid awkward questions from her hosts or her father, but she *hadn't* intended to leave this behind! Whoever tidied the room after she'd left must have shelved it automatically with the rest of the books.

Gervase probably thought she hadn't cared for it. Self-reproach washed over her. How ungrateful and unappreciative her silence must have seemed! He'd taken the trouble to give her a unique present, one that held so much meaning for her, and she'd neither read it—nor, she realized with chagrin, even thanked him for it!

So have a look at it now, you ingrate, she apostrophized herself. *And then thank him properly the next time you see him.*

Returning to the table, she opened her gift, taking care not to spill chocolate on it. After perhaps fifteen minutes, she turned back to reread the introductory pages more closely, then closed the book and set it aside, feeling more shaken than ever.

This was neither a new nor reprinted study on Richard III, nor yet some obscure scholarly work that Gervase had somehow managed to locate. This book was *hers*, in every sense of the word: a summation of her arguments over the years, collected, bound, and privately published for her particular use. *And* her name was on the title page; the giver had supplied only some light editing, the printing costs—whatever those had amounted to—and the inscription.

Oh, Gervase.

Her eyes stung, and she blinked them hurriedly. Ridiculous to tear up over a book! If Gervase could see her now... well, he wouldn't have to *say* anything; she could just picture that raised eyebrow of his! *"Tears over Crouchback? Surely not..."*

Margaret smiled, shaking her head over the image: no one could accuse Gervase of excessive sentiment where Richard III was concerned! All the same, he'd given her a lovely, thoughtful gift. She might be long overdue in acknowledging it, but better late than never!

She finished her toast and chocolate, then set the book carefully on her bedside table to enjoy later. Afterwards, she had a quick wash, then let Tilda dress her hair in a chignon and help her into a chocolate-brown skirt and jacket of velvety-soft wool plush, and a cream silk blouse trimmed with lace. A pretty gold-and-pearl brooch at the collar of her blouse added a touch of brightness to the ensemble, and neat black half-boots showed off trim ankles... of which she'd always been a trifle vain. The mantel clock was chiming nine when she went down to breakfast, hoping to find the gentlemen—Gervase, at the very least—still present.

Unfortunately for her hopes, only Juliana and Madeline were in the breakfast parlor, tucking into generous platefuls of eggs, toast, ham, and kedgeree. The Lyons women had never pretended to possess birdlike appetites; they enjoyed their food as thoroughly as the men did.

"Good morning," Juliana greeted her with a bright smile. "Did you sleep well?"

"Like a baby," Margaret assured her. "The tower was so delightfully warm, I almost didn't want to get up!"

"An understandable urge," Madeline remarked. "Especially on a morning like this. It snowed a bit more last night."

"But it's beautifully clear now," Juliana added, although her sister shuddered. "Try the kedgeree—it's delicious!"

"Thanks—I will." Margaret headed for the mahogany sideboard, laden with chafing dishes, their contents kept warm by spirit lamps. Savory aromas wafted up to her as she lifted off the covers, reawakening hunger. The toast and hot chocolate had taken the sharpest edge off her appetite, but she helped herself to some kedgeree, along with a coddled egg, a slice of fried York ham, and some crisp fried potatoes before joining the sisters at the table.

"So, where is everyone this morning?" she asked, pouring tea from the silver service.

"Well, Reg apparently insisted on going out riding—and my lunatic of a husband decided to accompany him," Madeline replied, with another exaggerated shudder. "Quite mad, in my opinion, but what can one do with a pair of avid sportsmen?"

"And Papa is in his study, attending to some sort of

business," Juliana said. "Mama may still be abed—she mentioned that she might take her breakfast upstairs today."

"Mama always eats more lightly in the morning," Elaine observed, coming into the breakfast room. "I'm not sure she ever acquired a taste for the typical English breakfast."

"Unlike the rest of us," Juliana said, grinning as she spread jam lavishly onto her toast.

"For which I've never been more thankful!" Elaine laughed, helping herself to a generous serving of kedgeree. "I simply couldn't face the day on nothing more than milky coffee and rolls, not when there's someone else's appetite to consider as well!"

"Eating for two," Madeline said with a sage nod. "Once I got over the morning sickness, my appetite was prodigious!"

"Mine too, especially at breakfast. Like a true Scot, Alasdair is always trying to press porridge on me. He has the best of intentions, poor darling, but I've never cared much for it." Elaine added an egg and some rashers of bacon to her plate, then took a seat at the table.

"So where is Alasdair?" Juliana inquired.

"I don't know. He got up much earlier than I did," Elaine reported, attacking her breakfast with gusto. "Perhaps he decided to go riding too."

"And the other men?" Margaret tried to sound casual. "My brother and Gervase?"

Lydgate, a silent sentinel in a corner of the room, gave a light cough that drew their attention. "The gentlemen all breakfasted earlier, Lady Bellamy," he informed Margaret. "After which, Lord Gervase and Lord Jason headed for the gymnasium, accompanied by both of the younger dukes. I believe a fencing match was under discussion."

"A fencing match? What fun!" Juliana glanced around the table at her companions. "Shall we go and watch?"

The level of interest, her own included, had risen visibly at the news, Margaret noted. She did not doubt that Augustus was responsible for much of it, but *her* pulse quickened at the prospect of seeing Gervase in action. He fenced regularly, but it had been years since she'd had the chance to watch him at it.

A wicked smile curved Madeline's lips, heightening her resemblance to her mother. "Four good-looking men with swords—even if two of them are our brothers. What better way to while away a winter morning? By all means, let us go."

❄

They finished breakfast quickly, then hurried to the gymnasium, a large, open room on the ground floor of the east wing, illuminated by morning light except on the very darkest days. The Lyons boys all tended to gather there when it rained, Margaret remembered, Hal and Reg frequently engaging in their less than friendly boxing or wrestling bouts. Or a net would be strung across the room for tennis matches, which were marginally more peaceful—or less likely to end in bloodshed!

As they approached the gymnasium, a series of metallic scrapes and clangs reached their ears, as blade met blade. Then a voice Margaret knew rang out imperatively. "Jason, *a moi!*"

Gervase. She quickened her step, just as Jason responded, his own voice almost cracking with excitement, "*En garde!*"

Amid the clash of swords, Margaret and her companions slipped into the room, taking care to stay on the periphery. Two pairs of fencers parried and thrust, attacked and defended along the length of the gymnasium floor.

Seating herself with the others on a bench against a wall, Margaret peered more closely at the combatants, seeking Gervase. No easy task, as all four wore close-fitting white jackets and trousers, along with wire masks over their faces, and the wan winter light from the windows seemed to turn everyone's hair to the same dull brown.

Then the nearer pair of fencers passed within a few feet of them, and she caught her breath. *There*—the slightly taller of the two, and the one defending rather than attacking. But the way he moved, the way he carried himself was unmistakable.

"Excellent form, I must say," Madeline observed, beside her. "Even if he *is* my brother."

"Which one?" Margaret asked, not taking her gaze from either man.

"Gervase, of course. Jason's not bad, either," Madeline added critically. "Though as yet, he has far more enthusiasm than skill."

Lower lip caught between her teeth, Margaret watched the brothers duel, part of her mind wondering how she'd come to recognize Gervase so quickly, from his movements alone. But every step, every motion of his was controlled, smooth, and precise, flowing from one position to the next with seeming effortlessness. Jason's style, by contrast, was more dramatic, but wild, and punctuated by occasional grunts of effort—as he tried but continually failed to break through his brother's guard.

Despite knowing little beyond the basics of fencing —thrust, parry, riposte—Margaret thought that Gervase could have easily disarmed his brother several times over. Instead, he was… not toying with Jason, exactly, but holding back a little. Continuing to fight in a mostly defensive fashion and letting the younger man try his strength. She almost missed the moment when his foil darted out in a sudden flick and Jason's weapon clattered to the floor.

"Again." Not even winded, Gervase picked up the foil and tossed it back at his brother.

Jason's breathing was more audible, but he caught the foil deftly and resumed his attack with redoubled vigor. Out of the corner of her eye, Margaret saw that Alasdair and Augustus had ceased their own bout, and were watching Gervase and Jason's match instead.

A subtle difference this time—Gervase had gone on the offensive as well, mounting his own attack in response to Jason's. They danced back and forth, thrusting, feinting, their foils meeting again and again. Jason landed a touch on his brother's arm and immediately grew overconfident, mounting a grandiose attack from above that stopped short when Gervase suddenly dropped into a lunge, the tip of his foil pointed at Jason's throat.

The boy yelped in surprise, the foil falling from his hand. This time, Gervase let it lie, and straightened up, exasperation visible in every line of his body. Neither displayed any awareness of their audience.

"This is *not* a Dumas novel, Jason." Gervase's voice emerged from behind the mask, sounding more than a bit testy. "Fencing requires control. Discipline. Precision. Flailing about like the villain in a melodrama is apt to get you cut to ribbons."

"But what about those plays we used to put on?" Jason protested, pulling off his mask.

"Stage fencing is different. Besides, actors are trained to make their duels look more dangerous than they are. And in any case, you left your guard open so often, you wouldn't have lasted long against Hamlet or Laertes, even without a poisoned blade." He glanced at the now-scowling boy, and added in a less severe tone, "On the other hand, you've got a bit faster on your feet, so there's been some improvement since last time."

"You think so?" Jason sounded just a little wistful.

"Yes. Your footwork is coming on well. But master the *basics* of fencing first, before you try anything more... flamboyant." He paused, then added with the dry humor Margaret knew so well. "And don't underestimate the advantages of a good defensive strategy. Like letting your opponent tire himself out before *you* go on the attack."

Jason stared at him for a moment, then his mouth twitched into a reluctant smile. "The way you did with me?"

"I leave you to draw your own conclusions," Gervase replied, more dryly still.

His brother huffed a laugh, then stuck out his gloved hand. "All right! Thanks, Ger."

Gervase took the outstretched hand and shook it punctiliously. "Well-fought, brother."

Margaret exhaled, relieved and unexpectedly impressed. Instruction... but not humiliation—and better for Jason than a too-easy victory that he hadn't truly earned or a trouncing that would have left him angry and embarrassed. The sort of defeat that Reg or even Hal would have handed out without a thought, she realized.

"Well fought, *both* of you!" Madeline called from the bench, and led the other spectators in a round of applause.

The brothers now turned to face their audience.

"Ah," Gervase remarked. "I see there are ladies present." He took off his mask, revealing tousled bronze-brown hair, and bowed to them; Jason followed suit, a little uncertainly.

Margaret studied her friend closely. He was breathing a little more quickly than usual, and a fine sheen of perspiration bathed his forehead. But other than that, he seemed unaffected, neither as flushed nor short of breath as his brother, who was gulping in air like water. Her fingers suddenly itched to brush back that fall of hair, card through its heavy softness...

Good heavens, what was she *thinking*? She glanced aside, seeking something other than Gervase on which to focus. Fortunately, Augustus and Alasdair were approaching the bench, their masks tucked under their arms.

"Good morning, love." Alasdair stooped to kiss Elaine on the cheek. "Come to watch me receive a drubbing from Langdale here?"

"From where I was sitting, you seemed to be holding your own," she said loyally.

"Castlebrooke is a worthy opponent," Augustus acknowledged, with his careful smile. "But I believe our thunder was stolen—and rightly so," he added, nodding towards Gervase and Jason. "Most impressive, gentlemen. Lord Gervase, I hope you are willing to match swords with *me*... perhaps some morning when we are both fresher?"

Gervase regarded him for a moment, then gave a brief nod. "I should relish the challenge, Langdale. Some other morning, then."

Margaret felt the back of her neck prickle at his words. Both men *sounded* perfectly cordial, but something about their exchange unnerved her. The assessing way they looked at each other, perhaps—their gazes, icy-blue and cool grey, locking like the swords of which they spoke.

She wondered if the others could sense it too.

Juliana broke the brief silence by inquiring brightly, "So, if you gentlemen are through dazzling us with your swordplay, shall we remove to the Great Hall? There's some holly and ivy calling for our attention—to say nothing of the Christmas tree!"

"A delightful prospect," Alasdair said warmly, then turned to Elaine. "Shall we fetch the children, *mo chridhe*? Beatrice, at least, is old enough to help with the decorating."

"So are Richenda and Harry," Madeline said, rising from the bench. "Which makes this the perfect time to introduce them to some Denforth Christmas rituals. Shall we meet in the Great Hall in half an hour? That gives the four of *you* a chance to wash first," she added, with an especially pointed look at Jason, who flushed in annoyance.

"We're all *'fat and scant of breath,'*" Gervase agreed with a hint of a smile, setting a placatory hand on his brother's shoulder. "So, half an hour it is, then."

❄

MARGARET WAS NOT in the least surprised when Gervase was the first man to appear outside the Great Hall, looking as fresh and immaculate as if he hadn't so much as *glanced* at a sword, let alone spent the morning wielding one. His linen gleamed white even in the shadowy passage, and she could glimpse the comb marks in his hair.

He sketched a lazy salute toward Juliana, approaching with a basket of greenery on her arm. "Reporting for duty, General."

"Splendid," Juliana greeted him with a sunny smile. "I thought we could use more ivy, so we could decorate the window bays as well as the mantel. And I found a bit of mistletoe to put up as well. What's Christmas without mistletoe—or stolen kisses?" she added, her blue eyes sparking mischievously.

"One *can* have the latter without the former," Gervase pointed out, an answering glint in his own eyes.

Margaret felt her cheeks grow warm. *Stolen kisses.* Like the one they'd shared on the train, the one that her body remembered all too well, even as her mind attempted to dismiss it. She glanced toward the doorway of the Great Hall, grateful for the shadows that concealed her flush. Then frowned, as a peculiar noise reached her ears.

"Juliana, do you hear something—from in there?" she asked.

Her friend paused, listening, then, "Yes! It's a bit faint... but it sounds like a cry."

They hurried into the Hall, Gervase just behind them. At first glance, the room appeared deserted. But as they approached the Christmas tree, the sound increased in volume—and the source became readily identifiable.

Juliana looked up and stifled a giggle. "Oh, dear!"

Gervase sighed as he followed her gaze. "One of Messalina's last litter, I presume?"

"How did you know?" his sister asked.

"Their reputation precedes them." And for a moment, they stood united in the memory of another tree and another cat. Then Gervase stepped forward with a resigned expression.

"At least there's a ladder this time," he remarked.

"And you don't have to tuck a fish paste sandwich in your sleeve," Margaret teased.

"Experience is a great teacher," Gervase said dryly. He extracted a pair of gloves from his pocket and tugged them on, before mounting the ladder set up beside the tree.

Standing on one of the higher rungs, he easily plucked the squalling ginger kitten from its branch. "Clearly, you have the same want of sense as your sire at that age," he told it sternly, as it squirmed and squeaked in his grasp. "Though I'll say this much: you have towering ambitions for one so small. However, as a Christmas tree ornament, you leave something to be desired."

"Well, if partridges can reside in pear trees," Juliana began mischievously, only to be cut off short as Gervase descended from the ladder and thrust the kitten at her.

"Ju, take him off before he aspires to climb something else he can't get down from—like the chandelier."

Juliana bore the kitten away, a thoughtful glint in her eye that Margaret did not miss.

"I think you may have acquired a kitten for Christmas," she murmured to Gervase, once they were alone.

His eyes widened in almost comical dismay. "She wouldn't!"

"Oh, don't be such a wet blanket, my dear!" she chided, laughing. "A kitten or two might liven up that stodgy townhouse of yours. Besides, didn't Sir Anthony have a cat himself?"

"Ozymandias was ripe in years and dignity, not a feckless infant," he grumbled.

"I'll bet he was every bit as silly when he was a few months old," she retorted. "And I challenge *you* to remain immune to a kitten's charms for longer than five minutes! For that matter, I wouldn't mind having one myself. I'll ask Juliana if the rest of the litter is spoken for."

"I'd have thought you already had a cat of your own. You usually did before—you named several after Greek goddesses!" he added. "Wasn't one of them called 'Persephone'?"

"*Purr*-sephone," she corrected, smiling at the memory. "Well, Alex certainly wouldn't have denied me one, if I'd asked. But he'd a pair of hounds who went almost everywhere on the estate with him, and it seemed a bit unfair to introduce a cat into the mix." And then, after Alex's death, she'd been too numb with grief even to think of acquiring a cat. His dogs had been inconsolable until Sandy and Charles had taken them in hand, humans and canines comforting each other in their shared loss. But now, perhaps, it wouldn't feel like a betrayal to have a cat...

A more recent memory tugged at her mind. "Talking of Christmas presents," she began, "you'll never guess what I found, in my chamber this morning! The book you gave me five Christmases ago—about Richard the Third's innocence."

Gervase stilled, his grey gaze sharpening. "I... hadn't known it was lost."

"Not lost, *exactly*. Misplaced might be a better word." She paused, fretting her lower lip, then resumed hesitantly, "I... forgot to pack it, when I departed that night. I suppose the maid found it, after I'd gone, and put it in the bookcase with everything else. I didn't mean to leave it behind. I'm so sorry. You went to so much trouble to give me something special."

Gervase cleared his throat, shifting his weight from foot to foot. Almost as if he were embarrassed—something she couldn't remember ever seeing from him before. "There's no need to apologize, Margaret. I imagine you were... much preoccupied, in light of your situation. If truth be told," he added, "I'd wondered if your interest in the subject had dwindled, over time."

"Not in the least," she assured him. "And I look forward to finally reading the book. Perhaps it will inspire me to new heights of rhetoric."

His lips curved in a lazy smile. "Should I be pleased at this prospect—or alarmed?"

The sound of approaching voices kept Margaret from replying exactly as she wished, so she contented herself with an eloquent eye roll as the others came trooping in: Madeline and Elaine with their elder children in tow, the men bringing up the rear.

Juliana returned, sans kitten. "Shall we get started, then?" she suggested.

Under her supervision, everyone took a lavish armful of greenery and chose a part of the Hall to decorate. By some design—whether hers or his, she could not be sure—Margaret found herself beside Gervase, sorting through holly and ivy to adorn one of the window bays.

Still wearing the gloves he'd donned to rescue the kitten, Gervase teased a particularly prickly cluster of holly from the pile. "Here—take some ivy. It's less likely to fight back."

Margaret complied, draping glossy leaves and tendrils over the sill. The panes before her reflected the cheerful domestic scene behind her, and she smiled, glancing over her shoulder for a better look.

Gervase's sisters were helping the children decorate the mantel, while Elaine's two-year-old son Simon watched from his nursemaid's lap, taking in everything with huge eyes.

Margaret smiled at the boy. "I wonder how much of this he'll even remember."

"Hard to predict at his age." Gervase's expression, as he followed her gaze, was oddly pensive. "Though *I* could swear to remembering as far back as my third birthday."

"Really? That long ago—what do you remember?"

"Mainly Hal and Reg, squabbling over something—our parents had to separate them for the day." He paused, brows creasing in a slight frown. "But then they squabbled so often that I might be confusing the occasion with a more recent memory."

Margaret pulled a face. "Pity they couldn't put aside their differences for *someone else's* special day!"

"Well, they were only five and seven at the time," he pointed out. "Fortunately, I have other, pleasanter recollections of the day. I believe it was the first time I ever tasted ice cream."

"That would be a *very* pleasant recollection," she agreed, smiling. "Which flavor?"

A corner of his mouth lifted. "Chocolate, of course."

Over by the mantel, Elaine began to sing, softly at first, then with more vigor as the children joined in: "*The holly and the ivy, / When they are both full grown...*"

Their enthusiasm was infectious, and soon everyone in the Great Hall was singing too, moving onto another carol when finished with the first. Gervase sang as capably as he did everything else, Margaret noted—in a well-trained baritone as warm as his grey eyes were cool.

They had just completed a rousing rendition of "Wassail! Wassail!" when a new voice spoke up sweetly from the threshold.

"But how delightful! I could not ask for a better welcome!"

Every gaze turned in the direction of the speaker—who could easily have served as the model for a Christmas angel: golden-haired, serenely beautiful, and exquisitely dressed in a traveling ensemble of sapphire blue velvet trimmed with swansdown.

Eyes of the same deep blue scanned the room, and came to rest on Margaret. "No greeting from *you*, Meg? *Tiens*, I see *I* shall have to make the first move!"

"*Alicia?*" Margaret exclaimed, and went forward in a daze to embrace the sister she had somehow failed to recognize.

Chapter Seven

For her own breakfast she'll project a scheme,
Nor take her tea without a stratagem.
—EDWARD YOUNG, *Love of Fame*

"*ALORS*, now I am home at last!" Alicia declared on a light, musical laugh, detaching herself from Margaret's clasp in an eddy of swansdown and expensive scent. "Or near enough," she amended, smiling about the room. "I am so happy to see all of you again!"

"As we are to see you," Augustus said, coming forward to embrace her in turn. "How was your crossing yesterday? I hope you passed a restful night at Bourne's."

"Cousin Ernest was hospitality itself. As for the crossing," Alicia gave a delicate shudder, "let us not speak of it! This morning's train journey was far easier, despite all the soot. I hope my face isn't covered in smuts!"

"It isn't—you look beautiful," Margaret told her. Alicia had always been a pretty child, although, like most young girls, she'd gone through a gawky, coltish stage during her teens. All that awkwardness had vanished, leaving only an exquisite young woman, burnished to a high gloss by her sojourn in Paris. Somewhat to her chagrin, Margaret felt almost dowdy by comparison: a plain brown sparrow beside a peacock. Even at her best, she'd never been as glamorous or soignée as Alicia was now.

"You do indeed," Juliana said warmly, approaching her new guest. "France has certainly agreed with you, Alicia. Welcome back to Denforth!"

They embraced lightly, cheek to cheek, though Margaret noticed a slight element of reserve between them. Which came as no surprise—while close in age, Alicia and Juliana had always been quite different in tastes and temperament, Alicia being far more conventional. Watching them, Margaret couldn't help wondering how Juliana—and her sisters, for that matter—felt about Alicia's engagement to Reg and her position as future Duchess of Whitborough.

Not that any of them betrayed the slightest misgiving. Madeline and Elaine greeted Alicia cordially, and the men appeared charmed by her. Jason was frankly staring, while Gervase... even cool, self-contained Gervase was regarding her with the appreciation men reserve for a lovely woman. The sort Margaret had seen in Alex's eyes when she dressed to please him.

Recognition shot a hot little needle through her, followed by a stab of what felt startlingly like jealousy. Jealousy of the kind Margaret had not experienced since her engagement to Hal, so many years ago. Shaken, she dropped her gaze to the floor. She couldn't *possibly* be jealous of Alicia, could she? Of her beloved younger sister—simply because Gervase was looking at her with admiration? Why shouldn't he, after all? Alicia was considered the beauty of the family; Margaret had long since come to terms with *that*, and they were far enough apart in age that they'd never been serious rivals—least of all over a man.

The sound of male voices and laughter roused Margaret from her thoughts, much to her secret relief. Moments later, Reg and Hugo strode into the room, flushed from their exercise, flakes of snow glistening upon their broad shoulders.

"Ah, the truants have returned!" Juliana announced with an air of triumph. "And just in time to help with the decorating!"

Reg gave her a lazily amused smile. "So, is that what's in the wind for today?" He glanced about the Hall. "The place does look more festive now, I must admit."

"*Bonjour*, Reg." The breathless catch in her sister's

voice sent Margaret's heart sinking to the floor. For all her newfound sophistication and elegant Parisian wardrobe, Alicia had not changed one bit in this regard.

Reg blinked, taking in her appearance. "Lady Alicia. Have you just got here?'

She smiled at him, her heart in her eyes, and extended a dainty gloved hand. "Yes, I arrived only a few minutes ago."

"You look different," he remarked, bowing over her hand with a perfunctory air.

"Do I?" Again that breathless note in Alicia's voice. "In what way?"

"More—fashionable," he said, after a moment. "Is that a new dress?"

Alicia smoothed a self-conscious hand over the velvet skirt. "Yes, from Paris."

"It suits you," he observed, making her glow as if he'd just recited an extemporaneous sonnet to her eyebrow. "They know about style, the French." He released her hand and turned to Juliana. "Well, infant—where do you want me to start?"

Some of the light faded from Alicia's eyes, and Margaret fought down the urge to hurl a basket of greenery at Reg's head. While Hal had taken *her* for granted during their engagement, Reg's indifference was on another level entirely, tepid compliments and all. Knowing the reason for it did little to lessen her annoyance, especially when she saw the disappointment on her sister's face. *Oh, my dear, if only you knew it* wasn't *going to get any better...*

"I hope that was carol singing I just heard," the duchess's throaty contralto observed from the doorway. "Christmas never quite seems like Christmas without music."

"You have ears like a cat, *ma belle Helene*," the duke remarked, from over his wife's shoulder. "But I thought I heard it as well. Along with a new voice or two."

"Alicia is here now, Papa," Juliana announced, beckoning her brother's fiancée forward.

Whitborough advanced into the room and bowed over her hand. "Lady Alicia, welcome to Denforth. You are lovelier than ever, I see."

Alicia flushed becomingly. "Thank you, Duke."

"My husband speaks no more than the truth," the duchess said, coming forward in turn to embrace the younger woman. "Paris appears to have done you a world of good, my dear! Is that Worth?" she inquired, eyeing Alicia's traveling costume with a knowledgeable air.

Alicia nodded, looking more like a schoolgirl who'd exceeded her allowance than the fashionable sophisticate she aspired to be. "Monsieur Worth designed most of my winter wardrobe. I know it was a trifle extravagant of me, but I simply couldn't resist!"

"Well, why on earth should you?" the duchess remarked with an indulgent smile. "A duke's daughter *should* dress according to her station."

"As should a future duchess, eh, Reg?" the duke added, shifting his probing blue gaze to his son.

Reg's face might have been carved from stone. "Lady Alicia should wear whatever she pleases." His tone was equally expressionless, and Alicia's face clouded a little more.

This time Margaret had to restrain the urge to throw things at *both* men. Reg's lack of interest in her sister was glaring enough without his father throwing fuel on the fire.

Fortunately, the duchess had things well in hand. "Quite right," she said briskly, putting an arm about Alicia's shoulders. "Now, *petite*, would you like me to ring for a hot drink, or would you rather go up to your chamber for a rest? From what I've heard about yesterday's weather, your crossing must have been rougher than mine."

"Oh, I'm quite recovered from that, Duchess. But I should be glad of a cup of tea, and a chance to help with the decorating," she added with her winsome smile. Margaret felt the knot of tension inside of her loosen at the sight.

"We should be glad of your help if you're not too tired," Juliana assured her.

"From what I can see, you've made a good start on Christmas-ing the Hall," the duchess said, with an approving glance around the room.

"Is 'Christmas-ing' a word, Helene?" her husband inquired, raising a brow.

"If it isn't, then it *should* be," she retorted, undaunted. "Come, Duke, let's do our part. We can't leave it all up to the children."

With so many hands at work, Juliana's baskets of greenery were soon empty, and all the window bays, along with the mantel, decked in holly and ivy. Even the mistletoe was up, fastened to a branch of the chandelier with trailing scarlet ribbons.

Sweeping over to the Christmas tree, the duchess eyed it appraisingly from top to bottom. "Shall we begin on this now? The Hall is so splendid that the poor thing looks underdressed by comparison."

"The ornaments are in that corner," Juliana informed her mother, gesturing towards a stack of wooden crates.

"Excellent!" the duchess declared, rubbing her hands together. "Let's get started."

One by one the crates were opened, and the ornaments, wrapped in cotton wool, tenderly lifted out. Sparkling globes of blown glass, dainty figures of porcelain or wood, brightly colored ribbons, and strands of silver tinsel... the children were especially taken with the sight, but their enthusiasm communicated itself to the adults. And soon everyone was occupied in transforming the Christmas tree into "a thing of beauty" and "a joy forever"—or rather, the next fortnight. The singing resumed as well, augmented by five more voices, until the Hall echoed with the merry sound. And *this*, Margaret thought, smiling as she did her part, was what made Christmases at Denforth special: these moments of gaiety and camaraderie, during which rivalries and squabbles were set aside.

By tacit agreement, the lower boughs of the Christmas tree had been reserved for the children. Madeline and Elaine solemnly helped them find places to hang the ornaments and strew the tinsel. Alasdair hoisted Beatrice onto his shoulders so she could hang a bauble on one of the higher branches. After which, Richenda and Harry immediately clamored for the same privilege.

"Save some branches in the middle," the duchess advised, lifting out a carved wooden chest from one crate, with special care.

The duke's expression altered when he saw the chest in her arms, and their eyes met in a very private exchange that made the air around them seem to crackle with electricity. What must it be like to be married for so long that you shared a secret language? Margaret wondered. For all their disagreements—for all their outright strife—over the years, the duke and duchess seemed wholly at one now. She liked to imagine that, if Fate had been kinder, she and Alex might have developed such an understanding—while sparing them the conflicts that had bedeviled the Whitboroughs' marriage. On the other hand, she could not deny that Their Graces had often appeared to relish their arguments, both giving as good as they got.

This, however, was no occasion for argument, Margaret realized, looking more closely at the chest the duchess was almost cradling in her arms, her expression soft... even wistful. And a faint thrill of anticipation rippled through Margaret as understanding dawned.

The ornaments. She'd always secretly envied the Lyons family this ritual—just a little. Her own mother had loved beautiful things and had known how to choose them, but she'd lacked the knack of *designing* them. By contrast, the duchess had been commissioning individual Christmas ornaments for the family—each marked with the recipient's first initial—since the early years of her marriage. Those of her own children first, then, as they married and started families of their own, those of their spouses and offspring. And every Christmas at Denforth, each member of the family put his or her ornament on the tree.

Whitborough, his own expression gentler than usual, turned to his wife. "Shall we begin, *ma mie*?" he inquired, holding out his hand.

Again that very private exchange of glances, then the duchess set the chest down on a chair, opened it, and took out two ornaments, one burgundy, one royal blue, each marked with an elaborately stitched and beaded initial "H" in gold. She handed the duke the blue ornament, and the Whitboroughs silently hung their ornaments on adjacent branches—almost side by side.

Returning, the duchess sat down with the chest on her lap, and beckoned to her eldest daughter. "Madeline."

Without a word, Madeline approached, her face pensive as she gazed into the chest. Margaret suppressed a shiver, knowing what she was seeing. Five Christmases ago, a similar moment had arisen... when the family had again been forced to confront their irreparable loss.

Then Madeline had spoken into the stricken silence that had descended on the Hall. "He is still with us, in spirit—and he is my twin, always." And then she'd taken Hal's ornament—gold and crimson—as well as her own rose-and-silver one and hung them up together.

"Very fitting, *chérie*," the duchess had said, her voice huskier than usual. And the duke, his eyes suspiciously bright, had only nodded, beyond speech at that moment.

The intervening years had dulled the edge of grief, so there was no awkwardness now when Madeline again took up both ornaments and placed them on this year's Christmas tree. But Margaret thought that the slight melancholy in the room dispersed afterwards, and the ritual took on a more festive tone as Hugo hung his ornament—dark blue with a gold tassel—on the other side of his wife's, then he and Madeline helped their children with theirs. The ornaments of all the grandchildren were white, Margaret observed, but enlivened with touches of color: pink for Richenda, gold for Harry, and dark blue for baby Oliver, who'd been left sleeping in the nursery.

Reg and Gervase followed with their ornaments: scarlet-and-gold and ice-blue-and-silver, respectively. Margaret couldn't help noticing that the brothers chose branches that were a fair distance apart, although they did not appear to be on bad terms. But then, she reflected with rueful amusement, the holidays had only just started.

Elaine and her family came next. Margaret remembered how touched Alasdair had been on receiving his ornament, soon after his and Elaine's wedding: a silver ball trimmed with tartan ribbon patterned in the Lennox red and green. She supposed if she'd married Hal, she'd have received an ornament as well, but she couldn't imagine exchanging fond glances with him as Elaine did with Alasdair as she hung her green-and-gold ornament alongside his. Five-year-old Beatrice wanted to hang her white-and-green ornament all by herself, but eventually agreed to let her father assist her, while Elaine put up Simon's white-and-tartan bauble for him.

"Next Christmas, you might be big enough to do it yourself," she told her son, who was gazing up at the tree in wide-eyed wonder.

Juliana's saffron-and-gold ornament shone like a small sun from one of the higher branches, and Jason placed his—dark green and silver—even higher, proving beyond a doubt that spirit of competition was alive and well in the Lyons family, Gervase murmured *sotto voce* in Margaret's ear. She stifled a giggle, but could not disagree with him.

Once the boughs were decorated, Reg, as the tallest in the family, mounted the ladder and placed an elaborately wrought crystal star on top of the tree, where it shimmered with iridescent hues even in the pale winter light. The rest of the tree was no less magnificent, glittering with tinsel, the jewel-toned ornaments glowing among the evergreen branches.

Around her, Margaret could hear the pleased murmurs and sense the satisfaction from all at a job well done. And something more, she thought: the growing anticipation and excitement that were intrinsically part of Christmas. Not just from the children either—the duke and duchess were standing together, almost close enough to touch, gazing up at the tree with nearly identical expressions of contentment, even delight.

"Isn't it beautiful?" Juliana exclaimed. "I think it's the best tree we've ever had."

"You say that every year, infant," Reg pointed out as he descended the ladder.

"And every year it's true!" she countered.

"You've done a wonderful job, all of you!" the duchess declared, smiling around the room. "I can't think of a single thing to be improved upon."

"Nor can I." The duke looked down at his wife—an intimate, lingering look that seemed to encompass the whole of their shared years together. "A triumph, *ma belle Helene.*"

She gazed back at him, hazel eyes into blue ones, and in that moment Margaret would have sworn that no one existed for them but each other.

"Grandmamma?" Richenda piped up from the corner where the crates were still stacked.

The duchess glanced towards her seven-year-old granddaughter. "Yes, *petite?*"

"I found this in one of the crates," the girl announced, coming over and holding up her discovery for all to see.

It glittered in the light—a sphere of royal purple, liberally encrusted with gold beadwork, embellished with a dangling gold tassel at the bottom *and* an elaborate bow of gold ribbon on top. Not hideous, Margaret judged, even attractive in a showy way... but far too garish—and ostentatious—to be the duchess's handiwork.

"It has an 'H' on it," Richenda went on, helpfully turning the ornament so her grandmother could see the initial. "Should it go on the tree too?"

A sudden chill descended on the room. Margaret glanced at Gervase and saw that he had stiffened slightly, though his face was unreadable. Not so some of his siblings: Madeline's lips were set in a tight line, Elaine had gone wide-eyed with dismay, and Reg looked positively thunderous. But it was the duchess whose face had undergone the most disturbing change. All trace of dreamy softness had gone, and her features now appeared sculpted from marble... or ice. The duke had paled as well, and a muscle twitched almost imperceptibly at the corner of his jaw. But his gaze never wavered from that of his wife.

Finally, the duchess moved, setting a light, reassuring hand on her granddaughter's head. "That, *petite*, is entirely up to your grandfather."

Her voice was quite calm; only someone who knew her well would notice the complete absence of warmth in her tone.

The duke cleared his throat, and stooped to Richenda's height. "I think, poppet, we have enough ornaments on the tree at present. So let's put it back in the crate."

"If everyone will pardon me, I must go and consult Mrs. Hill about dinner tonight," the duchess said, her voice still cool and utterly implacable.

"Helene," Whitborough began, and Margaret could hear the barely restrained frustration in his own voice.

"We will speak later, Duke." And without a backward glance at her husband, the duchess swept from the Hall.

Richenda glanced uncertainly from her grandfather

to the doorway through which her grandmother had vanished, her small face puckered with worry. "Mama, did I do something wrong?" she appealed to her mother.

Madeline gave her a reassuring hug. "Not a thing, sweetheart. Let's just put away the ornament, shall we?" Pointedly ignoring her father, she led Richenda back towards the crates.

The room emptied with astonishing speed after that, the duke being the next to leave, followed by Reg, then the Saxbys and Castlebrookes with their children. Alicia accepted Juliana's offer to escort her to her chamber, and Augustus departed in their wake. Jason lingered, clearly hoping that someone would enlighten him about the scene that had just taken place, but finally took himself off, his curiosity unsatisfied.

Alone in the Hall, Margaret turned to her companion, who'd been doing his best impression of an oyster ever since Richenda's inopportune discovery. He was standing in front the tree, making a wholly unnecessary adjustment to his ornament. The silver snowflakes surrounding his initial twinkled in the light.

"Gervase," she began tentatively, "was that from—?"

"Mrs. Clayton." His voice was as expressionless as his mother's. "Shockingly maladroit of Father—not to have kept his late mistress's gift separate from the family ornaments."

THE CONSERVATORY HAD ALWAYS BEEN one of his mother's favorite places at Denforth, Gervase mused as he stepped inside, closing the paned glass door behind him. Pleasantly warm, scented with oranges, lemons, and jasmine: the perfect haven on a winter's day.

So it came as no surprise that the duchess had gone to ground there, though he certainly hadn't expected to join her—and by invitation no less! He'd read her note several times just to be sure, though there was never any doubt in his mind about going—if only to find out what she intended. Curiosity was a besetting sin with *him* as well as the castle cats, he reflected wryly.

Peering into the room, he spied his mother sitting on a simple wicker chair, though her regal presence imbued it with the majesty of a throne. The Queen, about to grant an audience...

She turned her head and broke into that Circe smile he'd seen captivate rooms full of susceptible men, himself included. "Gervase!" She gestured towards the wicker chair beside her. "Do sit down, dear, and take tea with me. Mrs. Hill tells me that luncheon must be put back an hour to give her curry time to season, so I rang for some light refreshment to tide us over."

"Thank you, Mother. That sounds most pleasant." He seated himself, eyeing her covertly.

No sign of the brittleness she'd shown when Richenda had unearthed that painful reminder of her husband's infidelity. Rowena Clayton had died ten years ago, but he knew from experience that memories of betrayal tended to linger, like a chronic sickness. He'd been thirteen when he'd first heard from his furious older siblings about their father's mistress: a shy, soft-spoken —"mealy-mouthed," according to an enraged Madeline —young widow who couldn't be more different from his formidable wife. Gervase wasn't sure when his mother had found out, but he rather suspected that her periodic sojourns in France—alone—had resulted from that discovery. Surprisingly, given his parents' combustible natures, they had never quarreled openly about the duke's *affaire*, but Gervase did not believe for a moment that his mother had been happy about it, for all her sophistication and French pragmatism. And yet... after Mrs. Clayton's death, they'd reconciled—until Hal's untimely death had torn them apart again.

His mother's tranquil expression reflected none of this troubled history as she poured tea for them both. "I requested almond madeleines—your favorite, as I recall." She indicated a plate heaped with the shell-shaped, golden-brown cakes. "And the tea—our best Darjeeling."

He raised his brows. "Gracious, such a to-do! My birthday was in September, however, so unless this is a belated celebration, of sorts..."

Her golden-green eyes widened; it was as disconcerting—and about as convincing—as watching a lioness pretend to be a housecat. "Can I not have tea with my handsome, brilliant, most intellectually accomplished son?"

"Laying it on a bit thick, aren't you, Mother?" Gervase observed, unimpressed. "But I'll have some madeleines, thank you. No sense in hearing you out on an empty stomach."

She laughed then, the warm, throaty laugh he remembered so vividly. He and his siblings had all striven to make their mother laugh, when they were children. And Gervase felt his own mouth curving in reluctant response.

"My own fault, *mon cher*, for thinking I could pull the wool over your eyes!" she exclaimed, holding out the plate to him.

"I have learned *some* things since I was a boy," he informed her, taking two madeleines.

"*Sans doute*." The mischievous glint in her eyes made her look, for a moment, no older than Juliana. "Including how to trounce your father at chess—or so I've heard."

"Have you indeed? Word travels fast."

"The walls have ears, *mon fils*. As I am sure you are aware." The duchess broke off a morsel of her own madeleine, nibbled daintily with sharp little white teeth. *The better to eat you with, my dear...* "So, how much of a rout was it?"

"Checkmate in four moves," he reported with satisfaction. "However, I'm trying not to let it go to my head. Father was off his game last night. Too many distractions—and the only pieces he paid attention to were the pawns." Which was strangely apposite. At times Gervase suspected that *everyone* was a pawn to the duke, including—or rather, especially—his children.

His mother chuckled. "I'm sure he'll take that as a lesson. I doubt you'll have as easy a victory the next time you play."

"So do I. Which means I should savor it while I can." He bit into his madeleine, rich with butter and almonds. "Without being seen to gloat about it, of course. That would be rude."

Her lips twitched in amusement. "Perish the thought! Still, I think it's good for your father to be reminded that he is not omnipotent."

"Do you hold the same opinion when it comes to *your* designs, Mother?"

She smiled. "Unlike Harold, I'm *accustomed* to having

more than one string to my bow, when it comes to grand designs. And I happen to know that, despite the many pies your father has his fingers in, there's only one thing that truly matters to him at this point."

"The succession," Gervase stated flatly.

"What else?" The duchess finished her madeleine. "Am I correct in assuming *that* to be the reason your father wishes to engage your considerable legal skills?"

Gervase paused with his cup halfway to his mouth. The walls had ears, indeed—or else his mother had a preternatural understanding of the way his father's mind worked. Hardly surprising, after thirty-five years of marriage. "You would not be—incorrect," he conceded.

"I cannot imagine that bodes well for your brother."

He did not need to ask which brother she meant; in this case, there could be only one that mattered to her. "It's no secret what Father wants from Reg," he began levelly. "Likewise, it's common knowledge that Reg would rather be flayed alive than give it to him. And no surprise to anyone who knows them that each is capable of dragging things out *'even to the edge of doom.'*"

The duchess shook her head, her smile almost indulgent, save for the hint of steel beneath. "So much alike, those two—and so unwilling to see it! The very things that make your father such a force of nature are part of Reg as well—but he cannot abide having those things turned against him and his will!"

"Which is why he seeks to break the impasse—with my assistance."

Her eyes cooled, along with her voice. "And I suppose he has offered you considerable incentives to join him?"

"He has. Though you and I both know who the true beneficiary of his plans will be."

The duchess set her teacup down with a decided clink. "*Reg* is the next duke, not Jason. And the sooner Jason himself accepts that, the better off he'll be."

"But wasn't that what Hal always used to tell Reg?" Gervase asked quietly.

A brief spasm of pain crossed her face. "God grant that one misfortune of that kind is all this family will have to endure." She took a careful breath, regaining her composure. "And in any case, it's counterproductive to

live one's life in the hope that someone closer to the succession drops dead. I want better than that—for *all* my
sons."

"You sound very convincing," he observed, regarding
her with a critical eye.

"Well, I should certainly hope so, as I happen to be
speaking the unvarnished truth," his mother retorted. "I
have *always* wanted the best for my children—even
when we've disagreed about what that 'best' should be!
Although," she fixed Gervase with a penetrating hazel
stare, "it wasn't so long ago that you and I agreed perfectly about where your best interests did *not* lie."

"*Touché, Maman*," Gervase acknowledged, holding up
a hand. "And—I will always be grateful for your support
regarding my opposition to the Church."

"A cleric without a true vocation is one of the saddest
sights on this earth. I was happy to help you avoid such a
fate." A tiny smile played about her mouth. "You've gone
your own way, Gervase—forged your own path in life.
And whether you believe me or not, I respect you for it.
I suspect your father does as well, though he may never
admit it."

Loth as he was to admit it, her commendation
pleased him. "Yes, well..." He cleared his throat. "As you
said, the sooner younger sons learn to shift for themselves, the better. I preferred to plan my own life, rather
than have someone else plan it for me."

"As Reg does," she pointed out. "I should think you'd
have *some* sympathy for him, given the similarity of your
situations."

Gervase stifled a sigh at the hint of reproach in her
tone. Just as his father's thoughts revolved around Jason,
so did his mother's around Reg. "I am not wholly lacking
in sympathy for Reg, Mother. But as the heir, isn't it
time he spared *some* thought for the dukedom?"

"So you stand with your father on this?" she
challenged.

"Not necessarily. I am only saying that the remedy
lies partly in Reg's own hands. And he does himself no
favors by refusing even to consider a compromise."

The duchess uttered a ladylike snort. "Would you say
your father was any *more* amenable to compromise? For
as long as I can remember, it's been all or nothing with

Harold! If it were possible for him to disinherit Reg outright, I am certain he would try. As it is, he probably wishes him to beg for every penny—" She broke off, her gaze as sharp as a newly whetted knife. "*That's* what he intends, isn't it? To deny Reg the means to support his position—unless he does exactly as his father wishes!"

Gervase hesitated, but his silence was all the confirmation his mother needed. Hectic color flared on her cheekbones, a stark contrast to the icy glitter of her eyes and the chill precision of her next words.

"I will *not* see my son cheated of what's rightfully his. Whatever Harold has offered you, I am prepared to double that—if you give *me* the means to stop his scheme in its tracks!"

Chapter Eight

✦

Come and take a choice of all my library,
And so beguile thy sorrow.
—William Shakespeare, *Titus*
    Andronicus, IV, i

"Blow!" Margaret guessed as Alicia puckered her lips and puffed out her cheeks—which, rather unfairly, did nothing to diminish her beauty.

"Breath!" Alasdair called out from the other end of the circle.

"Whistle?" Jason suggested, a trifle uncertainly.

Alicia shook her head at all of them, clutched an imaginary cloak around her, and shivered dramatically as though chilled to the bone.

"Cold?" Elaine ventured with a dubious frown.

"Chill." Reg sounded just a touch bored, Margaret noted with a flash of annoyance. He'd *agreed* to play charades, after all. He could have declined; or taken refuge in a book like his mother, who looked up now and then with an indulgent smile as the game grew livelier; or purported to doze by the fire like his father, though Margaret secretly doubted that the duke was actually asleep. Unlike the brindled mastiff stretched out and snoring at his master's feet.

Still hugging her imaginary cloak around her, Alicia staggered from side to side as though buffeted by a gale.

Her sister had always been good at mime, Margaret mused, though not quite as skilled when it came to learning lines for their amateur theatricals as children.

"Storm," Gervase guessed, just as Madeline called out, "Wind!"

Alicia paused, smiling, and pointed at Madeline.

"First syllable: 'wind.'" Juliana wrote the answer on a slip of paper. "Second syllable?"

Alicia stood for a moment, frowning prettily, then angled her torso slightly backwards, moving her arms and shoulders in what looked like a rowing motion. And the guesses rang out once more, fast and furious.

"Boat!"

"Row!"

"Stroke!"

"Oar," Gervase said suddenly. "*Winds*. Oar. Windsor." He glanced at Alicia with a hint of a smile. "Windsor Castle?"

"That's right," Alicia said. "Very clever of you, Lord Gervase!"

Her answering smile was downright coquettish, which Margaret found inexplicably irritating. Really, there was no need for Alicia to flirt with *every* man in the room, just because Reg was being inattentive!

"We have time for one more," Juliana called, as Alicia, rosily flushed from her dramatic efforts, resumed her seat on the sofa beside Margaret. "Who's next?"

Hugo volunteered, and kept them all guessing for several minutes as he interspersed flourishing an imaginary sword with standing stiffly at attention. Then Elaine called out "Yeoman of the Guard!" and Hugo bowed deeply to her amid applause.

They called it a night soon after that, and everyone began straggling upstairs, some still chattering animatedly, others concealing yawns. Tonight's dinner had been as lavish as the previous evening's, followed by a huge bowl of trifle with lashings of heavy cream. If they continued to eat this well over the next fortnight, Margaret reflected ruefully, she'd have to take up some form of healthful exercise or have her new gowns let out at the waist!

Alicia's chamber was located just a few doors down the passage from Margaret's tower room, so the sisters fell into step beside each other. Alicia looked lovelier than ever tonight, Margaret thought: in a rose-pink satin gown that awoke an answering blush of rose in her fair complexion, The gown's décolleté neckline was just this side of daring, affording the barest glimpse of high, rounded breasts that Margaret had caught more than one gentleman eyeing covertly when he ought to have been attending to something else! Tempting as a newly opened flower, just begging to be plucked... and Margaret knew all too well whom Alicia wished to do the plucking. And how forlorn those hopes were. But how to tell her so, when she remained so deeply smitten? And without betraying a confidence that Margaret had promised to keep?

"Dearest," she began, as they neared her sister's door, "might we talk privately for a little while? If you're not too tired, that is."

"Not at all, Meg," Alicia said brightly. "I'd be delighted. We've hardly spoken since I got here—it will be just like old times!"

She opened the door and glided into her chamber, her skirts sighing around her. Margaret followed, still wondering how to broach the sensitive subject of Reg's continued indifference to his affianced bride.

Before she could say a word, however, Berthe, Alicia's pretty French maid, approached and immediately led her mistress off toward the dressing room.

"Come along and make yourself comfortable," Alicia invited. "I shan't be more than a few minutes, and I'm longing to get out of this gown—to say nothing of the corset!"

Margaret followed her sister into the small anteroom —furnished like the bedchamber in delicate shades of primrose and violet—and seated herself on a nearby armchair. Vanishing behind an elaborate dressing screen, Alicia emerged some minutes later in a peignoir that positively frothed with lace and sat down at the vanity, unfastening the strand of pearls still clasped about her throat. Berthe hung up the rose gown in the wardrobe, then came over to take down Alicia's hair for the night. Watching, Margaret felt a pang of nostalgia for the days when *she'd* brushed her little sister's hair, coaxing the spun-gold curls into ringlets around her finger. So many years had passed since then, so many changes... this so-phisticated, fashionable Alicia, with her little store of French mannerisms—affectations, their mother might have said—seemed half a stranger to her.

She was still debating what to say when Alicia broke the silence. "Meg, I just wanted to tell you again how sorry I am about Lord Bellamy." Her blue eyes, reflected in the mirror before her, were luminous with sympathy. "I did not know him well, but I know how fond you were of him. I hope that everything is all right with you —and your stepsons too."

"Thank you, pet." Margaret managed a smile. "We still miss him, but things aren't quite as—as raw as they were at this time last year. The boys are doing well at school, and I've started something of a new life for my-self, in London."

"And I see that you're out of mourning too," her sister observed. "You look simply marvelous, by the way. Not everyone can wear Prussian blue so successfully!"

A trifle self-consciously, Margaret smoothed the heavy skirts of her velvet evening gown. "I put off black in February. I know Alex wouldn't have wanted me to wear it forever."

"Certainly not. Lord Bellamy always struck me as the most generous of men." Alicia paused, then ventured delicately, "I hope—there are no *financial* worries? I know he had to provide for his sons first."

Margaret shook her head. "None at all. I'm quite well off, actually—Alex left me a generous portion *and* the Bellamy townhouse for the duration of my lifetime. He fully expected me to outlive him, you know." He just couldn't have known that their happiness would be cut short after only three years. She blinked back a sudden mist of tears, and added briskly, "I suppose I might find a small place in the country for myself once Sandy is of age—or sooner, if I've the inclination. The dower resi-dence at Bellamy Park isn't in the best condition. I'd probably do better to look for a cottage somewhere, as I won't require a huge household."

"In Yorkshire, perhaps?" Alicia suggested. "I know you've always loved it here. And you and I could see more of each other, once Reg and I are married."

As good an opening as any... but Margaret knew she'd

have to tread carefully, or risk alienating her sister. "Alicia, have you and Reg made any definite plans towards a wedding yet? It *has* been nearly five years."

"I'm fully aware of how long it's been, Meg." Was that a faint edge in her sister's voice? Alicia turned from the mirror, her golden hair now a cloud about her shoulders, and smiled up at her maid. "Thank you, Berthe. That will be all for the night."

The maid curtseyed and withdrew into her own room, closing the door behind her. Alicia turned back to the mirror and delicately began to wipe away her cosmetics with a damp cloth. The face that emerged from beneath the powder and rouge was no less exquisite, but softer, somehow. More *open*... closer to the face of the little sister Margaret remembered.

"I always knew Reg and I would have a long engagement," Alicia resumed, avoiding Margaret's gaze as she dabbed at her face. The Whitborough betrothal ring encircling her finger glittered in the lamplight, awakening a host of uncomfortable memories. "I *was* still in the schoolroom, after all."

"True, but you're of age now," Margaret reminded her. "And have been for several months. Has Reg spoken to you about setting a date?"

"N-no, not just yet," Alicia admitted, after a moment. "But I was in France—and I know how busy Reg has been, and how demanding the army can be as a career. Why, less than a year ago, the regiment was still in India! I imagine he's barely had time to catch his breath since returning to England, much less plan our wedding!"

He'd time to hunt foxes in the Shires, Margaret nearly said, but stopped herself before she could cross that line. Instead, she ventured, "It seems to me he *could* be more attentive to you, now that you're both back in England. Did you not find his manner a touch... brusque when you arrived today?"

Alicia paused, and for a moment Margaret saw a flicker of what might have been doubt in her eyes. Then she shrugged and peered more closely at her reflection. "Didn't you warn me that Reg hasn't a romantic bone in his body? He's a soldier through and through—a Mark Antony or a... a Richard *Coeur de Leon*, not a Romeo! I know how much the regiment means to him. It would be… silly to expect him to change his spots overnight."

"Neither Antony nor Richard the Lionheart was exactly what I'd call ideal husband material," Margaret pointed out, recalling the less than successful domestic lives of both. "Are you entirely certain that Reg is the one for you? Surely you've met other eligible young men over the last few years—when you came out, and in Paris. Did none of them appeal to you?"

The moment she asked, she knew how foolish that would sound. A brave and handsome soldier, who was also the heir to a dukedom, as well as to lands and fortune from his wealthy mother? What marriage-minded young lady wouldn't jump at the chance to be in Alicia's shoes?

Alicia's expression reflected much of the same incredulity as she turned from the mirror to face Margaret. "Yes, I've met other men. I've even *liked* some of them, but none could compare with my fiancé." Her blue eyes shimmered with confusion—and hurt. "Why are you asking me all this, Meg? I'm about to make a brilliant marriage to a man I adore, to whom I'm utterly devoted. I thought you'd be happy for me!"

Except that he doesn't return that devotion. And he never could. But she couldn't say that, and wouldn't even if secrecy *hadn't* already bound her tongue. Now, more than ever, she needed to chose her words carefully, or she'd bring about the very opposite of what she intended.

"Of course I'd be happy to see you well-married!" she temporized at last. "It's just that—I worry. I can't help comparing your situation with Reg to mine with Hal. *He* never got round to setting a wedding date either. He always found some reason to put it off. Getting married was the very last thing on his mind—an afterthought… just as I was." The memory could still sting, even after all these years. "He enjoyed his bachelor existence far too much to give it up."

"Oh, Meg!" Alicia breathed, her gaze full of sympathy now. "I hadn't realized it was as bad as that!"

"How could you have known?" Margaret summoned a reassuring smile. "You were little more than a child when Hal and I became engaged, and still in the schoolroom when he died. In any event, the point I'm trying to make is that, tragic as Hal's death was, it was perhaps a mercy that we did not marry, after all."

"Because of Lord Bellamy?" Alicia ventured, fretting her lower lip.

"No, because I think Hal and I would have made each other very unhappy." Margaret held her sister's gaze as she continued, "We weren't really suited, you see. And if Hal had lived, I would like to think we'd have realized that, and chosen to end our betrothal. But I'll never know for certain. Our parents had wanted the match for years—and a sense of duty can be a powerful thing. What I *do* know... is that no marriage, however advantageous, is worth being miserable for the rest of your life."

She infused the last words with all the authority she could muster, and Alicia flushed.

"I understand what you're trying to say, Meg, but Reg isn't Hal. Why, they couldn't be more different! And besides," she added, "didn't you just say that the main problem was you and Hal not being suited to each other?"

"That was the main difficulty, yes," Margaret acknowledged. "But, Alicia, are you sure that you and Reg are truly compatible? As you say, he's devoted to the regiment and army life. You, on the other hand, love Society and fashion—"

"Those aren't the *only* things I care about!" Alicia protested. "*I* can take an interest in things that matter to Reg."

"But will he do the same for *you?*" Margaret countered. "Because finding common ground is so important in a marriage. I might not have known Alex as long or idolized him as I once did Hal, but he was a good man and a good husband. And we shared a number of interests that brought us closer together, in spite of the difference in our ages." Seeing the mutinous set of her sister's mouth, she gentled her tone. "Dearest, I would just like to see you as—well, as happy in your marriage as I was in mine."

"Thank you. I have every intention of being happy with Reg," Alicia said stiffly. "And I have every hope that we'll find that common ground you speak of, in time." She gave a little Gallic shrug. "Rome wasn't built in a day, after all, and neither is a good marriage."

Margaret smothered a sigh; for a moment, she thought she'd been making some headway, but she could recognize the sight and sound of heels being firmly dug in. *None so blind as those that will not see.* For all her angelic looks and seeming pliability, her sister could be as stubborn and self-willed as the rest of them. Nonetheless, she tried once more. "I realize that, but—"

"Please, Meg, no more!" Alicia interrupted, shaking her head emphatically and turning back to the mirror. "I know you mean well, but I'm quite capable of handling my own life—*and* my betrothed." She leaned forward, examining her reflection more closely. "I really think you should concentrate on *your* life instead."

No good would come of pressing the issue further tonight, Margaret realized. She could only hope that some of what she'd said had sunk in, enough at least to get Alicia *thinking.* Aloud she said, "Actually, I've focused on little else since moving to London. There's always something to occupy oneself with in town—libraries, museums, the theater..."

"Oh, no doubt," Alicia interposed, "but that wasn't quite what I meant. What about the *people*? Have you met any interesting men in London? And I don't mean some fusty old scholar or antiquarian. I mean, attractive men close to your own age."

"A few," Margaret admitted, experiencing an all too familiar apprehension at the question. She was almost braced for what came next.

Alicia idly twirled one of her ringlets around her finger. "I understand you were devoted to Lord Bellamy, but... have you given any thought to remarrying, someday?"

"You too, Alicia?" Margaret forced a laugh. "You would not believe how often I've been asked that since I left off mourning!"

"Actually, I think I would." Alicia turned to study her appraisingly. "To tell the truth, I'm surprised that men weren't beating a path to your door the moment you set foot in town!"

Margaret shook her head. "Don't be absurd—the only man to call on me *then* was Gervase! Nothing out of the ordinary about that!"

"*Gervase?*" Alicia echoed, her eyes widening. "Reg's brother?"

"I don't know any *other* Gervase," Margaret pointed out dryly.

"And—have you seen him often, since you moved to London?"

"Gervase lives *and* works in London," Margaret reminded her. "We've had tea now and then. And gone riding in the Park some mornings—when his schedule permits," she hastened to add, lest Alicia get entirely the wrong impression.

"*Nom d'un nom d'un nom,*" Alicia murmured, her lips curving in a smile Margaret had never seen from her before. "That puts an entirely different complexion on the matter, I'd say!"

"What sort of 'complexion'?" Margaret demanded, more sharply than she'd intended. "There's nothing—unusual about two old friends taking tea or riding together."

"And what do 'two old friends' talk about, during those little interludes?" Alicia inquired, an arch note in her voice.

"Not marriage, certainly!" Did that come out a bit too emphatically? Margaret wondered.

Alicia shrugged. "Well, then, *don't* marry Lord Gervase. Take him as a lover instead."

MARGARET STARED STUPIDLY at her sister, the words echoing and re-echoing in her head until they seemed to lose all meaning. Then, "I—I beg your pardon?" she ventured faintly.

"Take Lord Gervase as your lover," Alicia repeated with a patient, almost patronizing air that would have annoyed Margaret at any other time. "Anyone can tell he's smitten with you. And probably has been for years."

The earth seemed to be falling away from her, and she struggled desperately for purchase on the shifting ground. "That's—that's nonsense! We're good friends, that's all."

Alicia's smile took on an almost feline smugness. "I

don't know of many 'good friends' who look as though they'd like to eat *me* alive!"

Margaret bit back an acid retort, even as her mind raced in tandem with her heart. Gervase, smitten? With *her*? And for years? Alicia *had* to be mistaken. Or perhaps she was trying to distract Margaret from further discussion of Reg—in which case she had succeeded beyond her wildest expectations!

"On reflection, *I* think Lord Gervase would make an excellent lover," Alicia went on, a speculative gleam lighting her eyes. "He seems the sort to attend to a lady's pleasures *very* thoroughly, if only as a matter of personal pride! Oh, I was always a little frightened—no, intimidated—by him when I was a child. He's so clever, after all, and has such a sharp tongue. I used to think he was rather cold too, but not after the way I saw him looking at *you* tonight!"

Margaret shook her head, as much from confusion as attempted denial. "Alicia, you *must* be mistaken," she began, though her tone lacked conviction even to her own ears. And just *when*, another part of her mind queried dazedly, had her innocent little sister acquired so much knowledge about lovers and ladies' pleasures? Surely not first-hand...

"*Au contraire*, I think I have it exactly right," Alicia retorted, rising from the vanity. "But have it your own way—if you must." She yawned suddenly, like a sleepy kitten. "*Mon Dieu*, I can hardly keep my eyes open! Forgive me, Meg, I simply *must* get some sleep."

Margaret got up from her chair, her own limbs moving with the stiff jerkiness of a marionette's. "I'll leave you to your rest, then."

The parting kiss she bestowed on Alicia felt equally mechanical, but she did not miss the amused glint in her sister's eye as she departed. Reaching her chamber, she closed the door and leaned against it, trying to still the thoughts circling relentlessly through her head. And because she had the strangest sense that if she tried to move just now, she'd topple right over the edge— like Alice falling down the rabbit hole.

Down, down, down... all the way to Wonderland, where everything known and familiar turned topsy-turvy in an instant.

What fire is in mine ears? Can this be true?

From Carroll to Shakespeare. A little laugh—sounding perilously close to hysteria—escaped her. Wasn't it always Shakespeare, with *him*?

Margaret pushed away from the door, forcing herself upright and feeling a belated surge of relief that she'd told Tilda *not* to wait up for her. Her own thoughts, more than twenty years' worth of them, were more than enough company for her at present. No sound in the chamber but the faint hiss of the gas lamps and the crackle of flames in the fireplace, but her ears were full of ancient echoes.

Gervase... she could not recall a time when he *hadn't* been a part of her life, if only peripherally. The Whitboroughs' third son, just two years older than she—the clever one, always at the top of his form in school. Not as charming as Hal or as athletic as Reg, but capable at whatever he turned his hand to. And well-spoken, with a ready tongue and a readier wit. The first to learn his lines for the amateur theatricals Madeline proposed, always willing to serve as prompter. Quick with a quip or a counterargument, able to soothe or infuriate with a few well-chosen words.

All those Christmases. All those summer holidays. A tapestry of memories—and Gervase was woven into so many of them. A constant—sardonic, exasperating, enigmatic... but there, as surely as sunrise.

An ever-fixéd mark / That looks on tempests and is never shaken.

She paced her chamber now, restless as a caged tiger. And the memories kept coming, in an unstoppable flood. Again and again she saw him: the boy with his nose in a book, looking up time and again to engage her in debate—over Richard's innocence or any other subject that happened to capture their attention. Threading his way from branch to branch, trying to rescue his sister's cat. Playing Lysander to her Hermia one Whitsuntide...

"Gervase, aren't you ready—" she broke off with a gasp as the sight of him, naked to the waist, the top of his pale blue chiton hanging about his knees. Blushing furiously, she turned her back. "I'm sorry—I just came to tell you we're on in five minutes!"

"Wait!" Was that a note of entreaty in his voice? "Don't go, please! The dressers are all tied up helping the fairies, and I'm having the devil's own time with this thing!"

Curious, she turned around as he continued, "Every time I try to pin it in place, I lose my grip on the cloth and prick my fingers into the bargain! Why couldn't Madeline have put the men in doublet and hose as usual?"

"Oberon identifies Demetrius and Lysander by their Athenian dress. Madeline wants as much authenticity as possible in this production."

"If it's authenticity she's after, then your part and Elaine's should be played by boys," Gervase pointed out. He scowled at his chiton. "And given how much trouble this authentic garment is proving to be, I for one would welcome some dramatic license!"

Margaret studied him as he tried once more to gather the chiton's folds about his shoulder. "It might help if you didn't have it on backwards. It's your right shoulder that's meant to be bare. Like mine." She stepped into the small dressing room to show him.

He stared at her for a moment, then closed his eyes and swore, softly but fervently, in French.

She stifled a giggle—it was rare to see self-possessed Gervase this ruffled over anything—and relented. "Here, let me help you."

He thanked her profusely, and between them, they turned the chiton right way around. Then, taking hold of the top, Margaret drew it up past his waist towards his left shoulder, which was... broader than she remembered it being. Good heavens, when had that happened?

For that matter, his chest seemed to have broadened as well —and acquired a faint dusting of bronze-gold hair. She stared at the last, her mouth suddenly dry and the chiton's linen folds wilting in her grasp. Stared... and suppressed the urge to touch, just to see if it was real.

He'd been a schoolboy, lanky and unfinished, when she saw him at Christmas. He was still a schoolboy—until he entered Oxford at Michaelmas—but he no longer looked like one.

Standing so close, she could feel the warmth of his skin and breathe in its scent: clean and healthy, with a slight tang that reminded her of her mother's herb garden on a summer day— but far headier.

"Margaret? Is everything all right?"

She started, forcing her thoughts back to the matter at hand. "Fine." She cleared her throat, resumed more briskly, "Just thinking how best to manage this. The pin, if you please?"

He handed it to her, and she quickly secured the chiton at his left shoulder, then busied herself draping the body of the tunic into graceful folds, doing her best to ignore the outline of his torso through the sheer linen. A lean, lithe torso that was somehow not at all boyish.

Striving for a light tone, she remarked, "You don't look half-bad, even in a chiton. Indeed, you could become quite good-looking... someday."

"You're too kind." Gervase glanced down at the skirts of his chiton. "I don't know whether to bow or curtsy in this thing."

She choked back another giggle at the latter image. "Madeline would have a fit!"

His eyes glinted. "Serve her right. But it wouldn't be fair to the rest of the cast. Shall we to the woods, fair Hermia?"

As they left the dressing room, she couldn't help observing that his bare calves, criss-crossed by Grecian sandals, were as strong and shapely as the rest of him...

Margaret surfaced, her face burning at the vividness of the memory that had ambushed her so swiftly, so *completely*. She might still have been that girl of sixteen, gawking at a friend's sudden transformation. So she'd noticed him as far back as that—why had she never acted on it?

Hal, of course. Hal who'd been golden and godlike while Gervase was trapped in gawky adolescence. Hal, who was to be her husband and who occupied all her thoughts once she'd emerged from the schoolroom. Regardless, Gervase had grown into an elegant, polished young man. Who danced with her at parties when Hal couldn't be bothered to attend. Who brought her wine and comfort when she despaired of her future with his brother.

Her thoughts floundered to a stop again.

That night, in the library, when he'd first suggested she go to Oxford... kissing him had been an impulse. A moment's gratitude for his understanding, kindness even. But as her lips had touched his cheek, she'd felt an increased awareness of his body, so close to hers. The light, lean frame, so different from Hal's, the mingled scents of warm skin and subtle, spicy cologne...

Kaleidoscope moments, in which the smallest turn led to the creation of a new pattern, each unique as a snowflake. How might the pattern have turned out, if she'd lingered—kissed him again, on the mouth this time? Slipped her arms about his neck and drawn him to her? Or might *he* have been the one to make the next move?

Because if what Alicia had said was in any way true... dear heaven, what those years of silence must have cost him!

Here, in the privacy of her room, she could admit—if only to herself—that she'd found him attractive even then. But it was a one-sided attraction... or so she'd always believed.

Cool, controlled, self-sufficient Gervase, who needed no one. Who'd shown no interest in any of the young debutantes casting their lures for him, because younger son or no, he was handsome, clever, and possessed of a comfortable fortune. She'd teased him about that, now and then. But how would she have felt if he *had* taken a fancy to one of them?

She had the uncomfortable suspicion that she wouldn't have liked it at all—any more than she'd enjoyed the admiration in his eyes when he looked at Alicia earlier today. The same sort of admiration she'd seen when he met her at the train yesterday, or when she'd come down to dinner last night. The sort a man displays towards a woman he enjoys looking at.

Here comes the Countess; now heaven walks on earth.

The compliment had unsettled her then. It did more than that now, sending arousal pulsing through her in a wave. And she saw him once more in her mind's eye—this time as the man he was now, smiling at her with that particular warmth in his gaze. Limned by fire-light in his London townhouse. Bandying quotations with her on the train. Kissing her when the train's sudden motion literally threw them into each other's arms.

Her hand stole to her lips. So light and fleeting a kiss... but the ghost of it seemed to linger on her skin, as memorable as any kiss she and Alex had shared.

Coming to a halt, she stared about the room, her gaze finally alighting upon the book lying on her bedside table. The book he'd had printed for her, that very personal book that held so much meaning for her...

Would he have given such a gift to anyone else?

Still staring at the book, she felt a conviction growing within her, terrifying and exhilarating at once.

But she had to know. Before tonight was over, she had to *know*.

❄

I NEED *you to find examples, find precedents, of entails being successfully broken, and present to me a detailed report of the results.*

Whatever Harold has offered you, I am prepared to double that—if you give me the means to stop his scheme in its tracks!

The voices dueled in his head, a relentless cacophony, and wasn't that just bloody typical of them, Gervase reflected mordantly as he mounted the stairs to his destination.

Caught between the Devil and the deep blue sea. Or perhaps more accurately, between the Scylla and Charybdis of his parents. But only if he chose to be.

Which was why he was here tonight, up in the library gallery, instead of in his chamber, sleeping the sleep of the virtuous.

He didn't actually *need* what they were offering him— or rather, proposing to offer him. Gervase had learned long ago that nothing was certain until it rested firmly in one's hand... or bank account. Perhaps it was just that, for the first time in his life, his parents were assiduously courting *him*, the son who'd long been an afterthought to both of them.

Candle in hand, he peered at the books' worn spines, wishing for the steady radiance of electric light to illuminate them... among the many disadvantages of country life. Well, at least the books were dusted regularly—even the most obscure ones. So he didn't have to contend with cobwebs, mildew, or worse.

He was just about to pull out a volume for closer inspection when he heard approaching footsteps and raised voices from the passage. Two loud *masculine* voices... and what were the odds, Gervase wondered wryly, that at least one of them belonged to a Lyons?

"—hardly spoke a word to her all evening!" That was the duke—just outside the door now, from the sound of it. "Good God, boy, anyone would take you for a eunuch!"

"Because I'm not lifting skirts on both sides of the Channel—like you?" Reg's voice was taut, but Gervase could hear the barely contained rage simmering under the tight control.

Frowning, he drew his hand back from the book and listened, bracing himself for the ducal explosion that seemed the inevitable outcome of such an exchange.

A moment of charged silence followed, then, "I'll let that pass for now," Whitborough replied, his voice deceptively even. "Whatever wild oats I sowed in my youth are entirely beside the point! I'm speaking of your fiancée, Reginald, and the respect you owe her!"

"Oh, that's rich, coming from *you*! What of the respect you owe *Mother*?"

Gervase's eyes widened. Good God, but Reg was sailing close to the wind! Almost as if he were deliberately *trying* to enrage their father.

"Your mother and I understand each other very well." The duke's voice was fraying about the edges—much like his temper, Gervase suspected. "And when you've been married as long as we have, perhaps you'll *also* understand! Although judging from your behavior tonight, it'll be a miracle if you and Alicia marry at all!"

"That's between my betrothed and myself!" Reg flashed back.

Oh, hell. They *were* coming inside. He sensed it even before the first foot crossed the threshold and he saw the glitter of lamplight on Reg's bright hair and gold epaulettes.

Now was the time to make his presence known. Or not.

Instead—almost without conscious volition—Gervase extinguished his candle and drew back into the shadow of a tall bookcase, as the duke strode in on Reg's heels. Intent on each other, neither thought to glance up at the gallery or even about the room for unwitting listeners.

"The devil it is, boy!" Whitborough snapped. "Your betrothal happens to affect us all, our family and hers!

Her brother's in a fine frenzy over your refusal to set a date—and I'll wager Lady Alicia is no happier about it!" He shook his head. "A beauty, by God! No man in his right senses would pass up a chance with her! Hell, if I were thirty years younger, I'd make a play for her myself!"

From his vantage point Gervase could glimpse only a sliver of Reg's profile, but he wagered it was every bit a match for the stoniness in his brother's voice. "Go ahead. Since when have you let age—or common decency stop you?"

Even from the gallery, Gervase could hear the sharpness of their father's indrawn breath, and his own gut twisted uneasily. He was no stranger to family rows. How often had he heard his father and Reg going at it, since Hal's death? But there was something different about it tonight—a sharper, more personal edge than he could remember hearing before. He felt as though he were watching a particularly messy domestic drama from a box at Drury Lane. What was it Tolstoy had said about happy versus unhappy families?

"Christ, Reginald—did you think I meant it literally?" Whitborough demanded. "This isn't about *me!*"

"Isn't it, Father? Isn't *everything?*" Reg fired back. "What you want, what you expect, what you demand—"

"For Whitborough, you callow cub, not for *myself!*" the duke thundered. "For Whitborough and for this family you treat so cavalierly, a family that includes that young lady you can hardly be bothered to court!"

"Alicia and I have been formally betrothed since the spring of '84," Reg pointed out. "I should think that eliminates the need for courtship. And may I remind you that the match was of *your* making and the late Duke of Langdale's, not mine?"

"You were of age, Reginald—you could have said no!" The duke paused, subjecting his heir to the probing scrutiny Gervase knew all too well. "Had you some other candidate in view? A lady whom you prefer? If so, you've been damned secretive about it!"

Reg turned away, went over to the fireplace. The line of his back was as stiff and rigid as the poker he used to stir the feeble blaze. "Alicia will do as well as any."

"That's a damned poor spirit in which to approach

marriage!" the duke retorted, and for once Gervase found himself wholly in agreement. "Fair enough—yours is an arranged betrothal. But that should not preclude esteem or affection. Even" his tone softened just a fraction, "even a touch of romance. No woman is immune to that."

The renewed crackling of the flames did not quite mask Reg's snort of derision, but the duke pressed on, "For the love of heaven, Reg, Alicia is to be your wife and the mother of your children! You'll both fare a damned sight better if you can feel some fondness or passion for each other!"

Reg turned from the fire and Gervase caught his breath at the hostility in his brother's face. "Passion—like yours and Mother's, you mean? No, thank you. I can't think of anything *more* likely to doom my marriage!"

Whitborough stilled, and so, it seemed, did the rest of the room. Then, "It was worth every minute," he said, almost gently. "The pain along with the joy. The quarrels *and* the reconciliations. And you—all of you, your brothers and sisters. And if I had it to do over again... so help me God, I *would*. In a heartbeat.

"But don't take *my* word for it. Ask your mother—and I suspect she'd tell you the exact same thing." He took a step towards Reg, stretched out a hand as though trying to bridge the gulf that had existed between them for almost as long as Gervase could remember. "You're sent my interference in your life, what you see as my attempts to control you. Well, then, set my mind at rest on one score and I will consider—I will *try*," the duke amended, "to compromise. To respect your desire for independence—and your commitment to the army."

Reg remained where he was, making no move to take his father's hand. "At what price?"

"Hardly an onerous one! Marry Alicia, that beautiful young woman who adores you. Marry her this Christmas, and get her with child as soon as possible." The duke took another step towards him. "Grant me the comfort of knowing that our line will go on. That Whitborough will go on."

Reg swallowed audibly. "As you've often pointed out, sir, you have two other sons."

"I once had *four* other sons," the duke countered. "Two of them died. And I'd a pair of younger brothers who were buried before you were out of leading strings. Life is fragile, Reginald. You know that as well as I." He paused, then resumed, "If you cannot feel what a husband *should* feel towards Alicia—though I cannot understand *why*—would you consider another bride? Perhaps one closer in age, for whom you already feel some affection?"

Reg tensed even further, if such a thing were possible. "Whom do you have in mind?"

Whitborough took a breath. "Margaret. She's a widow now, and you and she have always been friends."

Christ. Gervase stiffened in the shadows, the memory like a cold finger running up and down his spine.

That snippet of conversation he'd inadvertently overheard *that* Christmas. His father's tentative suggestion of a possible match to be made between Margaret and Reg, after a suitable period of mourning had passed.

"Margaret is *not* some garment to be handed down to a younger brother when the elder can no longer wear it!" the duchess had remarked with asperity.

"But she and Reg have always got on so well!" his father had protested. "Better than Hal and Margaret, in some respects."

"That does not mean they are suited to marry. They may well be better off as friends."

Gervase had been in full agreement with his mother—and not merely because his own heart was engaged. Sifting through his memories now, he could not think of a single incident in which Reg and Margaret had displayed any spark of romantic attraction. Surely, as competitive as his older brothers had been, Reg would have had no compunctions about wooing Margaret out from under Hal's nose if he'd desired her for himself.

Not that he would have succeeded. Margaret was loyal to the bone, even to those who did not necessarily deserve it, and for a time, she'd believed herself in love with Hal.

And now... Gervase took a careful breath of his own. He'd no choice back then but to accept her betrothal to his eldest brother or her marriage to Bellamy after that.

But he'd be damned if he'd give her up without a fight *this* time!

Then a new voice—the last he'd expected to hear—spoke from the doorway. "Gentlemen, I believe this matter concerns *me* as well."

Gervase froze in position as Margaret entered the library, the lamplight casting a gilded circle on her head, as bright as any ducal coronet she might have worn. Her face was pale but composed as she regarded the duke and his heir, who had the grace to look somewhat abashed as her gaze swept over them.

"I *am* your friend, Reg." Margaret began, her voice steady. "I have always been your friend. But I can be nothing more to you than that." Her gaze shifted to the duke. "And if *you* are pressuring Reg to make *me* the next duchess, then I cannot be that either. Especially if your goal is to secure the succession."

Whitborough cleared his throat. "Lady Bellamy —Margaret..."

For once he appeared at a loss for words. Out of his depth. In other circumstances, Gervase might have derived some amusement from the sight. But not now... not when he sensed that whatever revelation was to come would be acutely painful—for the person who deserved it least.

But Margaret was continuing. "As far as the world knows, Lord Bellamy and I had no children. That is not entirely accurate." She paused, as though steeling herself for some unimaginable ordeal, then resumed almost as steadily as before, "I conceived during our first year of marriage. It was—not an easy pregnancy for me, and so we told no one outside the immediate family. Our son was born at barely six months and lived less than an hour. The doctors told me... I was unlikely ever to conceive again."

Her words fell like stones into the silence, paralyzing them all where they stood. Then she turned on her heel and was gone in a whisper of velvet.

The sound of the door closing—not slamming—behind her broke the spell for Gervase. Shaking off his paralysis, he made for the stairs, no longer caring about secrecy or subterfuge.

His father and brother, still frozen in place, turned at

the sound of his descending footsteps, their faces registering almost comical dismay as he burst into view.

"You!" Reg exclaimed, recoiling.

"Gervase!" The duke was no less startled. "Good God, boy, have you been up there all this time?"

"Go to the devil, both of you," Gervase said tautly, striding past them.

Once outside the library, he broke into a run.

Chapter Nine

❧

Love sought is good, given unsought is better.
—William Shakespeare, *Twelfth Night,*
    III, i

She did not slow down until she reached the relative safety of the Long Gallery—and only then because of the growing stitch in her side. Pausing at last, she drew a shuddering breath, hugging herself in a fierce effort to hold on to her composure.

More than three years since that day... and the agony of her loss had passed, thanks to the healing power of time and Alex's loving patience. But all the same, the unfairness of it ached and ached. As it did for every unwillingly barren woman, she supposed.

"Margaret! Thank God—I hoped to catch up to you."

Gervase's voice, low and urgent... and she seized upon it like a lifeline, letting it tow her back to the still complicated but slightly less painful present. He stood just a few feet away, an almost palpable tension in his stance, scanning her with anxious eyes.

"Gervase." She tried for a reassuring smile, then abandoned the attempt, as it felt hopelessly wan and unconvincing. "Your valet told me you were in the library." It seemed a lifetime ago that she'd asked.

"I was. Up in the gallery." His mouth crooked. "Father and Reg entered in full spate. I couldn't find the proper moment to announce myself—and then, it seemed more prudent *not* to. Discretion being the better part of valor, after all."

"Then you heard."

After a moment's hesitation, he nodded. "My dear, I am sorrier than I can say." He paused again, then resumed gently, "I won't ask if you're all right. I know quite well that you're not. How could you be, after that?"

"We were going to call him Laurence. After my father." How was it she could remember, even now, the light weight of her doomed son in her arms, breathing so quietly, so shallowly? She hadn't wanted to let him go, even when that faint breath had stopped. Alex, his own eyes wet, had had to coax her arms open so... so that the proper arrangements could be made.

Gervase's mouth set, his eyes going as hard as flint. "I could take a horsewhip to both of them, for putting you through that again."

She shook her head. "They didn't force it out of me —I told them freely. So that the duke would stop thinking of me as... well, as a potential broodmare! Even if I could oblige him by producing a child, I'd still *never* marry Reg!"

He strode forward to put his arm round her, and she leaned into it, grateful for his warmth and strength. Who'd have thought that Gervase Lyons, of all people, would have become such a source of comfort to her? Closing her eyes, she let her head rest against his shoulder, breathing in the faint scent of bergamot and spice that clung to the heavy silk of his dressing gown.

"Besides Hal, my parents lost a son in infancy, long before I was born," he told her. "My mother says it's something one never forgets or truly recovers from."

"It's not." *And then to lose not only one's child but all hope of another...* Margaret swallowed, fighting the hot press of tears against her eyelids, and forced the words past the constriction in her throat. "But one learns to live with it. Come to terms with it. Endure it."

His arm tightened around her. "It need not be endured alone."

She drew a shuddering breath and opened her eyes. "No. And by God's grace, I *wasn't* alone—then or now." Reaching up, she laid her hand against his cheek, feeling its warmth even through her silk evening glove. "Thank you, Gervase."

She thought she felt the arm about her shoulders tremble, then, "What are friends for?" he asked lightly.

Friends. The words she'd spoken earlier to Alicia seemed so feeble, in light of what was stirring... *simmering* between them now. And the memory of *why* she'd sought him out tonight, driven from her mind by the shock of what she'd heard, came flooding back, like the rush of heat following a draught of strong spirits. Almost too heady a wine for her senses, drying her mouth and making her head swim. A single word or gesture on her part would free her from his embrace... except that she had no desire to move. No wish but to stay where she was, close within the circle of his arm.

She did not know if Gervase could sense any of this, but his arm remained where it was, and she could hear the slightly quickened rhythm of his breathing. Not since the train had they stood so close together...

"Margaret." His usually confident voice sounded almost tentative in the silent gallery. "You said—Farnsworth told you I was in the library. Were you looking for me?"

She swallowed, studying every plane and angle of that familiar face. "I was."

His brows lifted. "Why?"

Margaret took a breath, bracing herself inwardly. "Something Alicia said. About old friends... and how we don't always see them as clearly as we think we do."

Again she felt the quiver of his encircling arm, could sense the effort he was making to keep his voice and expression under control. "An intriguing subject. How did it arise?"

"As a corollary to something else entirely," she said, trying to match his light tone. "But it soon proved more interesting than the original topic. And far more pertinent." She paused, searching for the words that would carry her over the next hurdle. From friendship to... something deeper. Something that could well change both their lives.

"I suppose," she resumed, "when two people have been friends for years, they become accustomed to... to thinking of each other in a certain way. And not realizing that things might have *changed* between them."

"Changed." Something—apprehension, perhaps?—flickered behind his eyes. "In what way? And—for the better or worse?"

"Not the worse," she hastened to assure him. "I just meant that friends are so used to the way things are that they might not see the possibilities of something *more*. Not right away."

"Does that surprise you?" His voice was quiet and almost preternaturally level. "There's always a risk when friends venture beyond what is comfortable and familiar. I can understand not wanting to lose that. Especially if..."

"If?" she prompted gently.

"If only one person desires more than friendship."

"What if... *both* of them do?" Reaching out, she took hold of his free hand, lacing their fingers together and pressing her palm against his. *Palm to palm is holy palmer's kiss...*

This time she felt the tremor that went through his entire body at the contact, heard his sharp intake of breath, and saw his eyes darken to the color of storm clouds.

"*Margaret.*" Just her name, spoken about half an octave lower than usual, but enough to vanquish any doubts she might still have harbored and scatter them to the four winds... while the certainty growing inside of her took deeper root within her soul and sent out its first tentative blooms in her heart.

Smiling, she looked at the man before her, speechless for the first time that she could remember. Gervase fenced with words better than anyone she knew; they were his weapon—and his armor, concealing his deepest vulnerabilities. But now was the time for action. Still clasping his hand, she leaned forward and kissed him full on the mouth.

THE MOMENT MARGARET'S lips touched his, reason fled and desire flared to life in its wake, a white-hot blaze obliterating all else. Stifling a groan, Gervase pulled her closer, deepening the kiss until he heard an answering moan break from her and felt her arms twine about his neck.

All he'd wanted, all he'd dreamed of for so long—warm and pliant in his arms, kissing him with the same fervor and fire that were consuming him. *Fire ever doth aspire, / And makes all like itself, turns all to fire...*

They surfaced at last, breathless and dazed. Gervase could feel his heart racing, faster than he could ever remember, and his mouth was bone-dry—unlike his palms, damp as a schoolboy's before an examination. And a lifetime of self-control suddenly seemed no match for the mingled terror and exhilaration rioting through his veins, churning in the pit of his stomach. Was *this* how finally gaining one's heart's desire felt? If so, how did anyone survive it?

Margaret's eyes, dark and deep, gazed up at him as though seeing him for the very first time. Perhaps she was.

"Gervase." Her voice was low and husky, a voice meant for lovemaking, bedchambers, and midnight trysts. Some of her hair had come loose from its pins, and now lay in loose waves about her shoulders. Yielding to temptation, Gervase ran his fingers through it, and more pins pattered to the floor.

Sighing, Margaret closed her eyes, a smile playing about her lips, slightly swollen from his kisses. "Heavens, I've been such a *fool!*"

Gervase paused, raised an inquiring brow. "I beg your pardon?"

She opened her eyes, alight with rueful amusement. "I should be begging *yours,* dear friend. For not seeing—and understanding so much sooner."

He shook his head. "I didn't want you to see. Or burden you with sentiments that you did not share. I know how you felt about Hal—"

"As long ago as that?" she broke in gently. "Oh, my dear—"

He swallowed, tried for a lighter tone. "You're—the sort of woman it's easy to care for, Margaret. But I was a younger son, and you were destined to be my brother's bride."

"And a pretty mess *that* would have been, had it ever

come to pass!" she exclaimed, with the candor he'd always appreciated in her. "I fell out of love with Hal long before he died. Not that I didn't still care," she amended, "but not in the way that a wife should. He'd become more of a brother to me—and I know now that I was never more than another sister to him."

"And then there was Bellamy, to whom I know you were devoted."

"Yes, I was," she admitted. "And the memories of the life we shared will always be precious to me. But Alex was a kind and generous man—I know he would want me to be happy again." She lifted a hand to cup Gervase's cheek. "Even happy with someone else. Someone for whom I already cared—and thought of as a friend."

He captured her hand, pressed a kiss into her palm. "And now—as more than a friend?"

Her eyes glowed, their velvety softness seemingly lit from within. "*Definitely* as more than a friend!" She leaned into him, her body molding itself against his and sending a hot surge of arousal straight to his groin. "Make love to me, Gervase."

The request stole his breath for a moment. "What, here?" He glanced about the Long Gallery, inhabited by empty suits of armor and portraits of his various ancestors, none of whom he wished to observe or even imagine while making love to Margaret.

She smiled. "My chamber would be more appropriate... and far more congenial!"

"Margaret." Gervase studied her face intently. "Are you sure about this?"

Her smile did not waver. "Entirely sure, dear friend. Shall we go?"

HAND IN HAND, they hurried down the passage, and Margaret fought an insane urge to giggle. Country house parties, she knew, were notorious for nighttime assignations between amorous guests... she'd never thought she'd be among them, and trysting with a son of the house, no less! She stole a glance at Gervase and caught him looking at *her* with that familiar half-smile. But his gaze held warmth and a tenderness she'd never seen before, and she smiled foolishly back, her heart somersaulting in her breast.

The threat of laughter vanished, but she could not forget that other guests were asleep—or otherwise occupied—behind those doors, and the last thing she wanted was a witness. She could just imagine Alicia's reaction—surprise mixed with smug satisfaction. Augustus's she didn't care to imagine at all, though, as her younger brother, he had no say in whatever she chose to do!

Reaching the tower room, Margaret opened the door and they slipped inside, shutting out the rest of the world.

Leaving her alone... with her lover. With Gervase.

Suddenly shy, she turned to face him. Limned by lamplight and firelight, he looked at once strange and familiar—and very much a *man*. Not even the heavy dressing gown could conceal the breadth of his shoulders or the lean strength of his form, to which she'd clung so eagerly in the Long Gallery. The feeling of his encircling arms, the ardor of his lips on hers...

Those lips were now pursed, those woodsmoke eyes narrowed in a decidedly critical stare, a vivid reminder of all the times they'd disagreed and debated over the years. Her shyness vanished, and she raised her own brows inquiringly.

"*Belle amie*," he began in his flawless French, "I regret to inform you that you're wearing far too many clothes for the occasion."

"Perhaps I am," she agreed gravely. "What do you propose to do about it?"

His eyes held an unaccustomed smolder that kindled an answering heat low in her loins. "Oh, I imagine I can come up with something," he replied, slipping an arm about her waist and drawing her towards him.

She turned to smile at him over her shoulder. "My gown fastens down the back."

"So I observe." His warm breath ghosted over the nape of her neck as he brushed her hair aside and began to undo each tiny hook.

"So lovely," he murmured at one point, brushing his lips against her bare shoulder. "A pearl beyond price. You were aptly named."

Margaret shivered pleasurably. Leave it to Gervase to

remember that. "Would you take it amiss—if I asked you to hurry?"

"Not in the least." Was that amusement—even laughter—she heard underlying his voice? But he redoubled his efforts, his clever fingers making short work of the task and within minutes, her heavy velvet gown lay puddled on the floor, where it was soon joined by her petticoats.

He had her down to her combination when she decided a change in order. Turning around, she gave him her most winsome look and reached for the sash of his robe.

"One moment, my lord. As it is the Christmas season, I see no reason why *I* should be deprived of unwrapping a gift as well."

He smiled, spreading his arms obligingly. "As you wish, *ma belle*. Although I might add that yours is by far the easier task."

"I don't doubt that," she murmured, undoing the casually knotted sash with a flourish. The robe fell open over loose dark pyjamas, and for a moment, she paused, caught up in a sudden memory of Alex, who had always worn nightshirts. Then she set it aside—a different man, a different time—and pushed Gervase's robe down his shoulders until it slid to the floor.

Emboldened, she tackled his pyjamas next, removing his tunic... and pausing once again, this time in pure feminine appreciation of what she saw. The broad chest, lightly dusted with bronze-gold hair, the flat, well-muscled abdomen tapering to narrow hips...

Hers for the asking—and the taking. Lust speared through her at the prospect, sharper and more intense than any she'd ever experienced. The natural response of a widow who'd missed the physical side of marriage, or something more—something connected to the man now standing in front of her?

Gervase was no less affected by their proximity—she could tell as much by the way he was breathing, deeply and far more quickly than usual. Smiling, she laid her palm upon his naked chest, enjoying the warmth of his skin and marveling at the steady but gratifyingly accelerated rhythm of his heart.

"*What a piece of work is a man!*" she murmured, only

half in jest. "*In form and moving how express and admirable... the beauty of the world, the paragon of animals!*"

"Not exactly original, but thank you all the same," Gervase remarked, an amused glint in his grey eyes. "Now, with our mutual admiration duly expressed, shall we dispense with the rest of these inconvenient garments?"

"Growing impatient?" she teased, regarding him provocatively from under her lashes.

He huffed an exaggerated sigh. "Oh, my darling, if you only knew!"

He pulled her closer to him as he spoke, and within minutes, her combination and his pyjama trousers were on the floor with the rest of their clothes. Margaret bit back a startled gasp as Gervase lifted her off her feet in one swift motion and bore her to the bed. Astonishment and laughter tangled inside of her, the latter prevailing as he lowered her to the mattress.

"How masterful you are, my lord," she whispered, sliding her arms about his neck and drawing him down to her. "I declare, I'm all aflutter!"

He gave her that irresistible dimpled smile. "Do tell. No, on second thought," he laid a gentle finger over her lips, "it can wait. I can think of a far better use for that lovely mouth."

He kissed her again, with the same hunger he'd shown in the gallery and the single-minded focus she'd seen him bring to so many things. Closing her eyes, Margaret gave herself up to it, losing herself in the taste, scent, and feel of him. Almost to her chagrin, she heard a small whimper break from her when he pulled away, but then his lips were blazing a fiery path down the line of her throat and further down into the cleft between her breasts. When that clever mouth closed over one of her nipples, teasing it erect with his tongue, then tugging gently, she gasped and tightened her grip on his shoulders as sensations rippled through her in a series of tiny shocks. His hands were occupied as well, his long fingers tracing sinuous patterns down her belly and over the curve of her hips before coming to rest at her mound.

Margaret stifled another whimper as he stroked her *there,* then trailed his finger over her moist seam, coaxing her folds apart. What had Alicia said, about Gervase being thorough in attending to a lady's pleasures? He was certainly that—and more. She could lie here all night if she wished, blissfully adrift on the sea of sensations he was arousing in her.

But Alex had taught her to give pleasure as well as receive it, and Margaret considered herself a quick learner. Besides, she'd never been one to lie passive and inert during lovemaking. Intimacy was to be savored and shared, not merely endured. Releasing Gervase's shoulders, she let her hands explore what she could of him: the thick brown hair that was softer and finer than she'd ever imagined, the surprisingly sensitive nape of his neck, the expanse of his back, the lean, smooth flanks...

Gervase shivered as she skimmed her palm over the last... good heavens, was he *ticklish* there? Mischievously, she repeated the caress and received confirmation as his skin twitched beneath her touch.

He raised his head, his eyes wide, startled, and vividly blue in the lamplight.

"Discovered your secret, have I?" she murmured. "And after all these years too!"

His lips curved in a slow smile. "Shall I beg for mercy? Or just beg?"

She paused, considering. "Allow me to reflect upon that for a moment."

Gervase shook his head reprovingly. "Far too slow, *ma chere*." He surged forward, claiming her mouth once more.

Laughter rose within her again, bubbling out between kisses. Twenty-six years of knowing this man, and he could still surprise her... but then *this* Gervase was something of an unknown quantity—half a friend, half a stranger, and the best parts of both.

He lay on top of her now, skin to skin, his arousal hot and hard against the juncture of her thighs. But his gaze was soft as he stroked her hair back from her face, the touch of his hands and his lips infinitely gentle. She felt at once desired and cherished, treasured and as desperately craved as water in the desert.

His shaft nudged against her seam, and Margaret smiled, spreading her legs wide. Her body was ready for him now—primed and ready. Some things one did *not* forget, even after several years. Tilting her hips upward to meet his advance, she took him deep inside of her.

And the boy she had known forever, the man she was just beginning to know, shuddered as she tightened around him, his eyes going dark and dazed. A wave of tenderness suffused her. Cool, controlled Gervase... at this moment he was as unguarded as she'd ever seen him, as caught up in desire as she was. Framing his face with her hands, she brushed kisses over his brow, his eyelids, and finally sought his mouth again.

She felt his lips curve in a smile against hers, heard his low murmur in her very bones: *"A thousand kisses buys my heart from me; / And pay them at thy leisure, one by one."*

Then he was moving within her, slowly but purposefully, building up an irresistible rhythm to which she eagerly added her own embellishments, variations on an age-old theme. And the ripples became a cascade, then a coursing river that bore them along like storm-tossed flotsam, towards a fathomless, ever-changing sea.

She cried out as the wave flung them into the heart of the thundering surf, and a moment later, heard his answering cry. Locked in each other's arms, they trembled in the throes of their shared climax, then sank—together, always together—beneath the sounding sea.

SOME TIME LATER, Margaret raised herself on her elbow and contemplated her lover, supine and apparently still asleep beside her. His brown hair was tousled, glints of bronze and gold showing where the lamplight touched it, and his lashes, surprisingly long and dark, lay in a soft fringe upon his cheeks. With that knowing gaze hidden and that sardonic mouth relaxed, he looked years younger, more like the boy she had first known.

Except that no boy could have taken her with such skill and assurance, or roused such a response in her. She'd thoroughly enjoyed the marriage bed, and Alex had been a gentle and considerate partner, but this had been something... other than what she was accustomed to. A passionate joining that had left her limp and boneless, with every inch of her glowing from Gervase's ardent attentions.

Was it because of all those pent-up feelings on his part? All the times he'd had to hold back, during her engagement to Hal? And yet, even at the height of passion, there had been such care... and a melting tenderness that had made her want to weep.

She was just wondering whether to kiss him awake or turn down the lamp and let him sleep, when an arm reached up and drew her back down to the pillows. And a drowsy voice mused aloud, "*I wonder, by my troth, what thou and I / Did, till we loved?*"

"Awake, after all, I see." Margaret relaxed into his encircling arm, feeling like the cat who had got the canary, the cream, and just about every other delicacy known to feline kind. "*And now good morrow to our waking souls.*" She stroked his hair. "Dare I ask if you enjoyed last night?"

His eyes flew open at that. "Good Lord, *need* you ask?"

The surprise in his voice was all the reassurance she needed. Smiling, she rested her head upon his chest. "Just had to make sure the pleasure wasn't all on one side. I wouldn't have wanted to disappoint you—not after all these years."

She could not recall ever seeing him smile like this, all relaxed and unguarded, his body warm and slack in the aftermath of lovemaking. "You could never disappoint me, *belle amie*." Touching her face, he quoted softly, "*If ever any beauty I did see, / Which I desired, and got, 'twas but a dream of thee.*"

No doubting the sincerity in his eyes or voice. Margaret's own eyes stung, and she looked down quickly. "I can't believe how I missed all the signs!"

"Don't reproach yourself too much. I am a past master at concealing what I feel. In this family, how could I be otherwise? Elaine knew, though," he added, after a moment.

"Elaine?" Margaret echoed, incredulous. "Good heavens, for how long?"

"Long enough. Since Hal's death, certainly. Possibly before."

"But why didn't she—"

"Because I asked her not to," Gervase broke in. "And she respected the confidence. Recollect, *ma mie*, that you were to be my sister-in-law. And then..."

His voice tailed off, but she waited, sensing that there was more to come.

"I had a plan," he resumed at last. "I was going to wait another five or six months, until the year of mourning was up. And then—I meant to ask you... if you would consider letting me court you—"

She winced. "And then I eloped with Alex. Oh, Gervase..."

"Bellamy was a good man," he said on a sigh. "I tried to be happy for you. I *did* manage it, after a fashion, because you deserved to be happy. Even if it wasn't with me."

Margaret swallowed, more moved than she could say. Throughout her life, Gervase had been a friend, an ally, and a frequent thorn in her side. Not until this moment had she realized just how dear he could be. That he could have loved her, deeply and selflessly, for so many years... "I'd often wondered why you never married. There must have been dozens of women who'd have jumped at the chance to be your wife."

Gervase shook his head. "A solicitor isn't many women's idea of Prince Charming. Nor would I have wished to marry someone who only wanted me because I was a duke's son. Finally, I thought it would be unfair to propose to any woman for whom I could not feel strong affection. Under the circumstances," he added, a touch dryly, "I cannot bring myself to regret that decision now."

"Nor I," Margaret admitted. "In fact, I suspect I'd have been rather jealous if you *had* taken a wife." She trailed a finger down his sternum and glanced at him from under her lashes. "I was even a little jealous of Alicia tonight."

"Alicia?" Gervase sounded genuinely bewildered. "Good God, why?"

"Well, she's—grown up to be very beautiful, hasn't she?"

"I suppose," he conceded with a benign indifference that set any lingering fears at rest. "If one favors blondes. My preference is for something more... vibrant." He threaded his hands through her hair, admiring the strands in the lamplight. "Silk shot through with fire. Exquisite."

"You wax poetical," she teased, though the compliment warmed her to the core.

"Or a good chestnut horse, if you prefer," he resumed blandly.

She poked him in the ribs, and he laughed outright, a rare sound that delighted her. How many women had had the chance to see him so: open, uninhibited, and completely irresistible?

"Seriously, darling, why would you think I'd ever be attracted to Alicia?"

She savored the "darling," but explained, "I couldn't help but notice that she was flirting a bit with you, during charades."

"She was flirting a bit with *all* the men, during charades," he corrected. "I took it as no more than a bit of practice on her part—like a kitten trying its strength on someone. It's Brother Reg's attention she really wants, but unfortunately, she's chosen the wrong tree to climb."

Margaret tensed. "What do you mean, exactly?" she asked, trying to keep her tone casual.

He shrugged. "I've never *seen* Reg in love. But if I had to imagine him with a woman, it wouldn't be your sister, lovely as she is. It would be someone bold and dashing, who'd take to army life straightaway. Someone who could ride as hard, shoot as straight, and live as rough as any soldier. And look striking while doing it," he added with a faint smile.

So even Gervase, with his quick perceptions, had not figured *everything* out; she did not know whether to be relieved or sorry. "Sounds like a veritable Boudiccea—or an Amazon."

"A Hippolyta, as opposed to a Helen. That might suit Reg down to the ground. And she'd probably be like Mother, in personality at least." He paused, then continued not unkindly, "While I can't predict what will happen between Reg and Alicia, I have some difficulty imagining her getting all she wants from him."

He spoke more truly than he knew, Margaret reflected somberly. "Poor Alicia."

Gervase stroked her bare back. "I know it's not easy seeing your sister in such a situation. But we cannot always protect those we love from disappointment—or heartache. Sometimes all we can do is be there... to help pick up the pieces."

Who'd picked up *his* pieces, she wondered with a rush of self-reproach, all those years when she'd been engaged to Hal, then married to Alex? Elaine, perhaps—but knowing Gervase as she did, she suspected he'd borne most of his heartache alone and in silence. Suddenly remorseful, she wound her arms about him, letting an embrace say what words could not.

He stroked her back again, a more sensual caress this time, meant to arouse as well as soothe, and she arched into it, like a cat. Indeed, she wouldn't have been at all surprised to find herself purring. But touch was a game that two could play. Remembering his secret, she trailed her hand over his chest, then let her fingers drift innocently towards his flank...

Only to find herself pinned to the mattress again with Gervase poised over her. In the lamplight, his eyes shone a winter-sky blue, so clear as to be guileless, but his wicked grin belied all that. Changing tactics, Margaret twined her arms about his neck and kissed him until they were both breathless and she could see heat smoldering behind those cool eyes of his.

Which led inevitably to a second round of lovemaking, gentler and more leisurely than the first, but every bit as delightful. Afterwards, entwined in a delicious lassitude, they slid into sleep together.

SHE WOKE to find the place beside her empty, but on stretching out an anxious hand, she discovered that the hollow where he'd lain was still warm. Blinking heavy eyes, she scanned the chamber, noting from the quality of light that morning was approaching.

Her lover was standing, magnificently and unashamedly naked, in front of the casement, staring out at the landscape. Still only half-awake, Margaret eased herself up on her elbows and admired the view: the broad shoulders tapering to the narrow waist, the sturdy upper arms, the smooth ripple of muscle beneath the lean back...

He spoke without turning around. "*Merry Margaret,*

midsummer flower, gentle as falcon or hawk of the tower... it snowed again last night."

Margaret did not ask how he'd known she was awake. "Heavily?" she asked, stifling a yawn.

He glanced over his shoulder. "Let's just say, I doubt that anyone in this house will be going anywhere today. Not unless they've taken complete leave of their senses."

Their eyes met, then, "Reg," they said in unison and laughed.

"Well, I *was* looking forward to a white Christmas," Margaret said philosophically.

Gervase arched a dubious brow. "Even one with impassable roads and the unadulterated company of my family?"

"Don't forget *my* family as well," she reminded him. "One simply has to take the rough along with the smooth. Speaking of which..." She stretched luxuriously and let the sheet slip down just far enough to afford him a glimpse of what he'd so enjoyed the night before. Much to her satisfaction, interest sparked in his eyes. "Why don't you come back to bed? You must be freezing, standing there without a stitch on."

He hesitated, clearly tempted. "I should go back to my own room, before they come in to light the fires."

"That won't be for a while yet. Night's candles aren't entirely burnt out, are they?"

He left the window. "Not quite, but the sun will be coming up soon."

"*Busy old fool, unruly sun,*" Margaret quoted, leaning back against the pillows and patting the place beside her invitingly. "Stay until dawn? *My* bed is far warmer than yours is likely to be right now. And I won't even complain if you put those cold feet on mine."

He gave her that dimpled smile. "Greater love hath no woman. Very well—I'll stay."

Margaret stifled a squeak as he climbed in beside her; yes, his feet were decidedly chilly, but the rest of him warmed up with gratifying speed, especially once they began to kiss again. And to caress and fondle, like two people starved of touch.

"*She is all states and all princes I,*" Gervase murmured low in her ear, as they came together once more. "*Nothing else is.*"

And for another glorious interval, nothing else was.

※

As promised, he stayed until dawn, slipping cat-footed out of her bed and donning his pyjamas and robe again.

Margaret had protested sleepily, but Gervase had remained adamant. "As delightful as last night was, I think it best if we are discreet. I don't want to bring my whole family down upon you—which is what would happen if I were caught in your chamber."

She could not suppress a slight wince at the thought. And she did want to hold on to the sweetness of their new relationship, keep it close and secret, at least for now. All the same, she was reluctant to see him go, and said so.

He stroked her hair, smiled lingeringly into her eyes before stealing a farewell kiss. "This isn't the end for us, *belle amie*. It is barely the beginning."

"Shall I see you at breakfast?" she asked hopefully.

"Very likely, if you can make it downstairs by nine o'clock." He eased open the door, peered into the passage, then slipped out, throwing one last quick smile over his shoulder.

As it turned out, he was right to be cautious. It couldn't have been more than twenty minutes later that she heard footsteps in the passage and Tilda entered with her tray.

"Brought your hot chocolate, my lady," she announced brightly, seeing that Margaret was awake. "You'll be glad of it this morning. The ground's just *covered* in snow!"

So Gervase had said. Margaret rose, a little reluctant to leave the warm nest where they had so recently lain, and located her dressing gown. Tilda moved about the room, tidying up with brisk efficiency and no sign of suspicion that anything unusual had occurred. Gervase, with admirable foresight, had draped Margaret's discarded clothes circumspectly over a chair before leaving her chamber. She wondered if he'd made it back to his own room before his valet could notice that he'd spent the night elsewhere. Granted, if Farnsworth *did* suspect anything, he could be trusted to keep it to himself; discreet servants were worth their weight in gold! She smiled at the thought, hugging the memory of last night to her, happier than she'd been in years.

Pausing by the window, she looked out at a landscape blanketed in white. *Snow had fallen, snow on snow, snow on snow...* Gervase might disagree, but Margaret thought it a beautiful sight—as if the world had been made new while they slept.

The chocolate tasted especially good this morning, the toast positively ambrosial, and she enlivened her small repast by reading further into Gervase's gift. Strange to think of Richard III as a harbinger of romance, but the wronged Yorkist king had certainly managed to bring Gervase and herself together. Who needed Shakespeare or Byron, with such a matchmaker?

Afterwards, she washed—and was unable to resist singing or at least humming in the bath—and then chose a pretty suit of heathery tweed, flecked in two shades of green. Gervase liked her in green, and it brought out the red in her hair. Silk and fire, he'd called it last night... she found herself smiling foolishly at the remembered compliment, and was still smiling when she left her chamber to go down to breakfast, well within the appointed time.

GERVASE WAS ALREADY PRESENT, washed, shaved, sleek as a cat and looking twice as satisfied as he helped himself to ham and eggs from the sideboard. He glanced up as she entered, and smiled, the dimples forming deep crescents on either side of his mouth. That clever mouth that had done such interesting things to her last night.

Returning his smile, she joined him at the sideboard. "Are we the first ones down today?"

"Among the first. Lydgate mentioned that Father and Reg already breakfasted, and Mother is having hers upstairs, as usual." Gervase removed the lid of another chafing dish, and scooped a generous spoonful of fried potatoes onto his plate.

"Quite the appetite this morning, I see," Margaret observed as she filled her own plate.

"You have *no* idea," he murmured, brushing shoulders with her on his way to the table.

There were plenty of vacant chairs, but she sat down beside him, close enough for their knees to touch and their hands to meet under the table—if they so desired. And close enough to exchange intimate glances that promised more of last night's pleasure, as soon as they could safely manage it. For now, she contented herself with those and with the sight of his profile, admiring the angle of his cheekbones, the strong, sharp lines of nose and jaw, even the fine scrollwork of his ear. *Mine*, she thought with a possessiveness that surprised her.

Elaine and Alasdair were the next to arrive, both bright-faced and looking almost as pleased with themselves as Margaret suspected she and Gervase did.

Elaine glanced about the room. "Gracious, did *everyone* sleep in this morning?"

"Seems to be the most sensible choice, when one is snowed in," Alasdair observed, glancing fondly at his wife, whose blush left no doubt as to how they'd spent their waking hours.

Was Elaine watching *them* more closely? Margaret wondered. She'd known—and kept—Gervase's secret for years. Would she sense that things might have changed between them? Margaret lowered her gaze to her plate, took a sip of scalding tea, and carefully avoided looking at her lover, though she could feel amusement radiating from him like heat from a furnace.

The rest of the house party came straggling in soon after: Madeline and Hugo, Juliana, Jason, and Augustus. And finally Alicia, wearing a lemon-yellow morning dress that set off her bright hair to perfection.

They were all seated, laden plates before them, when Whitborough and his heir strode into the room. Margaret's heart sank when she saw how her sister straightened in her chair upon her fiancé's entrance. It sank further still when she looked more closely at the two men: the duke was smiling, his eyes alight with triumph, while Reg's expression was a match for Gervase's at his most impassive.

"Good morning," Whitborough announced jovially, casting a sweeping glance around the table. "I'm glad to see so many of you here. Especially since there's an announcement to be made." He set a hand on his heir's shoulder. "Isn't that right, Reginald?"

"Indeed, sir." Reg's voice, like his face, gave nothing away, and Margaret watched with mounting dread as he approached her sister's chair and lowered himself to one knee beside it.

"Lady Alicia," he began formally, "if it is agreeable to you, I thought we might marry on New Year's Eve, in the family chapel."

Chapter Ten

In time the savage bull doth bear the yoke.
—WILLIAM SHAKESPEARE, *Much Ado
About Nothing*, I, I

GERVASE BIT BACK A STARTLED EXCLAMATION. His family sat frozen in place like figures in a *tableau-vivant*, while Margaret had stiffened beside him, her eyes widening in her suddenly pale face. But to a one, every person in the breakfast room was now staring at Reg, still kneeling beside Alicia's chair.

To Gervase's critical eye, his brother neither looked nor sounded like an eager bridegroom. But Alicia—sweet, naïve Alicia—flushed rosily, her eyes aglow as she gazed at her betrothed.

"Oh, yes, Reg," she breathed, "I should be *delighted* to marry you this New Year's Eve!"

Reg's smile was closer to a grimace—and it certainly did not reach his eyes, Gervase noted. "Very well, then—it's settled." He took her hand and bestowed a perfunctory kiss upon it.

Covertly, Gervase studied the faces of those around the table. His sisters' reflected mainly surprise, although Madeline's narrowed eyes hinted at some suspicion as well. Hugo and Alasdair looked merely bemused, Jason startled and sullen, clearly aware that the forthcoming marriage meant that Reg was back in their father's good graces, and Augustus...

The flash of displeasure on the young duke's face lasted no longer than a second before disappearing under a smooth, unreadable mask, a mask that reminded Gervase all too well of the one he himself assumed for public purposes. And reminded him forcibly of what his father had said a few nights ago: that Augustus did not want this marriage either.

He did not look at Margaret... but then, he didn't have to. Her continued silence and rigid posture told him all he needed to know about *her* feelings regarding this latest development. Indeed, apart from Alicia, the only person who looked unequivocally pleased was the duke, surveying them all with a satisfaction bordering on smugness.

Hugo was the first to break the silence, declaring perhaps a shade too heartily, "Well, this is splendid news, isn't it? Congratulations, Reg, old boy—and to you as well, Lady Alicia!"

"Splendid, indeed." Madeline leveled a searching gaze upon her father. "And quite the surprise too, I must say."

"Isn't it, though?" The duke smiled beatifically at her, his own gaze as blue and guileless as a newborn infant's. "But a delightful surprise, you must admit, after so many years!"

Must we, indeed? Gervase cast another glance around the table. More of the family was chiming in with their good wishes, trying to compensate for that first, startled delay; Juliana, Elaine, and Alasdair even managed to sound as if they meant it. He himself murmured a vague benediction, aware that Margaret had not yet uttered a word. Alicia, still all smiles and with eyes only for Reg, did not appear to notice her sister's silence. Reg, for his part, accepted the congratulations with the stoicism of a soldier following a particularly unappealing set of orders.

"Alicia." Augustus rose from his chair and bestowed a ducal kiss upon his younger sister's cheek. "I am pleased to see your patience is to be rewarded at long last."

Gervase wondered if he was the only one who heard the faint edge under that smooth tone. Except for his father: the duke could be magnificently pur-blind when it came to his own children, to say nothing of his wife, but Gervase suspected that he had the measure of Augustus, on whom he now bestowed a brief, bland smile before turning his attention back to his heir.

"I believe there's someone else who should hear the happy news," he remarked. "Do you not agree, Reg?"

"Of course." Reg turned to Alicia. "Will you come with me, to tell my mother?'

She looked at him with her heart in her eyes. "I would be honored to go with you, and tell the duchess."

He offered his arm, and she rose and fairly floated out of the breakfast room with him. Gervase saw Margaret's hand tighten about her teacup and wondered if she were trying to stifle the urge to hurl it at his brother's broad back—for which he could not blame her in the least.

His father continued to smile benignly about the room. "I trust all of you will lend your assistance to ensure the wedding goes off as it should?"

"Of course we will," Elaine said at once, followed a moment later by Juliana. Madeline merely nodded, while Margaret remained silent, her gaze fixed on the tablecloth; fortunately, no one but Gervase seemed to be paying attention to her.

Augustus turned to the duke. "Whitborough, I believe we have some matters to discuss?"

"Indeed, we do, Langdale," the older man returned. "Shall we adjourn to the li—" he paused, and Gervase couldn't help wondering if he was remembering just how un-private the library had turned out to be the night before. "To my private study?" he amended smoothly.

Augustus inclined his head, and they strolled out of the room together, with every appearance of amity.

Not surprisingly, it was Madeline who broke the silence once the two dukes were out of earshot. "Well, nothing like starting off the morning with a bombshell, is there?" she remarked with an acerbity that would have done credit to their mother. "And now we've just a week to plan a wedding." A frown creased her brow. "I'm a little surprised that Alicia agreed to it. I'd have thought she'd prefer a big wedding in London or York, with more guests present."

"Augustus and Margaret are here," Elaine pointed

out. "Her family. That's really all one needs, isn't it?" But there was a note of doubt in her voice.

"We could work really hard to make it memorable," Juliana suggested. "Even if it's a small intimate ceremony rather than a grand one." Her face brightened in sudden inspiration. "I know! We can decorate the chapel ourselves, with holly and ivy. And perhaps some of the winter flowers from the conservatory—we've got some *beautiful* camellias. Or we could try to force some roses into bloom, just for the occasion."

Force. Interesting choice of word, Gervase reflected. And all too apposite, under the circumstances—had anyone besides himself and Margaret noticed Reg's indifference towards his impending nuptials and even his affianced bride?

As if on cue, Alasdair gave a slight cough and ventured, "Not to be a wet blanket, but did not anyone else find Reg's reaction a wee bit... lacking?"

An awkward silence fell, during which everyone at the table seemed to avoid looking directly at each other —although Gervase thought he saw a speculative gleam in Jason's eyes just before the boy lowered his gaze to his plate again.

"Well, Reg has never been one to wear his heart on his sleeve," Madeline said dryly.

"True, but he shouldn't look like he's facing the hangman, either," Hugo retorted.

"It wasn't *that* bad!" Elaine protested. "Surely, he'll come round by the time of the wedding. And Alicia seemed perfectly happy—didn't she, Margaret?" she appealed to her friend.

Margaret looked up, her face a polite mask that made Gervase's scalp prickle with apprehension. "Yes, very," she replied in a voice as flat as her expression.

Elaine studied her more closely, a worried crease between her brows. "And it's good news, isn't it? That she and Reg are to be married at last?"

"Indeed." Margaret stood up, forcing a smile. "Pray excuse me," she added, and headed for the door.

"Pardon me." Gervase pushed back his own chair and followed her out of the breakfast room. He could feel several pairs of curious eyes on his back, but did his best to ignore them. Let them speculate as they would—he could do nothing to stop them. At least Reg's wedding was the more pressing topic.

Just as he stepped out of the room, he heard Juliana ask whom they should ask to perform the ceremony: the elderly vicar or his new curate, young and rather green.

"Why not wire the Archbishop of Canterbury?" Jason inquired, the sneer evident in his voice. "I'm sure he'd drop everything to officiate at the heir to Whitborough's wedding!"

"That's enough, Jason!" Madeline's voice rang out sharply. "Father may tolerate your insolence and spite, but the rest of us aren't so indulgent! If you can't kept a civil tongue in your head, then leave the room!"

One could always count on Madeline to deliver a dressing-down when needed, Gervase mused; she took after their mother that way. And with Jason's faults being satisfactorily addressed, he could concentrate on Margaret, white-faced, agitated, and—to judge from her expression—moments away from an emotional outburst as alarming as it was uncharacteristic.

He reached out and caught her arm. "*Belle amie*, what is it you mean to do?"

Her eyes stared wildly into his. "I have to stop this, Gervase! I have to make them see—"

"Hush a moment, now," he soothed, taking her gently by the elbow and throwing a quick glance about the passage. "You'll not do your case any good while you're in such a state. Let's go somewhere private."

The library was deserted, fortunately. He escorted her inside, closing the door behind them—and then locking it, after a moment's thought. Turning, he saw Margaret pacing before the fireplace, all but wringing her hands in distress.

Striding up to her, he set his hands upon her shoulders and guided her to the nearest chair. "Sit," he instructed in the level tone used to quiet nervous barristers preparing for their first appearance in court. "And take several deep breaths before you even *try* to speak."

She flashed him a glance, half-surprised, half-resentful, but obeyed. After a few moments, a trace of color crept back into her cheeks and her restless hands stilled in her lap. Composure reestablishing itself: good.

He crossed to the liquor cabinet, poured out a glass of soda water, and brought it to her. "Drink this. Slowly."

She regarded the fizzing liquid quizzically. "What, no port this time?"

"Not this early in the day. Besides," he added with a wryness to match hers, "I suspect this morning's announcement had the rest of us doubting our sobriety already."

"Our sobriety—and Reg's sanity." She took a tentative sip from her glass, grimaced a little at the taste, then set it aside. "I still can't believe it!"

Gervase took the chair opposite hers. "Nor I. That was quite an about-face."

"He's all but ignored Alicia for five years—even last night, when she was doing her level best to captivate him. And now he's set to marry her, in a week's time?" She shook her head.

"Your sister is beautiful, virtuous, and as your brother pointed out, patient," Gervase replied, taking the devil's advocate position out of habit. "Not many young ladies would be willing to wait as long as she has for Reg, duke's heir or no. Some might argue that he's finally come to his senses and is prepared to do right by her."

Her mouth twisted. "Like Elaine?"

"Lainey's a romantic—she wants to believe there's a happy ending for every couple. And she's not alone in this," he added, "not even in *my* jaded, cynical family."

Margaret sighed, pressing her fingers to her forehead. "If I believed that was possible and not a disaster in the making, I wouldn't say another word! I know how long Alicia's waited for this—just as I know that Reg is the last man on earth who could ever make her happy!"

Her voice had risen on the last words, some of her earlier agitation returning, and he leaned forward to take her hands in hers. "Hush, love—"

"He'll destroy my sister's life. Maybe not intentionally, but he'll ruin it all the same!"

Gervase blinked, taken aback by her vehemence. "How can you be sure?"

She flushed, biting her lower lip. "I cannot tell you just *how* I know! But trust me, I have a good reason to feel as I do!"

"I do trust you." He gave her cold hands a gentle

squeeze. "And for what it's worth, I agree with you. Reg is not likely to make your sister happy, not if his demeanor at breakfast is any indication. I saw his face—he hasn't miraculously fallen in love with Alicia overnight."

"Then why, in heaven's name, is he marrying her?" she demanded. "What happened to change all that?"

"Not what, *who*," he corrected. "Did you see how Father was smiling? At a guess, he's promised something—or threatened something, to make Reg come round."

Margaret exhaled sharply, her eyes now holding a dangerous spark, and the hands he held balled into fists. "Pray don't take this the wrong way, Gervase, but sometimes I wish that someone would just *shoot* your father! Not fatally, just *painfully!*"

"The thought has doubtless crossed a number of minds," he remarked dryly. "My mother's, chief among them. But I'd settle for seeing him outmaneuvered instead."

"But how does one outmaneuver a master manipulator?"

She was fretting her lip again, and for a moment, he remembered those same lips, soft and sweet, pressed against his own. Had it really been just a few hours ago? The taste of her mouth, the warm satin of her skin, the glorious tangle of her limbs with his... simply being near her was enough to render him light-headed to the point of intoxication. And, after last night, as randy as a stallion in rut, he acknowledged ruefully. But they were still Gervase and Margaret, who'd known each other from the cradle onward, and right now she needed the cool-headed, analytical friend, not the ardent lover.

"Well, for starters," he began, releasing her hands and leaning back in his chair. "I don't recommend taking on Father directly. He's been at this longer than we've both been alive."

Margaret gave a reluctant nod. "Much as I'd love to give him a piece of my mind, I doubt he'd listen to *me*. Which leaves Reg or Alicia, who aren't likely to appreciate my interference either," she added, sighing. "But I can't just sit back and do nothing, not when my sister's future is at stake!"

"I know it's difficult in this situation, but try to keep your emotions in check," Gervase cautioned. "Take some time to consider how best to handle this, and plan your strategy accordingly. Or you could bring about the very thing you're trying to prevent."

She looked at him, and despite the worry shadowing her face, her eyes softened and the memory of last night flickered between them like a candle flame. "Dear Gervase. Thank you—For understanding."

He lifted a shoulder. "It's family. What is there to understand?"

A rueful smile tugged at her mouth. "True enough." She set her hands on either side of his face and gave him a sweet, lingering kiss before pulling away reluctantly. "Pray excuse me. I must go and think up some ways to stop a wedding!"

"Good luck," Gervase replied gravely, wondering if that was the appropriate remark under the circumstances. And the speaking look Margaret flashed him over her shoulder as she headed for the door showed that she too recognized the irony of the situation.

In spite of the complications that lay ahead, Gervase found himself smiling as he watched her go. Everything and nothing had changed between them. *A thousand kisses buys my heart from me...* but he'd parted with his after only one from her.

He shook his head ruefully. Utterly besotted. A complete mooncalf. How his family and friends would laugh if they could see him now! But the thought made no difference to his present mood. *A college of wit-crackers cannot flout me out of my humor.*

Still smiling, he started for the door in turn, only to stop short as it swung open to reveal an all too familiar figure.

"Ah, Gervase. Might I have a private word with you?" his father inquired in that mild tone that everyone most familiar with him knew better than to take at face value.

Gervase eyed him warily, remembering the last time they'd met in this room. "If this is about last night, sir—"

"Good God, I'm not about to rebuke you, boy! Given what this family is capable of, eavesdropping is a very minor peccadillo." The duke paused, regarding Gervase thoughtfully. "I had not realized that you and Margaret had become so close."

Gervase stilled, all his defenses rising like a castle

drawbridge, but he strove to keep his voice and expression neutral. "Margaret and I are friends," he said with perfect truth. "And she was in some distress, last night, after revealing such a personal loss."

The duke had the grace to look a little ashamed. "I did not intend to revive such a painful memory. You may rest assured that I will not do so again."

"Or attempt to promote a match between her and Reg?"

"No," his father said, after a moment. "There's no point in that, if they've neither of them the inclination. And Reg has confirmed what Margaret told me—that they are only friends." Again, his blue eyes scanned Gervase probingly. "But I realize that *some* friendships ripen into a deeper affection, with time. I would not be at all displeased if that should prove to be the case with Margaret and—another of my sons."

Gervase just managed to conceal his surprise. *Well, well.* A day of miracles, indeed: Reg set to marry Alicia— for now, anyway—and the duke giving a blessing, of sorts, to the relationship between Margaret and himself.

"Margaret is a fine woman, whom I would have been proud to call daughter," Whitborough went on. "Indeed, if you would like me to put in a word—"

"No! Thank you," Gervase amended in a milder tone. "I appreciate your support, Father. But I would prefer to handle *that* aspect of my life without assistance."

"So there *is* something between you then!" the duke remarked with satisfaction. "Well, I commend your taste, my boy."

Damn. He hadn't intended to reveal quite that much. But if the alternative was his father interfering in his careful courtship... well, he supposed he could part with a few details. "I care very much for Margaret, sir. I always have. But it's early days yet."

"Well, should your *friendship*," Whitborough emphasized the last word, "with her take a romantic turn... I want you to know that I would be glad to dance at your wedding."

The admission sent an unexpected rush of warmth through Gervase, even as he reminded himself to keep his defenses in place. While he did not doubt his father's sincerity, he knew from experience that the duke wasn't above using one's deepest, most personal feelings for his own purposes. Deflecting the subject, he said lightly, "You'll have the opportunity to dance at Reg's before long. Congratulations. Might I inquire as to just how you managed to talk him into it?"

The duke eyed him quizzically. "Would you believe the fine art of compromise?"

Gervase raised his brows in polite incredulity. "Compromise on what, exactly?"

"Your brother's career, for starters," his father replied. "I have agreed not to raise the subject of his leaving the army for the next nine months. After which time, he and I will renew our discussion... if certain events have not transpired."

The begetting of an heir, Gervase translated without difficulty. Whether that meant Alicia would accompany Reg when he returned to his regiment was unclear. Given her reaction to last night's conversation, Margaret would be furious either way over the terms of this arrangement, at the prospect of her sister being used as a broodmare.

"I see. Well, I am sure Reg will endeavor to do his duty." If Margaret didn't manage to stop the wedding, Gervase added to himself.

"Are you indeed?" the duke mused, regarding him through narrowed eyes. "You haven't given me an answer, you know. About those precedents for breaking an entail."

"I was not aware that you still required that information," Gervase temporized, feeling a sudden unease. "Especially now that Reg has come to heel as you desired, and is to marry Alicia, after all."

"On the contrary, I suspect I will need it even more," his father retorted. "Call it insurance. Because, between the two of us, I do not entirely trust your brother *not* to wriggle off the matrimonial hook, if he can manage it. Indeed, I'd expect nothing else from your mother's son." The duke's gaze rested almost broodingly on Gervase. "From *any* of your mother's sons."

Gervase suppressed a shiver, reminded of just how ruthless both of his parents could be in their ongoing campaign to outmaneuver each other. Scylla and Charybdis indeed.

"I was hoping perhaps to persuade you to be *my* son —at least in this," Whitborough went on. "And that I could rely upon your legal expertise and tenacity, to find the answers I seek." His tone softened suddenly, becoming warmer than Gervase could remember it being in some years. Towards him, anyway—Hal and now Jason had probably seen far more of their father's indulgent side. "And my offer still stands, you know. I'm prepared to give you *everything* I promised when we last spoke of this. And more."

Gervase felt his eyes widen. His father's proposed incentives already included a sizable retainer, a country estate, and shares in a possible silver mine. What other carrots was the duke proposing to attach to the stick? "More?" he echoed, allowing his skepticism to show. "At this rate, you will surely bankrupt yourself, sir."

"Not at all. When it comes to the future, I have limitless capital to invest." The duke paused, his keen gaze almost kindly. "Margaret has two young stepsons, does she not? Who would be part of your life as well, should you and she decide to marry someday."

So they would, Gervase realized with an inner start. The young Bellamys would surely want to spend time with their stepmother, even if she were to remarry—and why shouldn't they?

The possible shape of his future unfolded before him with dizzying, dazzling speed. If matters developed as he hoped, there'd be two boys to befriend. Or with whom he'd strive to build some kind of rapport, at least. A home to be shared, refurbished to accommodate two—no, four—rather than one. A few cats underfoot, perhaps a dog as well. And Margaret herself, always at the center, the most essential ingredient of all. He'd dared to imagine it before, on the train journey up to Yorkshire, but now, amazingly, it felt almost within his grasp.

All the more reason to be cautious, Gervase reminded himself. As he'd told his father, it was early days yet, and delightful as it was to imagine a future with Margaret, his lady was not yet won; time enough for castles in the air once she was.

The duke's voice broke into his thoughts. "You'll agree, I am sure, that two promising boys should be given a good start in life. I would be more than happy to assist you with that."

"Generous, but I am sure that Bellamy provided well for both of his sons."

"Oh, no doubt, but it can do no harm to offer extra assistance, if necessary. I know that *you'd* never underestimate the advantage of being connected to a duke, if only by marriage."

"That would depend on the duke," Gervase said dryly. But he couldn't deny that his father had a point. He'd risen to the top of his profession by his own efforts, but being one of Whitborough's sons had opened some doors for him in the beginning. And the Bellamy boys would receive that social advantage too, if he married Margaret.

If, not *when*. Those damned castles in the air again...

"True enough," his father acknowledged, an amused glint in his eyes. "But you must admit that my reputation in business is impeccable. Nor would I distinguish between grandchildren who are born—and grandchildren who are *acquired*. Although," he added gently, "it is not impossible that God might bless you with a child of your own, in time."

It was on the tip of Gervase's tongue to gibe that, based on his experience, children might be a mixed blessing indeed, but the flippant words died in his throat at the thought of how overjoyed *Margaret* would be if it happened, while he...

Rather to his surprise, he discovered that the idea did not displease him at all. Strange, when he'd given so little thought over the years to fatherhood, despite being fond enough of his nieces and nephews. Margaret's claim of barrenness did not alter his feelings for her—he doubted death itself would do that—but if by the grace of God, they had a child, a daughter, perhaps, with her velvety brown eyes...

The weight of his father's hand on his shoulder recalled him to the present. Startled, he looked up and felt himself caught by that keen blue gaze like a butterfly on a pin.

"Would you not agree, my boy," the duke's rich voice was a sonorous, almost hypnotic rumble in his ears, "that our children deserve every advantage that we can give them? That they're worth every sacrifice, every *compromise,* that we can make?"

KEEP CALM, Gervase had advised her, and Margaret had to admit he was in the right of it. In the first shock of the announcement, she would almost certainly have said the wrong thing. Now, at least, she'd taken the time to consider her approach, and discard the ones most likely to blow up in her face.

She would speak to Reg first. After all, he would understand her objections far better than Alicia would. Steeling herself, she knocked on his chamber door, only to learn from his valet that Lord Reginald had gone down to the gymnasium with Lord Saxby.

No word on whether Alicia was with him, Margaret mused as she headed downstairs. On reflection, she hoped not—it would be far harder to say what she needed to say to Reg in her sister's presence. Finding a way to speak to him alone would be enough of a challenge.

Pausing outside the gymnasium, she took a deep breath, then opened the door. Almost immediately, she caught sight of Reg and Hugo, stripped to the waist, and engaged in a vigorous wrestling bout in the middle of the room. Not surprisingly, they had an audience, much of it female and admiring, although—to Margaret's relief—there was no sign of Alicia.

Making her way towards the bench where Madeline, Juliana, and Elaine were seated, she glanced at the two wrestlers as they alternately circled and lunged. No denying that Reg was a fine figure of a man: tall, broad-shouldered and broad-chested. Even more impressive than Hugo, whose own build was also athletic and well-proportioned. Just now both men glistened with a fine sheen of sweat as they grappled with each other. From a purely aesthetic point of view, Margaret supposed many would find Reg irresistible, although she herself would have preferred to watch another man: not as tall, but lean, lithe, and elegant as the fencers' foils he wielded with such skill: Gervase, without a shirt, wrestling, fencing... or simply lying slack-limbed among her bedclothes, smiling at her with the lazy repletion of a recently fed lion.

Her face flamed at the memory, and she glanced down at her hands until her cheeks cooled. Keep your mind on the task at hand, she reminded herself sternly. She could not afford to be distracted by thoughts of her lover, however delightful.

A heavy thud accompanied by a grunt had her glancing up again. Hugo now lay on the mat, with Reg sprawled on top of him, pinning him in place. A scattered but enthusiastic round of applause broke out.

"Finished?" Madeline inquired sweetly of her husband, whose chest was heaving like a bellows. "Or haven't you been punished enough yet?"

Hugo shot her a speaking look, but made no other reply, rolling to his feet once Reg let him up and extending a congratulatory hand to his brother-in-law. "Well done, old boy," he half-gasped, with a rueful smile. "Listen to me, wheezing like a grampus! I probably should know better at my age."

"*Probably?*" Madeline murmured, but both men ignored her.

Reg grinned, relaxed as he always was when engaging in the pastimes at which he excelled. "Nonsense, that was an excellent bout! We should do it again sometime."

"Maybe in another year or so," Hugo puffed, reaching for a towel to mop his sweaty face.

"I commend your prowess, Major," a new voice remarked from the doorway.

Everyone turned at once to see Augustus approaching, his stride as smooth and powerful as... as a panther's, Margaret thought suddenly, and every bit as predatory. Gervase moved with a similar grace, but without that undercurrent of what felt unsettlingly like menace. Why had she not noticed it before? It was almost like watching a stranger instead of her baby brother.

Augustus's presence introduced a subtle change to the room as well, a lessening of the relaxed, almost convivial atmosphere. While the women still regarded him with undisguised admiration, the men, especially Reg, seemed a bit less welcoming. But then, Margaret reflected, he and Augustus weren't exactly friends. Even without the sensitive subject of Alicia between them, they were far too different in tastes and temperament to be truly compatible, and the seven years between them was an additional barrier.

"Thank you, Langdale." Reg inclined his head, his face a polite mask.

"Well done, indeed," Augustus continued, with a brilliant smile. "There's nothing like a good wrestling bout to help a man expend some excess energy. I hope the victor is willing to go a few rounds with *me*."

Without waiting for a reply, he shrugged off his coat and stripped off his shirt and waistcoat with almost lightning speed. A little to Margaret's discomfort, Juliana gave a soft murmur of admiration and Madeline's eyes glinted with unconcealed appreciation. Augustus's admittedly impressive physique emerged: slightly shorter than Reg and more willowy, but still handsome, well-muscled, and sturdy. The comparisons to Adonis and Apollo might be overblown, but they were by no means inaccurate.

"Shall we make it two out of three falls, Major?" Augustus invited, seemingly oblivious to the feminine attention he was attracting.

Reg's gaze flicked over Augustus, bare-chested and golden, smiling at him with blinding confidence. "Not today, Langdale—if you'll pardon me. After my match with Hugo, I should not be giving you my best effort."

"Oh, come now. You underestimate yourself," Augustus protested. "I met a friend of yours in London just last month. A Captain Andrew Hastings?"

Margaret froze, her gaze going at once to Reg, who had also stiffened at the name.

"As it happens, Hastings and I belong to the same club," her brother went on, his voice smooth as cream. "We struck up a conversation over dinner, and he told me there was no one to match Reginald Lyons when it came to wrestling. That he could take on half a dozen challengers, one after the other, and still prevail."

"Flattering of Hastings to say so," Reg returned. "But we were considerably younger then. I fear I would only disappoint you now."

"Come, Major, don't be so modest," Augustus chided, striding forward until he and Reg stood just inches apart. "After what I witnessed between you and

Saxby, I'm convinced you couldn't possibly disappoint me."

Margaret stilled, eyes narrowing as she watched her brother. They made a striking picture: the golden youth facing the powerful soldier, Adonis and Achilles, taking each other's measure. But what unsettled her even more was the intimate, almost confiding note in Augustus's voice... as if he and Reg were sharing some sort of secret.

Reg stiffened further, drawing himself up as though about to deliver a blistering snub, of the sort he dealt Jason. But all he said was, "Another time, Langdale. I must go and wash now. I promised your sister," he emphasized the last word, "a walk in the conservatory."

"*I'd* be happy to oblige, Langdale," Hugo offered, ignoring Madeline's glower of disapproval. "Once I've got my second wind."

"Or I," Alasdair spoke up for the first time, from his position leaning against the wall. "Mind you, I'm not in Reg or Hugo's league, so you're assured of an easy victory, Langdale."

"You see, you won't lack for challengers," Reg remarked, sidestepping the younger man.

"Now, if you'll excuse me—" he nodded to those assembled, and started for the door.

Bemused, Margaret glanced from Reg's retreating back to her brother's face, which wore the strangest expression. Far from appearing annoyed or offended by the older man's rebuff, Augustus seemed to radiate satisfaction, his well-cut lips curving in a faint but unmistakable smile. *What on earth...?*

But there was no time to think about that now, with the door just closing behind Reg. Recovering her wits, she hurried after him, thankful that everyone else's attention seemed to be focused on her brother.

Her quarry was already halfway down the passage. Stifling a most unladylike curse, Margaret caught up her skirt and quickened her pace, but she still had to take two strides to keep up with his one. "Reg, wait!" she called. "I must speak with you—about Alicia!"

He glanced over his shoulder, slowing his pace but not stopping; his expression was guarded, almost wary. "I haven't got time to talk, Margaret—"

"Then *make* time," she said tautly as she drew level

with him. "You wrote to me when your betrothal was first announced, that you knew what you were doing and that Alicia wouldn't be hurt!"

Reg's mouth set in a stubborn line as he resumed walking. "And I meant it—then and now. Your sister will come to no harm at my hands."

"How can you say that?" she demanded fiercely. "You've just set a wedding date, even though we *both* know that you could never make Alicia happy—and why!"

He did not look at her, nor did he slacken his stride. "Leave it to me, Margaret. I have things under control."

"If that were true, you'd never have allowed them to go this far in the first place!"

Now he paused, though he still avoided her gaze. "I will ensure that Alicia has every opportunity to change her mind before New Year's Eve."

"And if she doesn't?"

He made no reply, and Margaret stared at him in dawning horror. "My God, you'd actually go *through* with this?"

"Whitborough needs a duchess," Reg said curtly, walking on. "Alicia is available and willing. More than willing. I doubt she would thank you for your interference. If she is satisfied with our arrangement and our upcoming nuptials, I don't see that it's any of your business."

They were approaching the stairs now; Margaret caught hold of Reg's arm before he could ascend. "Alicia's well-being *is* my business! She has no mother to guide her now—and I won't stand idly by while she enters into a loveless marriage! If she seems willing, it's only because she doesn't know the whole story!"

Reg rounded on her, his eyes blazing. "Neither do *you*, I might add!"

Margaret matched him glare for glare. "Then enlighten me!"

He exhaled audibly. "A number of things have happened in the last five years, things of which *you* cannot be aware or hope to understand! Indeed, I doubt that any woman *could*."

Margaret ground her teeth at the patronizing note in his voice. "And just what," she began with saccharine sweetness, "are these *terribly* important things that you deem beyond my sex's comprehension?"

"*Private* matters," he emphasized in that same lofty tone, "which are none of your concern, but which have influenced my most recent decisions."

"As 'private' as your association with Captain Hastings?" she flashed.

Reg's expression hardened, and he started up the stairs, pointedly not looking at Margaret. "Hastings is ancient history. I haven't seen him in nearly four years. Nor have I any plans to see him in future, or impose his company upon my prospective duchess."

Margaret stalked after him grimly. "And you think *that*'s enough to make you a fit husband for Alicia?"

Reg shrugged a shoulder. "Time changes us all. Just ask Hastings himself if you don't believe me. Better yet," he added, with the barest hint of a wintry smile, "ask *his wife*."

Margaret halted on the stairs. "His *wife*?" she echoed faintly.

Reg's gaze was as cool and remote as his smile. "Indeed. Who can say what sort of husband a man might make, until he marries? Good morning, Margaret." He lengthened his stride to take two steps at a time, reaching the top of the stairs before she could frame a response.

Gripping the banister, Margaret stared after Reg, his last words ringing in her ears.

Andrew Hastings... he'd been a lieutenant five years ago, a darkly handsome young man, with a lithe, slender build that contrasted dramatically with Reg's broader, heavier frame. But they'd been a striking pair to look at —and apparently inseparable when they'd arrived at Denforth that first Christmas after Hal's death. Playing billiards and endless hands of cards, sharing brandy and cigars by the fire, riding out when the weather permitted, wrestling, fencing, and engaging in all manner of sport together... *He hath every month a new-sworn brother*, Gervase had quoted, watching them from a distance.

He'd spoken perhaps more truly than he knew, Margaret mused. The loss of Hal had left the whole family wounded and vulnerable, even Reg. Despite their fierce rivalry, he'd seemed almost adrift without his older brother to compete against and quarrel with. Initially, Margaret had wondered if Hastings filled some of that void, but without the abrasiveness that had been so much a part of Reg and Hal's relationship. Until the night she'd learned more than she'd ever *wanted* to, about how matters stood between Reg and Hastings.

And now Hastings was married. Was *that* what made Reg believe he could do likewise? Marry, beget children, and live a completely different sort of life? She supposed it was possible—clearly, other men with Reg's preferences did it—but she could not convince herself that it was *fair*. Least of all to the unsuspecting women caught up in such a deception. She had no wish to see Reg publicly disgraced and ruined for his proclivities—nor to be the agent of that ruin—yet neither could she support his marriage to her sister, knowing what she did. Alicia's happiness or Reg's security: why must one be sacrificed for the other?

She trudged upstairs wearily, burdened by a five-year-old secret as well as her own misgivings. No matter what Reg said, she could not believe that he would not ultimately hurt or disappoint Alicia. Her sister still believed she could win his heart. She would be devastated to learn the truth—but wouldn't it be far worse if she discovered it *after* the wedding? And that her own sister had known, but kept it from her? Her sister—and perhaps a few others as well?

Uneasily, Margaret's thoughts circled back to that moment in the gymnasium, when Augustus's seemingly careless remark had raised a ghost from five Christmases past. Did her brother know—about Reg and Hastings? Had he even guessed or sensed what effect his comment would have? Augustus had been only eighteen himself, down from his first term at Oxford, and self-absorbed, in the way undergraduates could be. But he'd never been stupid, or slow on the uptake. And if he hadn't pieced it together then, it was possible he'd done so later.

If Augustus *did* know... that put a whole new face on the matter, especially the way he had acted towards Reg this morning. Almost as if he'd been baiting him. Challenging him in a way that had nothing to do with wrestling matches.

Now that she thought of it, Augustus had never been particularly deferential to Reg—not since childhood, anyway. Even less so now that he'd acceded to the dukedom. Perhaps Augustus's awareness of his position partly accounted for that. Despite the seven years' difference between them, Augustus approached Reg as an equal, neither intimidated by nor envious of the older man. Likewise, Reg did not attempt to dismiss or belittle Augustus the way he often did Jason. Was that due to rank... or was there some other, subtler alchemy at work?

Margaret's temples throbbed, promising a headache of major proportions. At this moment she could not have said which troubled her more: Reg's evasions when it came to Alicia—or her inability to gauge her own brother's thoughts.

She'd reached the Long Gallery, and Reg was nowhere in sight, having most likely gone to ground in his chamber. For a moment, she considered following him and continuing their exchange, but common sense intervened; at this point she would almost certainly do more harm than good.

Keep your emotions in check, Gervase had warned... and so far, she was failing miserably. Crossing the gallery, she tried to focus on her next move. Reg might not have routed her, but he had certainly ambushed her. Defeat, however, was not an option.

She had almost reached her chamber when Alicia's door opened, and her sister peered out, flushed and radiant.

"Meg!" Alicia hailed her delightedly. "I've been *longing* to speak with you! Do you have a minute?"

Margaret's heart sank. All she wanted was her own chamber and a Beecham's Powder to soothe her aching head—along with time to consider her tactics, to formulate another plan. But here was her sister, positively aglow with happiness and no doubt brimming with plans for her big day. She couldn't rebuff her now, nor could she pass up the chance to see if there was some way to persuade Alicia to change her mind. If only she felt more equal to the task before her.

But she dredged up a smile somehow. "Of course,

dearest, for you," she replied, and let herself be drawn inside.

"Isn't it marvelous!" Alicia gushed, leading the way to her dressing room. "I hoped—oh, you know what I hoped—but I never dreamed it would happen today of all days!"

Margaret sat down on the nearest chair. "How did the duchess take the news?"

"Oh, she was wonderful, Meg! I admit, Her Grace used to *terrify* me, but she was so dear today! She kissed me on both cheeks, welcomed me to the family, and said she hoped that Reg and I would be very happy." Alicia danced over to the vanity and picked up a black velvet jewel box. "And just look what she's lent me to wear for the wedding." She opened the box with a flourish. "The Whitborough pearls!"

The pearls in question were a shimmering triple rope, accompanied by matching earrings and pearl-studded combs. Margaret had seen the duchess wear them on several occasions and had been told they would one day be hers, on her marriage to Hal.

"Aren't they splendid?" Alicia asked, beckoning to Berthe.

"Magnificent," Margaret admitted, watching as the maid fastened the pearls around Alicia's slim throat, where they gleamed like perfectly formed spheres of moonlight.

For every pearl a bride wears, she will shed one tear. Margaret shivered as the warning echoed in her head. Had it been their mother or their grandmother who'd said that? She wondered if Alicia remembered that wedding super-stition. If so, she appeared unaffected by it. Or perhaps she believed there would be only *happy* tears at this wedding.

Alicia sat down at the vanity, turning her head this way and that as she admired the necklace in the mirror. "Can you believe I'm to be a bride at last? Oh, Meg, do say you'll be my attendant!" she entreated, turning to stretch out her hands to Margaret. "And I was thinking of asking Juliana too—I know we aren't exactly close, but she's Reg's favorite sister. I'm afraid there's no time to have bridesmaids' dresses made, but I'm sure we can find something suitable."

Margaret forced a smile, giving Alicia's hands a brief squeeze. "I'd be honored to serve as your attendant, dearest." The lie that was not quite a lie left a bitter taste in her mouth; she would have been delighted to be a part of Alicia's wedding... if the groom were different.

Alicia turned back to the mirror. "I'm so lucky to have my gown already made! Monsieur Worth designed the most glorious white satin wedding gown for me when I first came to Paris! I didn't want to *mention* it—you know what they say about not counting one's chickens!—but I thought it might bring me good luck! And it has!" she concluded with a breathless little laugh.

Margaret clenched her hands in her lap, wishing with all her heart that she did not have to cloud her sister's happiness. "Alicia, are you—completely sure that this is what you want?"

Alicia turned around again, eyes wide. "Of course I'm sure! Why wouldn't I be?"

"Well, when we were girls, you used to talk of having a grand wedding," Margaret began. "With lots of guests, and in the spring when your favorite flowers were in bloom—"

"I'm perfectly satisfied with the current plan," Alicia said, a trifle stiffly. "I don't need some ostentatious ceremony at St. George's, Hanover Square. The most important thing is that Reg and I are finally getting married! Nothing else matters."

Margaret hesitated before asking as gently as she could, "Does Reg feel the same way?"

A tiny frown marred Alicia's smooth brow. "Well, surely he must—as *he's* the one who suggested we get married next week! Why would you think otherwise?" A hint of challenge colored her voice.

"It's just that he's dragged his feet for so long," Margaret explained, choosing her words with care. "Don't you find it, well, *odd* that he should have changed his mind so suddenly?"

For a moment, she thought she might have got through to her sister. Then Alicia shrugged and glanced aside. "They say that Christmas is the season of miracles," she remarked, rearranging the scent bottles on the vanity according to height.

And it would take nothing *less* than a miracle to

transform him into a fit husband for Alicia, Margaret reflected somberly. If only she could *say* as much... but she'd promised silence and discretion back then; a woman's word was just as binding as a man's. And as angry as she was with Reg—*and* the duke—for making a pawn of her sister, she couldn't bring herself to reveal a secret that could destroy his entire life. Not until every other approach had been tried. "I just wish I could be certain that Reg was as—whole-hearted about this as you are."

"As long as Reg is there to say his vows, I'll be more than content," Alicia countered, still avoiding her eyes. "After all, weddings are far more important to women than to men."

"Rubbish!" Margaret retorted, feeling her patience fray in spite of her resolve. "Weddings are equally important to men *and* women—or at least they *should* be! And a man who wants to get married usually shows much more enthusiasm about it. I know Alex did!"

Alicia whipped around so abruptly that one of the scent bottles fell over. "So you don't think Reg *wants* to marry me?" Her voice quavered, her blue eyes wide with hurt.

"I didn't say that!" Margaret protested, realizing her mistake too late.

"That's what it *sounded* like!" Tears pooled in her sister's eyes. "Is it because you think I'm too young, too frivolous, or too *stupid* to appeal to him?"

"That's not what I think at all!" Margaret insisted. "If anything, I don't feel Reg is good enough for *you!*" She gentled her voice. "You have so much to offer, dearest. I'd hate to see it wasted on a man who... who doesn't *appreciate* you as he should!"

"I don't believe you!" Alicia's face went stony. "After last night, I thought you'd be *relieved*—that I'm finally marrying the man of my dreams!"

"Alicia, all I meant was—"

"I'm not listening to another word!" Twin flags of scarlet flew on Alicia's cheeks as she leapt to her feet. "Oh, why didn't I see it before? All this nonsense about Reg not appreciating me—what you *really* mean is that you're jealous!"

"*Jealous?*" Margaret echoed incredulously.

"Yes, jealous! Jealous because *I'm* to be the next Duchess of Whitborough, not you! Jealous because Reg has named a wedding date—and Hal never did!"

The injustice of her sister's accusation shocked the breath from Margaret's lungs. "That's not true! Can't you see I just want you to be happy?"

"I'll be happy when I'm married to Reg!" Alicia stormed. "We'll be happy *together*, and no one is going to stop us, least of all *you*!" She stalked over to fling her chamber door open, her eyes steely through their sheen of tears. "And if you can't be happy for me, *dear sister*, then we have nothing more to say to each other!"

Chapter Eleven

HOW THE HELL had the old man managed to talk him into this?

Gervase stared at the stack of books before him, each fatter and more ponderous-looking than the last. Somewhere in those musty pages were the answers to the duke's questions on how to break an entail or—to be more accurate—how to keep his heir firmly under his thumb.

Manipulative bastard. He felt an unwanted twinge of sympathy for Reg. That his brother had agreed to marry Alicia, despite having no great love for her, was a major concession on his part. But still the duke wanted more control: he might accept—even embrace—compromise in the business world, but he shunned it with a vengeance in family life.

So what pressure had he brought to bear upon Reg, to get him to agree to this? It had to have been more than an appeal to sentiment, to judge from what Gervase had heard of their argument last night.

As opposed to Gervase himself, swayed by an unexpected show of fatherly support.

Surveying the stack of books with a jaundiced eye, he decided that he must be going soft in the head. How else could the duke have got past his carefully constructed defenses? If he'd any sense, he'd have told the old man to find another pet solicitor to do his bidding.

But even now he could feel his father's hand on his shoulder, see the keen blue eyes looking into his, hear the coaxing, almost gentle note in the older man's voice. Having seen the duke's tactics in action more times than he could count, he'd thought himself proof against all that. And yet a single appeal to his loyalty had been enough to blow him from his moorings.

No, that wasn't *entirely* accurate. It was more that, for the first time in recent memory, the duke had seemed interested in what might be going on with *him*, in *his* life. For once, just once, had his father seen the person instead of the pawn?

Gervase swallowed, his throat suddenly tight, even as he berated himself for this descent into sentimentality. Would he ever, deep down, stop wishing for his father's approval, or even just his attention? He'd made a success of himself without either, and he was damned proud of that. But... he couldn't deny that his father's support would have been welcome, then.

So, better late than never? Or was it merely that Whitborough now found Gervase's career convenient to his own schemes? And could it do any harm simply to *look* at these damn books, see what was in them? He could always change his mind later.

As if in a trance, he reached for a book, drew it towards him, opened the faded cover...

"Burning the midnight oil already, and it's not even noon," a familiar, acerbic voice remarked from over his shoulder.

Only a lifetime of training kept Gervase from jumping out of his skin. He took a moment to don his cool façade before glancing up from the book. "Good morning, Mother."

She regarded him with equal coolness. "Dare I ask what you've been set to work upon? Unless your exertions are your own idea, in which case I apologize in advance."

"What do *you* think I'm working on?" he inquired provocatively.

Her brows arched elegantly. "At a guess, whatever business your father has requested."

Again he strove to keep his face impassive; the woman was uncanny. "I congratulate you on your perspicacity. Either that, or your superior network of household spies."

True to form, the duchess did not deny the latter, nor did she appear the least abashed. "I like to keep my hand in things." She regarded the stack of books with a critical air. "They all look highly indigestible."

"They do," he agreed without enthusiasm, closing the one in his hands. "I'd as soon work my way through the whole of English common law again." Setting the book aside, he regarded her quizzically. "So what brings you here, *Maman*? I thought you'd be with my sisters, helping to plan Reg's wedding."

"I was looking for your father, actually," the duchess replied, seating herself in the chair directly across from him. "But he seems to have made himself scarce."

Wise man, Gervase thought, but was just prudent enough not to say. "Perhaps he's occupied with wedding business as well. There must be any number of details to oversee."

"Indeed. God—and your father are in the details."

The dry note in the duchess's voice had Gervase eyeing her with increased speculation.

He had, he realized, almost no idea of how his mother felt about her favorite son's impending nuptials —or his chosen bride. She'd been fond of Margaret and Alicia as girls, and had favored the match between Margaret and Hal, but that had been so many years ago. Might her sentiments have altered when it came to *Reg's* future?

"I gather the happy couple have informed you of their plans," he observed. "After so long a betrothal, doesn't it surprise you that they should be marrying so quickly now?"

She gave a Gallic shrug. "They've been altar-bound for nearly five years—I wouldn't describe that as 'quickly.'"

"I'm astonished that it wasn't ten years, given the way Reg has been dragging his feet," Gervase countered.

"Don't you find it the least bit odd that he's reversed himself like this?"

"It is Reg's decision to make." Was his mother avoiding his eyes? "I've told him that he has my support in whatever he chooses to do."

No surprise there, Gervase mused. The duchess had been Reg's staunchest advocate since the day he was born.

"And Alicia is a beautiful, accomplished, virtuous young woman," she continued. "If not perhaps the one whom I would have chosen right away for Reg."

"Whom *would* you have chosen, then?" At least he knew that Margaret was out of the running. "Or would you have preferred that he make his own choice and marry for love?"

"Marriages for love are frequently overrated," observed the woman whose tempestuous union had been the stuff of local legend for the last thirty years. "But I suppose—on balance—that they're preferable to the alternative. I can't really say that I had a prospective bride in mind for your brother. On the contrary, I found it difficult to think of a woman who would suit him. And so," she added on a sigh, "your father and Alicia's father made their arrangement."

"But they could have got out of it, though, couldn't they?" he pressed on. "If Alicia had met someone she preferred—"

"She'd have far to seek before she found a prize like Reg!" his mother declared emphatically. "Handsome, rich, heir to a dukedom..." She paused, a shadow flickering across her face. "I loved Hal dearly, and I grieved for him, but Reg is by far the stronger character. And Alicia's adored him since she was a little girl."

"Reg doesn't appear to adore *her* in return," Gervase pointed out.

The duchess shrugged again. "So he'll never rank among the great lovers of the age. He's marrying her on New Year's Eve—that should be enough for her. *And* for your father as well. Which reminds me," she fixed Gervase with a piercing stare, "eight years ago, I stood by you—and against *him*—when you wished to pursue a career in law rather than enter the Church. I exacted no promise from you then, but I would like you to remember it all the same."

"Because you wish me to promise you something *now*?" Gervase met her gaze squarely, recognizing the same appeal to loyalty that his father had made, though couched in different terms. His mother was attempting to call in a favor—and they both knew it.

She flushed slightly but her gaze did not falter. "I wish you to consider, very carefully, which side you should be on—not just for now but for the future. And as I am a woman of my word, I will make good on my other, more recent promise as well. Whatever Harold has offered you, I will offer more."

Her eyes bored into his, the eyes of a lioness watching—and assessing her prey. Gervase could not tell what she saw in his face, which he suspected was no longer as impassive as he wished, but after a moment, she drew back just a trifle. "Do we understand each other?"

It took him a moment to find his voice, another to master it. "Perfectly." To his relief, the reply emerged with a cool indifference worthy of the "Clockwork Solicitor."

"Splendid." The direction of the duchess's gaze shifted suddenly. "Ah, Margaret," she said in a very different tone. "Good morning, my dear."

Gervase stilled, then slowly turned his head to see Margaret standing in the doorway, regarding him and his mother with undisguised curiosity.

"GOOD MORNING, DUCHESS," Margaret replied, glancing uncertainly between mother and son. Was she just imagining the tension simmering between them? Or had her nerve-wracking encounters with Reg and Alicia that made her preternaturally sensitive to that? "And congratulations," she added, reminding herself that the duchess's view of the impending nuptials was likely very different from her own. "On the wedding—you must be so pleased."

"Thank you, *ma chere*." The duchess inclined her head, her exquisitely boned face a mask of perfect courtesy. "When it comes to the wedding, well... words fail me." Then, as Margaret blinked at her dry tone, the older woman rose from her chair. "Now, if you'll both excuse me, I have some business to attend to. Gervase," she turned to her son, "I trust you will remember what I said?"

"How could I not, *Maman?*" he returned, his voice equally dry.

The duchess patted his cheek with an elegant, long-fingered hand. "*Très bien, chéri.* I'll see you both at luncheon," she added over her shoulder, as she swept from the room.

Margaret stared after her bemusedly. "Just—what was that about?" she asked, turning to Gervase, still seated at the table and staring at a tall stack of books in front of him.

"Nothing you need trouble yourself with, darling." He pushed away the books, glanced up at her with the beginnings of a smile that faded as he regarded her more closely. "What's wrong, Margaret?"

The concern in his voice, in his gaze, made her own eyes sting. She blinked them furiously and tried for a reassuring smile, only to give up the attempt when she felt her lips tremble. "Does it show so blatantly?"

"Only to me. What happened, *ma belle?*"

Her sigh caught in her throat. "I tried talking sense into your brother and my sister—and failed abysmally," she confessed. "Reg essentially told me to mind my own business, and now Alicia isn't speaking to me because she thinks I'm jealous that she's to be the next Duchess of Whitborough. Oh, and she reminded me that, unlike Reg, Hal never set a wedding date."

Gervase winced. "I've heard women always go for each other's most vulnerable spots in a quarrel. Even *my* sisters, who rowed far less than my brothers and I ever did."

Margaret swallowed, still feeling the smart of Alicia's accusation. "It wasn't that scratch about Hal that hurt most—please don't think that! It's that she believes I'd let jealousy over something so petty spoil our relationship."

"Poor darling."

The caress in his voice warmed her more than the

finest brandy, and she fought back a rush of tears. "My own fault—I made a mess of the whole business, with *both* of them."

Pushing back his chair, Gervase held out his arms without a word, and she surprised herself by walking into them. And was even more surprised when he drew her down onto his lap and gathered her in, arms enfolding her as if she were something infinitely precious. Cherished, even. Breathing out in a tremulous sigh, she relaxed into his embrace. Until that moment she hadn't realized how badly she needed comfort just now. How strange—and yet *not* strange that Gervase should know that.

"Leave it be, then," he advised. "At least for now. No point in making bad worse." He brushed his lips against the crown of her head. "I suspect Alicia was too angry to think rationally and said what she knew would cause you the most pain. But she *is* your sister, and you do love one another. I am certain the rift will mend—if you don't force the issue too much."

"But how can I not?" Margaret protested. "I can't just stand by and let this disaster of a marriage take place!"

Gervase drew back just a little, scanning her face intently. "I have not asked before, darling, but *why* are you so adamant that Reg and Alicia not marry? When you said he wouldn't make her happy—"

"I meant every word," she broke in vehemently, "and I believe it with all my heart! But I *cannot* share my reasons with you. Can you not take my word for it?"

A faint frown creased his brow, but after a moment, he gave a reluctant nod. "Very well. I know this is not something that you would say lightly."

"Thank you. I *would* tell you, if I could! But it's such a *sensitive* matter—and I gave my word..." she trailed off, sighing again. "Conflicting loyalties are the very devil, aren't they?"

"They certainly are."

A strange inflection in his voice caught her attention; he was looking at the stack of books again, his expression unreadable. Margaret studied him thoughtfully, remembering that odd little exchange between him and the duchess.

"Gervase, what exactly did your mother want?" she inquired—and felt the sudden tension in his body, even though his arms remained relaxed around her.

"Oh, the usual," he replied, after a moment. "Ammunition against Father, and safe conduct for Reg. She believes I can provide both."

"Why would she think that?'

"Well, it's—complicated." His mouth crooked up. "But then, isn't everything, when it comes to my family?"

Margaret blinked, as bemused as ever by the inner workings of the Lyons clan. "Why does your mother think your father's working against Reg?"

"Because he is?" Gervase offered, a glint of wry amusement in his eyes. "My mother's instincts are all too accurate in this case. For as long as I can remember, Father has desired control over his children, especially his sons, and Reg has always resisted him."

"So have *you*," Margaret pointed out. "You might not make as much noise about it as Reg, but you've gone your own way and *not* let your parents tangle you in their schemes."

His gaze shifted suddenly, almost furtively, away from her. "Ah, well, as to that..."

"Gervase." Margaret eyed him with growing apprehension; on the rare occasions she could remember him losing his composure, his family had invariably been the cause. Slipping a finger under his chin, she turned his face towards her until they were eye to eye. "What *precisely* do Their Graces want you to do?"

He did not look away this time, but she could sense his discomfort. "As it happens, both of my parents wish to engage my services, in matters related to the estate."

"In what way? You might as well tell me, you know," she added. "Because, it's clearly troubling you, and no true friend would let you tie yourself in knots over this." She wound her arms about his neck, keeping him tethered to her side. "Let me help, Gervase. Please."

He drew a long breath. "This could—this could take a while..."

❄

HE TOLD HER FINALLY, choosing his words with meticulous care, feeling as tongue-tied and awkward as a schoolboy giving his first recitation. And watched the deepening confusion on her face as she tried to take it all in.

Afterwards, she massaged her temples and shook her head dazedly. "I took a Beecham's Powder half an hour ago. I now feel sorely in need of another. *And* the more I hear about your parents, the more convinced I am that I will *never* understand them!"

"You wouldn't be the first to reach that conclusion," he observed dryly.

"So, let me get this straight," she began, folding her hands in her lap. "Your father is offering you the earth to find ways to strip the wealth from the estate, to ensure that Reg accedes to all his demands. Your mother is offering you the moon to find ways to stop him. And for some inexplicable reason, you have not told them *both* to go to perdition—"

"I'm waiting to see which of them will throw in the sun and the stars as an incentive."

Margaret huffed an exasperated breath. "Has anyone ever told you that you're far too clever for your own good?'

"Yes, on a number of occasions. Sometimes I even agree with them." He felt his lips twist in a smile that mocked everyone—himself most of all. "*I eat the air, promise-crammed. You cannot feed capons so.*"

She pulled a face, whether at the quotation or its underlying sentiment he did not dare to ask. "It's like an eternal game of badminton, with you as the shuttlecock! Don't you tire of it?"

He exhaled wearily. "More than you can imagine, but... it's the Lyons way. Intrigue and manipulation are in our blood."

Notice me, Father. Notice me. He could hear the boy who still lived inside of him urging, *pleading*—despite his grown self's attempts to silence that plea. So many years as the forgotten son, vying for his father's attention. School honors, examination results, form reports... all the prizes he'd striven for in the hope that it might make a difference. It so seldom had. Perhaps a moment or two of approval, before the duke turned to praise Hal's score in a cricket match or even Jason's progress on his new pony.

Not that Hal had found their father's commendation so great a reward, laced as it always was with advice on how he could improve. He could remember his brother complaining on one such occasion, "If my team wins by ten points, Father will tell me how we could have won by twenty! He's never satisfied!"

And his mother, who tried to be more even-handed with her affections, but could never quite hide her own partiality towards Reg. That moment when she'd supported Gervase's wish to pursue a career of *his* choosing might have been the closest they'd ever been. How much did he owe her for that? Had she the right to demand his allegiance to Reg, who had always struck him as more than capable of fighting his own battles? If their positions were somehow reversed and *he* was the ducal heir, would she be pressuring Reg to help him avoid their father's subtle snares? He doubted it.

"Gervase." Margaret's voice and touch recalled him to the present; he turned his head to find her studying him with concern. "You *know* you don't need their approval, don't you?"

She nestled, warm and sweet, within his arms, but despite their physical closeness, he felt suddenly, almost overwhelmingly apart from her in that moment. She did not understand. Indeed, how could she? The Langdales had loved their children equally—or done a far better job of concealing their preferences. Easy for *her* to tell him to wash his hands of his parents!

He swallowed, doing his best to extinguish the spark of anger; she didn't deserve that from him, not after the morning she'd had so far. "Yes, I know." On a purely rational level, he understood that he did not need his parents' approval. Which didn't stop him from *wanting* it... and that was something he suspected even Margaret couldn't help him with. Still less would she understand the twinge of perverse satisfaction he felt at their attempts to win his loyalty, after years of inattention... a satisfaction of which he was almost—but not quite —ashamed.

Well, he'd be damned if he let this tug-of-war spoil things with Margaret. Or his Christmas, for that matter.

He'd waited almost all his life for his parents' recognition; they could wait a few more days for his—if he chose to grant it.

Resolutely, he turned again to the woman he held in his arms. So sweet and so good—a better, kinder, more generous person than he could ever hope to be—and far more deserving of his attention than his parents' ancient grudge. "I suspect that this, like my brother's wedding, is a subject better left for another time," he remarked, settling Margaret more firmly on his knee.

She raised quizzical brows. "Avoiding the issue?"

"Just—putting it aside for now. To focus on something a good deal pleasanter." He leaned in and kissed her, a long, lingering kiss meant to draw out the strain and tension from them both. From her soft sigh of response, he gathered he'd succeeded, and encouraged, he kissed his way down the smooth column of her throat, ending just before the topmost button of her blouse. Margaret shivered pleasurably, her dark eyes slumberous and half-lidded.

He caressed her cheek. "Might I come to you again, tonight?"

She smiled, twining her arms about his neck. "I'd be greatly disappointed if you did not."

"Heaven knows I cannot bear to disappoint a beautiful woman." Deftly, he unfastened the top two buttons of her blouse, slid his fingers inside to stroke the upper swell of a breast just above her corset. Margaret made a low, urgent sound in her throat, leaning into his touch and reaching for *his* shirt buttons. Heat rushed to his groin, an unnecessary reminder that his body was quite willing—and able—to resume what they'd started the night before.

The knock on the library door had them springing apart, breathless and wild-eyed.

"Damn," Gervase muttered, throwing Margaret an apologetic glance. "I knew I should have locked the door. Who is it?" he called, more loudly.

"Elaine. May I come in?"

Margaret all but leapt off his lap, hurrying to put the expanse of the table between them as she hastily buttoned up her blouse. Gervase took a few moments to smooth his shirtfront and grimly will his overeager body to quiescence before granting his sister admittance.

She entered the room with a buoyant step. "I thought you'd like to know, Ger—the actors have arrived. The ones who'll be performing tomorrow night. Father wants us all to come and meet them, show our hospitality—oh, Margaret!" she greeted her friend. "I didn't realize you were in here too. My heavens, have you both spent the whole morning in the library?"

Gervase shrugged, deliberately casual. "*I* have, but Margaret just got here. I'd be happy to come along in a minute, Lainey—what sort of company are they?"

As familiar with the Bard as he, she recited, "*The best actors in the world, either for tragedy, comedy, history, pastoral, pastoral-comical, historical-pastoral, tragical-historical, tragical-comical-historical-pastoral—*"

"*Scene individable or poem unlimited,*" Gervase finished for her, hearing Margaret stifle a giggle. "*Then came each actor on his ass.* Have you seen them perform before?"

"No, but Madeline has," Elaine replied. "She says they're quite a decent troupe, and you know how exacting *she* can be."

"High praise indeed," Gervase observed. Still, none of the Lyons family ever had to feign enthusiasm for the theater. Rising, he offered a decorous arm to both Elaine and Margaret. "Very well, Lainey. Take us to meet these '*abstracts and brief chroniclers of the time.*'"

"*The play's the thing,*" Margaret chimed in brightly, mistress of herself once more.

Linking arms, they left the library in perfect amity.

Chapter Twelve

When lovely woman stoops to folly...
—OLIVER GOLDSMITH, *The Vicar of Wakefield*

THE SPICY SCENT of evergreens perfumed the Great Hall, but even their fragrance was no match for the savory smells wafting from the laden plates and chafing dishes on the sideboard. Margaret eyed a platter of tarts hungrily, grateful for the hum of surrounding conversations that masked her stomach's unladylike grumbling.

"Oh, I'm absolutely famished!" Elaine declared, joining her at the sideboard. "I hardly know what to sample first, but those tarts seem an excellent place to start. Jam or mince, Margaret? Or," her dimples, as beguiling as her brother's, deepened, "would you prefer one of each, as I do?"

Margaret laughed, reaching for a small plate. "Oh, the latter, most certainly!"

Together she and Elaine helped themselves to two tarts apiece, and went to sit in the window embrasure of the Great Hall, buzzing with activity like an overturned beehive—which should come as no surprise on the afternoon of Christmas Eve. The children had been sent upstairs just ten minutes ago to take tea in the nursery. Now their distracted elders hurried hither and yon, to place brightly wrapped parcels under the Christmas tree.

Alasdair had just ordered Elaine off her feet for the time being, while he dealt with the heavier and bulkier of their children's presents. Over in one corner, Hugo and Reg were wrestling with the rocking horse—intended for Harry—beneath Madeline's critical eye.

"I don't know why you attempted to wrap the thing, Hugo," she remarked. "Harry will know exactly what it is just from the shape."

"But tearing off the paper is half the fun of Christmas, my love," he pointed out.

"He has you there, *chérie*," the duchess remarked, smiling at her daughter as she paused to survey Hugo and Reg's efforts. "And as the mother of several rambunctious sons, I can attest to that! Every inch of the floor would be *covered* with ribbons and paper on Christmas morning!"

Margaret chuckled, recalling her stepsons' enthusiasm about unwrapping presents.

"Daughters do their share as well!" Elaine called from the window seat. "Beatrice adores unwrapping gifts—the faster the better! *And* she's forever poking, prying, and trying to figure out her gifts by shape, beforehand."

"You were the exact same way," the duchess observed fondly. "And so was Madeline. Juliana was the only one of my girls patient enough to wait until the actual day."

"That's because I love surprises," Juliana chimed in from where she and Alicia were arranging a pile of parcels under the tree. "Although I'm sure Harry will love his rocking horse even if he does guess what it is," she added, smiling at Hugo, who grinned back.

"Next year, a pony," he predicted. "And I won't need to worry about wrapping *that*." He got to his feet and with Reg's help, carried the rocking horse over to the tree.

A footman entered the Hall and approached Reg, holding out a silver salver. "Two letters in the afternoon post for you, Lord Reginald."

Accepting his mail, Reg frowned briefly at one letter, slipping it into his breast pocket, but opened the second with alacrity. His face darkened almost at once. "Damnation!" he snarled, balling up the letter in his fist.

Everyone turned to stare at him, save for the footman, who made a strategic retreat.

"*Mon cher*, whatever is the matter?" the duchess asked, all concern.

"The Melton man has accepted a higher offer on the horse I wished to purchase," Reg replied, not quite through clenched teeth.

"Oh, that is too bad!" the duchess exclaimed, amid a chorus of commiserations from Reg's sisters and brothers-in-law. "Could you wire him back with a better offer?"

"No." Reg bit off the word. "According to him, the buyer was insistent on having the hunter delivered to its new home by Christmas Day."

"Bad luck, old boy!" Hugo remarked. "But you still have that splendid black of yours."

"Indeed," the duchess added with another sympathetic moue. "And I am certain you will find another hunter just as fine once you start looking again."

Reg's face remained stony, his mouth set in a hard line. "Except that I wanted *this* one, to ride in the St. Stephen's Day hunt!"

His mother laid a hand against his cheek. "You wouldn't be the first to be disappointed at Christmas, *chéri*. I feel for you, but pray don't sulk. It makes you look like a petulant schoolboy, which becomes you not at all."

Margaret looked away, hiding a smile at the astringent note in the duchess's voice. Doubtless it was her own vexation with Reg that made her relish the spectacle of his mother, usually so indulgent of his moods and tempers, treating him like a spoiled child, pouting over a denied sweet.

"It's Christmas Eve, *mon fils*," the duchess continued, her expression softening. "Far too magical a time to waste dwelling on regrets, instead of blessings. Now, come and taste the champagne I've chosen for tonight. Our guests should have only the finest reward for their efforts, and you know how I rely upon your palate."

Reg grunted, but allowed himself to be led from the room by Her Grace.

Margaret dropped her gaze to her plate and bit savagely into her jam tart. Reg showed more passion over that damned horse than he did over Alicia! The thought sent a pang through her and she glanced over at her sister, who had left the tree and was adjusting the garland of holly and ivy draped over the mantelpiece. She'd tried to make peace over breakfast that morning, but while Alicia had not exactly snubbed her, neither had she seemed overly receptive to the olive branch. Indeed, she'd avoided Margaret for most of the day, and even now, she clearly preferred anyone else's company to her sister's.

Don't force the issue, Gervase had advised. And as painful as Margaret found this distance between Alicia and herself, she knew that he was right. She had to give her sister time—and hope that they'd be speaking again long before New Year's Eve!

And she still had to find a way to stop the wedding. Or perhaps Reg would come to his senses and see how wrong this was. He'd said Alicia would have every opportunity to change her mind... and, despite being furious with him, she knew him to be a man of his word.

"Good heavens, what *are* they carrying?" Elaine's voice broke into her thoughts.

Margaret followed her friend's gaze to see Gervase and Jason entering the Great Hall, bearing a huge, gaily wrapped box between them. As they proceeded further into the room, Gervase happened to glance up at the chandelier and changed course immediately, skirting the dangling bunch of mistletoe en route to the Christmas tree.

"Gerry!" Juliana protested, glowering at him reproachfully.

"You'll have more than your share of unwary fellows falling victim to *that* later," he pointed out, as he and Jason set down the box with an air of relief.

"Spoilsport!" she accused.

He bowed, not bothering to deny it. "At your service, brat."

Elaine chuckled, polished off her mince tart, and left the window seat, heading for the tree. Margaret followed, as curious as her friend.

"Whatever is that, Ger?" Elaine asked, gesturing at the box.

"Richenda's Christmas present. And one of my better inspirations, if I do say so myself," he added with a dimpled smile of satisfaction.

"Is it a dollhouse?" Margaret asked. She'd owned a fine one herself when she was Richenda's age, filled with cunning, beautifully made miniature furnishings.

He shook his head. "She has one of those already. No, it's a toy theater, complete with stage, props, costumes, and actors. According to Madeline, Richenda's growing as partial to plays and performing as *she* ever was."

"It sounds marvelous!" Elaine declared. "Although," she glanced at their older sister, presently filling a plate at the sideboard, "I suspect Madeline will want to play with it too, once she sees it!"

"I suspect we all will." Margaret smiled as she remembered the countless plays and amateur theatricals that had enlivened their childhood.

"Ger's presents aren't half-bad," Jason remarked, with the air of one making a great concession. "Almost as good as Father's, sometimes."

"High praise indeed—thank you, Jason," his brother said dryly.

Impervious to irony, the boy went on, "I still have the pearl-handled pocketknife you gave me when I was twelve. It's better than anything I ever got from Hal or Reg."

"Talking of Brother Reg, we passed him on our way in, looking like a veritable thundercloud," Gervase observed. "Dare I ask what we missed?"

Margaret shrugged. "Just a bit of bad news for him. He got a letter saying that the horse he'd offered for was sold to another buyer."

"*Someone else* bought the horse Reg wanted?" Jason's eyes were bright with interest—and more than a touch of malice. "Ha! Do him good not to get everything he wants for once!"

"Keep your satisfaction to yourself, whelp," Gervase advised, eyeing him sternly. "Unless you want Reg taking it out of your hide the next time you see him."

Jason jutted out a defiant chin. "*I'm* not afraid of Reg!"

"Well, you *should* be, as he's got height, weight, and reach on you—as well as the devil's own temper when roused," Gervase pointed out.

"A temper that *you* seem to delight in rousing," Elaine

chimed in, quite tartly for her. "Really, Jason, must you *both* be such children about things? Why can't we all just have a peaceful Christmas for a change?"

Jason ignored her. "I'd like to see Reg try anything with Father there to stop him!"

"Who says Father will be anywhere near, when it happens?" Gervase countered, and nodded in grim satisfaction when the boy blanched visibly. "Act your age, Jason. Gloat if you must, but have the sense to do so in private."

Jason hunched a sulky shoulder, but made no further argument.

"Mama took Reg off to taste the champagne she wishes to serve tonight," Elaine reported. "I think she hopes to put him in a better mood."

"Inspired of her," Gervase remarked. "When all else fails, try liquor."

"Or food," Elaine suggested, nodding towards the sideboard. "Why don't we all go and have something to eat? I've heard we're to have only a light dinner, because of the play tonight. Though there will be a supper to follow."

"Are there mince tarts?" Jason inquired eagerly.

His sister dimpled at him. "Need you ask? A whole platter of them. But you'd best hurry before Hugo and Alasdair finish the lot!'

Jason strode off with alacrity, and Elaine prepared to follow, glancing over her shoulder at the other two. "Ger, Margaret—are you coming?"

"Oh, in a minute," Margaret replied a trifle vaguely, as—unseen by Elaine—Gervase's hand came to rest at the small of her back. An unspoken message she had no difficulty interpreting: *Stay*.

"I need to check something under the tree, first," Gervase added, smooth as ever.

Elaine eyed them with speculation, then gave a light shrug as she turned away. "Well, I'll see you presently, I suppose."

Elaine was halfway across the room when Margaret felt Gervase's hand at her elbow, guiding her around the Christmas tree, until they were shielded from view. Before she could venture a single question, he'd pulled her into his arms and into a kiss that made the room whirl around her. Relieved, she twined her arms about his neck and kissed him back.

"Mmm," she sighed against his mouth. "Who needs mistletoe?"

"My thoughts exactly. I hope I don't require the presence of holiday greenery in order to kiss you, *belle amie*," he murmured.

Margaret shivered, feeling his presence through every inch of her skin. Intimacy with Alex had been wholly satisfying, but with Gervase... she felt as though she'd stumbled onto some undiscovered country where everything seemed sharper, brighter, and far more intense than she was accustomed to. And yet, within that country, she felt more keenly alive than perhaps she ever had.

By night Gervase was a passionate, attentive lover. By day, he was much as he always was: her friend, confidant, and occasional sparring partner. Their love affair was a delicious secret, known only to themselves, although judging from Elaine's expression just now, Margaret wasn't sure how much longer it could *remain* so.

The prospect of discovery daunted her more than a little. Although, on reflection, she thought Gervase's siblings would have the least difficulty accepting the situation. His parents' reaction was less easy to predict—especially that of the duke, with his distressing tendency to meddle in his children's personal lives. Like his scheme to match her with Reg after Hal's death, which had sent her fleeing from Denforth five Christmases ago. What a disaster *that* would have been—even worse, perhaps, than Reg and Alicia's impending marriage was likely to be!

"Margaret." Gervase's fingers ghosted over her cheek. "Where did you go?"

She smiled up at him, leaned into his embrace. "Nowhere important, I assure you. In fact, I couldn't possibly improve upon where I am just now."

"Flattery will get you—somewhere." He stole another kiss.

"I was hoping it might," she whispered back. They already had plans to tryst tonight, after the play, and the prospect of seeing in Christmas morning together secretly thrilled her.

Approaching footsteps on the other side of the tree had them quickly drawing apart, smoothing their clothes, and assuming positions of complete decorum.

"Right over there, James," Augustus's voice ordered crisply.

"Very good, Your Grace."

Margaret exchanged a glance with Gervase before peering around the tree. Her brother, looking every inch the duke, was supervising the placement of several parcels. No doubt he felt it beneath his aristocratic dignity to handle Christmas gifts himself when there were servants in plenty to do it for him!

He glanced in her direction and that moment, nodded a greeting. "Good evening, Margaret. I hope you are enjoying Christmas Eve."

"Yes, very much." Margaret wondered when they'd grown so formal with each other. Had her younger brother always been so difficult to know, or had he merely become so, over the years? "I hope you are as well," she added, trying to lessen the constraint between them.

"Indeed." He favored her with a slight smile. "And looking forward to the play tonight."

"I believe we all are, Langdale," Gervase said, emerging from behind the tree in turn. "According to Madeline, Mr. and Mrs. Brand head a very talented company of actors, which includes three of their children."

Augustus's face became smooth and impassive once more. "I don't doubt their quality. Nothing but the best for Whitborough, after all."

Was there an edge to his voice? Margaret slid a glance at Gervase and saw from his narrowed eyes and his suddenly guarded expression that he'd registered the same thing.

"Well, I certainly hope they're the best!" she said brightly, trying to defuse the situation. "Madeline said the company spent the whole day rehearsing in the duke's private theater."

"Any word on what they will be performing?" Augustus inquired.

"Not a one," Gervase replied. "The production is shrouded in secrecy, despite numerous attempts by my sisters to discover more. Although as near as I can tell, it won't be a pantomime or a Nativity piece. Not tonight, anyway."

A peal of feminine laughter rang out just then, followed by a triumphant cry of "Caught!" from Juliana.

Reg was standing under the chandelier, the mistletoe almost brushing the crown of his head. Tipping his head back, he regarded the beribboned spray with mingled amusement and annoyance. "Are you serious, infant?"

"It's tradition, Reg," Juliana insisted. "And since you're the first man to pass under the mistletoe this afternoon—"

"An *engaged* man," he pointed out, and Margaret saw Alicia duck her head self-consciously. "Surely a bachelor would be a more appropriate choice for this."

Juliana shook her head, smiling. "No exceptions, Reg! If you're caught beneath the mistletoe, the forfeit is a kiss!"

"What forfeit could be sweeter?" Augustus spoke up, his voice silky. "And what could be more fitting than a mistletoe kiss between an affianced pair? Would you not agree, Major?"

Margaret tensed, hearing the challenge beneath her brother's words. "Augustus," she began in a low voice, but all his attention was fixed on their sister's betrothed.

Reg stood very still, but Margaret thought she saw his moustache twitch like the whiskers of an irascible tiger, as his gaze and Augustus's met and clashed. For a moment, the air between them seemed to crackle with barely suppressed hostility. Then, surprisingly, Reg glanced aside first and held out his hand to Alicia, whose fiery blush was visible even from across the room. "Well, my lady, shall we uphold tradition?"

Cheeks still scarlet, Alicia came forward and Margaret's heart twisted when she saw the hope in her sister's eyes. "Of course, Reg," she said, a trifle breathlessly, joining him under the mistletoe and turning her face up to him in happy expectation.

They were a striking couple, Margaret had to admit, despite or perhaps even because of their similar coloring. But Reg's tall, powerful build made Alicia's dainty figure appear slighter and more delicate.

Without a word, Reg lowered his head and kissed Alicia on the mouth—the first time Margaret could remember him doing so. And Alicia reached out, seeking, desiring more, her small hands coming to rest over her intended's heart.

As abruptly as he'd initiated the kiss, Reg ended it and stepped back, opening the distance between himself and his affianced bride. He did not push Alicia's hands away but they hovered uncertainly in the air for a moment, before—flushing for an entirely different reason now—she lowered them once more to her sides.

Margaret's own hands fisted, the world going sharp-edged and red-tinged around her. At that moment, she could not have said with whom she was angriest: Reg, Augustus, even Juliana with her innocent mistletoe gambit. Because surely everyone in the Great Hall must see it now: the extent of Reg's indifference. She could tell by the uncomfortable silence that succeeded the kiss, which might otherwise have been followed by laughter and cheers... if both halves of the couple had shown any enthusiasm for what they were doing. The only satisfaction she could sense was radiating from Augustus—in the form of a smirk she longed to wipe from his face!

Incensed, Margaret opened her mouth to deliver a stinging remark, when Gervase gave her elbow a warning squeeze that recalled her to her senses just in time. It would be Alicia, not Augustus, who would be hurt most by her outburst, who did not deserve further humiliation. With difficulty, she swallowed her anger, though the unspoken words seemed to burn under her tongue like hot coals, and tried to think of a way to dispel the tension that shrouded the room.

Fortunately, distraction arrived just then in the form of the duke and duchess, entering the Great Hall together—side by side, if not hand in hand.

"My children," the duke began in his most commanding tone, smiling about the room, "if I may have your attention?"

He hardly needed to ask: such was the Whitboroughs' combined presence that all eyes turned to them at once.

Smiling, the duke stepped aside and beckoned to a phalanx of footmen, who now entered, dragging behind them a sled bearing an enormous piece of wood—big enough to burn throughout the next twelve days, as tradition decreed.

Striking a pose, Whitborough recited with great dramatic flair: "*Come, bring with a noise / My merry, merry boys, / The Christmas log to the firing; /While my good dame, she,*" he gestured towards his wife, "*Bids ye all be free, / And drink to your heart's desiring.*"

More than one person exclaimed in delight at the sight of the log, and Juliana hurried to fetch the tinder-box, along with a remnant of the previous year's log, retained for the very purpose of igniting this year's blaze.

In the excitement of readying the log for the fire, the lingering awkwardness of Reg and Alicia's perfunctory mistletoe kiss dissipated, though Margaret knew her sister would not forget, any more than she would. But it was still Christmas Eve, a time of hope and magic, so she held her tongue and helped the other women drape sweet-scented evergreens over the log, watched as the duchess doused it in brandy, and stood back as the duke strode up to the fireplace. Looking as majestic as Prospero, he turned to face them and recited the last verse of Herrick's poem:

> *"With the last year's brand*
> *Light the new block, and*
> *For good success in his spending,*
> *On your Psaltries play,*
> *That sweet luck may*
> *Come while the log is a-tending."*

He nodded to Jason, who, aglow with his own importance, came forward to light the fire. And with a great roar, the log flared up, sending bright flames leaping toward the chimney. Margaret caught her breath at the sight—and in spite of everything, felt a glimmer of the joy and anticipation that was Christmas take root in her soul. Glancing at Gervase, she saw that same enchantment reflected in his eyes.

Unseen, her hand crept into his, felt the warmth of his answering clasp. Together, along with the others, they stood in silence, watching the Yule log burn.

※

THE APRICOT BROCADE, with its pattern of formal flowers in flame and gold, was the most brightly colored gown Margaret owned, and she almost lost the nerve to wear it after Tilda laid it out across the bed where it blazed like a bonfire against the counterpane. But gaslight would soften it, and she knew the vivid color flattered her more than pastels would. She decided to keep her jewels simple by comparison, choosing a delicate necklace of gold filigree and matching earrings. Looking at her reflection in the mirror, she felt a glow of satisfaction that warmed her to her toes.

"You look lovely, my lady," Tilda said, draping a gold tissue shawl about her shoulders.

"Thank you, Tilda." Margaret looped her gilt reticule about her wrist and started for the door. "Well, I shall certainly be difficult to misplace in a crowd! By the way, I don't know when I'll be back tonight, so please just go to bed! I'll see you in the morning."

"Very good, my lady."

To Margaret's surprise and pleasure, Gervase was waiting for her at the foot of the stairs. His eyes widened most gratifyingly, and she barely resisted the urge to preen.

"*O, she doth teach the torches to burn bright.*" His smile was as brilliant as the torches he spoke of.

Margaret blushed. "Too flattering, dear friend! I might not dare to wear this color if we weren't spending the next three hours or so sitting in the dark!"

Gervase shook his head. "Don't hide your light under a bushel, *ma belle*. Take pride in it—*I* certainly intend to," he added, the wicked glint in his eyes promising all manner of delights to come.

Smiling, Margaret took his arm, and they made their way over to Denforth's private theater in the east wing. The room had been freshly painted since Margaret had seen it last, but otherwise it was as she remembered: a handsome salon furnished with rows of padded seats surrounding a stage shielded from view by a red velvet curtain. While not nearly as large as Drury Lane's or Covent Garden's, the stage was wider than it looked, as Margaret knew from experience. Hadn't Madeline commandeered this theater countless times for *their* productions?

Several family members were already present, including the Saxbys, who'd seated themselves in the front row. Not surprising, given Madeline's keen interest in the theater. "Where would you like to sit?" Gervase inquired.

"Second row," Margaret decided. The Whitboroughs would almost certainly be occupying the first row, and she would just as soon avoid their scrutiny for now. And judging from Gervase's contemplative expression, she suspected he was thinking along the same lines.

So, in perfect accord, they chose seats in the middle of the second row and sat down together. A few minutes later, the two youngest Lyons children approached, Juliana radiant in her favorite turquoise, with a strand of aquamarines about her milky throat.

"What a lovely gown, Margaret!" she exclaimed. "And such a striking color!"

"Thank you—as long as it's striking, rather than *blinding*!" Margaret laughed, smoothing her skirt self-consciously.

"It's beautiful. Alas, I'd look like a lighted torch in apricot!" Juliana added ruefully, tugging at a lock of coppery hair. "Mind if we sit here?"

"Not at all," Margaret assured her, smiling.

"Found out which play they'll be performing?" Gervase asked his sister, as she took the seat on his right.

She shook her head. "Not yet. Papa says it's a secret, but it will be one we all enjoy."

"It's bound to be Shakespeare," Jason said, affecting an air of resignation.

Juliana smiled at him. "Remember the first time *we* went to the theater, Jason? We weren't old enough for Shakespeare, so we got taken to the pantomime instead. What was it—*Ali Baba*? I know it had an Arabian Nights theme."

"*Aladdin*," Jason corrected, breaking into a reminiscent smile. "I remember, because I wanted to *be* Aladdin! And have a flying carpet and a genie to grant all my wishes!"

"Was one of them to be an only child?" Gervase inquired dryly

Jason widened innocent eyes. "How ever did you guess, big brother?"

"Oh, the merest shot in the dark, I assure you."

They exchanged a smirk, younger sons sharing a moment of perfect understanding.

Juliana rolled her eyes, but laughed. "Well, *Aladdin* was great fun, as I recall! Perhaps we can persuade the Brands to put on something a bit lighter tomorrow for the children, since Shakespeare is a bit over their heads just now."

More people were filing into the room—including Alicia, Margaret observed with a start of surprise at her sister's appearance. Tonight Alicia had eschewed the softer colors that she usually chose, and now wore a dashing gown of deep scarlet, trimmed with gold accents. A compliment to Reg's dress uniform, perhaps?

Margaret tried to catch her sister's eye and send her a smile, but Alicia's gaze was sweeping the room— seeking Reg, no doubt. Wishing her sister were less transparent, Margaret looked as well, and finally located him sitting on the aisle seat of the front row, a little apart from the rest, wearing somber black and white evening dress like the rest of the men. Alicia had spotted him as well, if the wistful longing on her face was any indication. For a moment, she stood where she was, then with a lift of her chin, she glided forward.

Margaret held her breath as Reg's head turned towards her sister, but he rose at her approach, a tacit acceptance of her presence beside him. Lowering her gaze, Margaret exhaled with relief. Much as she opposed Reg and Alicia's wedding, she could not bear to see her sister snubbed by her own fiancé. Fortunately, Reg was being courteous to her in public—perhaps a way to atone for that less than impassioned mistletoe kiss?

"Gerry." Juliana's low murmur reached Margaret's ears as well, and she glanced over in time to see Juliana nudge Gervase and nod significantly towards the doorway. Margaret followed the line of his gaze as well.

Their Graces had just come in together, the duchess resplendent in her favorite deep wine, with priceless rubies at her throat, while the duke was elegant in black and white. Arm in arm, they made their way to the seats left vacant for them and sat down, side by side.

Once everyone was seated, the lights flickered and all eyes turned toward the stage to see Mr. Brand, splendid in a fur-trimmed velvet robe, emerge from behind the curtain.

"Your Grace," the actor bowed profoundly towards the duke, "Thank you for engaging our company to perform at Denforth. We are deeply honored by the invitation, and we hope tonight's performance will please you. Lords and ladies all, we present *The Winter's Tale*."

Goodness, now there was one that wasn't performed every day! Glancing at Gervase, Margaret saw a similar look of surprise on his face. Well, at least this play had a happy ending, she mused, though there was considerable tragedy to be got through first. And it was certainly appropriate to the season.

One of the junior members of the company, a boy dressed as a page—or perhaps as the young Prince Mamilius—made a circuit about the room, handing programmes to the audience before disappearing into the wings. A few minutes later, the lights dimmed completely and the curtains parted with a sigh. Two men, kings and friends, clad in royal robes, and a beautiful woman, just as richly arrayed, but with a significant swell to her middle, entered from stage right. One of the men stepped forward and declaimed, "*Nine changes of the watery star hath been / The shepherd's note since we have left our throne...*"

Margaret leaned back in her chair and let the stately dialogue carry her away.

THE COMPANY WAS A SKILLED ONE, speaking the verse with lyricism and intelligence. Even better, they were audible—Madeline had spoken scathingly of actors who mumbled and otherwise mangled their lines. And like his sister, Gervase tended to watch plays with a more critical eye. *The Winter's Tale* was by no means an easy play, made all the more difficult by Leontes's lightning-fast shift from devoted friend to insanely jealous husband. But when performed well, it could be sublime—a truly satisfying evening of theater.

Hermione, played by Mrs. Brand herself, had an open, smiling warmth that reminded him a bit of Margaret, the sort of warmth men were drawn to—as he himself had cause to know. And Polixenes played that angle most effectively, as a man charmed by his hostess's wit and hospitality, and willing to let himself be persuaded. Gervase watched Leontes closely, knowing that the success of the drama often hinged on how convincingly the king swung from acceptance to jealous rage. Fortunately, Leontes showed with a range of subtle expressions the deepening disquiet when Hermione succeeded where he had failed, convincing Polixenes to extend his visit.

Gervase wasn't sure when he began to feel uneasy. Around the time that Leontes and Hermione's marriage truly began to disintegrate, perhaps, and a growing sense of familiarity began to gnaw at him. A once-harmonious union strained by jealousy and suspicion, and later the tragic loss of a child... surely he wasn't the only one to notice the parallels?

And as the sad news of Mamilius's death rang through the room, Gervase found himself glancing towards where his parents sat—and saw his father take his mother's hand. Even more significantly, his mother let him, keeping her hand in his throughout that tense, dramatic scene.

Staring at their linked hands, Gervase felt a suspicion gradually take hold in his mind, but it seemed so outlandish that he did not quite dare to put it into words. Then he heard a soft rustle beside him and slid his gaze toward the sound: Margaret, surreptitiously reaching for a handkerchief. Granted this was possibly the saddest moment in the play, but he did not doubt that her own lost child had crossed her mind. Tentatively, he reached for her free hand, felt a rush of exultation when her fingers twined with his.

They sat that way for the remainder of the act.

As applause thundered through the theater, Margaret dabbed at her eyes, not for the first time that evening. The end of *The Winter's Tale* might strain credibility, but there could be no denying that, when done right, it was powerful and moving. The presumed-dead queen stepping down from her pedestal and into her penitent husband's embrace, then turning to welcome the daughter she had lost. Glancing at Gervase, she saw that his expression was quite soft, for him, and a faint smile played about his lips. Except that his eyes were not turned towards the stage and the reunited royal family but towards the couple sitting almost directly in front of them.

Intrigued, she followed the direction of his gaze—and barely kept her mouth from dropping open in shock. Their Graces' hands were linked, the duchess's eyes shining with the brilliance of what looked suspiciously like unshed tears. And the duke, looking not at the stage but at his wife, wore an expression of almost ineffable tenderness. Margaret could not remember the last time she had sensed such accord between them.

Consumed with curiosity, she gave Gervase a gentle nudge, then tilted her head inquiringly in his parents' direction once she had his attention.

He smiled crookedly, one dimple deepening in his cheek, and shrugged. "*Plus ça change, plus c'est la même chose*," he murmured under cover of the continuing applause.

The more things change, the more they stay the same. Well, that was certainly true of the Whitboroughs' contentious relationship, Margaret reflected.

"Let's see how long it lasts," he added, then turned back to applaud the actors as they came to take their bows.

IN THE SUPPER ROOM, a sumptuous buffet had been laid out, while champagne flowed like a river to toast the company's thespian efforts. Gervase's parents, apparently still in harmony, were lavish in their compliments and eager to discuss tomorrow's production.

Gervase offered his own compliments to the actors, especially the senior Brands, who had brought so much passion and pain to their portrayals of Leontes and Hermione. Then he made his way over to the buffet to fetch supper for Margaret and himself. Mrs. Hill had surpassed herself with a wide selection of French and English delicacies that included petit fours, lobster puffs, *pâté de foie gras*, smoked oysters, and several kinds of cheese.

Heading back towards the corner where he'd left his lady, he spied her in conversation with Alicia and quickly changed course for the nearest alcove. If the sisters were on the point of resolving their differences, far be it from him to interrupt that.

The alcove turned out to be already occupied by his elder sister, sipping champagne and looking unusually abstracted. She looked up as he entered, one elegant brow arching inquiringly.

"Good evening, Madeline," he greeted her. "Mind if I join you for a moment or two?"

"Not at all." She gestured towards the vacant chair beside her. "Make yourself at home. Hugo just left to get us some supper."

He sat down, balancing the laden plate on his lap. "Enjoy the performance?"

"The one onstage—or the one off?"

Gervase stilled. Needle-witted Madeline. All his sisters were intelligent, but Madeline's mind was as sharp and incisive as their mother's. And like their mother, she did not suffer fools gladly. If anyone could be counted on to notice what *he* had noticed...

"If you're referring to the play, I found it very pleasing," she continued. "Although Polixenes turned a little bombastic in the second half, and Camillo remains a largely thankless role. If, however, you mean our Aged P.'s not so secretly holding hands and doing their best impressions of Darby and Joan... and if you failed to notice, I shall be seriously disappointed in your waning powers of observation."

Gervase exhaled. "I noticed. I just—wasn't sure how much emphasis to put on it."

"Understandable." Madeline stared into the depths of her champagne flute. "Well, then, I shall go out on a limb and express my own theory. Which is that Father doesn't merely want Reg to come home and take up his duties as heir. And he doesn't just want all of us together for this sentimental family Christmas. I think he wants Mother back—permanently."

Gervase opened his mouth, and closed it again,

frowning. "Are you sure about the 'permanently'? Their truces seldom last beyond a few weeks at most."

"True enough. And I have doubts myself whether they could sustain a long-term reconciliation. But I suspect tonight's play was chosen quite deliberately." She swirled the last of the champagne in her flute. "An estranged couple torn apart by jealousy and the death of a child. Who finally reconcile years later, when *'what is lost is found.'* Shakespeare meant Perdita, as we all know—but I suppose, speaking figuratively, this Christmas could be considered Father's attempt to recoup his losses. Starting with Mother."

"Even supposing you're right," Gervase began slowly, his frown deepening, "he's playing a dangerous game. The tactics he's using are as likely to fail spectacularly as to succeed. He could end up driving her away instead. To say nothing of what he's doing to Reg."

"But I think that's part of it. He knows how Mama favors Reg—and always has." Madeline's lips quirked. "What else would bring her from France or the ends of the earth, for that matter, but a threat to *his* interests?"

Gervase shifted in his chair, thinking of their father's current scheme against their brother, but Madeline was continuing. "Everything changed when we lost Hal, and Reg is to be the next duke, no question of that. But I know that Father's broached the subject of Mother making... someone else the heir to her French properties now."

"No need, I suppose, to guess whom he had in mind," Gervase interposed.

"No need whatsoever. Nor does it seem to have crossed his mind that Mama could just as easily name you, me, or either of our sisters as her heir. She's unlikely to do so, but that's more probable than her choosing Jason."

"Thanks for the mention," Gervase said, a touch dryly. Although if truth were told, he'd never coveted Reg's French inheritance all that much. His mother had been training her favored son in the management of the family winery for more than fifteen years, so Gervase could readily understand her reluctance to supplant him with his baby brother, who was a stranger to *her* in so many ways. "I should have thought Father would be providing Jason with all he needs."

"No doubt he will—as Jason himself enjoys pointing out. But it's a point of pride with our father to manipulate our mother into yielding more than he does." Madeline's changeable eyes glinted with wintry humor. "And heaven forbid that he should ever just come out and simply confess that he misses her and wishes to live as husband and wife again."

"The Lyons pride," Gervase murmured, aware of both meanings. "God, what a family."

They traded a glance of wry understanding, but any further conversation was cut short by the arrival of Hugo, bearing a plate of "Maddie's favorites," as he fondly informed his wife. Gervase excused himself and went in search of Margaret, whom he found standing close to where he'd last seen her but alone.

"You've been quite an age coming back," she observed as he joined her.

"I saw you with Alicia, and thought I'd give you some time to talk." He held out the plate of supper to her. "Is everything all right there?"

"A *little* better, perhaps. We talked mostly of the play."

He scanned the crowd but saw no sign of a scarlet and gold gown. "Where is she now?"

"She pleaded a headache, and thought she'd retire early," Margaret replied, helping herself to a lobster puff. "I offered to escort her to her chamber, but she said there was no need."

"At least you're speaking again," Gervase pointed out, snagging champagne flutes for them both from a passing footman's tray.

She managed a smile. "Yes—thank heavens for small mercies! I'd have hated it if we were still estranged on Christmas morning."

They found a quiet corner—no small feat, given the number of people still milling about the room—and shared the supper he'd brought. Margaret did look a little happier, now that she and Alicia had taken a step towards mending fences. Gervase only hoped that their sisterhood could survive Margaret's continued opposition to Reg and Alicia's wedding.

He glanced towards where he'd last seen his brother, in conversation with Juliana, but there was no sign of him. Indeed, the crowd in the supper room had thinned out considerably; even some of the actors appeared to have retired to their guest chambers.

Leaning forward, Gervase murmured in Margaret's ear, "Ready to go, darling?"

"I thought you'd never ask. Would anyone notice if we just slipped away?"

"Not at this point, I believe. Besides, Elaine's already left with Alasdair, and Reg seems to have departed as well."

She set aside her empty glass and stood up, smiling. "Then, by all means, let us go."

Free of scrutiny, they made their way back towards the west wing, walking hand in hand through the Long Gallery and stealing the occasional kiss as they went.

They'd just entered the passage, when they heard what sounded like a cry issuing from one of the chambers. Alarmed, Gervase halted in his tracks, feeling Margaret stiffen beside him. But before either of them could react further, a door ahead of them burst open, and Reg strode out, carrying Alicia, clad only in a sheet and her long golden hair.

Even in the dim light of the passage, Gervase could see that his brother's face was set like stone. Without a word, Reg deposited his trembling fiancée none too gently on the floor, then turned on his heel and disappeared into his room. Seconds later, Alicia's gown, undergarments, and slippers hurtled through the open doorway before the door itself slammed shut.

Chapter Thirteen

Quoth she, 'Before you tumbled me,
You promised me to wed.'
(He answers) 'So would I ha' done, by
yonder sun,
An thou hast not come to my bed.'
—WILLIAM SHAKESPEARE, *Hamlet,* IV, v

WHAT THE DEVIL...?

Gervase stared at Reg's door, then at Alicia, huddled on the floor in mute misery. Then another sound reached their ears: the faint but emphatic click of a key turning in the lock.

Alicia's face crumpled like a child's, and she began to sob. Margaret shook off her paralysis, rushing forward to kneel by her weeping sister.

"Hush, dearest," she soothed, wrapping her arms around Alicia. "Hush, now..."

Gervase followed more slowly, trying to decipher what he'd just seen. Had sweet, innocent Alicia attempted to seduce his brother? It seemed impossible, given what he knew of her character, but the other scenario—Reg bedding and then repudiating her—was even less plausible. His brother was many things, but not a despoiler of innocents. And to judge from his expression, he'd been angered rather than aroused by his fiancée's presence in his chamber.

Frowning, Gervase regarded his brother's door again. If he and Reg had a different sort of relationship, he could ask to be let in, try to talk this out. Should he make the attempt, at least? Approaching the door, he cleared his throat and ventured, "Reg?"

"*Go away*." His brother's voice, low and dangerous, issued through the paneling—a tiger's warning growl before it sprang. "*All* of you."

Recognizing the tone, Gervase stepped back. Well, so much for *that* idea. Right now the wisest course would be to respect Reg's wishes and leave him alone. Confronting him in his present humor would most likely result in a fist to his own face and make bad worse.

Apropos of which... he glanced at the girl weeping in her sister's arms, noticing as if for the first time the scarlet-and-gold gown lying in a crumpled heap beside her.

"Margaret," he began in a low voice, "I think we should take Alicia to her chamber *now*."

Comprehension lit her eyes, and some of the color drained from her face. More of the family would be coming soon, and it would do Alicia no good to be found like this, all but naked and crying outside Reg's chamber. Regardless of their betrothal, questions would certainly be asked and accusations most likely made, which could damage Alicia's reputation beyond repair.

Stroking her sister's hair, Margaret murmured, "Come, dearest, you're making yourself ill. Let me help you to your room."

Gervase gathered up the scattered clothes as Margaret tenderly coaxed Alicia to her feet, then followed the sisters down the passage, the back of his neck prickling over the dread of discovery. Fortunately, they encountered no one else on the way to Alicia's chamber.

Opening the door, Margaret ushered her sister inside at once, then turned to accept the bundle of clothes. "Gervase, I know what we'd planned, but—" She gave a helpless little shrug.

He shook his head. "No need to explain. Alicia needs you now. I'll just head off to my own chamber."

She threw him a grateful look in lieu of a kiss, and slipped inside the room, closing the door behind her, though Alicia's muffled sobbing was still audible.

Alone in the passage, Gervase raked a hand through

his hair and sighed. *So far this evening, we've had the tragedy, the comedy, and now the melodrama. Or is it farce?* Who knew what the rest of the night might hold?

Still bemused by what he had seen, he started back the way he had come. Pausing again outside Reg's door, he listened intently, but no sound came from within. He was just debating whether to knock when he heard voices approaching from the gallery, one of which he recognized at once.

Madeline. Who would want to know why he of all people was lurking outside Reg's chamber and who would *not* be easily put off. Stifling a curse, Gervase turned away and made for his own room at top speed before his sharp-eyed, sharp-witted older sister could catch him.

✳

TO MARGARET'S RELIEF, Berthe was waiting up for her mistress and came forward at once, no questions asked. Crooning endearments in French, the maid wrapped Alicia in a dressing gown and helped her into bed before bearing off her discarded clothes. And through it all, Alicia wept inconsolably, tears coursing down her cheeks. Once in bed, she rolled over, burying her face in her pillows.

Torn between concern and a slowly building anger, Margaret regarded her sister's prone form. No doubt in her mind about what had happened in Reg's chamber, and to judge from the way Alicia avoided her gaze, *she* knew that as well.

"You never had a headache, did you?" It wasn't a question.

Alicia shuddered and sobbed, her slender form shaking. Swallowing her anger, Margaret said more gently, "Dearest, why on earth did you try something so..." Foolish? Reckless? Destined to fail? But her sister did not know that. *Could not* know that.

Alicia lifted a tear-ravaged face from her pillow. "I had to, Meg! I just had to! My whole future *depended* on it!"

"Your future?" Margaret stared at her sister, bewildered. Much as she disapproved, Alicia and Reg were betrothed, and their wedding was proceeding apace. Unless... "Alicia, has Reg said anything—about changing his mind?"

"N-not in so many words." Alicia drew a hiccupping breath and thrust a hand across her eyes. Sighing, Margaret handed her sister the extra handkerchief from her reticule.

Alicia gulped, wiped roughly at her face with the handkerchief before continuing. "Yesterday—after you and I h-had words. I went to find Reg." Her chin trembled. "His valet said he was in the study, with his father. I p-probably shouldn't have gone, but I just *had* to see him! I was g-going to show you how wrong you were, about us! That he *did* want to marry me! And then—and then..." More tears spilled from her eyes.

Hard as it was, Margaret forced herself to remain silent, waiting for the rest.

Alicia swallowed, dabbing again at her eyes. "I could hear them arguing, even from the passage! I t-tried not to l-listen, but I c-couldn't help overhearing... and I wish I *hadn't*!" Her voice rose to a near-wail. "Oh, M-Meg, Reg loves *someone else*! A woman in India!"

"A woman in India?' Margaret echoed, thunderstruck. How could this be *possible*? Memories crowded her mind at a dizzying speed: Reg and Hastings, their hands lingering a moment too long in each other's grip, exchanging smiles over a hand of cards, almost leaping apart when she found them together, their expressions telling her all she needed to know...

But Hastings had *married*—and from what Reg had implied earlier, turned his back on what had come before. And if *he* could, then—?

Alicia's tearful voice broke into her whirling thoughts. "Reg told the duke not to interfere, or he'd call off the wedding!' Her hands fisted in the bedclothes. "I had to do *something*, don't you see? My whole *life* was at stake!"

Margaret laid a hand upon Alicia's shoulder. "Oh, my dear..."

"I saw her photograph," her sister continued. "He keeps it on the dresser. She was *beautiful*." Her voice broke, fresh tears welling in her eyes. "So dark and exotic..."

Captain Hastings had been dark too, Margaret remembered with an inner wince.

"I know what I did w-was wrong," Alicia went on. "B-but I thought if I could just let him see, if I could just make him *care*—" She looked up with brimming eyes at her sister. "What if he despises me, Meg? I acted like a... like a..." Flushed with shame as well as tears, she sank her wet face back into the pillows and wept anew.

Heart aching, Margaret stroked her sister's shaking shoulders, wishing she knew how to comfort her. How to fix this whole ungodly mess.

Because whomever Reg loved, whether man or woman... he'd made it abundantly clear tonight that it *wasn't* Alicia.

NOT QUITE THE Christmas Eve he'd anticipated, Gervase reflected, kneeling to stir the dying blaze in his fireplace to life again. But considering what he'd witnessed and the distressing scene that had followed, he must make an effort not to be selfish. Margaret's place was at Alicia's side right now; he only hoped her presence was doing them both some good.

He felt an odd twinge of what might have been regret that he and Reg—he and any of his brothers, for that matter—had never shared that sort of closeness. The fires of rivalry and competition had burned too hot between them, especially as boys. But even as men, they existed in a state of uneasy truce at best. And he knew from bitter experience that it took only an ill-timed jest or barbed remark to ignite hostilities again.

A knock at the door roused him from these decidedly morose thoughts, and the soft call that followed brought him to his feet at once. Opening the door, he drew Margaret inside, threw a quick glance around the passage, noting with relief that it was otherwise deserted.

He closed the door and turned to his visitor. "Come over to the fire, *belle amie*," he invited, observing that she, like himself, had changed into a dressing gown, and her chestnut hair was plaited for the night.

She obeyed with alacrity, sinking down upon a chair

and holding her hands out to the blaze. "Thank you. I'm glad of the new radiators, but nothing *brightens* a room like a fire."

Gervase took the chair opposite hers. "Not that I'm not delighted to see you, but I thought you'd still be with your sister. How is she?"

Margaret's smile wavered. "Still in some distress. I stayed with her for a while, but she said she wanted to be alone. I think Berthe is more of a comfort to her right now than I am." Her gaze dropped to her lap. "I don't—I don't know what to say to her."

"It's hard to know what to say, in this situation. I take it that she—initiated whatever led to that scene we witnessed?"

Her silence was answer enough, even without the sudden flush mounting to her cheeks.

"What on earth possessed her to do such a thing?"

Margaret shook her head, her eyes still downcast. "I think—she hoped that, if she and Reg were... intimate, he would *want* her. That she could make him feel for her the way she feels for him." She looked up at last, a hint of defiance in her gaze. "Foolish, I know, but what woman doesn't dream of that, when she loves someone who doesn't love her back?"

"I'll wager *you* never did anything so reckless, even for Hal."

"Only because I fell out of love with him. Unfortunately, Alicia hasn't fallen out of love with Reg. And now she's terrified that he'll repudiate her. That he'll reveal her shame in front of the family and cast her off."

"He won't," Gervase said with sudden certainty. "Because he has as much to lose as she does, if this gets out. Possibly more."

"How do you mean?"

"It's not as if Alicia were some nobody trying to trap a man into marriage. She's a duke's daughter and Reg's fiancée—they're to marry in a week. What she tried to do was certainly improper, but she wouldn't be the first to anticipate the wedding." Gervase strongly suspected that Alasdair and Elaine had done so, given Beatrice's appearance slightly less than nine months later. "And if my parents found out, they'd be far more likely to insist that the ceremony be moved *up* than to allow Reg to call it off. In other words, *his* best interests lie in keeping silent."

Though he'd made his feelings devastatingly clear tonight. Gervase felt a twinge of pity for the girl, as foolish and selfish as her actions had been. Reg had been within his rights to remove her from his room, though he could have done so more kindly.

Margaret leaned forward, her eyes anxious. "Have you any idea what he'll do?"

"I'm afraid Brother Reg is a mystery to me, when it comes to matters of the heart."

"Do you think he'll go through with the wedding, after what's happened?"

"I'd say that depends—on whether he feels he has more to gain or lose by doing so."

Her mouth twisted. "You mean he'll consider his own advantage first, and to the devil with everyone else."

"It's the Lyons way," Gervase reminded her, not un-kindly. "Reg may find he has too much to lose by calling things off with Alicia."

"What about what *Alicia* has to lose?" Margaret challenged.

"You've just told me that her greatest fear is that Reg will cast her off. Is that what you want for her?"

She caught her breath, an indignant denial already forming on her lips. Then she stopped, sighed, and said more temperately, "You know that I oppose this mar-riage, and that I've been racking my brain trying to come up with ways to stop it, but I don't want my sister shamed or humiliated in the process. Does that sound strange?"

"Not at all. Of course you'd prefer her engagement to end painlessly—if that's possible." He paused, then said gently, "Margaret, how do you *want* to see this resolved?"

"What I want..." She took a breath. "What I want is for Alicia to wake up and see what a mistake marrying Reg would be! I want her to realize that she deserves a husband who will truly love her, who will devote his life to making their marriage a success!"

"A husband like Bellamy," Gervase translated without difficulty.

A flush mantled her cheeks. "Well, let's say a husband who'd be as attentive to *her* as Alex was to me," she amended. "But above all, I want to see my sister happy and fulfilled, not eating her heart out over a man who cares more about his regiment and his damned... *horses* than he ever will about her!"

Harsh words, but honest ones. Gervase took one of her hands—chilly despite the fire—and tried to warm it between his own. "Alicia is fortunate indeed to have a sister who cares so passionately about her happiness. And I can't disagree with a word you've said. But—"

She sighed. "*Must* there be a but?"

"I'm afraid so," he conceded ruefully. "You can't make Alicia want the same things *you* want for her. Ultimately, she must make her own choices—even if you disagree with them."

"But if she knew how *wrong* he was for her—"

"Don't you think she might have some idea of that now?" Gervase countered. "Your sister may not be as clever as you, but neither is she completely obtuse. What more can you do, if after tonight—after five *years* of indifference—she still wants him? Darling, even if you were to reveal the worst you know of Reg, if you were privy to all his deep, dark secrets—"

He felt the sudden jump of her pulse beneath his fingers, just before she pulled her hand free of his. "Gervase, I can't speak of this—"

"I know." Again he wondered what knowledge was fueling her opposition to the match. A sensitive matter, she'd said before. Had Reg taken a mistress? A possibility, given their family's history of infidelity—and Margaret would never want Alicia to suffer the heartaches *she'd* endured over Hal's faithlessness. "And I promise not to press you on it. But even if you were to disclose... whatever *this* is to Alicia, it might not sway her. What if she doesn't believe you—and cleaves still more closely to Reg? Could you live with that outcome?"

She dropped her gaze again. "I don't know. I—haven't thought that far ahead."

"Sometimes the hardest lesson is that you can't always save people from themselves."

"I can't *not* try, Gervase!" she protested.

"I wouldn't expect you to. But, in the end, it must be Alicia's decision alone, and if you can't support *her*, you could be risking permanent estrangement. And I would hate to see that happen—for both your sakes."

Margaret looked up, a telltale shimmer in her eyes. "So I speak and risk losing my sister altogether, or remain silent and let her throw her life away on a man who doesn't love her?"

The slight quaver in her voice affected him even more than her tears, but he forced himself to speak calmly. "Those are two of the possible outcomes. But if there is another, happier resolution, I have every confidence that you'll find it."

She sighed again, her shoulders slumping. "Thank you for your faith, but I can't see my way clear to *anything* just now. Or bear to think about this a moment longer."

"Then don't. Just come to bed. To rest," he added, as her dark eyes lifted to his. "It's been a long day for us both, and you'll be the better for a good night's sleep."

Margaret tilted her head to study him more closely. "That hardly seems fair to *you*."

"Having you near will be more than enough for me," he assured her. "Unless you'd rather return to your own chamber?"

"I think," she rose from her chair, took a step towards him, "I think I am perfectly satisfied with my present surroundings—and my present company. I would like to stay."

He rose as well. "Then stay. And as it's long past midnight, let's call it Christmas now."

"Christmas." She hesitated as though nerving herself up for something, then glanced at him with a faint answering smile. "Then, may I offer you the first of your gifts?"

Intrigued, he raised his brows. "My gifts?"

A delightful blush stole into her cheeks as she undid her sash and let her robe fall open.

Gervase stilled, gazing at the gloriously naked form she'd just revealed. "*Ma belle...*"

"I remember how long it took you to undress me the first night," she explained in a rush. "I thought—I would save us both some time. Do you... do you approve?"

He exhaled, love and lust tangling in his veins. "*But beauty's self she is, / When all her clothes are gone*. My dear,

Lady Godiva herself could not have been half so bewitching."

She smiled brilliantly. "Another apt quotation! You have a lawyer's mind and a poet's soul, dear friend."

"More like a good memory and a misspent youth." He drew her to him for an embrace, a lingering kiss. "Let me look after you tonight, *chérie*."

Her answering sigh warmed his skin. "I should like that, very much indeed."

He reached out to touch her plait. "May I?"

At her nod, he loosed the ribbon and began to unweave the strands, teasing them out until they rippled over her back and shoulders like a burnished mantle.

"Probably not as long as Lady Godiva's," she murmured.

"But still beautiful," he countered, and led her over to the bed.

Discarding their robes and slippers, they sank together into the warm nest of blankets. Go gently, Gervase told himself, because she *needed* gentleness tonight. So, first he soothed the tension from her neck and back, working out knots with patient fingers and taking satisfaction from every sigh and stretch as her limbs relaxed beneath his touch. And only after he'd finished and she was lying there, supple and boneless as a drowsing cat, did he stoop to brush his lips against her nape. "Asleep yet?" he whispered, noting her closed eyes and even breathing.

For answer, she opened her eyes and turned over so that they were face to face. "Not even close, my dear." She slid her arms about his neck and pulled him down for a kiss. "Tell me, how does that Campion poem go? *The summer hath its joys, / And the winter its delights—*"

"*Though love and its pleasures are but toys, / They shorten tedious nights.*"

She laughed softly, running a hand down his bare chest. "And so they do. *My* turn now."

Without warning, she locked her limbs about his and rolled until she sprawled atop him, the cool silk of her hair spilling across his chest.

Too surprised to resist, he stared up at her. "Margaret..."

She shifted her weight, pinning him more firmly to

the mattress. "Yield, sir!" Mischief danced in her velvety eyes. "And I *might* be merciful."

Although Gervase could have freed himself with little effort, he chose to remain quiescent beneath her. "Surrender is anathema to a Lyons, you know."

"I do, indeed." She lowered her eyelids to half-mast, her gaze sultry, "But I promise to make it worth your while."

He could not recall the last time one of his lovers had taken the initiative like this—and that it should be Margaret, of all women... Intrigued as well as aroused, he conceded, "Then, just this once, I will make an exception." *Surrender to love.*

Her laugh, warm and throaty, reminded him of a blackbird's chuckle. "A wise decision." Straddling his hips, she rose, erect and graceful as a caryatid above him. "And now that I have you in my power..." She trailed her fingers over his chest in a languorous caress, pausing to tweak one of his nipples.

Gervase just managed not to flinch. "You're enjoying this," he accused.

Her eyes widened, deceptively demure. "Should I not? I was three years a wife, and Alex saw to it that I had—a *very* thorough education."

She drawled the last words seductively, and Gervase's estimate of Bellamy rose several notches. Something else rose as well, and he saw Margaret smile—a smile as old as Eve, laced with satisfaction, even triumph. Cupping her hands about his rearing shaft, she rolled the ball of her thumb over the tip.

He sucked in a breath at that, and saw her smile deepen, even as her eyes softened. "Fear not. I *will* be gentle with you."

As *he* had meant to be with her—the irony did not escape him. "I am yours, *ma perle*," he said lightly. "Do as you like with me... only not at such a distance." He reached up to clasp his hands at the small of her back, seeking to draw her closer.

She angled her hips, positioning herself over him. "Allow me to remedy that."

He swallowed a gasp as she sank down, taking him wholly inside of her, enveloping him in the moist, silken heat of her passage. Margaret's head tipped back, her lips parting and her eyelids fluttering shut, absorbing every sensation just as he was.

Sheathed in her, enclosed by her. "You surround me." Was that *his* voice—hoarse, almost guttural, with desire?

"You fill me." Her whisper echoed through his soul.

Nothing else is. He caught his breath as she began to move—gently at first, then with a faster, more insistent rhythm that rippled along his length. Heart racing, sparks dancing before his eyes, he strove to keep pace with her. Dear God—yielding control had never felt more intoxicating!

Their joined bodies pulsed in unison, the warmth between them kindling from a smolder to a blaze. Arching up, Gervase caught Margaret in his arms as she shattered around him with a cry. His own release speedily followed, and they soared and fell together like mating eagles, tumbling into a void where only *feeling*—only joy —existed.

Later, when Gervase felt as though he could move again, he stroked the tousled hair back from her face, watched her lips curve in a slow, sweet smile. "Happy Christmas, *ma mie*."

"Happy Christmas, you aggravating boy." The drowsy syllables were a stroke of velvet against his ear, and his heart seized at the sweetness of it all.

I want you. I want this. *Forever.* The words sang through him in an impassioned serenade; it was all he could do not to shout them aloud, for the whole world to hear.

Margaret shifted in his embrace, her breathing settling into the steady rhythm of sleep, and he smiled, albeit a touch wryly.

Timing. He needed to work on that. But what he had to say would keep—for now.

Closing his eyes, he followed his beloved into slumber.

Chapter Fourteen

MARGARET ROUSED to the sensation of clever fingers stroking through her hair, and the sound of a steady heartbeat in her ears. Then, as she prised open her eyelids, warm lips brushed against her brow.

"Mmm. I can't think of a lovelier way to be awakened," she sighed.

She heard Gervase chuckle, low and deep. "The prince always awakens the Sleeping Beauty with a kiss."

"What a flattering comparison, though I'm sure any mirror would give you the lie." Her hair, loosed from its plait, must be a mass of knots by now.

"*I can see yet without spectacles and I see no such matter.*" His woodsmoke gaze traveled over her face. "Indeed, I cannot complain of the view."

"Nor can I." She reached up and stroked his jaw, feeling the rasp of stubble beneath her fingertips. Not even Gervase was immaculate first thing in the morning, which she found oddly reassuring. "Any idea what time it is?"

"Hard to say. After sunrise, I think. I heard the maid come in to light the fire."

Heard but not saw, Margaret noted, grateful for his foresight. At some point last night, he'd drawn the bedcurtains around them for warmth and privacy. She'd done the same to *her* bed before coming to his chamber. Some of the servants might suspect that she and Gervase were spending their nights together, but one should make an effort to be discreet. Besides, she liked the sensation of being closed in with her lover. *Make of one little room an everywhere...*

"Six o'clock, perhaps. I should return to my chamber, I suppose," she added reluctantly. But lying here, her head pillowed on Gervase's chest, felt so comfortable—and comforting.

His hand traced lazy circles over her back. "'*Tis true, 'tis day. / What though it be, / O, wilt thou therefore rise from me?*"

She laughed, was about to reply in kind, when a sound reached her ears and she froze.

"I hear footsteps."

He stilled, listening. "Farnsworth. I think—he's about halfway down the passage now."

"Oh, God!" Margaret sat bolt upright, clutching the sheet to her. Even with the bedcurtains drawn, she couldn't hope to escape detection indefinitely—not to mention that Gervase's valet was sharper than most. "I never meant to stay so long—"

Gervase put his arm around her. "Don't panic, *chérie.*"

She pushed away his arm. "Easier said than done! When I think about what happened last night, with Alicia—"

"There's no comparison, darling—heart up!" He gave her shoulders a little bracing squeeze before releasing her. "You're hardly the first to be caught unawares. Go into my dressing room—through that door—and I'll get you out as soon as possible."

Margaret hurtled out of bed, catching up her robe and flinging it on as she went. The dressing room smelled pleasantly of shaving soap and Gervase's cologne. Arousal spiked through her at the latter scent, but she forced it back, leaning against the door and listening with bated breath as Farnsworth entered his master's chamber.

"Good morning, my lord," the valet began. "I've brought your morning coffee."

"Thank you, Farnsworth." Amazingly, Gervase sounded as serene and unruffled as ever. "Happy Christmas."

"Happy Christmas to you as well, my lord. By the fire, as usual?"

"Yes, that will be fine."

In an agony of suspense, Margaret strained her ears as Farnsworth moved about the chamber with brisk efficiency. She heard the clink of china and silver, could imagine coffee and toast being set out. Once or twice, the valet ventured some remark that she could not quite make out, and Gervase's replies were likewise inaudible.

Finally, the clinking ceased, and she began to relax. Gervase was clever, no doubt he'd come up with some pretext to send Farnsworth out of the room so she could make her escape.

Then the valet spoke again, every syllable clear and distinct. "Shall I—bring more toast, my lord? And perhaps a pot of chocolate?"

Margaret tensed against the door, her face burning and her mind racing in frantic circles. How on earth had he guessed?

Gervase paused for only a fraction of a second, then, "That sounds... like an excellent idea, Farnsworth. Thank you."

"Very good, my lord."

She heard the chamber door close again, waited a few minutes more, then opened the dressing room door the barest crack and listened intently.

"I believe it's safe to come out now, darling," Gervase announced with perfect composure, as if hiding women in his dressing room were quite an everyday occurrence.

Peering around the door, Margaret found him gazing back at her, his mouth crooked in that familiar half-smile, his grey eyes alight with sardonic amusement. Odious man.

Expelling a pent-up breath, she demanded, "How did he—"

"This, at a guess." Gervase held out one of her unmistakably feminine slippers. "My apologies for the oversight, Cinderella."

She made a face at him, tugged on the slipper, and went in search of its mate, which she located under the bed. Shod again, she sank down onto the mattress with a distressed moan. "I don't know how I'm going to look your valet in the face again!"

"If *I* can, then so can you," Gervase retorted, coming to sit beside her. "They say that no man is a hero to his valet, and by now, I suspect my life is an open book to Farnsworth. Besides," he added bracingly, "he appears to have twigged to your presence, so why not stay a while longer? Otherwise a perfectly good pot of chocolate will be going to waste. And Farnsworth will likely have a private word with your maid, so she won't be alarmed by your absence."

"Don't you think I'm a bit underdressed for the occasion?" Margaret reminded him.

He studied her with a lingering appreciation that both warmed and flustered her. "*I* wouldn't say that, necessarily." Then, at her exasperated glare, he relented. "Very well. You can borrow one of my old nightshirts—there should be some in that chest-of-drawers."

The nightshirt was soft and limp with age, but fragrant with lavender; more importantly, it covered everything of her that needed to be covered. She also plaited her hair again, so she was quite decently arrayed when Farnsworth returned with another tray.

"Lady Bellamy has accepted my invitation to take some early morning refreshment," Gervase informed him with unshakable aplomb, as he and Margaret seated themselves at the small table by the fire.

"Very good, my lord." Farnsworth's *sang-froid* was clearly a match for his master's. "Toast and chocolate, Lady Bellamy?" he inquired with perfect courtesy.

"Thank you," Margaret replied, trying to sound as composed as the men. As Farnsworth set the plate and the chocolate pot before her, she found herself wondering if he'd ever waited like this upon other women who might have shared Gervase's bed? She felt what she knew to be a completely unreasonable stab of jealousy at the thought and hastily suppressed it.

Pas devant les domestiques. While Gervase had assured her of his valet's discretion, it seemed prudent not to add fuel to the fire by acting clingy or possessive.

Once Farnsworth had served her, he withdrew into Gervase's dressing room, closing the door behind him. Margaret flushed, despite knowing that she had left no trace of her presence in that inner sanctum. Hiding her lingering embarrassment, she took a sip of the rich chocolate, nibbled at the lavishly buttered toast.

"Is everything to your satisfaction?" Gervase inquired, sounding almost anxious.

"Everything's fine, thank you," she assured her. "And your valet is a marvel of efficiency. I wonder how he knew to offer chocolate instead of tea."

"Farnswoth is nothing if not observant. It wouldn't surprise me if he'd somehow learned all the guests' preferences during his time at Denforth."

"Sounds like a servant worth his weight in gold," she remarked.

His eyes crinkled. "Indeed. Which is about what I pay to keep him in my employ. More toast?" He nudged the rack closer to her.

They ate and drank in companionable silence, broken now and then by desultory conversation. There was something almost delightfully decadent, Margaret reflected, about this early morning interlude with her lover. Alex had always been too busy about the estate to linger abed in the mornings, and while she'd admired his energy and dedication, she'd sometimes felt a bit wistful that he seldom stayed with her once he was awake. Would Gervase be the sort to let his wife breakfast alone? She knew he worked hard at his profession, so perhaps he too would be similarly hard to hold once the sun rose.

"Do you rise this early in London?" she asked.

"More or less. There's usually something to be done at the office. But even when there's not, I find I rather enjoy the earliest part of the day because it's so peaceful and unspoiled. Although," Gervase paused, his expression pensive, then resumed almost diffidently, "I find that even the loveliest morning is the better for... someone to share it with."

Warmth shimmered through her at his words. "As it happens, I quite agree with you," she managed to get out, then added more lightly, "Although we should enjoy the peace while it lasts, because I suspect the children will be stirring at any moment. Remember how *we* used to be on Christmas morning?"

Gervase groaned. "One occasion when Denforth never seems big enough to hold us all! But seriously, *belle amie*," he sent her a smile over his coffee cup, "the chaos of Christmas notwithstanding, I could grow accustomed to mornings like this one."

She smiled back at him and gave his hand a brief squeeze. "So could I, dear friend."

MUCH TO MARGARET'S RELIEF, no whisper of Alicia's indiscretion appeared to have circulated, and she offered silent thanks to heaven that Gervase had judged his brother's response accurately. Otherwise, Christmas morning turned out to be as noisy and tumultuous as she had predicted. Once awake, the children proved unstoppable, rooting through their laden stockings and gleefully tearing open brightly wrapped parcels, while their parents—roused earlier than they might have preferred—attempted to smile and stay awake. While Simon and Oliver were too young to participate in this ritual, Richenda, Harry, and Beatrice more than compensated for their siblings' absence, chattering like magpies as they opened their gifts, littering the floor of the Great Hall with shreds of paper and coils of ribbon.

Harry fell upon his rocking-horse with a jubilant shout and immediately started to ride for "Banbury Cross." Richenda grew wide-eyed over her toy theater, examining every prop and costume that came with it. Madeline was no less captivated, and mother and daughter were soon engaged in moving the "actors" about in miniature dramas. While Beatrice divided her attention between a skipping-rope and a doll almost as big as she was, with eyes that opened and closed.

The adults opened their own gifts more sedately, but with just as much pleasure. Margaret had purchased cashmere shawls for the women and woolen mufflers for the men. Still, even practical gifts could be handsome—and she'd taken particular pains over Gervase's scarf, choosing a deep blue with a narrow stripe of silver-grey. He'd not got round to opening it yet, but she looked forward to seeing how the colors would complement his changeable eyes.

Meanwhile, Gervase was giving books to most members of his family. Smiling over the memory of his gift to *her* five Christmases ago, Margaret felt certain that he'd picked the ideal title for each of them. Hadn't Jason, of all people, commended his brother's gift-giving ability?

"Open this, please, Meg?" Alicia, her new blue-and-cream cashmere shawl draped over her shoulders, had come to sit beside her and was holding out a large parcel. "Happy Christmas."

The diminutive reassured Margaret more than anything that their tentative peace was still in place. She was likewise relieved by Alicia's apparent composure this morning—Berthe had successfully repaired the damage from last night's storm of tears—though she noticed that her sister avoided glancing in Reg's direction, at the far end of the Great Hall. "Happy Christmas, dearest," she replied, and began to unwrap her gift.

From a nest of tissue wrappings, she lifted one of the most beautiful gowns she had ever seen—of lush silk-velvet in a rich shade of emerald green. "Oh, Alicia, this is just—"

"It's cut in the very latest style," her sister explained. "So there's hardly any bustle, though it does have a bit of a train. I thought—perhaps, you might want to wear it tonight, at the party? It ought to fit," she added, "I asked Tilda to send me your current measurements before I ordered it from Monsieur Worth, though there's still a little time to alter it, if necessary."

"It's lovely, dearest," Margaret assured her. "Exquisite. And I should be delighted to wear it tonight." She kissed her sister's delicately perfumed cheek.

Alicia relaxed and smiled with all her old sweetness. "And there are slippers to match, exactly. Paris can't be bettered for that sort of thing!"

"*Mais, oui,*" Margaret agreed in an exaggerated French accent, and Alicia rolled her eyes.

They laughed together, and Margaret saw Gervase glance in their direction and smile.

Alicia demurely excused herself a moment later, saying she hadn't given Madeline and Elaine their presents yet, and once she'd withdrawn, Gervase strolled up to Margaret.

"So, all's well, then?" he inquired, taking the chair her sister had just vacated.

"Better, at least. And she gave me the most beautiful gown to wear tonight, at the party." Folding back the wrappings, she allowed him a glimpse of the green velvet, and saw his eyes brighten most gratifyingly.

"I look forward to seeing you in it." From his breast pocket, he drew out a small parcel that was decidedly *not* a book. "And perhaps—you can find an occasion to wear this as well."

Margaret caught her breath as he handed her the box. Because it *was* a box—she could tell that through the brown paper wrapping—and from its size and shape, it most likely held...

"Ah, there you are!" Juliana's voice hailed them gaily. "Just the two I was looking for!"

Annoyance flashed across Gervase's face but was quickly suppressed. Dropping his gift into the hanging pocket of her dress, Margaret strove for a similar expression of polite interest.

"Are we indeed? Dare I ask the reason, Ju?" Gervase inquired with resignation.

"Because your Christmas presents are becoming impatient."

Despite her apprehension, Margaret had to smile when Juliana placed a wicker basket on her brother's lap —a basket that quivered noticeably once she set it down.

He examined it dubiously. "Should I open this, or drop it down the nearest well?"

"You do, and I'll never speak to you again!" Juliana retorted, glaring at him.

Still keeping a wary eye on the basket, he lifted the lid. And Margaret was not in the least surprised by the sound that emerged—or the head that now appeared over the basket's rim.

Gervase regarded his present in silence for a moment, then gave an almost imperceptible sigh and extended a hand. The ginger kitten with the propensity for high places mewed imperiously and swiped at it, though Margaret could see that his claws were retracted.

"I thought you might do very well together," Juliana explained, her face the picture of innocence. "You're already acquainted, after all."

Gervase surveyed the kitten, who had seized his forefinger in two tiny paws and was pretending to bite it. "Feste," he said at last. "If you're going to insist on playing the fool like that. And clearly you require someone to keep an eye on you before you run through all your nine lives at record speed."

Margaret consulted the pocket watch she wore on a pretty braided chain. "Well under five minutes," she observed. "You're growing soft in your old age, dear friend."

"Soft in the *head*, it would appear." Gervase gently disengaged his finger and ran it between Feste's ears in a brief stroke before lowering the basket lid again over the kitten's squeak of protest. "Go back to sleep, little pest, and dream of fresh mischief."

Juliana grinned outright and produced another basket, which she handed to Margaret.

This kitten was female, a dainty little thing with bright green eyes and tortoiseshell and white patches that reminded Margaret of motley. "Touchstone," she decided, lifting her new pet out and cuddling her close. "Your name is Touchstone."

The kitten appeared to have no objection, turning three times in Margaret's lap before settling into a softly purring heap.

Gervase's lips twitched. "That one's clearly no fool, in spite of the name!" He glanced at the basket that housed Feste. "Perhaps he can learn a thing or two from his sister."

"*All* brothers could stand to learn a thing or two from their sisters," Juliana remarked pointedly. "And I'm glad to see that *someone* appreciates my gift properly!"

He favored her with a wry smile. "Well, life with this one certainly won't be boring. So thank you for that at least, brat."

"Hmmph." Juliana put her nose in the air but looked slightly mollified all the same.

Just then, the duke, who'd been in and out of the Great Hall for much of the morning, strode back in, bringing with him a swirl of winter wind and a palpable air of satisfaction.

"If I may have everyone's attention," he began, smiling broadly. "Another present—a *very important present*—is being delivered in the courtyard at this very moment. And I would appreciate all of you coming out to see it."

Curious murmurs and speculative glances greeted his announcement, and the duchess shook her head indulgently. "You're as big a schoolboy at Christmas as any I've seen, Harold."

He flashed her an unrepentant grin, not denying it. "But you *will* come, my lady?"

"But of course." She rose like a queen from her throne. "We shall *all* come."

And such was her presence that no one even considered declining. Instead, they rose practically as one to follow the Whitboroughs from the Great Hall.

THE FIRST THING Gervase saw as they trooped out to the courtyard was one of the Denforth grooms standing before the front steps, holding the reins of a horse. A hunter, to be precise, at least fifteen hands high, its chestnut coat gleaming richly in the pallid winter sunlight.

A sharp exhale behind him drew his gaze to Reg, surprising a look of hope, even longing, on his older brother's face, such as he had not seen in years.

Oh. Enlightenment dawned with breathtaking swiftness. But before he or Reg could utter a word, their father's voice rang out jovially in the still morning air, "Jason, come down and meet your Christmas present!"

Chapter Fifteen

Rich gifts wax poor when givers prove unkind.
—WILLIAM SHAKESPEARE, *Hamlet,* III, i

REG STIFFENED, the color leaching from his face until it was as white as bone. By contrast, Jason was flushed and wide-eyed, glancing incredulously between the horse and his father.

"*Mine?*" he breathed.

"All yours," Whitborough confirmed, smiling. "As you see, I could not wait until your birthday, after all. Happy Christmas, son."

Dazedly, the boy descended the steps and held out his hand to the horse. The hunter snorted and tossed his handsome head before bending down to nose at Jason's palm.

"Isn't he splendid?" Jason marveled, running a hand up and down the proud arched neck. "I've never *seen* one so fine..."

Gervase eyed his older brother covertly; Reg's face was still set, but he had more control over his expression and demeanor now. Fortunately, most of the family was busy congratulating Jason on his new mount.

Their father smiled, clapping his youngest son on the shoulder. "I'll have you know, my boy, he comes from one of the best horse breeders in Melton Mowbray."

Was it his imagination, Gervase wondered, or did

those last two words ring through the courtyard like a challenge? And was he also imagining the uneasy silence that followed? Jason, intent on the horse, seemed oblivious, as did most of their sisters, but their mother...

Gervase slid a glance towards the duchess, standing straight as a ramrod and studying her husband through narrowed eyes. And just beyond her stood Hugo, looking uncomfortable, even a touch guilty. After all, he and Reg had discussed that coveted hunter's various excellences in the duke's hearing that very first evening. Not that that was likely to have made a difference, and Gervase doubted that Reg blamed their brother-in-law for how things had fallen out. How could straightforward, good-natured Hugo have predicted such a development? Dealings within the Lyons family were a law unto themselves.

A hand touched his arm, and he turned to find Margaret watching him, comprehension dawning in her eyes.

"Gervase," she began, under her breath, "is that—?"

She tilted her head towards the horse, and he gave her the barest nod of confirmation, before glancing around for Reg.

Only to find that his brother had somehow managed to slip away unnoticed.

HE RAN Reg to ground in the library, standing by the fireplace, a cigar in one hand and a glass of whiskey within reach of the other. His brother glanced at him as he entered, glowering through a haze of smoke.

"Come to gloat?" Reg bit off each word with icy precision, drew on his cigar again.

Gervase refused to take umbrage. "I think you know me better than that."

Reg exhaled, blowing out an angry cloud. "True. *Jason* would gloat." He picked up his glass, tossed off half the contents in one swallow. "So, did Mother send you?"

"No. But only because I left before she could ask." Gervase paused, then ventured without any real conviction, "Any chance this *might* have been a coincidence?"

"Coincidence, my arse," Reg said thinly. "This is the duke our father's way of keeping me in line. Of telling me that he has the power to take away something—anything—that I want, if I don't give in to his demands." He seized the poker, thrusting it into the flames as though they were opponents he longed to skewer.

"He can't take away the dukedom," Gervase pointed out.

"He can try. Isn't that what he's asking *you* to do for him?" Reg's eyes raked him from head to foot, a silent accusation of complicity.

"He may *ask*," Gervase retorted. "He may not get the answer he desires. And whether he likes it or not, he'll still have to pay me for anything I *might* choose to do for him." *And I haven't chosen to do anything... yet.*

Reg stared at him, then huffed a reluctant laugh. "At least you're honest about it."

"About what?"

"About being on no one's side but your own."

"Whom else can I trust not to change alliances at the drop of a hat?" Gervase inquired dryly. Who else had ever been consistently on his side *but* himself—with the possible exception of Sir Anthony? And it might not be admirable, but keeping *both* of his parents on a string, waiting for his answer, was undeniably satisfying.

Reg snorted, whether in amusement or acknowledgment Gervase could not tell. "I can't argue with that, brother. Especially where this family is concerned!" He drew on his cigar again, visibly attempting to master his still-smoldering anger. "Well, then. You can reassure Mother that I'm *not* planning to murder Father or Jason in their beds over a damned horse! But I wish to be left alone, for now."

"Understood." Gervase inclined his head and withdrew, closing the door behind him.

It wasn't often that he sympathized with Reg, but remembering how his brother had looked in the courtyard, he found it easy to do so today.

Because what Gervase suspected—and what he knew Reg would never admit—was that, for a moment, Reg had dared to hope that their father had bought the horse for *him*.

❄

COOING SOLICITOUSLY, Tilda bore Touchstone and her

basket off to the dressing room, leaving her mistress to contemplate Gervase's still-unopened gift on the vanity before her.

It's just a box, Margaret told herself firmly for what felt like the hundredth time since she'd unwrapped it. A black velvet box. A *jewel* box... just big enough to hold something that could change her life forever.

She swallowed, her throat suddenly as dry as her palms were damp. But she was being nonsensical: if the contents were something of life-changing significance— say, a ring—surely Gervase would have insisted on being present when she opened it. Instead, he seemed to have forgotten about it—as she had, temporarily, over that drama with the horse.

Margaret shook her head at the memory. However long she lived, she would never understand Gervase's parents—especially his father! While she'd known for years that the duke tended to play his sons off against each other, this morning had provided a particularly obnoxious example of that. She could almost pity Reg, and she thought Gervase *did* pity him; indeed, she suspected that was why he'd gone discreetly in search of his brother, afterwards. He'd returned—alone—just as the rest of the family was sitting down to breakfast, but made no mention of Reg. Probably the most tactful thing he *could* do, she mused. Reg would hate for anyone to know he was affected by his father's blatant act of favoritism towards Jason.

The mantel clock's chiming roused her from her thoughts. They would be leaving for church within the hour; time to stop procrastinating. Taking a breath, she pried open the box.

Not a ring. A cameo brooch. Margaret sat quite still, unsure what to call the emotion flooding through her. Relief perhaps, tinged with something that *might* have been regret—though that struck her as nearly as absurd as her earlier anxiety had been.

In any case, Gervase's gift deserved appreciation. She had inherited a cameo or two from her mother, but this one was especially lovely: a delicate female profile carved in white shell, against a warm coral ground, in a scalloped frame of gold filigree. There was even a tiny loop through which she could thread a chain if she wished to wear it as a pendant.

A beautiful, tasteful, well-chosen present that any woman would delight in. Why, then, did she find herself suddenly wishing he'd just given her a book, as he had everyone else?

Furious at her own ingratitude, Margaret closed her eyes, struggling to master her ambivalence. There were gifts a man could safely give a woman without arousing comment or undue curiosity: books, sheet music, sweets —even flowers were deemed acceptable. But an article of clothing or a piece of jewelry... those were far more personal. Not just in themselves, but in what they represented.

Opening her eyes, she stared at the brooch as though it could unlock ancient mysteries. Gervase must have purchased it before they'd left for Yorkshire. Which meant that, even then, before matters between them had taken the turn they had, he'd been preparing to venture beyond the safe, familiar shoals of friendship into deeper, far riskier waters.

That discovery unnerved her as much as the gift.

"I had a plan," he'd said, the night they became lovers. A plan to approach her once her mourning period for Hal had elapsed. And she'd been so touched by his confession that she hadn't really considered how she might have received his suit, if she hadn't eloped with Alex. What would she have said—and how might her life have been different?

It's only a brooch, for heaven's sake. But she knew that to be untrue. At the very least, it was a challenge: to think beyond the moment, to consider the future and what it might hold. Just now she was enjoying a delightful love affair, a carefree holiday romance... but what would happen once the holidays were over, and everyday life beckoned? To her chagrin, she hadn't thought that far ahead—but she was willing to bet that Gervase had.

Once back in London, would they carry on there, as they did here? Discreet assignations by night or day, intimate meals *á deux*, perhaps secret jaunts to the country under assumed names. Some couples, she'd heard, believed that intrigue lent a certain spice to an affair.

Others were simply content to settle for what they could get, especially if marriage was not an option.

But there was no reason why she and Gervase could not marry, if they wished. And five Christmases ago, Gervase *had* wanted to marry her, and while he'd so far avoided bringing up the subject, it was not inconceivable that he still did.

Which left the question: what did *she* want?

The emotions swept over her in a giant wave: grief, shock, and remembered pain, still sharp enough to take her breath away, make her eyes sting and blur...

Alex coming in from a morning about the estate, complaining of chills and a sore throat. Within a fortnight, he'd been gone. And even before that, Hal— falling in that stupid race, succumbing to his injuries three days later. Two men she'd pledged her life to, and she'd seen them both buried. And for a time, she'd felt that Alex's death would physically *crush* her.

Shaken, Margaret pushed away the box and braced her forehead against her folded hands as she fought for composure. She'd believed the worst of her grief was behind her, but this—visceral response to the very idea of remarrying seemed to prove otherwise. Not rational, perhaps, but no less real. To give her heart completely to someone, to build a future together, and then to lose him... was that something she even *wanted* to try again?

"My lady? Are you feeling unwell?"

Margaret raised her head to find Tilda regarding her with concern, and quickly summoned a smile. "No, no, I'm fine, Tilda. Just a little—distracted, that's all."

The maid relaxed, smiling back. "Then, shall I get out your clothes for church?"

"Yes, thank you," Margaret replied, gratefully abandoning the turmoil in her head.

"Is it to be the green tweed or the grey merino?"

"The merino, I think," Margaret replied, a touch absently. "It will be warmer. With the black half-boots and the black velvet bonnet."

As Tilda laid out her clothes, Margaret took a last peek at the cameo. But to wear it... might raise too many questions—and expectations at this point, neither of which she was ready to deal with. Resolutely, she closed the lid and placed the box in a drawer of her vanity, ignoring the twinge of guilt as best she could. Besides, as lovely as the brooch was, its colors would look quite wrong against a grey dress. Surely Gervase, with his discerning eye, would understand.

❄

As THE WEATHER was fairly mild for Christmas Day, the family chose to walk the short distance to church. Jason, still cock-a-hoop over his new acquisition, suggested riding there, but was quietly discouraged by several family members. Reg had resurfaced, stony-faced and seemingly in control of his temper, but Gervase suspected the sight of Jason astride that coveted horse would seriously strain his older brother's self-command.

Swathed in wool and furs against the chill, they set off for the village. Gervase's parents led the way, stately as the heads of a royal procession, his mother's gloved hand resting lightly on his father's arm. A Christmas truce appeared to be in effect, although Gervase wondered how long it would endure, in light of his father's recent horse-dealing. The rest of the family followed in groups of two or three. He saw a wistful Alicia glance at Reg—walking with Hugo, Madeline, and their two eldest children—before dutifully accepting Augustus's escort.

Gervase fell into step beside Margaret, cheered by the spark of welcome in her eyes. His own eyes went instinctively to the high collar of her day dress... and found it unadorned.

He glanced away, concealing a sharp pang of disappointment that he told himself was unreasonable. Perhaps she hadn't got the chance to open his gift yet?

Margaret's hand touched his arm. "Gervase."

The timid note in her voice was so unexpected that he glanced at her in concern. She looked like a guilty schoolgirl, right down to her flushed cheeks and the lower lip she was worrying. "Thank you, for such a lovely gift. I just—wasn't sure this was the right occasion to wear it."

"I see." And he did, though he wished it were otherwise. But Margaret sporting an unfamiliar piece of jewelry might attract attention, especially from his fashion-conscious sisters. "You would prefer not to arouse speculation, at this point. I understand completely."

"Thank you." Eyes warm with gratitude—and a hint of contrition, she reached up to adjust the muffler at his throat. "And I knew these colors would suit you. That shade of blue does wonders for your eyes."

He was no peacock, but the compliment pleased him, as did the implication that she'd chosen his gift with particular care. He'd taken similar pains with hers, trying to decide between several cameos, including a very pretty Wedgwood-blue one ornamented with a spray of white flowers. But the young girl's profile, the roses in her hair, had reminded him of Margaret as a debutante. He'd also preferred the richness of the coral background, as he so often associated Margaret herself with warmth and color.

He could share none of this with her now, however, given her present skittishness over their romance. Not that he blamed her, but a part of him wondered uneasily if the "right" occasion to wear his gift would ever arise for her.

As the Whitborough party neared the church, Gervase sternly reminded himself to count his blessings. The woman he'd loved for years had spent Christmas morning in his arms and was even now walking beside him. In all likelihood, they'd be spending the rest of the day—and the night—together. With that prospect before him, it would be sheer greed to hanker after more.

He offered her his arm, and they went in together.

THE SERVICE, which included a reading from Luke, was brief but heartfelt, and a splendid Christmas lunch awaited them on their return from church. Roast goose with all the trimmings, followed by flaming pudding in which several silver charms had been hidden, as supposed portents for the future. And while Margaret did not consider herself superstitious, she had been secretly relieved that her serving had contained only pudding, rather than a ring presaging marriage or a thimble predicting spinsterhood. But Gervase unearthed a silver sixpence, much to her amusement and, she suspected, his as well. The only awkward moment came when Reg found the horseshoe and pushed it to the side of his plate, without comment. Fortunately, Juliana located the ring seconds later and the table erupted in lively speculation regarding the lucky man.

The rest of the afternoon had passed in a pleasant post-prandial haze, enlivened by some carol singing about the piano and the Brand Company's performance of *A Christmas Carol*—one of the less mawkish adaptations, Gervase had murmured in Margaret's ear during the interval. Richenda, Beatrice, and Harry had attended, sitting spellbound through the play—though the latter fell asleep towards the end, owing to what his mother deemed an excess of pudding.

Now, with the evening sky darkening to black outside her window, Margaret let Tilda help her into Alicia's gift. Much to her relief, the green gown fit perfectly, even after a Christmas feast. Better still, it was every bit as becoming as Alicia had promised, the rich emerald velvet brightening her hair to auburn and making her skin look almost translucent. And the skirt fell in sweeping folds, so much more graceful without the weight of a bustle in back. She barely resisted the temptation to twirl before the mirror like a little girl trying on her first party frock.

"The gown looks a treat on you, my lady," Tilda declared, smiling as she did up Margaret's long evening gloves. "Now, will you be wearing the diamonds or the pearls tonight?"

Either would suit the low neckline, but on consideration, Margaret decided upon a third option. "Neither. The emerald pendant that was my mother's." The chased gold setting was perhaps a touch heavy and old-fashioned, but its simplicity would complement that of the gown.

Tilda murmured approval and went to fetch the necklace. Margaret thought with another pang of Gervase's gift. She'd noticed his disappointment that she hadn't worn the cameo to church, though he'd quickly concealed it—as he did so many of his deeper emotions —and uttered not a word of reproach. Nor would she be wearing it tonight, as the colors wouldn't suit her evening gown any better than her day dress. That Gervase would doubtless be as understanding this evening as he'd been this morning made her feel guiltier than ever.

Biting her lip, she stared into the troubled eyes of her own reflection. It wasn't that she didn't *want* to wear the brooch; she just needed to find the right *time*. When they were back in London, perhaps, away from the prying eyes of their families. *If* they were still together by then.

Her heart lurched at the thought, even as she chided herself for being ridiculous. Much to her relief, Tilda returned with the necklace, fastening it deftly about her mistress's throat.

"My goodness!" Margaret exclaimed involuntarily, looking down.

The emerald solitaire on its heavy gold chain had settled just above the shallow cleft between her breasts, ever so slightly exposed by the gown's décolletage. Not unbecoming, but far more daring than her usual style. For a moment, she almost lost her nerve and asked Tilda to bring her the pearls or even a fichu, to fill up that expanse of bare skin. Pride—or perhaps only vanity—stopped her: the jewel matched the gown's color perfectly... as a certain pair of woodsmoke eyes would be quick to notice.

So instead, she let Tilda finish dressing her, accepted her reticule and a white lace fan that made her think of snowflakes mounted on ivory sticks, and set off for the ballroom.

Entering, she caught her breath in instinctive pleasure. The walls had been hung with champagne-gold silk, lending them a much-needed warmth against the chill of a winter night. Miniature arrangements of holly, ivy, and mistletoe brightened the window bays, larger ones of red and white camellias were placed strategically throughout the salon, and the lighted chandelier cast a soft glow over everything.

"Margaret!" Elaine rustled up to her in a billow of cream brocade. "What a beautiful gown—and you look simply ravishing in it!'

"Thank you. Alicia wanted me to wear it tonight," she added, smoothing the skirts a little self-consciously.

"I can see why." Elaine eyed the gown with appreciation. "Clearly, I shall have to make a trip to Maison

Worth myself, once the baby is born and I have my figure back."

Margaret smiled at her. "You hardly show at all right now, and you look, well, radiant." *Just as an expectant mother should*, she thought, masking a pang of wistfulness. Her own pregnancy had been marred by sickliness, perhaps an omen of the loss to come. She changed the subject hurriedly. "The ballroom looks magnificent tonight."

"Doesn't it? Mama and Juliana have outdone themselves."

"They certainly have," Margaret agreed, wondering how Her Grace could work so harmoniously with her daughters when her husband was such a disaster with his sons. She glanced around the room, surprised to see it so sparsely occupied. "Are we the only ones here?"

"For now." Elaine's smile held more than a trace of mischief. "But that's mainly because of the War of the Wassail being waged in the supper room."

"The War of the Wassail?" Margaret echoed, but before Elaine could elaborate, Gervase strode into the ballroom.

Again, Margaret caught her breath. While she'd seen Gervase in full dress every evening so far, he looked even more elegant tonight, the black tailcoat emphasizing his lean form, his shirt and waistcoat appearing blindingly white by comparison, and a single white camellia gleaming on his lapel. The light of the chandelier shone upon his hair, picking out threads of gold and bronze among the brown.

Elaine regarded him with sisterly approval. "You do us credit, Ger."

He raised a brow. "Do I? Well, then, my existence is now complete. Although," he added, eyeing them, "I would be honored to play the stem to such a pair of roses."

"What, no quotations from you tonight?" Margaret inquired lightly.

The intensity of his gaze seared her. "I could resort to a chorus of 'Greensleeves' if you like, but even Shakespeare seems inadequate to convey how well you look in that gown."

Greensleeves was all my joy, Greensleeves was my delight...

Margaret glanced aside, plying her fan to combat the sudden warmth in her cheeks.

"How about Byron?" Elaine suggested. "Do we not walk '*in beauty, like the night*'?"

"Most assuredly—both dark and bright." He smiled at them without a trace of reserve. "Now, did I hear someone mention wassail?"

"Not only wassail, but a wassail *war*," Elaine informed him. "I was just telling Margaret. Madeline has taken charge of preparing tonight's wassail punch, aided and abetted by Reg."

"Reg and Madeline?" Gervase's brows rose. "Now *there's* a combination seldom seen!"

"And with reason," Elaine observed, stifling a giggle. "They practically came to blows over the spices, and when I came away, they were arguing over the right proportions of cider to brandy. Reg, you may be sure, prefers the latter, Madeline the former. Alasdair was foolhardy enough to suggest the addition of whiskey, but they ignored him, fortunately. He and Hugo stayed to keep the peace, but I wouldn't lay odds on their success!"

"I'm almost sorry to have missed the excitement," Gervase remarked. "However, I had a rescue mission to undertake."

"A rescue mission?" Margaret glanced at him inquiringly.

He sighed. "The newest member of my household contrived to escape from his basket and climb up to the canopy of my bed. It took twenty minutes, the combined ingenuity of Farnsworth and myself, and a plate of chopped chicken to coax him down again."

"By the sound of it, he's got you wrapped round his forepaw already," Margaret observed, making no attempt to hide her amusement; Elaine was laughing outright.

"He's only getting away with it because it's Christmas," Gervase insisted. "Once we're back in London, Master Feste can learn to make himself useful —somehow."

"I'm sure your household will be the better for '*a harmless, necessary cat*,'" Elaine assured him. "Oh, look— here comes the wassail!"

A footman bearing a tray laden with steaming cups

had just entered from the supper room. A rich scent of apples, spices, and spirits followed him like a cloud.

Margaret breathed in the aroma. "Well, it smells wonderful anyway."

"As it should," Madeline said crisply, entering with Reg, Hugo, and Alasdair at her heels. "And you may taste the results for yourself. I adhered to our traditional recipe and used plenty of fruit and spices. Even though *someone*," she shot a pointed look at Reg, "thought we should leave out the clove-studded oranges."

Reg, splendid in his scarlet regimentals, shrugged a shoulder. "It's punch, not a pomander ball. I merely said reduce, not omit altogether. *And* I let you have your way about the cider too."

She regarded him through still-narrowed eyes. "I'd be more impressed by your magnanimity if I hadn't caught you trying to sneak in extra brandy at the last minute!"

"At least you finished before the guests arrived," Elaine said, ever the peacemaker. "They should be arriving any minute now, and they'll be glad of something hot to drink. I know I am," she added, accepting a cup of wassail from the footman.

"Who else is coming tonight?" Margaret asked, taking a cup as well. The punch looked as traditional as it smelled: flecked with spices and bits of fruit, but topped with a tiny square of toasted bread. The wassail toast.

"The Middletons, of course," Madeline replied. "And the Lovells, who may be bringing additional guests from *their* house party."

"Including a few Mama wouldn't mind Juliana meeting," Elaine added significantly.

Reg sighed. "Do women never tire of match-making? We've enough maudlin sentiment at Christmas, without adding in romantic drivel."

"And '*Bah, humbug*' to you too, big brother!" Juliana's laughing voice remarked from the doorway. Clad in a shimmering gown the color of candlelight, she glided into the room, Alicia trailing behind her. "As an unmarried, unbetrothed lady, should my ears be burning?"

"If they're not now, they will be once you drink this," Reg retorted, nodding towards the footman and his tray of cups.

Juliana perked up. "Ooh, wassail! Just the thing for Christmas night!"

Margaret studied her sister covertly as the two young women approached. Alicia wore a soft blue gown that made her look as pale and delicate as a snowdrop; it couldn't have been more different from the daring scarlet and gold confection she'd worn last night—the gown Reg had tossed so disdainfully after its wearer, along with the rest of her garments. Berthe had powdered and tinted her mistress's face with an expert hand, but Margaret could see the shadows beneath Alicia's eyes, the slight puffiness of the lids that hinted at recent tears, and her heart ached to see her sister's unhappiness. The confident young sophisticate had been replaced by a subdued penitent, mortified by her failed seduction and desperate for her fiancé's forgiveness. A forgiveness that Reg might be unable to express, even if he *felt* it, Margaret thought sadly. For as long as she could remember, Reg had shied away from emotional scenes involving women. His continued silence regarding Alicia's indiscretion might be the best her sister could hope for.

Much to her relief, Alicia's chin rose and a tinge of color crept into her cheeks as she drew near. "Meg, how lovely you look—I knew *that* was your color!"

Her bright tone sounded a bit forced, but Margaret was willing to overlook that to help her save face. "Thank you, dearest—your taste has been much admired. Have some wassail," she added, thinking that her sister might benefit from a bit of Dutch courage.

Alicia obeyed, blinking as the heady fragrance wafted up to her. "Goodness, this is strong! But I'm sure it's very warming, on a winter's night," she added hastily.

The rest of the party was filtering in: Augustus, looking more than ever like a golden Adonis, and Jason, wearing a new set of evening clothes that accommodated his recent growth. He appeared much the better for them, Margaret decided: not as sullen or self-conscious. Indeed, he was carrying himself with the pride of a young man who knew he looked his best tonight.

But that could be said of everyone—including Their Graces, now entering the ballroom together. The duchess in silver, her diamond coronet glittering upon

her dark head, looked like the Queen of Winter personi-
fied. The duke wore the same black-and-white evening
dress as the other men, but a sprig of holly glowed bright
as a jewel on his lapel, and his tawny head shone more
gold than silver beneath the light of the chandelier. Lord
of the Revels, Margaret thought irresistibly, *and* of all he
surveyed.

His sapphire gaze swept the room, and he gave a satisfied nod. "Ah, glad to see you're all here! The musicians
are settling into the gallery even as we speak, and Lydgate informs me that the arrival of our first guests is
imminent. Madeline, my dear, is that wassail punch I
smell?"

"It is," she confirmed, smiling more indulgently at
her father than was her usual wont. "Prepared *exactly* according to tradition."

"Excellent. I knew I could count upon you to see
things done properly." The duke turned to his wife.
"Well, madam, shall we have a toast to the occasion?"

"But of course, Duke." The duchess took the last two
cups remaining on the tray and handed one to her
husband.

Raising his cup, Whitborough faced his family. "To
an evening of merriment, and a happy Christmas to us
all. *Waes hail!*"

"*Waes hail!*" they echoed, and drank deep.

THE ADDITION of guests increased the company to some
three dozen people, a small turnout for a ball, but perfectly respectable for a Christmas night party, considering that most of the Whitboroughs' neighbors had
probably stayed at home, sleeping off their goose and
pudding.

But the evening was proving gay and convivial so far,
conversations humming from all corners of the room,
while the wassail punch flowed freely. Music lilted from
the gallery, and couples swirled about the dance floor,
with enough space to avoid collisions. There were several eligible young men pleased to make Juliana's acquaintance—and that of the other ladies as well.
Margaret was both surprised and amused by the

number of admiring male glances she received. Alicia's present, no doubt, which had her looking her best tonight. Although, if she were being wholly honest with herself, there was only one man whose opinion on that score mattered, and his response had proved most gratifying.

Nonetheless, she smiled at her partner—one of the Middleton sons—as he escorted her back to her corner after their polka. But the next dance was a waltz, which she had promised to Gervase. Anticipation fired her blood like wassail punch, leaving behind a similar warm glow.

Strange to think that, in all their years of knowing each other, they had never waltzed together. But it had always been Hal who'd laid claim to those, little as they'd meant to him and much as he might have preferred a different partner. But in the expectation that they would one day marry, he'd been automatically given first pick of the dances on her card.

Margaret sighed over the memory. So many years and waltzes wasted on her indifferent fiancé, when all the time there'd been a man who would have actually *enjoyed* dancing with her! Well, tonight she and Gervase could make up for those lost opportunities.

If he ever showed up. Scanning the ballroom, she finally located him in a far alcove, talking to his father. Or rather, the duke appeared to be talking, while Gervase listened with a faint half-smile. Curious and a touch apprehensive, she made her way towards them.

"—hope you've given what we discussed earlier some serious consideration," Whitborough was saying as she approached.

"I assure you, Father, I've given it all the consideration it deserves," Gervase replied.

His tone and expression were as smooth as country cream, and Margaret's disquiet grew. This was the Gervase she'd never quite understood: the guarded young man who kept his own counsel and weighed all his options before making his next move. The consummate chess player and occasional manipulator whom she respected but with whom she seldom felt at ease. She preferred the Gervase who climbed trees—complaining all the way—to rescue his sister's kitten, who challenged her on subjects she held dear, who lay relaxed and smiling beside her in bed, his limbs tangled with hers...

Father and son caught sight of her at the same moment, and their postures eased, Gervase unbending enough to give her a genuine smile. "Ah, Margaret! I was just about to claim our waltz. If you'll excuse us, sir?" he added to his father.

"By all means." The duke waved them off benignly. "Enjoy your dance."

"Dare I ask what that was about?" Margaret asked, as Gervase led her on to the floor.

He shrugged. "The usual. Am I in or out regarding his latest scheme, and when can he expect an answer?" A faint edge crept into his tone. "I am in no hurry to give one, and it will do him no harm to wait a little longer."

Spoken like a true Lyons. Margaret shivered, and he was immediately all solicitude. "Darling, are you cold? Would you care for some wassail, to warm you up?"

She shook her head. "No, thank you—one more cup and I'd be floating. As it is, I'm feeling no pain whatsoever," she added, striving for a lighter tone.

"The punch does seem unusually strong," he agreed. "Even *my* hard head is feeling the effects somewhat. I'm not sure that Reg didn't manage to slip in extra brandy, after all."

"Let's see if waltzing warms us up instead," she suggested.

He smiled, looking more like *her* Gervase. "I like the way you think, *belle amie*."

She moved into his arms as the music began, conscious as never before of the warmth of his hand at her waist, and the breadth of his shoulder as she rested her left hand upon it. A shoulder every bit as strong and muscular as his older brothers'.

It shouldn't have surprised her that he waltzed well, moving in perfect time with the music, his clasp light but firm. She might never have partnered him in that particular dance, but she'd seen him waltzing with his sisters numerous times. Still, a dance with a sibling was entirely different from a dance with a suitor—or a lover.

Her lover. As the dance progressed, she found herself leaning into his embrace, the space between their bodies dwindling until it seemed there was hardly any distance separating them. His eyes smiled into hers, more blue than grey at the moment, and holding more than a hint of desire, which her own eyes must surely reflect. Lowering her gaze, she breathed in his scent, a heady mingling of warm male skin, clean linen, and bergamot. Savor the moment, she told herself. Forget the past, don't think about the future... the present was all that mattered.

As the last strains of music faded away, she murmured, "So, was it worth the wait?"

His lips curved in a full smile. "Darling, you have no idea. And I could not have asked for a more beguiling partner."

She smiled back, absurdly pleased by the compliment. "Nor I." Hal had danced well, Alex tolerably, but Gervase moved with a lithe grace that surpassed them both, she thought.

"Are you bespoke for the next dance?"

She shook her head. "I thought a respite might be in order."

"Good thinking," he approved, offering his arm to lead her from the floor. "Perhaps we might take a walk in the conservatory? I've heard it's very romantic, by moonlight."

"Are you speaking from personal experience?" she teased.

"From my sisters', actually." His eyes glinted. "I have never before had a particular desire to stroll with a lady among the shrubbery. So this is an evening of firsts."

Hal had never taken her walking in the conservatory, not once in their entire betrothal. "It sounds delightful. Let us go."

Arm in arm, they strolled towards the doorway, only to find themselves halted by the duchess, who emerged seemingly out of nowhere, looking as brilliant and brittle as an icicle.

"Mother," Gervase acknowledged, inclining his head.

"Gervase." Her tone was crisp, even astringent. "Enjoying the party, I trust?"

"Yes, very much." To Margaret's disquiet, his face had become the polite mask he usually donned when dealing with his parents. She wondered if the duchess had ever noticed—or cared to notice—just how guarded Gervase became around her and the duke.

"*At Christmas play and make good cheer, / For Christmas comes but once a year*," Her Grace quoted. "Still, play must yield to work eventually, and childish games cease. Do you not agree, *mon fils?*"

The muscles of Gervase's arm tightened beneath Margaret's hand, though neither his face nor his voice betrayed his tension. "That depends, *Maman*. Some games continue long past childhood—with no clear outcome in sight."

"They might end sooner, if the players would cease straddling the fence and choose a side," the duchess pointed out.

"Ah, but without the proper incentive, the fence is the only sensible place to be," he countered silkily.

Margaret glanced between mother and son, aware that a silent battle of wills was going on. Then, unnervingly, the duchess's gaze shifted to *her*. "Ah, Margaret! I meant to tell you before how well you look in that gown! *Très belle*, my dear."

"Thank you," Margaret said, disconcerted by the sudden change in direction.

"On that we certainly agree, *Maman*," Gervase observed.

"You and my son look well together too," the duchess continued, ignoring him.

Margaret hesitated, unsure how to respond, though she knew quite well what Her Grace was attempting to discern. Quickly, before those probing eyes could somehow strip her secret bare, she said with a bright, superficial smile, "Oh, Gervase is an excellent dancer."

"As is Margaret herself," Gervase interposed smoothly. "Although, after our exertions, we are both finding the ballroom a trifle warm. Would you excuse us, Mother?"

Annoyance flickered in the duchess's eyes, but after a moment, she stepped gracefully aside. "But of course— enjoy the rest of the evening. And Gervase," she laid a hand upon his sleeve, "I hope you realize that, should your *personal* circumstances change, I am prepared to be... as generous as your father."

He inclined his head. "Thank you, Mother. Happy

Christmas."

"Gervase," Margaret began, as they finally made good their escape, "was that—"

"My mother demonstrating that she can be every bit as controlling and manipulative as my father?" he finished with a tight smile, as they made their way along the dimly lit corridor outside the ballroom. "Yes. Very astute of you to notice."

She suppressed a shiver. "Do you think she suspects —about us?"

"Perhaps." He glanced at her, his softening expression visible even in the shadows. "Don't worry, *ma mie*. I'll make sure *you* don't get caught up in their ridiculous schemes."

"That's all very well, but what about you?"

He shrugged. "What about me? I'm a Lyons—I grew up surrounded by such intrigues."

"You have no idea how much that fails to reassure me," she retorted.

"Margaret." He paused to cup her face briefly, his hands warm through his evening gloves. "I assure you, there's no need to worry. And when you think about it," he added more lightly, "the whole situation is not without its amusing side."

"*Amusing?*" She shot him a disbelieving glance.

"Think about it." Humor as black as a winter's night edged his voice. "The all-powerful Duke and Duchess of Whitborough, falling over themselves to court the son they've virtually ignored for the last twenty years! I keep wondering what extravagant offer they'll make next, to sway me to their side. Not that I set much store by *that*, but I would have to be a saint not to find their antics vastly entertaining. It's a refreshing change to be the one holding the strings."

Margaret gritted her teeth. "Very diverting, I'm sure —until someone gets hurt!"

"Thank you for your concern, darling, but I can take care of myself."

"That's what Hal thought too."

The words flashed out, as swift and sharp as a sword stroke, shocking them into silence.

After a seeming eternity, Gervase spoke, his eyes dark in his pale face. "I'm not Hal."

Margaret bit her lip, half-wishing her words unsaid. "No," she managed. "No, you're much stronger than Hal. Which is why it's so hard to watch your parents twist you up inside."

He exhaled, his breath forming a cloud in the chilly passage. "I can handle my parents—"

"Can you?" she challenged. "I once compared them to badminton players bashing a shuttlecock back and forth. But now I think they're more like *grindstones*, crushing everything and everyone that comes between them into powder!"

His eyes widened at her vehemence. "Margaret—"

"You say that you're holding the strings, but strings can be pulled both ways!" she reminded him. "How can you be sure that *they're* not the ones in control, just as they've always been? That you're not playing right into their hands, by playing this game at all?"

"You don't understand." Anger roughened his voice, kindled a blaze in his eyes. "How could you, when you were raised so differently? *Your* parents—"

"Loved their children equally," she finished. "For which I am forever grateful. But I understand better than you think, Gervase. I spent years watching you and your brothers compete for your parents' attention—and watching *them* feed those rivalries for their own purposes, instead of encouraging you to be friends. Or even allies. That was *their* folly." She swallowed again, her eyes stinging. "But letting them continue to manipulate you... that would be *yours*."

He stared at her, lost for words for the first time she could remember. Holding his gaze, she strove to reach him, infusing her words with a conviction rooted in her soul. "You made your own life, Gervase, and your own success. I was so proud of you for that. Don't risk losing everything you've gained by involving yourself in your parents' war. Don't risk losing *us*."

"Losing us?" he echoed, his voice scarcely above a whisper.

Margaret forced herself to go on, past the emotions clogging her throat. "I don't know if I could be with a man who does not ultimately belong to himself. I *know* I can't stand by and watch a man I—care for be consumed by family strife... as Hal was."

Chapter Sixteen

*And this same progeny of evils comes
From our debate, from our dissension;
We are their parents and original.*
—WILLIAM SHAKESPEARE, *A Midsummer
Night's Dream*, II, i

GERVASE STARED at the woman he loved, shock and in-
dignation flooding through him.

He *wasn't* Hal! That feckless, charming boy who'd
never grown up, who'd immersed himself in frivolous
pursuits because he could never match—nor be *allowed*
to match his father's success in the business world! *He'd*
seen, years ago, which way the wind was blowing and
charted his own course accordingly. And now he was at
the top of his profession: respected, admired, sometimes
even feared... someone to be taken seriously. A player in
the game, as he'd told his father—with nothing to lose
by participating.

Except *her*, apparently. *Except us.* An impasse he'd
never foreseen.

His hands fisted at his sides, and he lowered his gaze,
fighting the irrational urge to... what, roar and bluster,
like his father or Reg? Furiously deny that her words
held any truth, as Jason might have done? Neither way
was his; he'd always striven to keep the Lyons temper in
check. He was the levelheaded, analytical one, who

channeled hot rage into cold purpose and dissected opposing arguments with surgical precision. Hard to remember that now, with so many emotions—anger,
frustration, even hurt—churning inside of him like a tur-
bulent sea.

Unclenching his hands, he took a slow breath, willing
himself back to calm. Lashing out would be childish and
accomplish nothing. Surely, with the application of reason, he could *make* Margaret understand...

Then he saw the betraying shimmer in her eyes, and
reason bled away, leaving him feeling drained and oddly
defeated.

"I'm sorry." There were tears in her voice as well as
her eyes, and his heart ached dully in response. "I never
meant to hurt you. But I can't help what I feel—"

He cleared his throat, endeavored to speak normally.
"No need to apologize—you spoke from the heart. And
we have always been honest with each other, have we
not?"

Margaret made a sound between a laugh and a sob,
brushed impatiently at her eyes. "Yes, but we're not usually so—*brutal* about it."

"The wassail, perhaps?" he suggested. "We've both
drunk a bit more than usual tonight."

*In vino veritas. In wine there is truth. Perhaps we've had a
little too much of both.*

"That's possible," she conceded, after a moment.

Gervase drew another steadying breath, "Then, shall
we return to the ballroom? I can fetch us some coffee or
soda water, to help clear our heads." He spared a moment to regret their walk in the conservatory, but neither of them happened to be in a romantic mood
just now.

She hesitated, then gave a tiny nod of acquiescence.
"Perhaps... that would be best."

He offered her his arm, and they retraced their steps
in silence.

❄

MUCH TO GERVASE'S RELIEF, no one intercepted him on
the way to the supper room. He'd left Margaret seated in
a quiet alcove, partly hidden from view by a tall vase of

camellias; she'd been grateful for the privacy, hinting that she would appreciate some time to think.

Gervase supposed they could both benefit from that. They might have patched things up, but Margaret's words continued to gnaw at him all the same.

A familiar voice floated out from the supper room, halting Gervase in his tracks. Instinctively, he drew back into the shadows on the far side of the doorway.

"—never waltzed especially well," Reg was saying, sounding gruffer than usual. "I am sure you could find a more graceful partner among our guests."

"But I saved some waltzes just for *you!*" Alicia protested. "Please, Reg—it would mean so much to me."

Gervase winced at the naked pleading—just bordering on desperation—in her voice. *Use me but as your spaniel, spurn me, strike me, / Neglect me, lose me...*

Reg said stiffly, "I'm afraid my dancing is done for the night, Alicia. An old... cricket injury has been giving me trouble all day. I need to rest it, if I'm to ride out tomorrow."

Old cricket injury? Gervase shook his head. *Lame, brother—even for you.*

"Now, if you'll excuse me, I need to speak to Sir George Middleton—"

"Reg!" A world of yearning in that one word. "*Why* do you keep pushing me away? Is it because you can't forgive me—for last night?"

Oh, God. Gervase steeled himself for his brother's reply.

A charged pause ensued, then, "Last night is best forgotten, by both of us," Reg replied, every syllable clipped and curt. "Enjoy the party."

Gervase flattened himself against the wall as his brother strode into the passage, looking neither right nor left in his haste to escape from his fiancée. A moment later, a choked sob issued from within.

Gervase sighed. He did not know Alicia well, but he could hardly leave her alone, weeping over the punch bowl, without making some effort to help her—if only for Margaret's sake. Squaring his shoulders, he walked into the supper room.

Alicia was in a corner by the window, dabbling at her eyes with a lacy wisp of a handkerchief, her breath hitching in tiny, barely audible sobs. Gervase eyed her, torn between pity and exasperation. Had the girl no pride—or backbone—at all?

The usual admonitions crowded his mind: Reg was a brusque, unsentimental soldier, not given to romantic speeches or displays. But unless Alicia had spent the last ten years with her eyes closed, she must know that already—even if the reality was more difficult to live with than she'd expected. Perhaps it was time everyone stopped treating her as though she were made of blown glass.

"Pardon me," he began, as those tear-drenched blue eyes turned in his direction, "but I could not help overhearing."

She froze, the flush mounting to her hairline making her look no older than sixteen. "If I may offer some unsolicited advice," Gervase continued in his most lawyerly tone, "I think you should dry your eyes, compose yourself, and go back into the ballroom. There are any number of attractive young men who would be delighted to dance with you, fetch you drinks, and attend to your lightest wish all evening."

Alicia practically goggled at him. Whatever she'd expected him to say, it wasn't this. "B-but how can I—"

"Show some pride in yourself," he advised. "Some dignity, as befits the daughter of a duke. You might contrive to enjoy the party, after all. At the very least, you might feel less miserable than you do now."

"Pride?" Alicia bristled like an affronted kitten. "Dignity? How dare you? How can *you* presume to know what I'm feeling?"

Gervase refused to take umbrage. "I would say it was obvious to even the most casual observer. Happy women seldom spend Christmas—during a party, no less— crying in a corner."

"And observing is what you do best, isn't it?" Alicia struck back. "How superior you must feel, Lord Gervase, *watching* the human race instead of actually *engaging* with it!"

So, the kitten had claws. "Not bad," he approved. "Show *this* side of yourself, and Reg might take more of an interest."

Tears sprang to Alicia's eyes, but before she could

launch into fresh sobs or reproaches, he continued, "Brother Reg admires strength, Alicia. And independence. He has no use for soft, clinging females who beg for his attention." He added more gently, "He is close to our mother and sisters because they are women of spirit, who can stand on their own."

"I just wanted to show him how much I *care*!" she defended herself. "You talk of pride and dignity! What does *that* get you except loneliness?"

"There's no lonelier place on earth than in a loveless marriage." Or a marriage where the love has soured, he thought—like his parents'.

"Did Meg put you up to this?" Alicia demanded, her eyes accusing.

"She has no idea I'm even speaking to you now." But the memory of Margaret's disillusionment with Hal rose in his mind, along with the advice he'd offered then. Different though the sisters were, Alicia might benefit from similar counsel.

"I don't know what sort of marriage you hope to have with Reg," he began, meeting her gaze levelly. "But it would be better in any case for you to have interests that *don't* revolve around him. Build your own life, and don't depend on him to supply everything you need."

Alicia's mouth opened in instinctive protest, then, unexpectedly, closed, and her brow creased in a pensive frown. Had what he said actually penetrated? "That's... not such bad advice," she conceded, sounding a bit surprised.

"Offered *gratis*, from your future brother-in-law," Gervase said lightly, and saw her lips twitch into something resembling a smile.

"I never thanked you properly for last night, did I? For keeping quiet about..." She dropped her gaze, flushing again.

"That, too, is *gratis*," he assured her.

She looked up with a more genuine smile. "Thank you."

"You're welcome. Now, have you seen the soda water by any chance?"

❄

It would be all right, Margaret told herself for the hundredth time. She and Gervase hadn't *quarreled*. After the first shock of what she'd said, he hadn't even seemed angry—only startled... and maybe, just a little hurt.

Her eyes stung, and she looked down, nervously pleating the folds of her fan. Hurting Gervase was the last thing she'd ever wanted to do. She knew what a sensitive subject his family was for him. And he hadn't been wrong when he said she did not understand what it was like to grow up as a Lyons.

But neither had *she* been wrong, to point out what he was risking by getting caught up in his parents' schemes. If she could just make him see that he didn't *need* their validation, that what he'd achieved on his own already made him worthy of respect. Could whatever amusement he derived from playing Their Graces off against each other—an impulse she *did* understand to some degree—truly outweigh his satisfaction at becoming one of London's top solicitors... and his own man?

Her pulse quickened when she heard male voices approaching, but none belonged to Gervase. After a moment, however, she recognized the man currently speaking as Sir George Middleton, the local Master of Foxhounds.

"Ready for the meet tomorrow, Lyons?" he inquired jovially. "Yorkshire may not be Melton, but I can promise you some good sport all the same."

"More than ready, Sir George," she heard Reg reply. "Lord Roland and I are looking forward to an excellent run with your pack."

The two men paused just outside Margaret's alcove. Peering around the vase of camellias blocking her view, she caught a glimpse of Sir George's back and one of Reg's scarlet sleeves.

"He's that big black hunter of yours, isn't he?" Sir George was saying. "I heard in the village that you'd had a new one delivered this very morning—a handsome chestnut."

Margaret tensed, but after a moment, Reg replied calmly, "No, that was a Christmas gift for my brother Jason. Father thought it time he had a proper hunter of his own."

"A princely gift," Sir George remarked. "Is the horse up to the task?"

Another infinitesimal pause, then, "He seems sound enough."

"If you say so, Lyons, then he must be. Ah, Langdale —good evening to you! Lyons and I were just discussing the St. Stephen's Day hunt. Will you be joining us tomorrow?"

"Indeed, Sir George," Augustus replied. "I wouldn't miss it for the world."

"Splendid!" the older man exclaimed. "Glad to hear you young fellows are so keen on sport, and not planning to spend tomorrow dozing by the fire! Ah, there's my lady—if you'll pardon me, gentlemen, I promised her the next dance." He set off, his step as lively as that of a man half his age.

"Good evening, Major," Augustus greeted his sister's fiancé cordially.

"Langdale," Reg returned evenly.

Margaret shifted in her chair, wondering if she should announce her presence now. The last time she'd seen her brother and Reg share more than the most perfunctory exchanges had been in the gymnasium, when Augustus had challenged the older man to a wrestling bout—and brought up Captain Hastings. And while nothing catastrophic had occurred, the memory still unsettled her.

"Pardon me," Augustus began, after a moment, "but I could not help but overhear what you told Sir George. And commend you on how well you've handled your disappointment—over the horse, I mean."

Margaret frowned. What Augustus was saying sounded perfectly polite, but she felt a growing unease that he'd brought the subject up at all.

"Not at all, Langdale." Reg's tone was still perfectly even. "I am sure that I'll find another hunter just as suitable when I go looking again."

"Nevertheless, I feel I must apologize—for my role in this morning's little drama."

"*Your* role?" Reg's surprise mirrored Margaret's own.

Her brother continued smoothly, "I was, I confess, rather put out by what I saw as your neglect of my sister. Which led me to say some things in anger, in your father's hearing, that I now regret. But I never once thought Whitborough would take my suggestion so literally."

"What, exactly, did you suggest?" A certain tautness had crept into Reg's voice.

"I merely intimated that you would be far more... upset over losing a horse than losing a bride. Forgive me —an excess of port, along with temper, must have been to blame."

Margaret sat immobile, the realization creeping over her like a freezing fog.

"No need to ask forgiveness, Langdale." Reg's voice seemed to come from a long distance off. "My father is responsible for his own actions, inexplicable as they seem." Another pause ensued, then he added, "Will you excuse me? Saxby gave me a box of Cubans for Christmas, and I have been craving a good cigar this age."

"By all means, Major."

Reg strode away, and Margaret's misgivings grew as she tracked his progress along the perimeter of the ballroom floor. He moved like the soldier he was, heading swiftly and purposefully towards his destination.

The distant corner where Whitborough was standing alone.

And in that moment before father and son came face to face, Margaret heard something that struck an even deeper chill into her heart: the soft, satisfied huff of her brother's laughter.

As if... he'd *expected* this to happen. More—as if he'd deliberately set it in motion.

Reg was now speaking to Whitborough. While unable to hear what was being said, Margaret could tell from Reg's expression that it wasn't likely to be anything good. Her suspicions were confirmed when she saw how the duke's expression changed—or rather, vanished completely, his face becoming an unreadable mask. The way Gervase's did, she realized, when he didn't want anyone to know what he was thinking or feeling. Then His Grace held up a hand, and replied briefly to whatever his son had said. Reg gave a curt nod in response, and the two men left their corner, heading out of the ballroom.

Uneasily, Margaret watched them depart. Then, out of the corner of her eye, she spied further movement:

Augustus, serenely decamping after having sown his seeds of discord—and blithely unaware that anyone else had overheard his exchange with Reg. Even his retreating back radiated complacency. *What's* your *game, brother dear?*

Well, she wasn't going to find out just sitting here. Quietly, compelled by some unknown instinct, she rose from her chair, slipped out of the alcove, and followed him at a distance.

She spared a moment to be thankful for all the childhood games of hide-and-seek and sardines, which had taught her to move with stealth; even full ball dress didn't impede her movements too much. Fortunately, Augustus appeared unaware of her presence.

Where was he planning to go now? After Reg and the duke, to eavesdrop on their conversation? Surely, that piece of spite was beneath him—but then, so was setting them against each other in the first place, and he'd done that without hesitation. A sudden impulse—or something far more calculated and malicious?

At present, Augustus seemed content to drift along the periphery, paying no heed beyond a cursory nod or smile at the other guests. Margaret likewise avoided attempts to engage her attention as she focused upon her brother's aimless wanderings.

"I say, Langdale!" Much to her surprise, Jason was hurrying towards Augustus. Hurriedly, she stepped back, hiding her face behind her fan and turning slightly aside as though absorbed in her surroundings. She was, however, still close enough to hear what was said.

"I just saw Father leave the ballroom with Reg," the young man went on, not troubling to lower his voice much below its usual volume. "Do you know anything about that?"

"Ah." Augustus stood where he was, regarding the youngest Lyons brother. Something about his stance reminded Margaret uncomfortably of a cat watching a bird flutter within reach. "Why would you think that, Lord Jason?"

"Because I saw you and Reg talking, just before."

"Ah," Augustus repeated, infusing that lone syllable with a wealth of significance that set Margaret's teeth on edge. "I must confess to an unfortunate slip of the tongue there. I only hope I haven't made an... awkward situation worse."

Jason frowned. "I don't follow you, Langdale."

"I happened to commend the Major on his graciousness, knowing how disappointed he must have been when your father purchased that hunter for you instead—"

"What?" Jason interrupted, his eyes widening. "*That* was the horse Reg wanted?"

"You didn't know?" The astonishment in Augustus's voice sounded almost genuine, and Margaret's hand clenched around her fan. "Oh, dear. I've put my foot in it again, apparently—"

"Never mind that!" Jason's face was flushed, his eyes ablaze with excitement—and an unholy glee that made Margaret's stomach sink. "It's really true? Father gave *me* Reg's horse?"

"It would seem so." Augustus's tone managed to convey reluctance, sympathy, and regret all at once.

Quite an improvement over his wooden performances in their amateur theatricals, his sister reflected caustically. And Jason's gloating grin was so insufferable that Margaret no longer wondered why his siblings often longed to wipe it from his face.

"Did you see where Father and Reg went?" he asked now.

"I really couldn't say," Augustus demurred.

"No matter. I can find out easily enough." Still grinning, Jason turned away—without so much as a word of thanks for the news he'd been given.

Not that Augustus appeared to mind. Indeed, he could not have looked more satisfied as he watched the younger man stride off. Smirking visibly, the Duke of Langdale strolled off in the opposite direction as Jason, still oblivious to the presence of his seething sister.

Margaret's mind raced, trying furiously to calculate her next move. What could she do, exactly? Nothing that Augustus had told Reg or Jason was untrue—and some small part of her thought it might serve Whitborough right to have to deal with the consequences of his latest manipulation. But it was another thing entirely to watch her own brother fan the flames of that already bitter rivalry. Why was he doing this? What could he possibly hope to gain by it?

"Margaret." Relief flooded through her at the familiar voice, and she turned to find Gervase beside her, holding a glass of soda water. "I couldn't find you in the alcove—"

"I'm sorry," she blurted out, all in a rush. "But I *had* to find out what Augustus was doing! I swear, I think he's gone stark staring mad——"

"Shh," he soothed, handing her the glass. "Calm down, my dear, and tell me what this is all about."

Margaret took a sip to steady herself. "I'm not sure *I* know! Except that my brother seems to be going out of his way to cause trouble tonight!"

"Trouble? How so?"

"Well, first I overheard him talking to Reg," she began. "And confessing that *he* might have inadvertently given your father the idea to buy that horse!"

Gervase raised his brows. "Did he indeed? I can't imagine *that* pleased Brother Reg!"

"He went to confront your father, and then they left the ballroom together," Margaret informed him. "And I heard Augustus actually *laughing* about it. Then, to make matters even worse, he not-so-inadvertently told Jason that his new hunter—"

"Was the one Reg had his eye on," Gervase finished for her. "Well, I can't begin to guess your brother's motives, but he's certainly been busy tonight!"

"He has indeed," Margaret said grimly. "And I'm about to see that he becomes much *less* so." She was, after all, Augustus's *older* sister by a good three years.

"I recommend the Yellow Saloon for the purpose you have in mind. Reasonably close, but far enough away that you shouldn't be disturbed by noise from the ballroom. Talking of which," he glanced about the salon, "where did Jason go?"

"After Reg and your father, wherever that is."

His eyes flashed annoyance. "Damn the boy! I should have known he wouldn't be able to resist the opportunity to crow." He grimaced. "It appears that *I* have a fire to put out as well."

"Must you go?" Margaret tried not to sound forlorn.

"Tempting though it is to let the three of them simply have at each other, one should probably make an effort to restore peace at Christmas. I might be able to retrieve Jason; he listens to me—occasionally." His mouth crooked in a wry half-smile. "And someone needs to see that the blood is cleaned up afterwards. Courage, *belle amie*," he added more gently, resting a hand upon her shoulder. "We're more than a match for the lot of them."

As GERVASE STRODE out of the ballroom, Margaret approached her brother, who was sipping a newly acquired cup of wassail punch. That punch might have a great deal to answer for, she reflected darkly.

Aloud she said, smiling, "Happy Christmas, Augustus."

He inclined his head, his own expression benign but unreadable, and once again, she wondered how they'd become such strangers to each other. "Happy Christmas, Margaret."

"It occurs to me that we've hardly spoken this past week," she observed, still smiling. "I was wondering if I might have a private word with you."

He regarded her quizzically over the rim of his cup. "Indeed you may, but might I inquire what this is about?"

Margaret assumed what Elaine had called her "doe-eyed look" during their shared season. "Oh, a matter of some delicacy, I assure you."

"Very well." Augustus drained his cup and set it aside. "Where might we go?"

Remembering Gervase's advice, she proposed the Yellow Saloon, to which her brother readily acquiesced, and they quietly left the ballroom.

On reaching their destination, Margaret locked the door behind them, earning a surprised glance and a raised eyebrow from Augustus.

"This must be a sensitive matter indeed," he observed.

"Just making sure we won't be disturbed." Margaret turned around, letting her blandly smiling mask drop away. "First of all, Augustus, I would appreciate an explanation for why you've been doing what you're doing."

Both eyebrows rose this time. "I wasn't aware that I was doing anything."

"You were deliberately trying to stir up trouble between Whitborough and his sons tonight." She spoke with all the sisterly sternness she could muster. "Don't bother to deny it! I overheard you telling Reg about that blasted horse, and how *you* might have inspired the duke to buy it for Jason instead."

Surprise, followed by irritation, flickered across his face. "Eavesdropping, Margaret? That's hardly to your credit."

"I wouldn't call it eavesdropping when the speaker can't be bothered to lower his voice in a crowded ballroom," Margaret retorted, refusing to be put on the defensive. "And unlike you, I was *not* trying to make mischief! You must have known Reg would confront his father, after what you told him! And Jason," she went on heatedly. "Setting *him* off after them—that can't possibly end well! What ever were you thinking?"

She might have abandoned her mask, but Augustus's remained firmly in place. "Pardon me if I don't share your concern about Whitborough or his sons, dear sister. The thought of that manipulative bastard being torn apart by his own progeny affords me the deepest satisfaction."

Margaret caught her breath, stunned by the venom in his tone and the malevolent gleam in his eyes. "Augustus, this—this isn't like you..."

"No?" He shrugged a shoulder. "Considering how seldom we have seen each other since your marriage, perhaps you don't know what is 'like me' as well as you think you do."

She had to concede his point, if only to herself. Their lives had diverged years earlier, and her marriage and subsequent removal to Gloucestershire had only widened the gap. "Augustus," she tried for a more temperate tone, "what is this all about, really?"

He stilled, his fine features growing stony. "Has it never bothered you, Margaret—how often Whitborough got the best of our father?"

"Why ever should it?" she asked, in genuine bewilderment.

Augustus folded his arms, his expression chillingly remote. "I heard about it over and over from Grandfather. And I've thought about it even more since becoming Langdale. How Whitborough stole Father's bride right out from under his nose—"

"They weren't married," Margaret reminded him. "They weren't even betrothed—"

"A double heiress," he continued, as if she hadn't spoken, "whom Grandfather picked out just for his heir, and Whitborough convinced her to elope with him—"

"Papa didn't even want to marry her, not really," she pointed out. "He loved Mama. He always had, even before he became the heir."

"Every chance Father had, every opportunity to get ahead, in business or in life—Whitborough bested him at every turn."

It was like speaking to a brick wall, but Margaret kept trying nonetheless. "Papa didn't mind. They even used to laugh about it together."

"Well, *I* mind for him." Her brother's voice hardened. "And once, just once, I mean to get the better of that old man. He won't ride roughshod over *me* the way he did over Father. And he won't be laughing either, once I'm through with him."

"Augustus, Papa was *happy*!" she insisted. "He had everything he truly wanted—Mama and us. He had a family he loved. And I don't think he'd have traded any of it for the Duke of Whitborough's life." She paused, hoping that her words were sinking in, then resumed somberly, "They haven't led the charmed existence you think they have. They lost their eldest son—their heir." *My betrothed.* "And they've been estranged for years. Their other sons are at each other's throats more often than not. Do you think Papa would have wanted to live like that?"

"It no longer matters what our father would have wanted," he countered. "He's dead, while Whitborough, his termagant wife, and their litter of snarling curs are still alive. Toss even the hint of a bone their way, and they'll rend each other limb from limb over it. I'm shedding no tears for any of them."

Shocked into silence, Margaret stared at her brother. The handsome features, taut with implacable anger. The sculpted lips set in a hard line, the pale eyes colder than the ice they resembled. No, not Papa's face—Grandfather's.

She'd always been just a little afraid of the old duke. And she'd gathered that he'd been none too pleased that her parents' first surviving child had been a daughter instead of the all-important son and heir. He hadn't been cruel or even unkind, so much as indifferent to Margaret. But when Mama had been ill after Alicia's birth, the duke had taken it upon himself to spend more time with his young grandson, whom he'd shaped in his own image.

Over the years, she'd looked in vain for Papa's warmth and generosity in her brother's character. Instead, he was the old duke all over again: ruthless, competitive... and cold, even when he professed to care.

Unfazed by her scrutiny, Augustus strolled over to the sideboard and poured himself a glass of whiskey from one of the decanters.

Somehow, Margaret found her voice again. "What about Alicia?"

He glanced over his shoulder. "What about her?"

"Whatever your feelings about the Whitboroughs, you might consider *her* happiness. This is the family our sister wishes to marry into."

"Is it, indeed?" His tone was indifferent. "Well, she may need to prepare herself for disappointment. I have every belief that this marriage will not come off." Satisfaction practically oozed from him. "Moorhaven will be back in the family again, soon enough. That's one prize Whitborough won't be getting his talons on."

"What makes you believe that?" she demanded. "You know how Alicia loves Reg!"

"And we all know how Reg *doesn't* return the sentiment."

"That doesn't matter to Alicia," Margaret pointed out. "She's determined to go through with the wedding."

"Ah, but is *he* as determined?" Augustus mused, holding his glass up to the light as though admiring the color of the liquor. "Personally, I think not. The Major may be willing to call his father's bluff for now, but I'll lay odds that his nerve will break at the altar as it never has upon the battlefield." A faint smile curved his lips. "Of course, the cream of the jest is that even the all-knowing, all-powerful Duke of Whitborough hasn't tumbled to the secret yet."

"Secret?" Margaret husked, a sick feeling growing in her stomach at the words.

His eyes glittered with malice. "That his heir, the celebrated soldier, the very model of manliness, would far rather take *me* to bed than our sister!"

All the breath seemed to rush out of Margaret's lungs. "You *know*?"

His gaze sharpened. "*You* know?"

They stared at each other for what seemed an eternity, then Augustus uttered a soft laugh that froze his sister to the marrow. "Well, well... Alicia may lack the brains of a butterfly, but clearly you're not as innocent or naïve as you seem." His eyes narrowed in a probing stare. "How did *you* happen to discover the Major's dirty little secret?"

"Never mind that," Margaret said tersely. "I know. Let that suffice for now."

"A good thing you ran off with Bellamy when Whitborough was thinking of passing you along to your late fiancé's brother. Or," his eyes flared wide in comprehension, "was that *why* you ran off with Bellamy in the first place?"

"That's not your business," she said curtly.

He raised mocking brows. "Oh, come, Margaret! Surely one good secret deserves another. Besides, shouldn't a brother and sister be in each other's confidence?"

She found herself shaking with unaccustomed rage. "Go to hell, Augustus!"

"In due course, perhaps," he replied, unperturbed. "But I'll see Whitborough there first."

Sick at heart, she turned away and made for the door on unsteady legs, leaving Augustus behind to drown his sorrows—or, more likely, to celebrate his success in setting his enemies at each other's throats. Her brother and sister: the latter so desperate for a man's love that she'd sacrifice her self-respect, the former so calculating that he'd sacrifice everything and everyone to his personal vendetta. Both of them strangers to her... and now she wondered if she had ever truly known either of them.

All of the sudden, she wanted Gervase desperately, hoped fervently that his crisis would prove far more manageable than hers just had.

But knowing who was involved, that seemed a forlorn hope indeed.

ACCORDING TO A FOOTMAN, His Grace and the major had last been seen heading towards the former's private study. Gervase thanked him and quickened his pace. Just as he'd suspected: his father's study and the scene of countless family rows. How the walls had rung with the battles between Father and Mother, Father and Hal, Father and Reg, Father and himself—on those rare occasions when Whitborough took more than a cursory interest in his third son's affairs. Which happened mainly when they conflicted with the duke's own agenda, Gervase reflected wryly, remembering that long, acrimonious argument over his refusal to enter the Church.

He spared a hope—probably futile—that he might intercept Jason before reaching the study. Or, if he were too late on that score, that he might be able to extract the whelp and keep him from making a bad situation worse. Now that Reg had confirmation of their father's horse-dealing scheme, he was unlikely to hold back his rage at him—or at the beneficiary of that scheme. Not for the first time, Gervase wondered why the hell his parents, so accomplished at so many things, were so inept at hiding their partiality for their favored sons—and so incapable of seeing how much that favoritism had damaged their family as a whole.

Even if he hadn't known Denforth like the back of his hand, the sound of raised voices would have guided him unerringly towards the study. Grimly, he headed down the passage just as Jason's voice, cracking with excitement and triumph, rang out through the half-open door.

"—really true, Father? That you gave *me* Reg's horse?"

could detect a hint of defensiveness. As if, deep down, their father knew his latest manipulation had been just a bit... petty. "The sooner you accept that, the better!"

"And what about you, Father?" Reg challenged. "When are *you* going to accept that *I* am the next Duke of Whitborough? The rightful heir, by law, and none of your schemes will change that. I'll have what is *mine*—the title, the estate, and the wealth to sustain them! I will not lose anything more to this... festering boil, this walking pile of horse sh—"

"That's enough!" their father thundered. "None of it's yours *yet*, or have you forgotten that little detail?"

"How could I, when you hoard power the way a miser hoards his pelf?"

"Did you hear what he called me?" Jason's voice soared indignantly over the other two. "You're just jealous, Reg—you've *always* been jealous—that I'm Father's favorite!"

Gervase had heard enough. "And *you* have no sense of self-preservation, whelp!" he remarked, pushing open the door and wading into the fray.

A trio of faces turned towards him, and he took quick stock of them all: Jason, scarlet with rage, Reg, pale and flint-eyed, and Whitborough, his own color up, his blue eyes sparking with a mixture of temper and defiance.

"Listening at doors again?" Reg sneered.

And such was the power of her presence that, to a man, her husband and sons immediately fell silent, all their attention fixed on her.

She stepped into the room, her coolly assessing gaze alighting upon each of them in turn.

"A family reunion, and no one thought to invite me?" She glanced about the study. "I see the girls aren't here either. Shall I dispatch a footman to fetch them?"

"That," Gervase said, "would be a singularly bad idea, Mother."

"Indeed, and on a day that has seen plenty of those already," she said dryly.

"Madam," the duke began, looking and sounding almost apprehensive, much to Gervase's surprise. "Had this been a matter that required your presence—"

"I learned long ago to pay close attention when all the Lyons men leave the room at approximately the same time," his wife interrupted. "How else would I have discovered the truth about so many things—including my husband's latest equine investment?"

A muscle twitched at the corner of the duke's jaw as he absorbed her words and her unwavering scrutiny. The tension in the study spread like a thickening layer of ice, holding everyone fast in its frozen grip. Gervase glanced at his brothers and found them as apparently disinclined to speak as he. Even Jason was holding his tongue— proving that discretion was indeed the better part of valor.

The duchess's eyes and voice were equally frigid. "That should have been beneath you, Harold. I was fool enough to think it was."

"It was a fair deal," he insisted, though the defensiveness had crept back into his tone.

"Undertaken for the most *unfair* of reasons," she countered.

His eyes narrowed. "You are hardly the best judge of what is fair or unfair, Helene! Wasn't financing our eldest son's attempted *coup* supposed to be beneath *you*? Or do you still consider it my just punishment for infidelity?"

Gervase winced inwardly. Christ, that *was* a low blow. And there were ghosts in the room now, not just of a dead son, but of an old betrayal. Eleven years ago, Hal, frustrated by their father's refusal to allow him any real power or authority, had tried to acquire a controlling interest in one of the duke's businesses—with their mother's backing. Ultimately, he'd been thwarted, but Whitborough had neither forgotten nor ever really forgiven his son or his wife.

The duchess stilled, her fine-boned face as stark as it was beautiful, but she did not flinch beneath her husband's attack. "I have told you many times that your dalliance with that little bauble," a contemptuous flick of her fingers relegated Rowena Clayton to the periphery of their lives, "was *not* the reason for my decision then. But your *amour-propre* could accept no other explanation. Just as your overweening pride can accept no equal, even among your heirs!"

Ice yielded to fire as the duke's eyes blazed at her. "Is it *my* fault that my sons have no patience?" he demanded. "That they want to snatch the reins of power before they're capable of handling them?"

"If you had your way, they'd *never* handle them!" his wife struck back. "You'd rule from the grave if you could! I've already seen one son ruined by your controlling ways—"

"I gave Hal *everything*!"

"Except what he needed most—the chance to grow!" There was urgency as well as anger in the duchess's voice. "To make mistakes, and *learn* from them! To become his own man, not merely an extension of you!"

The familiar words lanced through Gervase, a sharp reminder of times past. Eight Christmases ago, preparing to fight for his chosen profession, he'd expressed that very desire to Sir Anthony. To be his own man—was he jeopardizing that even by being here, watching his parents fight and re-fight their old battles?

The duke's face hardened, but pain shone in his eyes. "I only wanted what was best for him—"

"Which, in your mind, was to be wholly dependent on you! And now you're making the same mistakes with another of our sons," she added, casting a half-pitying, half-dismissive glance at Jason, who flushed anew at her appraisal. "Fortunately, not all of them are as willing to dance to your piping! *Your heir*," she emphasized the words, "won't stand for your tyranny, any more than I would!"

The duke eyed said heir with disfavor; Reg returned his glare with interest. "That's because he's *your* creature! He absorbed your perversity along with your milk from the day he was born! And by God, I won't see everything I've built as Whitborough dashed to pieces by a hot-headed, self-willed fool who won't listen to my advice on even the smallest matter!"

"So instead you'll place your faith in a feckless boy with nothing in his head but what you put there yourself?" the duchess fired back.

Stalemated, the Whitboroughs locked gazes, their anger a tangible presence in the room. Oberon and Titania, Gervase thought—the fairy couple whose discord upset the whole balance of the natural world. *Ah, but who's wearing the ass's head*, an irreverent voice in his head mused.

Probably all three of us, for getting caught up in this. He glanced at his brothers, noting Jason's scowl and Reg's hard-eyed stare. Foot soldiers like himself in their parents' war... just as Margaret had said. The thought of her sent a spear of longing through him, for her sanity and sweetness—his touchstone against the madness that was his family.

Did either Reg or Jason see this situation as he did? Probably not, as each had a parent in his corner to advance his cause. While *he* was once again the forgotten son... until his parents wished to make use of him.

As if on cue, he heard his father say, "I'll see that my heir does his duty by the family and the dukedom, if it's the last thing I do!"

His mother's brows rose. "And just how do you propose to do that, my lord and master?"

"By calling upon one of the most brilliant legal minds currently in practice," the duke informed her.

"The same brilliant legal mind to which *I* have recourse?" she inquired dulcetly.

And as one, they turned towards Gervase, their eyes bright with avid speculation. A speculation that had little to do with him as a person—and all to do with how he might fit into their plans. A cog in the machinery, a piece in the game...

He felt it then, the anger stirring beneath his carefully constructed façade, the layers of indifference he'd built up to shield himself from the sting of never coming first with either of his parents. Not once had he let them see how much he'd *minded* being the son they continually overlooked; perhaps he hadn't even known that himself. And now, like a geyser, it rose steadily to the surface, all the stronger for its years of suppression: his version of the Lyons temper.

"Well, Gervase?" The duchess's voice, with its throaty Gallic lilt, caressed his ear. "You've had your fun, *mon fils*, manipulating us both. Now it's time to commit yourself, one way or the other."

"For once I agree with your mother," the duke remarked. "You've done more vacillating than Prince Hamlet, son. High time you decided where you stand—and with whom."

"I happen to like my current position, thank you," Gervase retorted. "The view is more entertaining by far."

Whitborough's brows drew together in irritation. "Damn you, boy, this isn't a game!"

"Isn't it, Father?" Gervase challenged. "For as long as I can remember that is how you and Mother have played it—as an eternal tug-of-war with your sons in the middle. The girls have no idea how fortunate they were to be spared all that."

"Stop acting so damned pious!" the duke growled. "You were willing enough to participate before, especially when you believed there was something in it for *you!*"

"Bloody typical," Reg muttered, not quite under his breath.

"Traitor!" Jason accused, for once in accord with his eldest brother.

Gervase ignored them both. "A belief that you and Mother actively encouraged, as I recall." He sketched his parents a mocking bow, no longer trying to hide the anger that surged through him. "You could always be counted on to enliven the proceedings with your seemingly inexhaustible supply of sticks and carrots! A property here, an increased allowance there, a new house, a new horse," he nodded towards his brothers. "Granted, I put more faith in the sixpence I acquired today than in any of your promises, but it was amusing to see what you'd come up with next!"

"*Amusing?*" his father sputtered, his color mounting dangerously.

"Vastly so." Gervase paused, then resumed in a voice colder than an arctic winter, "After all those years in Hal's shadow, and Reg's, and now Jason's, do you truly begrudge me my bread and circuses?"

"*Mon Dieu.*" The duchess stared at him as though seeing him for the first time; perhaps she was. "I—had not realized you were so bitter."

Gervase offered her a bleak smile. "Why does that surprise you, *Maman*? Bitterness was the one legacy you and Father shared equally among us all."

Color drained from her face as the shaft went home, and for a wonder, the duke also appeared lost for words.

"And now, at long last, you and Father want me to pick a side," Gervase went on, crossing his arms and regarding his family with cool appraisal. "Dear me, how shall I ever choose between such allies? My lady mother and a swaggering bully who rides roughshod over everyone?" He slid his gaze over to the duke. "Or my noble father and a spoiled schoolboy who expects Daddy to fight his battles for him?"

He heard Jason's outraged gasp, sensed Reg stiffening in offense, but his attention remained fixed on his parents—and theirs on him, as perhaps never before. His powerful, charismatic father, his clever, beautiful mother: continually at war with each other... and warping their children in the process.

A sudden weariness, tinged with regret, swept over him. Nothing between his parents would change, unless *they* changed—and Gervase was not sure that they could. All he could change was his own response to them.

"There was a time," he began, almost gently, "when I would have done just about anything for your notice and approval. But after nearly thirty years, the only thing either of you sees when you look at *me* is a tool to thwart the other."

Straightening to his full height, he stepped away from them—in every sense of the word. A lifetime's worth of caution and calculation rushed to the surface, urging him to reconsider his next move, his next words, but he pushed it down and held it under like the head of a drowning man. No turning back.

"A plague on both your houses. I'm done with the lot of you."

Suiting the action to the word, he left the study without a backward glance.

Chapter Seventeen

MARGARET REENTERED the ballroom to the strains of a polka—gay, sprightly, and wholly incompatible with her mood after her confrontation with Augustus. Grimacing, she sought out a quiet corner, to be alone with the thoughts circling wildly through her head.

Augustus... her little brother, who'd grown up to be the sort of man she could neither like nor admire. A cold-blooded manipulator who cared only for family pride and his own advantage. And he knew Reg's secret too: why hadn't he used it yet, to get back whatever it was he felt entitled to?

The answer came to her almost at once. Because Reg's secret was her brother's trump card: the one he'd play only after his other resources were exhausted. Margaret couldn't begin to imagine what else Augustus had up his sleeve, but she suspected she wouldn't like it above half. As it was, she could have kicked herself for betraying—even indirectly—part of the reason for her elopement with Alex. It was only a small consolation that she'd given him no more ammunition than that.

Why must I be surrounded by all these clever, unscrupulous people?

Perhaps she should have gone elsewhere for Christmas, after all. Joined her stepsons in Wales. Or decamped for Italy, the Riviera, or the south of France, as Gervase had suggested. Despite her bleak mood, she found herself smiling ruefully as she recalled his pungent observations about Christmas in Yorkshire, especially with his family in attendance. Who'd have thought that *her* family would contribute so significantly to the ensuing drama?

Margaret's smile faded. Had she been perhaps a trifle smug all these years, believing that the Carlisles were somehow above the kind of tempestuous scenes in which the Lyons family engaged? If so, she'd learned a sharp lesson this holiday, thanks to Augustus and Alicia.

A pang went through her at the thought of her sister, and she scanned the ballroom for a slender blonde in pale blue. Much to her relief, she spied Alicia among the couples romping through the polka, and while it was difficult to tell from this distance whether her sister was enjoying herself, she did not *appear* to be unhappy. And she was mingling with the other guests, rather than moping in a corner over Reg's continued neglect.

Margaret dropped her gaze, mulling over what she and now Augustus knew of Reg and what Alicia claimed to have heard. Surely her sister was mistaken about Reg having a woman in India? Perhaps in her agitation, she had misheard what he and the duke had been arguing about. Or perhaps this mysterious woman represented Reg's attempt to follow Hastings' example? Either way, the circumstances boded ill for Alicia's future happiness, which Margaret highly doubted was a priority for Reg, Whitborough, or Augustus.

She expelled a breath. There were times when she could almost *hate* men, for the power they wielded so unthinkingly, so *carelessly*, over women.

"Hullo, Margaret!" Elaine, flushed and slightly breathless, peered into the alcove. "Mind if I join you?"

"Not at all." Margaret moved aside, gesturing towards the solitary chair she'd been far too agitated to occupy herself.

Elaine sank down upon the chair with a relieved sigh. "Thanks! I simply must get off my feet for a bit." Unfurling her fan, she plied it vigorously. "Quite a party, isn't it?"

"Most eventful," Margaret agreed, trying to keep the strain out of her voice.

"I do like seeing people enjoying themselves at Christmas," Elaine went on. "Just like old times."

Not *quite* like those, Margaret thought, but she had no wish to spoil her friend's pleasure. "The guests look very happy," she agreed.

Elaine dimpled. "Especially the ones who drank the wassail! Like Lady Middleton—dancing my poor Alasdair right off his feet! And you should see Madeline—she's positively mellow! And I don't think Juliana's been without a partner all night."

"Who's that dark-haired man she's dancing with now?" Margaret asked, idly curious.

"Mr. Lovell's nephew. He's been working in France as an architect, and just returned to England. No title, but he does have expectations, or so I've heard. And he's not bad-looking, if one likes them lean and angular." Elaine's smile broadened. "Which *I* do, very much indeed!"

So do I, Margaret nearly replied but stopped herself in time. "Lean and angular" described not only Juliana's partner and Elaine's husband, but *her* lover as well. Flustered, she returned her attention to the ballroom. No sign of Gervase so far, and uneasiness gripped her.

"*Some* people are conspicuous by their absence, don't you think?"

Startled, Margaret turned to find Elaine regarding her with disconcertingly shrewd hazel eyes—the duchess's eyes. "The ballroom still looks quite full to me," she temporized.

"Well, I don't see my parents or my brothers anywhere," Elaine observed. "And their being gone at the same time... tends not to augur well."

"True enough." Margaret hoped Gervase had been exaggerating about the possibility of bloodshed, but one could never tell—especially with *those* particular members of his family. The duke and all three of his sons, and if the duchess were also involved...

"Oh, there's Gervase!" Elaine exclaimed, relaxing visibly.

Margaret followed her gaze, and relaxed as well when she spotted him, skirting the dancers but otherwise moving with swift purpose through the crowd. He paused, his gaze sweeping the room, and she felt the jolt within her very bones when their eyes met, his glittering with an almost feverish brightness. *Dear God, what had happened?*

REACTION DID NOT HIT until Gervase had almost reached the ballroom, the strains of the polka cacophonous in his ears. Without warning, his hands began to shake, a subtle tremor that he combatted by shoving them in his trousers pockets. Closing his eyes, he silently recited the names and reigns of the English monarchs, as he'd done at school to quell his nerves before an examination. Leaning against the wall also helped, projecting the illusion of nonchalance and taking the weight off his knees, which were threatening to follow his hands' example.

He made it through the Plantagenets, then opened his eyes and forced himself upright, pushing down the turmoil that threatened to resurface when he remembered the scene he'd just left. The world would *not* end because he'd taken a stand—a stand he should have taken long ago! His parents would always be his parents, but he would no longer be their puppet. He'd left his past behind him, in his father's study, and his future... waited for him in the ballroom.

Margaret. The thought of her was like a beacon, illuminating everything warm, good, and *sane*. He passed through the doorway with a firm step, his hands now steady at his sides.

The dancers were still engaged in the polka. He paid them only cursory interest as he navigated the ballroom floor, seeking, seeking...

There. The emerald-green of her gown glowed against the pale walls, as vibrant—and as welcome—as an oasis in the desert. He set his course for the alcove where she was standing, her dark eyes gazing directly into his, a faint pucker of worry between her brows. *Ah, my love.*

He quickened his pace, saw on approaching that she was not alone; Elaine was sitting in the alcove's one chair. Assuming his customary cool façade took longer than usual—for once, he actually *felt* how much of a façade it was. Fortunately, his sister did not appear to notice.

"There you are, Ger!" she greeted him with a smile. "We were wondering where you'd got to. Have you seen our parents—or our brothers?"

Oh, God. He took a breath before replying, aware that Margaret was watching him intently. "Rather more of them than I care to, if you want the honest truth."

Elaine's bright expression clouded. "Oh, dear! A row?"

"*Birds in their little nests agree,*" Gervase quoted piously. "*And 'tis a shameful sight / When children of one family / Fall out and chide and fight.*" He added in his normal tone, "I'd stay well away from this, Lainey. Matters were bad enough when I arrived, and they hadn't improved by the time I left."

"I suppose it was too much to hope for, that the Christmas truce would last," Elaine said resignedly. "Couldn't we—no, I suppose not," she amended, sighing.

"Try not to fret about it," he advised gently. "The peacemaker's lot tends to be a thankless one." Glancing around, he saw his brother in law, flushed and panting from some unknown exertion, staggering towards them. "Here's Alasdair. Let him fetch you some supper."

"Poor lamb!" she exclaimed, caught between sympathy and laughter. "From the looks of it, I should be fetching *him* a doctor! Pray excuse me." Leaving her chair, she hurried out of the alcove to meet her husband.

Margaret turned to Gervase. "How was it, really?" she asked, her voice low and urgent.

"No bloodshed, except of the metaphorical kind." But he could feel the tensions from that last encounter rippling through him, knew that for all his resolve he was still perilously close to the edge. He needed—*they* needed—to escape, to find some place where they could truly be alone together. "I'll tell you more, but in private.

Shall we try the conservatory, after all? I'd be... glad of the quiet."

"So would I," she confessed. "Plants and moonlight sound very soothing, especially after the last hour or so!"

He summoned a smile, just for her. "I couldn't agree more. Let's go."

STEPPING INTO THE WARM, scented air of the conservatory was like stepping into a comforting embrace. Margaret closed her eyes and inhaled the mingled fragrance of citrus and jasmine, letting it soothe her frayed nerves and troubled thoughts.

"It's like entering another world," she murmured, half to herself. "An indoor garden."

"*Who loves a garden loves a greenhouse too*," Gervase quoted. "A pity to disturb it."

Hearing the strain in his voice, she opened her eyes and studied him with concern. Back in the ballroom, she'd noticed how *brittle* he'd seemed, his movements almost crackling with nervous energy, his eyes overbright. She could not recall ever seeing him like that; for as long as she'd known him, he'd prided himself on his cool composure. Whatever had happened tonight, with his family, must have shaken him to the core.

"Gervase, what happened with—"

"How did your conversation with Augustus go?"

They spoke at the same time, paused awkwardly, then Gervase turned his hand palm-up. "After you, *belle amie*."

Margaret sighed. "I'd just as soon not talk about it at present, if you don't mind. All I can say is... I feel as though I never really knew him. We're strangers to each other—perhaps we always were. He's full of anger and resentment, most of it directed at your father. On *our* father's behalf," she explained, as Gervase's brows rose in astonishment. "For all the times your father supposedly got the best of him. So anything Augustus can do to cause trouble for Whitborough..." She shook her head. "Please don't ask me to explain what I can barely understand myself."

"While I, on the other hand, understand all too

well," Gervase observed wryly. "Holding grudges being another sterling quality of the Lyons family."

She touched his arm, felt the muscles harden beneath her fingers. "What happened, Gervase?"

"About what you'd expect, with my father and brothers involved. Threats, insults, all manner of abuse... and then my mother showed up."

"Oh, God."

"Needless to say, things instantly went from bad to worse." He paused, then exhaled slowly. "I've heard my parents quarrel before, fling the same accusations at each other over the years, but before God, it never felt as visceral... or as *vicious* as it did tonight. Not to me."

He fell silent again. The moonlight shining through the conservatory's glass walls illuminated the strain on his face, the skin stretched taut over the sharp, strong bones. *Pushed to the limit*... and her heart ached for him.

"As you can no doubt imagine," Gervase resumed at last, "no one escaped unscathed. And in the end, it came down to my mother and Reg on one side, my father and Jason on the other, demanding that I choose between them... and I walked away."

She stared at him. "You did *what*?"

"I walked away," he repeated more strongly, and in his voice was wonder, along with a growing conviction. "From both of them. Because you were right all along. God help them, they'll never change, and I've wasted enough of my life hoping for the impossible from them. It was past time for the games—*this* game—to stop."

"That—can't have been easy for you," she ventured.

"It wasn't. I can't decide whether it feels more like amputating a limb—or breaking a chain. The latter, I think." He paused, then said softly, "*For what shall it profit a man, if he shall gain the whole world, and lose his own soul?* It took me a long time to see that, but I did, finally. Nothing my parents could offer me would be worth the loss of... what I've already gained."

Relief swept through her, so intense her knees nearly buckled. "That's all I ever wanted for you, Gervase—to realize your own worth!" she exclaimed, catching his hands in hers.

He gripped them almost convulsively, the grey fatigue ebbing from his face, light kindling in his eyes. Life on its way back. "I might never have understood—if *you* hadn't shown me everything I stood to lose."

"You'd have figured it out, eventually," she began, but Gervase shook his head.

"I think I was too close to see it clearly," he confessed. "To realize how trapped I was by the past. But I'm done with looking back. It's the future that matters now. And I hope very much—that you will be part of that future." He raised her hands to his lips, kissed them both in turn, gazing at her all the while. "*Ma belle Marguerite*. My pearl beyond price. Will you do me the great honor of becoming my wife?"

MARGARET CAUGHT HER BREATH, taken aback not only by his words but by his face—open, unguarded, and more vulnerable than she'd ever seen it. And the tenderness in his eyes that she knew was all for her. Panic rose to the surface, writhing and clawing like a trapped animal. *Too soon, too soon*, something inside of her keened, followed by the mocking echo of Alicia's voice: *Don't marry him, take him for your lover instead.* "Gervase, I don't know what to say—"

His lips curved in a very faint smile. "How about 'yes'?"

She shook her head, dazed. "I can't…" Then, as some of his hopeful anticipation dimmed, she amended hastily, "This is so sudden! I never expected this, or anything like it."

"Never?" His brows arched. "Did you not consider the possibility, even once?"

Margaret dropped her gaze, reminded forcibly of a cameo brooch and all it signified. "Briefly, perhaps," she admitted to the floor. "But all this came on us—on *me*, anyway—unawares. How can we be sure that we're even suited to be married?"

"We've known each other all our lives, Margaret," he pointed out. "Shouldn't we have some idea by now, of how we'd deal together?"

"As friends and companions, yes, but we've been lovers for only a few days!"

"Wouldn't you agree that friendship and companionship are as vital to a good marriage as desire?" he countered. "Although I think we've proven that there's no lack of *that*, either."

"I've just started to get used to our—new arrangement! It's not as if I were particularly experienced in this. *You*, on the other hand—" she broke off, realizing how unfair that sounded.

Gervase flushed slightly, but his gaze did not waver. "I won't deny that there have been other women in my life. But I have never been a rake, nor would I be an unfaithful husband. I have seen for myself how much pain infidelity can cause."

He was speaking of his parents, Margaret realized and felt about two inches high. "I don't doubt that you'd be true to your marriage vows. But I—I cannot promise you children..."

His expression softened. "I understand, and I am sorry, mainly for your sake because I know you'd make an excellent mother. But I would rather have you as my wife and remain childless than marry and have a dozen children with someone else."

Her eyes stung. "You say that now, but what if—"

"I am not wholly convinced that *I* would excel at fatherhood," Gervase interrupted. "Consider the example I've had, after all. But your stepsons would always be welcome in our home, and if, by some miracle, we *were* to have a child, I would do my—doubtless imperfect— best with him or her." He paused, his eyes intent on her face, then spoke with such gentleness it almost undid her completely. "*Belle amie*, what is this about, really?"

She blinked back tears. "Can we not go on as we are —at least for a while longer?"

"Is it that you wish to be courted?" He gave her a faint smile, though his eyes still held concern. "I promise you'll have all the time you need to grow accustomed to the idea."

"I don't know that I could *ever* grow accustomed to the idea!" she burst out, swiping furiously at her eyes. "Not after—after everything that's happened."

His gaze sharpened. "Is this about Bellamy?"

All pretense dropped away like a discarded cloak, leaving her defenseless against the chill of remembered grief. "In part," she conceded. "But... it's about Hal too."

His face changed, almost imperceptibly, at his brother's name, but he waited for her to continue.

Margaret made herself go on. "I—have been married only once. But seeing my betrothed and then my husband buried... was like being widowed twice. I pledged my life to both of them, and they *died!* Long before their time, when they still had everything to live for!" She looked away, unable to bear the sympathy in Gervase's eyes. "Call me superstitious, call me a coward, but I don't know that I could endure that sort of pain again!"

Her voice broke on the last words, and she pressed a hand to her mouth, fighting desperately for composure. After a moment, she felt Gervase's arm encircle her shoulders, almost tentatively—and her mind flashed back to four nights ago, in the gallery, when he'd comforted her in the same way, but she dared not respond as she had then. Resisting the temptation to turn into his embrace, she held herself stiffly aloof. "And you needn't tell me that my response isn't rational. I know that. It is simply—the way that I feel."

His breath stirred her hair as he pressed a light kiss to the top of her head. "You've known more than your share of loss, *ma mie*. I don't dismiss it."

Margaret closed her eyes, fighting the too-easy urge to yield to him. "Then... I hope you can understand why I cannot give you the answer you want."

"Not now?" he queried. "Or not ever?"

"Gervase—"

"Do you regret marrying Bellamy?"

Her eyes flew open. "Of course not!"

"Would you not say that the happiness you shared during your marriage was worth the risk?" he continued. "And would you do it again, given the choice?"

Gentle, but relentless. And seeing every counterargument there was. The disadvantages of arguing with a lawyer. Unable to deny his words, unwilling to admit their truth, she remained silent, refusing to meet his gaze. A deeper worry gnawed at her heart: after nearly two years of widowhood, was she still unable to see herself as anyone but Alex's wife?

Gervase's arm dropped away from her shoulders, and he stepped back. "*This world uncertain is.*" His voice was still impossibly soft. "Not even the most devoted couple can promise each other not to die someday. All they can do is fill the time between with precious moments and memories of a life well-lived—together." He paused, then she felt his finger glide beneath her chin, turning her face towards his. "You are the one woman with whom I wish to build such a life. To share the joys and even the sorrows, though God willing there won't be many of those. An affair—even one as delightful as ours has been—would not be enough, *ma belle*. Not with you. I wish to give you all that I have, not merely the parts that are convenient."

This time, she did not try to hide her tears. "I'm sorry, Gervase! I understand what you're saying—I do— but I can't help how I feel! And if I must give you an answer now—"

"Don't, then," he cut in, almost brusquely.

Margaret gulped, wiping futilely at her cheeks. "What?"

"Don't answer me tonight." He reached into his coat pocket, handed her a handkerchief. "Give it some time— give us *both* time—before you decide. And in the meantime, I shall wait."

She blotted her cheeks, balled the handkerchief in her fist, resenting her lack of control. "That hardly seems fair, when I can't promise you that my answer will change."

His face, so open and expressive a moment before, had become an impassive mask, and her heart ached at the knowledge that she'd hurt him. "I believe that is *my* risk to take. Now, do you wish to return to the ballroom, or would you prefer to retire for the night?"

She swallowed the tears clogging her throat. "The latter. And... alone, if you please. Forgive me, Gervase, but—I think, perhaps, we need some time apart. I'll see myself upstairs," she added, before he could offer his arm.

He stilled, then inclined his head. "Very well. I bid you goodnight then."

Margaret nodded as she turned away, trying not to think about how alone *he* looked at that moment: a lean, upright figure sharply limned by winter moonlight, standing in the middle of the deserted conservatory. "Goodnight, Gervase."

She had just reached the door when he spoke again.

"Happy Christmas." The valediction, no louder than a whisper, mocked them both.

Closing her ears and her heart to it, she left the conservatory and did not look back.

Chapter Eighteen

St. Stephen's Day dawned grey and overcast, a fitting counterpoint to Margaret's mood when she woke. Listlessly, she nibbled her toast and sipped her chocolate, though both tasted oddly savorless this morning. The aftereffects of too much wassail, perhaps. In the end, she pushed them both aside half-finished.

Tilda helped her into a navy-blue day dress that, on closer inspection, looked almost black in the wan morning light. Staring at her reflection, Margaret had the uncanny sense of being in mourning again, the somber hue of the dress leaching the color from her face and emphasizing the faint shadows under her eyes. With a shudder of distaste, she turned away from the mirror and asked Tilda to fetch the rouge.

Once the necessary repairs had been made, she headed downstairs. There was usually chaos on a hunt morning, with people dashing in to wolf down breakfast before hurrying outside to mount up. And today was no exception; as she approached the breakfast room, Hugo and Alasdair—both in riding dress—strode past her with only the hastiest of greetings. Outside the door, she hesitated, wondering whom she might find there. Sternly admonishing herself not to be a coward, she went in.

The man she half-longed, half-dreaded to see turned from the window as she entered, and her heart gave a painful little start. He looked well enough, if a trifle pale, in a dark green riding coat, black trousers and riding boots. Better than *she* did, Margaret thought with a faint twinge of resentment. Sleep had eluded her for most of the night; she had told herself firmly that it was *not* because she'd grown used to Gervase's presence in bed beside her. As she'd said last night, they'd been lovers for only a handful of days. Hadn't she slept alone for almost two years?

"Good morning." Did her greeting sound a touch tentative?

"Good morning. Would you care for some porridge or kedgeree?" He gestured towards the sideboard with its silver chafing dishes; as always his company manners were impeccable.

The thought of either made her slightly queasy this morning. "No, thank you. Just tea, for now." She crossed over to sit at the table, poured herself a cup from the silver service.

Gervase picked up his own cup from the window ledge, glanced without interest at its contents, then turned to set the cup down on the table. "I suspect there are several uneasy stomachs this morning, thanks to the last night's punch."

Including mine, Margaret thought, but she knew that her own malaise had little to do with wassail and everything to do with how they'd left things between them. She took a sip of tea, hoping the hot liquid would dissolve the knots in her stomach. "Gervase, about last night..."

His face grew still more expressionless at her words, and she swallowed, her eyes stinging. "I'm sorry. I never wanted to quarrel—"

"We have not quarreled." A trace of warmth crept into his voice, his eyes, though his posture remained formal. "We are friends, still. But... we both have much to think about."

She nodded, mutely accepting the olive branch. *I missed you last night*, she wanted to say, but that was hardly fair, given that it had been *her* decision that they sleep apart. A change of subject seemed in order. "So, how many of you are riding out this morning?"

"All the men, your brother included. Juliana and, much to my shock, Madeline."

"Really?" Surprise startled a laugh from her.

"She yields upon great persuasion—and partly to remind Hugo not to take foolish risks on the hunting field. Elaine is staying behind, along with Mother and Alicia."

"Very prudent, given her condition." Margaret was glad that *her* sister would not be hunting, either. Riding was not among Alicia's strengths, and Reg, as single-minded on the hunting field as he was everywhere else, would have scant time or inclination to look after her.

"Indeed. However, if *you* wish to come, there's probably still time for you to change."

Margaret shook her head; the days when she'd tried to impress Hal with her riding were far behind her. "I haven't hunted in years. Besides," she added, smiling, "I was once tactless enough to voice the hope that the fox would get away."

"Not a popular opinion with sportsmen," Gervase agreed, his mouth softening in an answering smile. "Although *I* personally have no objection to such an outcome, being less enamored of blood sports than some members of my family." He consulted his watch and retrieved his hat from the window ledge. "I should be going. The others will be gathering in the courtyard about now."

Margaret pushed her teacup away and stood up. "Let me see you off, then."

They went out together, close but not touching. Gervase made no move to offer his arm, and she did not know whether to be relieved or sorry. She kept her hands at her sides and told herself to be grateful that their friendship was intact.

The sound of dogs barking greeted them as they stepped into the courtyard. The Middletons had arrived, their hunting pinks vivid in the grey dawn, and the foxhounds milled about underfoot, a seething mass of tan, black, and white, eager to begin the chase. Unexpectedly,

Margaret felt her pulse quicken. While she was largely indifferent to the object of the hunt, she had to concede that there was a certain thrill in riding out on a crisp winter morning, with the pack in full cry.

"*My hounds are bred out of the Spartan kind,*" Gervase quoted softly.

And she smiled at him, constraint forgotten for a moment. "*I never heard so musical a discord, such sweet thunder...*"

Over the next quarter-hour, as more hunters assembled, the courtyard swarmed with riders, horses, and dogs. Margaret stood on the steps, alongside the duchess, Elaine, and Alicia, watching as the rest of the house party mounted up. She had to admit it: a Lyons man on horseback was an impressive sight, whether it was the duke—his seat as erect as a young man's—mounted on his sturdy bay, or Gervase, who had just swung himself fluidly into the saddle of a rangy dun. The feeble sunlight turned the horse's tawny coat to pale gold, a dramatic contrast to his dark mane and tail.

A short distance away, Reg sat astride his black horse, pointedly ignoring Jason perched atop his new acquisition, which was snorting and stamping in the cold. Even in the gloom, the chestnut's coat shone like molten copper. Impossible not to wonder if the frictions of last night still existed among the men, Margaret mused. Gervase must surely wonder the same. She caught his eye, saw a corner of his mouth curl up, the faintest flicker of a dimple, and he touched his riding crop to the brim of his hat in an ironic salute. The gesture warmed her, and she smiled at him, wishing him an enjoyable day in the field—even if she still hoped for the fox's escape.

The women of the family looked equally good on horseback. Juliana, as fearless as her brothers, was mounted on a lively, dapple-grey mare, while Madeline, wearing a resigned expression, was on a placid bay gelding that looked half-asleep.

Augustus rode into the courtyard now, on a red roan with a hint of fire in its eyes. Meeting Margaret's gaze, he inclined his head in a cool, slightly amused nod that made her seethe inwardly. She mustered a thin smile for form's sake, and looked away, preferring to focus on just about anything else.

Like the footmen now circulating with the stirrup-cup. Flushed with cold, their breaths clouding the wintry air, the riders eagerly quaffed the small measure of spirits, toasting to the day's success. Then, following a blast upon Sir George's horn, the hunt rode out, their horses' hooves seeming to echo on the cobblestones even after the last rider passed through the gate.

Margaret smothered a sigh, and turned back towards the house with the other women.

"ALMOST TWO HOURS and no sign of a fox yet," Hugo reported, glowering at the scarlet-clad backs of their leaders, fruitlessly combing the coverts for the desired quarry. An occasional whine or growl drifted back to them, betraying the hounds' frustration.

"Maybe they're sleeping off Christmas dinner too?" Alasdair suggested with a grin.

Hugo grunted in annoyance, but Gervase fought a smile, gazing off into the distance to conceal his amusement.

On leaving Denforth, they'd ridden south and east, deeper into hunting country. Stubbled fields stretched before them, bleached to the color of straw beneath a weak winter sun. But the current absence of snow made conditions favorable for hunting, though Gervase would have been just as content to remain at Denforth. Still, being outdoors, in the open air, might clear his head—and give Margaret the time she needed to consider his proposal.

It *wasn't* over. Until the day she replied with an unequivocal "no," he would continue to wait... and hope.

"View halloo!" The cry echoed across the field.

And to a man, Gervase observed, the hunters visibly revived, discontent yielding to excitement. The pack broke into full cry, and just like that, the chase was on, hounds, horses, and hunters surging after their long-sought quarry.

Hugo, grinning broadly, spurred his grey forward, determined to catch up with the riders at the forefront. Gervase and Alasdair followed at a more moderate speed, keeping the leaders within sight but not rushing to overtake them.

The hunters raced over the fields, the most daring of them leaping hedges and fences with reckless abandon. Gervase wasn't in the least surprised to note Reg among their number and their father not too far behind him. The duke had been a tireless hunter in his youth, and even now gave a good accounting of himself in the field, not even regretting his aches the following day. Gervase's sisters were also visible: Juliana further in front than Madeline, but both women successfully keeping up with the pack.

A tall chestnut thundered past at a full-out gallop, its rider lurching in the saddle like a sack of laundry. With a start, Gervase recognized his younger brother, face taut with strain, lips drawn back over clenched teeth as he clutched the reins.

"By God!" Alasdair panted. "That's a spirited beast!"

Perhaps a little *too* spirited, Gervase thought with growing alarm. While his father and Reg preferred to be out in front and had established their dominance in the field years ago, Jason was comparatively new to hunting. Granted, he might have improved markedly as a horseman since Gervase had last seen him, but even so...

He urged the dun onward, following in Jason's wake. Despite the current hostility between them, he did *not* want the whelp to break his neck.

The dun's long legs soon closed the distance between them, but the chestnut continued his headlong rush, determined to overtake the leaders. Other hunters galloped past them, sparing not a glance for the white-faced youth struggling vainly to control his mount.

"Jason, pull up!" Gervase shouted as he pulled alongside his brother at last.

"I—can't!" The wind tore away the gasped reply.

Gritting his teeth, Gervase kneed the dun forward and again caught up with Jason... just as a hedge loomed up before them.

Gervase swore as he saw the chestnut's muscles bunch and gather in readiness for the leap. And just at that moment, Jason lost his grip on the reins, lunging frantically for them as the chestnut rose into the air. The dun, only half-a-stride behind, took off as well, soaring up and up... and Gervase leaned over, grasped a handful of cloth, hauling his brother back into the saddle with a wrench that made the muscles in his shoulder scream in protest.

Winded, Jason collapsed onto the chestnut's neck as they came down, but before Gervase could right his own balance, something rammed into *his* horse's side. The dun staggered, fighting to regain his footing, and Gervase felt himself falling, the unforgiving ground rushing up to meet him.

ST. STEPHEN'S Day was also Boxing Day, and the duchess, every inch the gracious chatelaine, presented servants and tradesmen with gift boxes, inviting the latter inside for cups of mulled cider. If last night's scene had disturbed her—and Margaret couldn't imagine that it hadn't—no sign of anxiety or strain showed on that still-beautiful face.

The last tradesman had just left the Great Hall, when Margaret heard the sound of voices coming from outside, accompanied by the clatter of horses' hooves.

"It sounds like they're back," Elaine observed with surprise. "But it's barely noon..."

The duchess frowned, half-rising from her chair, when the front door burst open, and the entrance hall filled with noises: a housemaid's shriek, a startled exclamation from Lydgate, and the heavy tromp of booted feet.

The duke's voice rang out imperatively over the tumult, "Fetch a doctor at once!" Then, even more loudly, "Helene!"

But Her Grace was already in motion, her skirts billowing behind her as she made for the doorway. Margaret followed hurriedly, a nameless dread forming about her heart, barely aware of Alicia and Elaine at her heels.

The duchess halted so abruptly that Margaret almost collided with her. Peering around the older woman, she took in the sight of several grim-faced men bearing a hurdle between them. Her gaze dropped automatically to their burden... and everything inside of her—blood, breath, and heartbeat—froze.

A green coat, stained with mud or worse. Bronze-brown hair, framing a still—*too still*—face streaked with blood. So much blood.

A distant roaring filled her ears. She was dimly aware of the duke striding forward to catch his wife by the shoulders, the duchess demanding to know what had happened, her throaty voice gone shrill and strident. Of the pale, tense faces of the returned hunters. Of Juliana visibly fighting tears as she turned her face into Madeline's shoulder. But her own gaze remained fixed on the man lying motionless on the hurdle.

Open your eyes, she willed him silently. Move. Say something.

He heareth not, he stirreth not, he moveth not.

It might have been *his* voice, laced with sardonic amusement, murmuring in her ear.

The room swayed, swimming in and out of focus, and she felt her knees buckle.

"Meg!" Alicia's voice, sharper than she'd ever heard it, and then a hand closed about her arm, steadying her. Gratefully, she leaned against her sister, still not taking her eyes from her lover's limp, bloodied form. *They bore him barefaced on a bier...*

The duke's voice sliced through the fog shrouding her senses. "The doctor's been sent for." He stepped in front of the men, blocking Margaret's view of the hurdle. "Take Lord Gervase—take *my son* up to his chamber."

MARGARET STARED at the closed door, willing it to open, yet dreading what would happen once it did. Fear hung like a pall over the corridor, where the whole house party —except the children—had gathered, a fear intensified by the memory of another riding accident, another badly injured son of the house...

Despite her own distraction, Margaret noticed that Madeline and Elaine had both sought comfort in their husbands' arms, that the Whitboroughs were standing together, united—for a change—in concern for their child. Jason looked haunted, Reg grimmer than usual, and Augustus... well, if her brother felt any satisfaction over this horrific turn of events, he was at least concealing it behind a polite mask. Alicia had remained at Margaret's side, her presence an unexpected comfort.

Just then, the door opened, and a dozen pair of eyes turned towards the doctor, a lean, fair man perhaps in his forties. The family physician had retired some years ago, Margaret recalled.

"A severe concussion," Dr. Marshall reported, his somber gaze sweeping over them all. "No broken bones that I can discern, but he was badly bruised, and I have had to stitch the cut on his scalp."

Margaret's heart remembered how to beat again, and she exhaled shakily, feeling almost sick with relief. Scalp wounds—those always bled copiously, looked much worse than they were. Why hadn't she thought of that before?

"But he *will* recover, yes?" the duchess asked, her voice huskier than usual.

"Lord Gervase is young and strong. But he will need complete rest," the doctor temporized. "And peace and quiet." He paused, frowning abstractedly. "Of the most concern to me is that he has not yet regained consciousness. That often happens with a concussion, but if he does not revive within the next day or so..."

Margaret shivered, not wanting even to contemplate the possibility.

"He will," Whitborough predicted, steel in his eyes and voice. "It would take more than a knock on the head to keep a Lyons down. And from the sound of it, my son's injuries could be far worse."

"True enough," the doctor conceded. "However, I would caution everyone not to take them too lightly. Someone should be with Lord Gervase at all times—"

"Someone will be," the duchess cut in. "He will *never* be unattended."

Marshall nodded in approval. "Excellent. I've prescribed a tonic for the pain, and I'll return tomorrow to check on the patient. But if his condition should worsen before then—"

"We'll send for you at once," the duke finished. "Thank you for coming so promptly, Marshall. I'll see you out."

A collective sigh of relief shuddered through the corridor in the wake of the doctor's departure. Margaret leaned against the nearest wall, thanking God and every saint she could remember with silent fervor. Elaine swayed slightly, and Alasdair steadied her at once.

"All right, *mo chridhe?*" he asked tenderly, stroking her hair.

"I am, *now*," she assured him. "Thank goodness Ger will recover! How did he ever come to fall in the first place? He's not one for taking foolish chances on the hunting field."

"*He* isn't," Reg interposed, his voice harsh. "Unlike a certain scrub showing away on a horse he couldn't control—"

"Reginald!" the duchess said sharply, even as Jason gasped as though he'd been struck.

"It's true, *Maman*." Reg raked the boy with a contemptuous stare. "Gervase was injured trying to keep *him* from breaking his worthless neck."

"Bastard!" White-lipped, red-eyed, Jason spat at his brother, "I wish it had been *you!*"

"He should have let you fall," Reg countered stonily.

Anger surged up in Margaret like a tidal wave. "Will both of you just *stop?*" she exploded, pushing away from the wall and striding into their midst.

The feuding brothers stared at her in shock. Margaret swallowed and lifted her chin defiantly, refusing to back down. Mindful of the man lying unconscious in the chamber behind them, she lowered her voice but spoke no less intensely, "Nothing is more important now than Gervase's recovery. So, keep your quarrels, your recriminations, and your petty grievances to yourselves! They have no place in a sickroom."

She could feel them *all* staring at her now, too astonished even to be offended. In other circumstances, it might have been comical. Stifling her anger, she continued more evenly, "My younger stepson suffered a concussion a few years ago, falling out of a tree, so I have some experience in tending this sort of injury." She turned to Gervase's mother. "Duchess, I would like to take the first watch, if I may."

Her Grace regarded her in thoughtful silence for a moment, then nodded decisively. "Yes, *ma chere*, I rather think you should."

❄

FOR THE FIRST time in his life, Gervase's welfare became the primary concern of his family. And he wasn't even conscious to appreciate the irony. The thought was like a knife thrust deep into Margaret's guts every time she looked at him, lying there so silent and still, his face almost as white as the bandage wound about his head.

His parents loved him, in their way. It was merely Gervase's misfortune that they expressed it so poorly, through a combination of neglect and manipulation that might have warped a weaker man. It said something for Gervase's own strength of character that he hadn't been fully twisted awry by their mistakes, that he still cared for *them* as well, although Margaret suspected there were times when he wished he didn't.

The Whitboroughs had sat with Gervase in their turn, though the vigil exacted a heavy emotional toll on them. Both had paled at the sight of him, the duke abruptly quitting the room after only fifteen minutes. The duchess stayed longer, but never spoke, sitting mutely beside her son's bed, her hand covering his. Margaret suspected that Her Grace's thoughts had flown back in time to another bedside, where Hal had succumbed to his injuries. And perhaps she was also haunted by all the things left unsaid and undone where Gervase was concerned. In less charitable moments, Margaret rather hoped so, though she could still find it in her heart to pity the woman who'd already buried two sons.

Gervase's sisters were more than willing to help. To sit with him, so Margaret could nap or take some refreshment... although she did not like to be away from him for long. Farnsworth, who almost never left his master's side, accepted her presence with equanimity, and possibly appreciation. Margaret was likewise grateful for the valet's loyalty and unshakable calm, especially as the hours dragged on with no sign of change. And as the day drew to its close, *that* became the hardest part for her to bear. Seeing his face, slack in its unconsciousness, with no glimmer of the formidable intelligence behind it.

Dawn found her sitting at his bedside again, rubbing her tired eyes and fighting back the memory of another still face on a pillow: Alex's, when all hope had been lost. But she would *not* let those fears conquer her now. Youth and strength were on Gervase's side, and by some miracle, he did not appear to have suffered internal injuries beyond the concussion.

So, why wouldn't he wake up? It had been more than half a day. Charles, by contrast, had been insensible for only a few minutes after sustaining *his* concussion.

According to Farnsworth, Gervase appeared slightly more responsive today—or at least, not as deeply unconscious. Studying her lover's still-wan face, Margaret hoped that wasn't wishful thinking on the valet's part. Strange how empty the room felt, without even a hint of its owner's personality to enliven it. The sound of his breathing, while reassuring, was less comforting than it might have been. She longed for him to wake, to say something, however acerbic. Or profane—who would have thought she'd yearn to hear Gervase swear?

She closed her eyes against the hot pressure of tears. Gervase... all the years of friendship and camaraderie that she'd taken for granted. And the things she'd just begun to discover about him: his skill as a lover; the kindness concealed behind the razor-sharp intellect and equally sharp tongue; the care and forethought he put into choosing gifts; and the deeply ingrained family loyalty that had led him to risk his life for his spoiled younger brother.

Despite her resolve, tears seeped from beneath her closed lids. She dashed them away, opened her eyes, and rose, a trifle stiffly, from her chair. This *wasn't* over. There was a battle to be waged—and won. And she would fight it with every weapon at her disposal.

Gervase's sisters had spoken to him yesterday—as had she—in low, hushed tones appropriate for a sickroom. But if Farnsworth was right, and he was trying to find his way back to them, perhaps he needed a stronger stimulus.

Engage his mind. Wondering why she hadn't thought of this sooner, she headed for the bookcase, scanning the shelf directly at eye level. Several familiar names leapt out at her, but it took no more than a split second to make her choice. Who better than the Bard to reach Gervase?

Book in hand, she returned to his bedside. "Good morning, my dear," she greeted him, not loudly but at a volume closer to normal speech. "I thought you might like to be read to. That's what I do for my stepsons when they're feeling poorly. Mind you," she added as she resumed her seat, "their tastes aren't quite as elevated as yours. I hope you appreciate being spared the latest blood-and-thunder piece from *Boys' Own*."

Margaret settled more comfortably in the chair, the volume of Shakespeare on her lap. Should it be the sonnets, or a play? The latter would be more entertaining, she decided; maybe one of the comedies, or *Hamlet*, which they both knew well. On closer inspection, however, she discovered that he'd marked his place with a faded strip of silk. Curious, she opened to that page—and choked back an almost-hysterical giggle. *Of course. What else* would *it be?*

She bent a severe gaze upon her prone lover. "Very amusing. If I didn't know any better, I might think you'd chosen that page deliberately. As it is, I hope you understand what a major concession I'll be making. *And* I reserve the right to skip the boring parts."

She turned back to the page and cleared her throat. "*Richard the Third*, Act One, Scene One. *Now is the winter of our discontent / Made glorious summer by this sun of York...*"

She read on into the morning. At one point, Farnsworth came in to check on his master, but did not appear to disapprove of what she was doing. Shortly after, he set a tray holding a pot of tea and a jar of honey on the nightstand and withdrew discreetly. Margaret gratefully partook of both; the hot, sweet liquid soothed her throat and made it easier to continue reading.

Gervase was right about the play being brilliant theater, even if the historical inaccuracies made her want to gnash her teeth. And whenever Shakespeare's villainous Richard was onstage, the scenes fairly crackled with demonic energy. She was even sorry when his schemes unraveled, and the ghosts of his victims appeared to him on the eve of Bosworth Field, predicting his defeat and enjoining him to "*despair and die.*"

"*I shall despair, there is no creature loves me. / And if I die, no soul will pity me...*"

The words, unexpectedly poignant, clogged in her

throat, and the page blurred before her eyes. She closed them, all the pent-up emotions of the last day catching up with her at once, her longing for Gervase's voice and presence a soul-deep ache.

You are *loved, Gervase. You are wanted. Come back. Come back to me.*

I love you.

The sound, when it came, was so faint that it barely registered with her at first. Until the words reached her ears, spoken haltingly and no louder than a whisper, but still intelligible.

"Nay, wherefore should they... since that I myself... find in myself no pity to myself?"

Hardly daring to hope, Margaret opened her eyes—and saw his gazing back: blue-grey as woodsmoke, unfocused as a newborn infant's, but open. Better than open, *present*. The mind that animated and informed them had returned.

She stifled a wild urge to weep. "About time you woke up."

Gervase exhaled, a jagged sigh, his brows furrowing in what must be a hellish headache. "Might... live to regret it."

Not if I have anything to say about it. "Here." Margaret reached for the bottle and spoon on the nightstand, relieved to see that her hands shook only slightly. "Tincture of willow bark—I know it tastes awful, but Dr. Marshall said it would help with the pain. He didn't want to prescribe opiates for a concussion."

Obediently, he swallowed the dose she gave him, though his mouth twisted at the taste. She poured him a glass of water, held it to his lips as he drank. Greatly daring, she brushed back the hair that fell in a disheveled shock over the white bandage. The ends were tacky with dried blood; fastidious as Gervase was, he would hate it if he knew.

"Do you remember... what happened?" she probed gently. The doctor had suggested that they ask, once Gervase was awake. Memory loss was one complication of a concussion.

He closed his eyes, frowning. "Hunt. Fell off my horse."

Margaret breathed out a relieved sigh. "Yes. You were

trying to keep Jason from losing his seat going over a jump, but another horse rammed yours on the way down." She knew the details by now, thanks to the other hunters. An image rose in her mind of Gervase falling, buffeted by hooves on the ground, trying to cover his head and face with his arms...

She swallowed, then resumed quickly, "Your head's the worst of it—fortunately, we all know how hard *that* is. And you've got some magnificent bruises—most of them hoof-shaped. Rather miraculously, nothing's broken."

"Rolled... like a jockey."

"Yes, I heard." And she thought it had shortened her life by a good ten years, but she wasn't about to tell him so.

He took a careful breath, mind working behind his closed lids. Then, "Jason..."

"He didn't fall, Gervase—you made sure of that. And he'd damned well better be grateful for it," she added tartly.

His mouth quirked up ever so slightly. "Nice to have... a partisan."

"I think it's high time you had one." She drew a shaky breath, reached for his hand. "Sorry. I don't mean to chatter—or babble. It's just... you gave us all such a scare."

"Gave... myself one too," he admitted, wincing as he opened his eyes.

"So I should think." She stroked his hair again with her free hand. "Your family's been here, you know, keeping vigil. Do you want to see any of them?"

His hand closed on hers with surprising strength. "Not... yet. Just you."

Margaret blinked stinging eyes, her heart almost too full for words. "All right." She gave his hand a gentle squeeze. "Anything else I can do for you?"

"Finish—the play?"

She gave a put-upon sigh, eliciting the faintest of smiles from the patient, and picked up the book again. "Oh, very well. If you insist."

By the time Richard had met his end, shouting for a horse, Gervase's eyes had drifted shut again, and his breathing had assumed the steadier rhythms of sleep.

But the face on the pillow, while relaxed, was no longer wholly oblivious or remote.

Smiling softly, Margaret closed the book and set it aside, before leaning forward to touch her lips to his brow.

He would live. He would recover. For now, that was enough.

That was everything.

Chapter Nineteen

Three days later

"So, the invalid is now up and about?" Madeline inquired, raising a quizzical brow as she gazed about Gervase's room, from which Gervase himself was conspicuously absent.

"The *convalescent*," Margaret emphasized the word, "decided to resume walking today." *And would not listen to a word of advice to the contrary.* At least he'd taken a cane with him.

Elaine hid a smile behind her hand. "Oh, dear. You have my sympathies. Convalescents are always hard to manage, and Lyons men more than most."

"Tell me about it," Margaret sighed.

Like most people who were seldom ill, Gervase was a difficult patient, especially after the dazed docility from the concussion wore off. She'd tried not to hover, knowing it would make him even testier, but her heart had whimpered over every wince, every sign that he was in pain. And yet another part of her had taken comfort simply in the knowledge that he was *here* to be snappish over his lingering aches, to scowl in a rare display of temper over the tonic and teas she made him drink. To be fair, he seemed angriest with himself and the current limitations of his body rather than with anyone else. But he'd grown increasingly restless and irritable in the last day or so.

Messalina brushed against her leg, meowing plaintively. The cat had somehow found her way into the room yesterday, settling herself in a purring heap beside the patient, who had given a martyred sigh, but neither ousted her from her position nor demanded her removal. He'd seemed to find stroking her soothing. Feste, much to his displeasure, was denied access to the bedchamber until Gervase was stronger; Juliana had taken charge of the kitten until then.

Elaine stooped and picked up the cat for a cuddle. "Poor Messalina! She's utterly besotted with him, you know."

She wasn't the only one, Margaret reflected with a bittersweet pang. Love had its hooks deep in *her* as well —as she'd finally acknowledged on the night of her vigil. When she'd realized she still might lose him, without even the joy of having had him—fully and completely— as her husband and her life's companion. The thought of remarrying, of opening herself anew to the potential loss and grief, still frightened her... but not as much as life without Gervase.

Distractedly, she fingered the cameo pinned to the collar of her shirtwaist. She'd donned it just this morning, but if Gervase had noticed—surely, he *must* have noticed—he hadn't said a word. Nor had he brought up the subject of his proposal, not once since he'd awakened. She told herself that he was only giving her the time he'd promised, but it was hard not to wonder—and even harder not to fear that *he'd* been the one to have a change of heart.

Her own heart ached at the possibility, the heart that she'd believed irreparably broken by Alex's death. This wasn't exactly love as she'd known it for *him*, but they were such different men. Alex had been all comfort and reassurance, while Gervase was challenge and fulfillment: a man whose physical presence made her pulse quicken, whose incisive intellect stimulated her own, who could rouse her to fury with a few well-chosen words and melt her heart like butter with one dimpled smile. And she was almost embarrassed to admit how much she desired him, even in his present condition—battered and somewhat surly. Where was he now? She hoped he wouldn't jeopardize his recovery by trying to do too much too soon.

Madeline's voice broke into her thoughts. "What a lovely brooch, Margaret! Is it new?"

Margaret roused herself quickly. "Yes, it is. A Christmas gift, from a dear friend," she added. *That* was still true, whatever else happened between her and Gervase.

"Well, that friend has excellent taste," Madeline approved.

Elaine put down the squirming Messalina, who promptly vanished under Gervase's bed, and admired the brooch in turn. "How pretty! I do love cameos—Alasdair gave me a cameo necklace for my last birthday. I'm thinking of wearing it for the wedding tomorrow."

"Tomorrow?" Margaret echoed, dumbfounded. "I thought it had been postponed, because of the accident?"

The sisters exchanged a look. "That was discussed, yes," Elaine admitted. "But since Gervase is recovering well, Papa suggested that the wedding go forward as scheduled—to give us additional reason to celebrate."

"I see." Margaret cursed the duke inwardly, along with her own preoccupation. She'd had no thought to spare these last four days for anyone but Gervase—and assumed that held true for the rest of his family. How naïve of her to think that an injured son might take precedence over His Grace's marital schemes!

Again Madeline and Elaine traded significant glances. "Margaret, I hope you're not *too* upset—at being left out of the wedding plans," the latter began. "It's just that we all knew how busy you were, taking care of Gervase."

"And thank God for that," Madeline added, more warmly than usual. "We couldn't have done without you. I suspect even Farnsworth was glad to have you in charge of the sickroom."

"Thank you," Margaret acknowledged mechanically, suspecting that Alicia had probably been relieved that she'd been too busy to interfere. "I appreciate all the support you offered during that time, and I know Gervase does as well. He'll be sorry to have missed you."

"We'll come back later," Madeline promised. "Even Lyons men need their rest."

Margaret closed the door behind them, then leaned against it, one thought uppermost in the chaos swirling through her tired brain.

One day left to stop a wedding... how was she to manage it?

❄

GERVASE PAUSED, ostensibly to catch his breath, but really to let the aches subside. Stubborn as a mule, Margaret had declared in exasperation when he stated his intent of being up and about today. He hadn't denied her charge, though he was rather relieved she wasn't presently about to witness his efforts. He'd walked the length of the Long Gallery and back, and to his chagrin, found himself as weary as if he'd traversed the entire estate.

Braced against the wall, he contemplated the journey back to his chamber without enthusiasm. Ordinarily, he made nothing at all of the distance, but today that length of corridor stretched like a trek through the Sahara, even with a cane to help him along. Nor was he looking forward to Farnsworth's disapproval—his valet had made it clear that he sided with Margaret on this. Not to mention Margaret herself, who could not always resist the temptation to say, "I told you so"—one of his least favorite phrases in any language.

The door just down the passage opened, and Reg looked out. "Oh, it's you. Should you be out of bed?"

The note of concern in his voice, muted though it was, came as a definite surprise. "Probably not, if you ask Margaret," Gervase admitted ruefully. "But I couldn't face another day flat on my back, with nothing but the canopy or the opposite wall to look at."

Reg grunted in what might have sympathy. He himself was a terrible patient, Gervase remembered vividly; short-tempered, impatient, and forever attempting to circumvent the doctor's orders. It must run in the family.

"I was about to have a drink," his brother announced abruptly. "Care to join me?"

An invitation, from Reg? "All right," Gervase said after a moment. "Thank you."

Reg turned and went back into his room, and Gervase followed.

"So, what's the occasion?" he inquired, closing the door behind him.

"Have you not heard? My wedding is tomorrow. Postponement was considered," he added as Gervase raised a questioning brow, "but as you're making a good recovery, our father suggested that we keep to the original plan."

Gervase wondered what it said about him that he was neither surprised nor hurt by the duke's suggestion, though perhaps he should have been. "And you agreed to it?"

Reg shrugged, not quite meeting his eyes. "It's what Alicia wants." He strode over to the sideboard, where several crystal decanters stood. "Brandy or whiskey?"

"Brandy, thanks."

His brother unstopped one of the decanters and poured a measure of amber liquor into a pair of snifters. "So, come tomorrow, I shall be Reginald the married man."

The prospect did not appear to fill him with delight. Gervase had seen enough friends and acquaintances married to know that the night before a wedding tended to be a festive occasion for men. Grooms would be spirited off by friends to observe their last night of bachelorhood with stiff drinks at a pub—or rowdier entertainment elsewhere. No such revelry tonight, however... just Reg, stoically drinking by himself in his chamber.

Did that stoicism hide loneliness? Gervase thought about his own mask, carefully constructed to hide any sign of weakness or vulnerability. Perhaps he and Reg weren't so different after all.

Accepting one of the snifters, he sank down upon one of Reg's well-padded leather armchairs, thankful to be off his feet. He could not remember when he had last been in his brother's room—not since boyhood, perhaps. But now, as then, it was a study in darker hues and solidly masculine furniture, as well as being scrupulously neat and orderly, the way one imagined a soldier's room to be.

Reg took the armchair opposite, and set his glass on the table between them. "Well, shall we have a toast?"

"To..." Given his brother's somber demeanor, it seemed inapposite to toast to the wedding. "To the future," Gervase said at last, lifting his glass.

"To the future," Reg echoed, touching his glass briefly to Gervase's before tossing off a healthy swallow of brandy.

Gervase drank as well, savoring the smooth caress of the brandy. "Better than tincture of willow bark any day," he observed.

Reg's mouth crooked in what might have been a smile. "Oh, God—yes. You have my sympathy, brother." He held up his glass again. "To courage. Yours, in particular."

"Mine?"

"Saving the pup from his folly on the hunting field." He paused, then added with the air of one making a confession, "In your place, I don't know that I'd have done the same."

Gervase frowned. "You ride like a centaur, Reg. Of course you could have done it."

"Could have. I just don't know that I *would* have." Reg's mouth tightened. "God help me, I saw him struggling with that damned horse, and my first thought was that it served him right. Riding to his rescue... never occurred to me. Hell, I actually thought it might do him some good to fall."

"In ordinary circumstances, perhaps," Gervase conceded. "We took *our* share of falls over the years, didn't we? But this was a hunt—and I couldn't forget Hal."

"*I* did. Until it was almost too late." Reg took another swallow of brandy. "Jason and I—may never be on the best terms, but... this family did not need to bury another child."

"Exactly." Rare to find himself in such accord with Reg. He was reluctant to lose their present amity. "Those happened to be my thoughts as well. Jason's been thoroughly spoiled by Father, and he can be an ass at times—like most young men—but he didn't deserve to die for it."

Reg grunted, whether in agreement or amusement Gervase could not tell. "He's in a somewhat chastened mood these days. I suggest you enjoy it while it lasts. *I* plan on doing so."

"Perhaps some of it will take," Gervase suggested. Soon after he'd regained consciousness, Jason had visited, almost babbling with relief and touchingly grateful for Gervase's intervention—more the engaging boy and less the overindulged brat. Margaret, he recalled, had been quite thoroughly disarmed.

"Mm." Reg did not look overly convinced. "I'm tempted to make him an offer on that horse—it's far too strong for *him* to ride."

"That may be, but you'll undoubtedly set his back up if you put it that way," Gervase warned. "And then he'll hang on to the horse just to spite you."

"True enough," Reg conceded.

"But you still want the beast."

"Guilty, Your Honor," his brother confessed. "Do you know, when the horse first showed up at Denforth, I deluded myself into thinking that he was meant for *me*—as some sort of reward for doing what the old man wanted."

"I wondered that as well," Gervase admitted, taking another sip of brandy. "It's like Father, isn't it? To give with one hand, and take away with another. And dangle the grandest prize of all in exchange for complete obedience."

"You'd think we'd have learned better by now." Reg brooded over his glass. "And our mother's a match for him, in good ways and bad."

Gervase raised an eyebrow. It wasn't often that he heard Reg criticize their mother.

"You may have the right idea—washing your hands of them both," his brother went on. "And for what it's worth, I'm relieved that you weren't killed or maimed that day."

"Thank you. Though I find *this* tedious enough as is," Gervase added, gesturing towards the cane he'd propped against the arm of his chair.

"But necessary. Your lady wouldn't thank us for letting you overtask yourself."

Gervase eyed his brother warily. "You know, then?"

"About you and Margaret?" Reg smiled, just a little. "Hard to overlook it, especially after she took charge of the sickroom and threatened us all with bodily harm if we interfered with your recovery in any way. You mean to marry her, I trust?"

"I hope to. But I suspect it'll take some persuading on my part." He thought of the cameo he'd seen pinned to her collar, the flash of hope followed by a surge of caution. She might have chosen to wear it out of simple friendship; he did not yet dare to read anything more into it.

"Try your luck tomorrow. They say one wedding is the making of another." Reg's tone and expression had gone flat again. He lifted his glass, drained the last of the brandy, then gestured towards Gervase's own nearly-empty snifter. "Care for another?"

"Maybe a small one. Let me get the decanter." Gervase reached for his cane. "I should move around, or I'll stiffen up."

"If you're sure you can manage," Reg began, eyeing him with genuine concern.

"I'll be fine." Gervase levered himself out of the chair and made his way slowly to the sideboard. A little stiffness, but not too bad—a brief rest seemed to have eased the aches... or perhaps he was sufficiently numbed by the brandy not to feel them.

Reaching for the brandy, he noticed a photograph sitting at the end of the row of decanters. Two photographs, rather—facing each other in a silver frame: a dashing young man wearing the uniform of an army captain, and opposite him, a dark, almost exotically beautiful woman holding a dark-haired baby. Gervase studied both faces, but could not identify either.

"Second decanter from the left." Reg spoke from over his shoulder. Then he saw what Gervase was looking at, and stilled abruptly. "I meant to put this away." He picked up the photographs, stared at them as though no longer sure what to do with them.

"Were they friends of yours?" Gervase kept his voice low, even gentle.

"In a manner of speaking," his brother replied, after a moment. "Adrian Markham was a captain in my regiment. We were both stationed in India three years ago.

"He was… a good officer. And a brave man. I was honored to serve with him." To Gervase's surprise, Reg's eyes had moistened, and there was just the slightest tremor in his voice. He cleared his throat before resuming. "He died quite suddenly—a border skirmish."

"I'm sorry." Gervase had heard of the bond that could exist between fellow officers. Perhaps Reg had found "a new-sworn brother" in the army, one far more satisfactory than any of those he'd been born with. "And the other photograph is of his wife? And their child?"

Reg hesitated just a fraction too long before replying. "His wife, yes. Priya was half-caste. Her mother was a native, but well-born and very beautiful. All the same, it's not easy for a child of mixed blood, not even in India. She and Markham had known each other for years—their marriage suited them both." He cleared his throat again, turned away, still cradling the photographs to his chest. "I should like that brandy now. How about you?"

Taking the hint, Gervase picked up the decanter. Questions crowded his mind—chief among them why Reg was brooding over pictures of a dead comrade and his family on the eve of his wedding. And why Reg should have revealed this much to *him,* of all people. Their mother was usually his preferred confidant. Was it simply that Reg needed to talk? And about something that he felt more comfortable discussing with another man? Whatever the reason, Gervase found himself increasingly curious about this unexpected glimpse into his brother's past. When all was said and done, they really didn't know each other that well as adults. Their lives had diverged after Oxford: Reg vanishing into his regiment, while Gervase focused on his apprenticeship.

Returning to his chair, he poured more brandy for them both. Reg had placed the Markhams' photographs on the table before him and was still gazing at them, his expression characteristically stoic—but Gervase recognized melancholy when he saw it.

"I hope Mrs. Markham found comfort in her child at least," he ventured.

To his surprise, Reg stiffened, something flickering behind his eyes. Then he said in a voice carefully devoid of emotion. "Surya… was born almost ten months after Markham died."

Not "her father" but "Markham." Did that mean...?

Reg's next words confirmed his suspicions. "There was a lover—another childhood friend of Priya's. He died in a cholera epidemic, six weeks after she was widowed. And to complicate matters further, *he* was a native. Fortunately, Surya favors her mother.

"Priya was a good woman," Reg went on, his tone strangely gentle. "Her marriage to Markham had always been one of friendship and convenience, not passion. I do not judge her for seeking comfort elsewhere, least of all when newly bereaved."

Gervase just managed to conceal his surprise. Reg had blamed their father most bitterly for his infidelity. And yet here he was, expressing sympathy for an unfaithful wife. Granted, Markham might not have been an ideal husband. Had Reg harbored tender feelings for the lady? Gervase knew what it was to covet a woman bound to another man, a hell made even worse when that man was a friend—or brother. But, if so, why was Reg not hurt or outraged that she had turned to someone else after Markham's death? Just where did his brother fit into all this?

"There must have been a great deal of unkind gossip —and speculation," he said.

"You'd be right on both counts. Priya spent her confinement in seclusion, but that didn't stop the whispers, or," Reg's expression hardened, "the wagers about Surya's true paternity."

Enlightenment did not so much dawn as strike like a hammer blow. "*You?*"

Still tight-lipped, Reg nodded confirmation. "I called on her several times after Markham died—he'd have wanted to me look after her. I suppose it was inevitable that our names would be linked... especially after I suggested that we marry."

Gervase stared at him. "You *proposed* to her? Even though—"

"Even though I was engaged to Alicia," Reg finished. "Yes, I did. It wouldn't have been a love match, but we were friends—and I could protect her and the child." He picked up his glass, swirled the contents around, but did not drink. "But she said that one marriage of convenience in her lifetime was enough. And if the child was a boy, she didn't want him thrust into the position of being Duke of Whitborough someday, when he'd no right to the title."

Dear God—the dukedom. Gervase pushed aside his own brandy. His head was already swimming without it, especially when he tried to envision their father's reaction to Reg jilting Alicia *and* bringing home a half-caste bride with an illegitimate child. He'd speculated before about Reg having a mistress, but this was far more disconcerting.

"Priya agreed to have me as Surya's godfather," Reg continued. "And we correspond—more frequently, now that we're both in England. She's living with her father's relations, in Cambridgeshire. They've accepted Surya—but it hasn't been easy."

"Do our parents know anything about this?"

Reg's smile was blade-thin. "I don't know about Mother, but our father's—informants are nothing if not thorough." His hand tightened around his snifter. "He thinks Surya is mine. I couldn't convince him otherwise. He's relieved that I did *not* marry her mother, but he's... prepared to be generous."

"Generous in what way?" Gervase inquired, but he suspected he already knew.

Reg stared into the depths of his glass "He's offered to help provide for Surya—to make sure she and her mother never want for anything. That she'll have the proper advantages when the time comes. Schooling, a dowry, possibly even a Season..." He looked up and Gervase saw the strain on his face, the storm of emotions in his eyes. "How could I refuse, when I know how hard it will be for her—for both of them —otherwise?"

"And, in exchange, you marry Alicia tomorrow?"

Reg's silence was answer enough. Gervase reached for his glass and drank some brandy after all, remembering the Duke's promises to *him* regarding Margaret's stepsons.

"Wishing to help a comrade's widow and her child is certainly commendable," he said finally. "But you don't lack other resources, Reg—and Mother would probably be happy to champion your goddaughter *and* Mrs. Markham. Not even the Duke of Whitborough's support is worth binding yourself in marriage to someone you do not care for." .

Reg flushed. "I never said I did not care for Alicia—"

"In the last half-hour, you've spoken more warmly of the Markhams than you have of Alicia in the last five years," Gervase pointed out. "You were prepared to break your betrothal for Mrs. Markham, despite not being in love with *her* either."

"With our parents' example before us, *you're* recommending marriage for love?"

"*I* wouldn't marry without it," Gervase retorted. "Permit me to enlighten you. I have cared for Margaret for years—through her engagement to Hal *and* her marriage to Bellamy."

Reg's gaze sharpened. "I—I never knew that..."

Gervase shrugged. "No reason you should. I did not know that she would ever return my affections or be in a position to do so. I could have married at any time, but I chose not to. Not because I was pining away, but because I knew how unfair it would be to marry a woman I did not love... as I loved Margaret. Unfair to her—and unfair to me. And now," he added softly, "it's as well that I didn't, don't you think?"

Reg said tautly, "It's not the same. No one is out there waiting for *me*."

"You can't know that for certain. And what about Alicia?" Gervase persisted. "What if there's someone out there for *her*? Someone who could give her—more than indifference? Who could actually make her happy?"

"You think that *I* would make her unhappy." It was not a question.

"I think you'd make *each other* unhappy," Gervase replied evenly. "You by not giving Alicia what she most wants, Alicia by wanting more than you can give. And in the end... I believe the guilt would eat you alive."

Reg swallowed and looked down, his hands white-knuckled about his glass. Gervase breathed out a sigh and set his own empty snifter down on the table.

"Think carefully, brother, about how you wish to live the rest of your life." Gervase rose with the aid of his cane. "Thank you for the brandy. I'll see myself out."

Chapter Twenty

※

This looks not like a nuptial.
—WILLIAM SHAKESPEARE, *Much Ado*
About Nothing, IV, i

THE CHAPEL of Denforth Castle was decked in ivy and winter roses, the latter of which must have cost a fortune. But what was that to a duke's son about to marry a duke's daughter? Even though that duke's son had no business marrying anyone at all.

From the doorway, Margaret stared stonily at the tall, broad-shouldered figure, splendid in his scarlet regimentals, standing alone before the altar. *One last chance.* Yesterday she'd tried to persuade Alicia to reconsider, or to postpone the wedding, at least. Once again, her sister had burst into tears and accused her of being jealous, and once again, Margaret had placated and soothed. They might have patched things up, but the strain was still there. And now, unless good judgment or a miracle prevailed, Alicia would become Reg's bride in an hour's time.

The groom had made himself scarce for the last day or so, but he could hide no longer. Raising her chin, Margaret stalked down the nave towards him.

He glanced briefly at her when she joined him, and she felt an unwilling twinge of pity at the sight of his face: pale as chalk, the handsome features fixed and rigid.

"Do you really mean to do this, Reg?" she asked without preamble.

A muscle twitched at the corner of his jaw. "I have no choice."

"There's *always* a choice!" she said sharply. "It's not too late to call things off—for whatever reason!"

He gave an infinitesimal shake of his head, his eyes fixed on the altar before them.

Margaret gathered up all her resolve. "If you don't put a stop to this, Reg, then *I* will. By telling my sister what *you* should have told her long ago."

His gaze snapped over to her. "You gave your word!"

"I did, but that was before you and Alicia were betrothed! And before I knew you were all set to consign her to a lifetime of misery! If I'd known *then*..." With an effort, she swallowed the bitter words collecting on her tongue. Recriminations were useless. So was hindsight, for that matter. She continued more temperately, "I've never betrayed a confidence. I would prefer not to do so now—especially one of *this* magnitude—but I've exhausted every other option. Just think of what you're doing to her, Reg. What you *would* be doing to her, by going through with this."

"She'll be well-provided for, and a future duchess. And God willing, there would be children someday." Reg cleared his throat. "I am—prepared to do my duty by Alicia."

"Duty?" Margaret echoed incredulously. "If you think *that's* enough to content my sister, then you don't know her at all! Alicia *idolizes* you, just as she did when she was a child! She thinks that all she has to do to overcome your resistance is be beautiful, attentive, and affectionate. That someday you'll feel the same way she feels about you. We both know that will never happen —and *why*.

"And one other thing—I'm *not* the only one who knows your secret. Augustus has discovered it as well. And unlike me, he would feel no compunction about revealing it."

That got his attention. "Good God, why? What could he possibly hope to gain by it?"

"Among other things, vengeance against your father —for all the times he supposedly bested *our* father." She paused, remembering Augustus's diatribe on Christmas night. "He's no more in favor of this marriage than I am. I don't know what he intends, but I suspect he would like nothing more to expose you in front of your entire family—just to humiliate the duke!"

She'd thought Reg was pale before; now he resembled a walking corpse as the remaining color drained from his face.

"It's the duke, isn't it?" she breathed, the realization almost blinding in its brilliance. "*That's* why you haven't called off the wedding!"

"I don't know what you're talking about—"

"You can't bear for him to know, can you?" Margaret shook her head, wondering how she could have missed something so simple. What was it about the Duke of Whitborough that he could tie his grown sons in knots like this? "Telling him the truth might be the *one* thing that could stop this wedding—but you won't do it! Because, after all this time, in spite of *everything* you two have fought over, you still hunger for your father's approval!"

His gaze slid away from her, and she saw his throat work convulsively. "Leave me."

"Reg—"

"Get out, Margaret. Please."

WEARILY, Margaret made her way along the passage towards Alicia's chamber. She'd done all she could with regard to Reg, laid every card upon the table... only time would tell if it had made a difference. And now, she must make one final attempt to reach her sister.

The door opened, disgorging the duchess and her daughters into the passage. They greeted Margaret with smiles and assurances of Alicia's loveliness as they passed. Margaret returned their pleasantries, then, once they were out of sight, let herself into her sister's room.

Despite her ambivalence, she caught her breath. All brides were said to be beautiful, but Alicia was a walking dream in white satin and lace, a misty veil of tulle floating nearly to her knees. And on her face was a radiant smile, the smile of a bride seeing her dearest wish about to come true. A vision of loveliness to tempt any man... unless that man were Reginald Lyons.

She glanced towards the door as Margaret entered, and some of that radiance dimmed.

"You look beautiful, dearest." That at least Margaret could say with total sincerity.

"Thank you." Alicia relaxed just the slightest bit, but her eyes were wary.

Margaret steeled herself before approaching her sister. "I hoped... we might have a chance to speak privately."

"Please, Meg, I don't wish to quarrel anymore!" Alicia turned away in a rustle of satin. "I know you don't approve of this marriage, but it's what I *want*! You should be happy for me, not trying to spoil it!"

The quaver in her voice made Margaret's own eyes sting, and she resented Reg and his father all the more for what they'd forced her to do. "Alicia, you know that I'd never say *anything* to hurt you deliberately! Please, just hear me out—five minutes, that's all I ask!"

Alicia hesitated, her blue eyes filling. Then she turned to her maid, hovering discreetly in the background. "Berthe, would you leave us, please?"

The maid dropped a curtsy and left the chamber, closing the door behind her.

Margaret drew a shaky breath. "Thank you, dearest. I promise you won't regret it!"

Alicia swallowed, blinking hard. "I hope that I won't." She dabbed at her eyes with a wispy handkerchief. "Just one thing, Meg—I forgot Mama's prayer book in the dressing room. Would you get it for me? And then, I promise, I'll listen to whatever you have to say."

"Of course." Relieved, Margaret hurried into the dressing room, her mind racing as she turned over what she had to say and how she might say it.

Then she heard the door slam shut behind her, followed by the snick of a lock.

"Alicia!" She flew to the door, wrestled with the knob, wondering furiously how she could have been so stupid. "Let me out this instant!"

"I'm sorry, Meg!" Alicia's voice wavered between remorse and triumph. "But I can't let you do this! I'm marrying Reg today, and you can't stop me!"

"He won't make you happy!" Margaret shouted through the door. "He can't make *any* woman happy!"

But the sound of another door closing and the subsequent silence told her that Alicia had already flown.

❄

SOMETHING WAS WRONG. Gervase knew it the moment the bride floated down the stairs, her color too high, her eyes too bright... and her chief attendant—her only sister—nowhere in sight. And the dismay on Alicia's face when she caught sight of *him* confirmed his suspicions.

"Where is Margaret?" he asked.

Alicia did not quite meet his eyes. "She felt too unwell to come down."

"Unwell?" Gervase didn't believe that for a second. "Should we summon the doctor?"

"No, no—I meant that she *won't* come down!" Alicia amended hastily. "Meg doesn't wish to attend the wedding."

She really was the most awful liar. "Perhaps I'd better go and see which it is."

Her eyes widened. "No, please—"

"Alicia?" Langdale, sleek as a cat in impeccable morning dress, approached with his arm outstretched. "Everyone's waiting. Shall we go in?"

Alicia hesitated, glancing between her brother and Gervase. Then, resolutely, she stepped forward and laid a hand on Langdale's arm. "Yes, let's go. I can't *wait* to be married to Reg!"

They swept down the passage, Alicia's veil trailing behind them like the tail of a comet.

Instead of following, Gervase mounted the stairs as quickly as his cane would allow. Thanks to a hot bath that morning, he found it easier to move, though he doubted he was up to a footrace. Nonetheless, he crossed the Long Gallery at a speed approaching normal and was soon making his way along the passage towards Margaret's chamber.

Long before reaching the Tower Room, however, he

heard muffled pounding and a voice demanding release. From Alicia's room, he noted without surprise—and let himself in at once.

It was the work of a moment to free Margaret. Breathless and disheveled, she all but fell out of the dressing room when he opened the door.

"Gervase, thank God!" Her dark eyes showed wide and panicky. "Has the wedding begun? I must get to the chapel right away!"

"They were just about to start when I left. You mean to stop it, then?"

"I must." She thrust the combs more deeply into her slipping knot of hair, twitched her rumpled skirts straight. "Reg has no business marrying Alicia, or any woman for that matter! And if I don't speak, someone else might, and that could be ten times *worse!*"

For whatever reason, she *had* to do this—and nothing he might say would dissuade her. Recognizing this, he stepped aside. "Choose your moment carefully, *belle amie.*"

She flashed a grateful smile and hurried past him in a blur of blue satin.

Hefting his cane, Gervase followed.

Despite his lingering stiffness, he found he could keep up fairly well, lagging only a few paces behind Margaret. No telling how this would turn out in the end, what unpleasant consequences might ensue, but he meant to stay as close as she would let him. She was acting out of sisterly love and concern—he would not let her suffer for that.

Her last words echoed in his head as they passed through the Long Gallery. *No business marrying Alicia, or any woman for that matter!* Words spoken in anger and agitation—and yet... might there be a little more to them than that?

Memories of last night niggled at him: Reg drinking brandy, gazing at the Markhams' photographs, confiding in him about the child their father believed to be Reg's own. Gervase had wondered at the time how Reg had fit into his friends' unconventional union, but the picture now taking shape in his mind was drastically different from the one he'd first imagined.

Is't possible? And if it were... it went a fair way towards explaining not only this Christmas, but the last five years as well. Possibly the last fifteen. Hal had sown his wild oats—as had Gervase, on a smaller scale. He'd assumed that Reg had done so too, only more discreetly; in all that time, there'd never been so much as a whisper about his middle brother's ladyloves. Which argued extraordinary circumspection... or something else entirely.

He no longer questioned Margaret's desire to stop the wedding. Lengthening his stride, he drew almost level with her as they reached the main staircase and started down.

The trouble with a small wedding, Gervase reflected as they arrived at the ground floor, was that one couldn't depend upon pomp and circumstance to delay the proceedings. Bed-ridden as he'd been for the last few days, he had no idea how elaborate the ceremony would be, and he suspected Margaret did not know either.

The vicar's sonorous voice floated out to them as they approached the chapel. "Not by any to be entered into unadvisedly or lightly..."

Barely in time. Pausing in the doorway, Margaret glanced back at Gervase, her face showing equal amounts of relief and apprehension. He gave her an encouraging nod that drew a faint smile from her before she turned and started down the nave.

Gervase followed, letting the tip of his cane strike the floor audibly as he walked. The faces of both families turned towards the sound, their expressions ranging from surprise to mild irritation that he was making such an uncharacteristically noisy entrance. Ignoring them all, Gervase focused on the couple standing at the altar—particularly, the groom.

Reg's pallor was visible even in the shadowy, candle-lit chapel. As Gervase drew nearer, he could see the sheen of perspiration on his brother's brow: he looked as though he'd rather be facing a firing squad than marrying the woman beside him.

Their eyes met and held across the diminishing distance. *I know*, Gervase told his brother silently. *And I understand. You poor devil. It wasn't* Priya *whom you loved, was it?*

"Into this holy estate—" The vicar, who had presided over Madeline and Elaine's weddings, broke off, frowning at the new arrivals. Alicia, who'd been gazing adoringly up at Reg, now turned her head as well. Even through the veil Gervase could see the mingled dread and defiance on her face when she spied Margaret approaching.

Turning back to the altar, Alicia gestured entreatingly at the vicar, who resumed, "Into this holy estate, these two persons present come now to be joined. If any man can show just cause, why they may not be lawfully joined together, let him now speak, or else hereafter forever hold his peace."

Mere steps from the altar, Margaret prepared to speak.

"No." Half-strangled and barely audible, the voice was still recognizable as Reg's own. He cleared his throat and repeated more clearly, "No."

Shock rippled through the chapel, everyone staring at the pallid, sweating groom.

"Reg," Alicia breathed, her eyes huge and beseeching. "*Please.*"

He swallowed, looked at her with what appeared to be genuine regret. "I'm sorry, Alicia. I can't—I can't do this…"

Margaret hurried forward to steady her swaying sister. Alicia clutched at her supporting arm, but managed to remain upright, though her face was as white as her gown.

"Vicar," Gervase pitched his voice to carry over the growing murmurs of dismay and disbelief. "I think, before anything else, my brother and Lady Alicia need to talk—privately."

Shaking his head, the vicar gestured wordlessly towards the small antechamber just off the chapel. Hardly the first time a Lyons wedding had deprived the officiant of speech, Gervase reflected wryly. Reg threw him a quick, grateful glance as he guided Alicia gently towards seclusion—and the conversation they should have had years ago.

"WHAT THE HELL JUST HAPPENED?" the Duke of Whitborough demanded with a fine disregard for their present surroundings.

"Well, for a start, our son just called off his own wedding," his wife replied astringently.

His face set in obstinate lines. "Weddings can be held again."

"Not this one," Gervase spoke up firmly. "Let it go, Father."

The duke glowered at him. "Why should I? Just because your brother has cold feet—"

"It goes far beyond that, sir. It always has." Gervase paused, then added with careful deliberation, "*Formosum pastor Corydon ardebat Alexin.*"

"What the devil do you m—" His father stopped abruptly as the words sank in. No one could call the Duke of Whitborough slow; he'd been a fine scholar in his youth, with a quick ear and tongue for languages. He could hardly fail to recognize one of Virgil's most notorious opening lines, nor—ultimately—its significance.

The shepherd Corydon burned with love for the handsome Alexis.

"How very apt." Langdale remarked, his amusement as obvious as it was annoying. "I commend your gift for quotation, Lord Gervase."

Ignoring him, Gervase watched the emotions crossing his father's face in rapid succession: anger, disbelief, denial, and finally, a gradual—but by no means happy—acceptance. Harold Lyons was too worldly and experienced to bury his head in the sand, though learning such a thing about his heir must come as an unwelcome surprise to a man who placed so much importance on the continuance of his line.

Gervase could sympathize with him, but he was more concerned about Reg. This secret could cost his brother dearly, if it ever became public knowledge: his reputation, his career, even his freedom might be at stake.

"Ger's right, you know." Hugo spoke up from the pew where he and Madeline were sitting. "About Reg not... being the marrying kind."

"*You* knew?" Madeline demanded of her husband, who shrugged uncomfortably.

"You can't attend public school and *not* pick up on

that sort of thing. Not that it's completely obvious in Reg's case," he added hastily. "But one learns to recognize certain signs."

Gervase glanced at his other siblings, absorbing this revelation about their brother in stunned silence; even Jason seemed subdued. And his mother...

"Did *you* know, Helene?" the duke asked in a low voice.

The duchess gave a short, sharp sigh. "I... suspected. And in time, I think Reg came to realize as much. But we did not speak of it." She met her husband's gaze squarely. "It made no difference to me, Harold—he is my heir still. He is my son—*our* son—still, and it would be cruel to force him into a role he can never play. And this line," her golden gaze swept over her children, "will go on. It already does."

The duke exhaled, looking every day of his fifty-six years. "No word of this is to go beyond the chapel," he ordered. "I expect that promise, from *all* of you."

Murmurs of assent immediately followed—with one exception.

"You are not the head of *my* family, Whitborough," Langdale reminded him silkily. "Nor have you the legal authority to silence me." Malice sparkled in his eyes, and Gervase understood why Margaret was so disgusted with her brother. "Indeed, a number of my acquaintances would be *fascinated* to learn of today's occurrences. However... I could be persuaded to give my word—on certain conditions."

The duke favored him with a cool stare. "No doubt you could, Langdale. Well, then, we can discuss that elsewhere, at some other time."

A door opened, and they glanced toward the sound. Reg and Alicia were reentering the chapel. Margaret, who'd been sitting slightly apart from the rest of them, leaned forward in her pew, all her attention on her sister.

Alicia had folded her veil back from her face, which showed traces of tears but was otherwise composed. She walked a little ahead of her betrothed, carrying herself with a dignity befitting a duke's daughter. Reg looked drained to the point of exhaustion, yet strangely at peace, as though the weight of the world had been lifted from his shoulders.

Unexpectedly, Alicia spoke first, her voice low but clear and perfectly steady. "Reg and I... have agreed that we do not suit. I hereby release him from our engagement."

THE NOW-DESERTED CHAPEL smelled of wilting evergreens and melting beeswax—the aroma of disappointed hopes? Margaret wondered, then dismissed the fancy. It might have been the smell of relief—that a secret responsible for so much anxiety and fear had finally been exposed to the light. True, things would never be the same... but some things *might* be better, with time.

Retrieving what she'd sought, she turned to go—and encountered Gervase coming down the nave towards her.

"Mama's prayer book," she explained, holding it up. "Alicia left it in the anteroom."

"Fortunate you came back for it, then. I was hoping to find you, but I thought you might still be with your sister."

"Berthe's tending to her now. Making her eat something, and then rest."

"Will she be all right?"

If she hadn't already loved him, that would have tipped her over the edge: that, with his family undergoing yet another dramatic upheaval, he could express genuine concern for Alicia. "I think so, in time. She's had a shock, of course—it can't be easy discovering that the man you've idolized since girlhood is incapable of ever returning your affections. Mainly because his... preferences are for another sex entirely."

"For which Alicia herself is not to blame. Perhaps she can take comfort from that."

"Yes," Margaret acknowledged with a sigh. "Reg told her as much, though it might take her a while to believe it. Still, it's best that she knows, and from Reg himself. I was prepared to tell her, if he did not, but I don't know if she'd have believed me."

"Probably not," he agreed. "She locked you in the dressing room rather than hear what you were trying to say."

"Thank you for letting me out, by the way."

"I knew something was afoot when she came to the chapel without you. Even before she began making such lame excuses for your absence."

"And how is Reg?" she asked, as they left the chapel together.

"He'll be all right too, eventually. He had a long talk with our parents, trying to clear the air, and now Hugo and Alasdair are plying him with strong drink."

Margaret found it possible to smile. "The typical masculine remedy!"

"What else? He may feel worse tomorrow than he does today." Gervase paused, then resumed more seriously, "Margaret, when you ran away from Denforth five Christmases ago... I thought it was because you knew Father was hoping to arrange a match between you and Reg."

"That was part of it," she admitted. "And that was also the night I discovered his secret. That he preferred men to women. I found him and Captain Hastings together in the library."

"When you eloped, you kept all the attention on yourself," he mused. "Everyone was so busy reacting to what *you'd* done that no one thought to look to Reg for answers."

"Reg had nothing to do with my marrying Alex," Margaret pointed out. "But even if Alex hadn't been a factor, I still wouldn't have consented to your father's scheme."

"I know. I'm merely saying that your elopement made it easier for Reg to hide what he was. *Continue* to hide, I should say."

And the hiding was over now—from the family, anyway. "Did you truly never guess?"

Gervase gave her a wry smile. "I wish I could say that I did, but, no, I only put the pieces together before the ceremony. It's easy to say, in hindsight, that the signs were there. That Reg never showed any partiality for a woman, that he seemed happiest and more at ease in the company of men, but I've known men who were like that while growing up and went on to marry contentedly enough. I even thought he might have a mistress. In any case, telling our parents about his true inclinations might be the bravest thing Reg has ever done. I'll be sure to tell him so." He paused. "It can't be easy—hiding your true self from the world."

And he'd still have to, especially in England, Margaret reflected somberly. "Do you think he'll remain unmarried?"

"Who can say? He might decide to take a wife eventually, if only to do his dynastic duty. But it would be a marriage of convenience, I suspect—to a woman who expects nothing more. Unlike your sister."

"If he doesn't marry, *you* could be the duke one day."

"The same could be said of Jason," he reminded her. "But I've given up living my life according to what might happen *someday*. Life in the here and now tends to be more satisfying—and the rewards more immediate."

Ahead of them in the passage, two people emerged from the shadows. The duke and duchess, arms linked, heads close together, speaking in voices too low for anyone else to hear.

"Do you think they'll reconcile?" Margaret asked in a low voice, watching as Their Graces ascended the main staircase and vanished from sight.

Gervase shrugged. "Who knows? I've likewise given up trying to predict anything at all where my Aged Parents are concerned. Still," he added reflectively, "I think they are on better terms now than they've been in years. That's something to be thankful for, this Christmas."

Margaret nodded, thinking of everything else there was to be thankful for. Like this man standing beside her: friend, companion, and lover. With the brilliant mind he exercised freely and the generous heart he guarded from all but those he loved most: his family— and her. The man she could not do without. "They value you more now. Your parents."

"Perhaps," he conceded with a faint smile. "And I won't deny that pleases me. Although, strange as it sounds, I find I no longer mind not being his favorite. Or hers."

Margaret slipped her hand through the crook of his arm. "You're *my* favorite."

"Then what more could I ask?"

"Quite a lot, actually. And you've a better than average chance of getting it."

He raised quizzical brows. "I'm afraid I don't follow you."

She took a breath, preparing to leap the chasm between past and future. *Their* future. "You maddening, infuriating, brilliant, *stupid* man... will you marry me?"

His own breath caught, his body tensing like a wound spring. "If I said anything other than 'yes,' I would deserve the epithet of 'stupid.'"

"And heaven knows we can't have *that*," Margaret teased.

His eyes glinted as he pulled her to him. "*For God's sake, hold your tongue and let me love,*" he murmured, and proceeded to kiss her breathless.

UPSTAIRS IN HER CHAMBER, they made love with leisurely sweetness, mindful of Gervase's healing injuries. Not that those affected the quality of his performance, Margaret reflected with hazy contentment.

She traced a fading bruise with a gentle finger. "*I do love nothing in the world so well as you. Is not that strange?*"

He smiled lazily, his eyes half-lidded. "*As strange as the thing I know not.*" His hand trailed over her back in a lingering caress. "But strange or no, I can only rejoice that you do."

Margaret pillowed her head on his chest, listening to the steady beat of his heart. "Talking of rejoicing, where should we have the wedding? It seems a shame to let your family chapel go to waste."

"Convenient though that is, I think it would be bad luck to marry in a place where the last wedding failed to come off," he pointed out. "How about the Minster instead?"

"That would be lovely," she approved. "And how soon can we be married?"

"Unless you'd prefer a more fashionable time like spring or summer, as soon as I'm rid of that thrice-blasted cane! I don't want to be hobbling up the nave like the Ancient of Days!"

"A very reasonable concession," Margaret said demurely.

"To say nothing of maintaining the tradition of carrying my bride over the threshold," he added. "I flatly refuse to allow you to carry *me*."

She stifled a giggle against his chest. "Well, I don't care about being fashionable. I just want to be married to you as quickly as possible!"

His arms tightened around her. "My sentiments exactly. But let's have ourselves a splendid wedding anyway, because you deserve one."

"*We* deserve one," she corrected, snuggling closer to him. "Though our wedding could hardly fail to be splendid, with our families in attendance."

His eyes took on a reminiscent gleam. "A Whitborough-Langdale marriage at last! That should please Father—in spite of the groom being a mere younger son."

"*Mere*, forsooth!" Margaret waved a hand airily. "As far as *I'm* concerned, I'm marrying the best of the Lyons boys!"

The dimples deepened about his mouth. "*Merci du compliment, ma mie*! Although, given how your brother feels about my father, *he* might not approve of our marriage."

"Augustus has nothing to say about it, now or ever. Shall I enrage him by laying claim to Moorhaven?" she suggested. "It was originally part of *my* dowry when I was engaged to Hal."

"I understand the temptation, but let him have his victory. It matters little enough to us."

"You don't mind giving up possible shares in a silver mine?"

He shook his head. "*My* treasure happens to be above ground—and God willing, shall remain so for the next forty years at least. *For thy sweet love remembered such wealth brings—*"

"*That then I scorn to change my state with kings*," Margaret finished triumphantly, and kissed him.

Epilogue

> *Here lies a she-sun and a he-moon there,*
> *She gives the best light to his sphere,*
> *Or each is both, and all, and so*
> *They unto one another nothing owe...*
> —JOHN DONNE, *An Epithalamion on the*
> *Lady Elizabeth and Count Palatine, Being*
> *Married on St. Valentine's Day*

14 February 1889

THEY MARRIED at York Minster on St. Valentine's Day.

Margaret's gown was ivory lace over shell-pink satin, cut in the latest fashion, with a lovely train but no bustle. No tiara either, but a delicate wreath of orange-blossoms in her hair: the only coronet she wanted. She wore Gervase's cameo about her neck on a fine gold chain and carried his silver sixpence from the Christmas pudding in her left shoe—for luck.

Gervase, impossibly handsome in morning dress, waited for her at the altar. Alasdair was his best man, which worked out nicely as Elaine, along with Alicia, was Margaret's attendant. Both families were present in their entirety, along with young Earl Bellamy and his brother. To Margaret's relief, her stepsons appeared to approve of her future husband, and they had an open invitation to visit her whenever they wished.

While neither the duke nor the duchess had confirmed their reconciliation, Margaret thought that Her

Grace's continued presence in Yorkshire was an encouraging sign. Gervase refused to speculate one way or the other, reiterating that his parents were a law unto themselves.

To the relief of the bride and groom, their guests were on their best behavior, even Reg and Jason. Better still, Augustus and Whitborough had called a truce for the time being. Augustus had negotiated a fair price with Gervase's father to ensure that Moorhaven would remain part of the Carlisle family. To his credit, the duke did not seem to mind losing access to whatever lay on the property, while Augustus appeared satisfied with his triumph. Margaret only hoped it would last, and he'd feel less inclined now to perpetuate their grandfather's grudge.

Despite a hint of wistfulness in her eyes when she'd helped Margaret dress, Alicia had come to terms with the end of her betrothal to Reg and was making plans for her own future. They were polite, even cordial, towards each other now, Reg showing Alicia an almost brotherly warmth that contrasted sharply with his indifference during their engagement. Margaret hoped fervently that her sister would someday find a real love, who would appreciate everything she had to offer. Perhaps she would find him in Paris, where she planned to return in the spring.

Margaret and Gervase had decided to live in his townhouse on Half Moon Street. They might look for a country house as well, though Sandy had assured Margaret that she and her new husband would always be welcome guests at Bellamy Park. She thought they would visit from time to time when the boys were in residence. The memories of her life with Alex were forever a part of who she was, and she knew Gervase did not begrudge her those.

But today was about Gervase and herself, and her heart turned over when he looked up at her approach and smiled without even a trace of reserve or irony. Her love—and her dear friend... she smiled back and quickened her pace, wanting only to reach his side and begin their new life together.

❄

WINTER SUNLIGHT GILDED the Minster's walls and shone through its stained-glass windows, casting colored shadows over the congregation, the altar, the nave, and the approaching bride.

Gervase would always remember the sight of Margaret walking towards him through a shower of brilliant reds, blues, and greens, as though emerging from the heart of a rainbow. But nothing outshone her smile or the light in her eyes, and his non-clockwork heart thudded against his ribs when she joined him at the altar. He was surprised that his voice sounded firm and clear when they spoke their vows. Margaret's voice trembled slightly—with emotion, not uncertainty, she assured him later—but remained audible. Afterwards, he did not hesitate to pull his wife into his arms and kiss her quite thoroughly before the whole congregation.

His wife. The reality of it had yet to sink in. He barely tasted their lavish wedding breakfast, held at one of York's most splendid hotels, where they would also be spending the night before leaving for Italy the next day. Still in a daze, he accepted the congratulations and good wishes of family and friends, conscious all the while of Margaret, never more than a few feet away—laughing, blushing, radiant. More than once, their eyes met in an unspoken promise of the night to come.

Some hours later, while their guests were still making merry, they stole upstairs to the luxurious suite the hotel —appropriately named The White Rose—had provided for them.

Margaret vanished into one room with the ever-faithful Tilda to remove her wedding finery, while Farnsworth performed a similar service for his master.

Clad only in a silk dressing gown, Gervase waited for his wife to admit him to their bedchamber. Even now, the marriage still felt like a dream to him—*too flattering-sweet to be substantial.* He could almost believe that, if he opened the door, he'd find an empty room, rather than the woman he had loved and longed for since he was a stripling of nineteen.

Then he heard Margaret's voice calling to him from within, and all the joy, the certainty, he'd felt that morning at the Minster came rushing back. Entering with alacrity, he found her already in bed, her bare shoulders gleaming like pearl through the rich mahogany of her unbound hair. His sisters had given her a negligee of sheer silk in varying shades of green, but he was glad she'd dispensed with it for tonight. *He comes, and passes through sphere after sphere, / First her sheets, then her arms, then anywhere...*

Her velvety eyes scanned him from head to toe. "One of us is wearing too many clothes."

He smiled, untying the belt of his dressing gown as he approached the bed. "My apologies, *ma mie*. I shall remedy the situation at once."

"Not a bruise in sight," Margaret noted with satisfaction, as he disrobed before her.

"As you already have cause to know," he reminded her, tossing the dressing gown over a nearby chair.

"But never tire of observing." She gave him a languorous smile and stretched out her arms. "Oh, I thought this day would *never* end! Come to bed now, husband."

"As you command, wife." Gervase drew back the sheet and climbed in beside her. "*Let not this day, then, but this night be thine,*" he quoted, as he gathered her close. "*Thy day was but the eve to this, O Valentine.*"

Thank You

THANK YOU for reading *Devices & Desires,* Book One in my new historical series, **The Lyons Pride**. I hope you enjoyed it.

Would you like to know when my next book is available? You can find out by signing up for my newsletter at pamelasherwood.com. Or follow me on Twitter at twitter.com/pamela_sherwood or like my Facebook Page at facebook.com/PamelaSherwoodAuthor.

Reviews help readers find books, so I hope you will consider leaving a review at your venue of choice. I appreciate all reviews, whether positive or negative.

What's next for The Lyons Pride?

I have at least three novels and three novellas planned in this series. *The Advent of Lady Madeline* and *Devices & Desires* will be followed by Elaine and Juliana's stories, *A Bride by Michaelmas* and *Women & Wine*, respectively. I also plan to explore the Duke and Duchess of Whitborough's complicated relationship in the past and present.

Meanwhile, read on for an excerpt from *Intimate Delights*, a pair of novellas covering the last days of the Christmas house party in *Devices & Desires*! In "Epiphany"—the longer work—two clever, resourceful servants find romance while aiding and abetting a love affair between their employers.

Anything else in the works?

My first two novels, *Waltz with a Stranger* and *A Song at Twilight*, will be reissued as Blue Castle titles—with new covers and bonus material, starting in late 2019 or early 2020! These books, along with the novellas *A Scandal in Newport* and *A Wedding in Cornwall*, form *The Heiress Series*. While this quartet is now complete, several secondary characters may be getting their own stories soon...

Further details of all upcoming works will appear on my website.

Intimate Delights: Excerpt

AVAILABLE FROM BLUE CASTLE PUBLISHING

'Tis the season for romance...
Upstairs, downstairs, and in my lady's chamber!

Tilda James is an impeccable lady's maid. Simon
Farnsworth is an ideal gentleman's gentleman. Both
agree that their employers are perfect for each other and
decide to encourage their budding romance. But will an

upstairs match lead to a downstairs love affair, especially when old secrets come to light?

❄

> *"Hail, fellow, well met,*
> *All dirty and wet..."*
> —JONATHAN SWIFT, *My Lady's*
>   *Lamentation*

London, 19 December 1888

FIVE MINUTES after Tilda left the haberdasher's, the rain —a manageable drizzle up to that point—intensified with a rumble and a roar. Water cascaded from the sky as though a giant tap had been turned on.

Squinting from under her umbrella, Tilda stifled an unladylike desire to swear, even as her mind sifted through possible ways to escape the downpour. Wasn't there a bookseller's shop not far away? She'd make for that, take refuge until the rain slackened off. Grimly, she hugged her parcel closer to her chest and set off at a rapid pace.

Too rapid, perhaps, as her toe caught the uneven ridge of a paving stone and she pitched forward with a cry, losing her grip on both umbrella and parcel. But before she could crash to the ground, strong hands seized her shoulders and she felt herself caught and held against a broad chest. A broad, *masculine* chest.

"Miss James? It *is* Miss James, is it not?"

Breathless, Tilda pushed straggling hair out of her eyes, and looked up at her rescuer. Relief, along with recognition, flooded through her: Lord Gervase Lyons's valet. She'd met him over the summer, after Lady Bellamy had moved to London. Her mistress had called upon his lordship, whom she considered an old and dear friend, on several occasions. "Mr. Farnsworth?"

He nodded, steadying her on her feet. "Indeed. Are you all right?"

"Yes, thanks to you." Tilda straightened her hat brim and smiled up at him, trying not to show her embarrassment. "Sorry—I'm not usually so clumsy."

"No need to apologize." He stooped to retrieve his

fallen umbrella. "It is hard to see anything in such a downpour."

Tilda glanced about for her own umbrella, spied it lying a few feet away, still open and twirling in lazy circles on the pavement. Her parcel had landed to the left of it.

Mr. Farnsworth picked up Tilda's umbrella and gallantly held it over her, while she inspected her parcel, splashed with rain but otherwise intact. At least it hadn't landed in a puddle, which meant that its contents were likely safe enough. Sighing with relief, she wiped off the worst of the splashes. "At least I shan't have to go back to the haberdasher's! There's a bookseller's just round the corner, isn't there?"

"There is," Mr. Farnsworth confirmed, handing her back her umbrella. "Indeed, I've just come from there. But the owner had to close up shop early today—he was locking the door when I left."

"Oh, no!" Tilda exclaimed involuntarily.

"If you would like a place to wait out the storm, there's a tea room not far from here," Mr. Farnsworth suggested. "I usually take some refreshment at this time of day. Would you do me the honor of joining me, Miss James? The tea-cakes and crumpets are particularly good there."

Tilda hesitated. A bracing cup of tea and a plate of toasted teacakes sounded like heaven, especially given the wretched weather. And it had been several hours since she'd eaten.

"Unless Lady Bellamy is expecting you?"

She shook her head. "Lady Bellamy is taking tea with a friend and won't be back for some hours yet. And this is my afternoon off, as well."

"I too am at liberty. Lord Gervase is at his office, seeing to some last minute details before our departure for Yorkshire."

An ominous rumble overhead had Tilda glancing up at the sky. "Thank you for the invitation, Mr. Farnsworth," she said quickly, before she could change her mind. "I would be happy to accept."

He smiled, which did wonders for his rather solemn face, and offered his arm. After a moment's hesitation, she accepted. Looping the string of the parcel about her wrist, she let her companion lead her where he would.

LIKE MASTER, like man.

Tilda had often heard that saying during her years in service, and did not always agree with it. But in the case of Mr. Farnsworth, she had to admit that the words held true. Like his employer, the valet was every inch a gentleman.

She stole a glance at him as they walked. Tall, lean, not at all bad-looking... and younger than he first appeared, despite the white in his dark hair. No more than thirty-five at a guess. Despite the newness of their acquaintance, she felt oddly secure in his company, as though this was a man upon whom one could rely.

And whose taste in tearooms proved impeccable. The establishment to which he led her was clean, cozy, and wonderfully warm—a welcome respite from the wind and wet. Delicious aromas of tea, coffee, and hot buttered toast scented the air, and Tilda had to force herself not to inhale too deeply, lest she betray how ravenous she was.

But soon enough she and Mr. Farnsworth were seated at a quiet corner table. Tea in a squat brown teapot that reminded Tilda of her mother's, a plate of toasted teacakes and another of Welsh rarebit, arrived in short order, and they fell to with relish, sharing their provender between them. Food and drink eased any lingering constraint and before long, they were chatting comfortably together. A good thing, Tilda decided, as they, along with their employers, would be spending the Christmas holidays at the same house party. Hosted by Lord Gervase's parents, the Duke and Duchess of Whitborough.

"Have you been to Yorkshire before, Mr. Farnsworth?" she asked, dipping a corner of toast into hot, bubbling cheese.

He shook his head as he buttered a teacake. "I have never traveled so far north, Miss James. Lord Gervase has warned me about the climate, however, so I have packed for us both accordingly."

"As have I. I've never been to Yorkshire either. Lady Bellamy told me how cold it gets in winter, though she also mentioned how beautiful it can be there, when everything is covered with snow." She smiled. "I suspect she misses it now and then. We tend to receive more rain than snow in Gloucestershire."

"His lordship is somewhat less enamored of heavy snow. Although he maintains that Yorkshire is very pleasant in the spring and summer."

"According to Lady Bellamy, her family and his have been friends for years."

"Indeed. The children grew up together." He paused, as though weighing his words, then resumed a touch diffidently, "Many years ago, Lady Bellamy was betrothed to Lord Gervase's brother, the Earl of Denforth, but he died from injuries in a riding accident."

Tilda winced. "I hadn't heard *that* before. But I know she's experienced a great many losses for such a young woman."

"His lordship, too, is no stranger to sorrow." Mr. Farnsworth steepled his fingers, his eyes thoughtful. "How long have you been in Lady Bellamy's employ?"

"Three years this past autumn. She was still in mourning for her father when she engaged me." And a little more than a year later, Lady Bellamy would be wearing mourning for her husband, who succumbed to pneumonia at forty-two. Not for the first time, Tilda reflected that she'd seen her mistress in black more than in any other color.

"The late Duke of Langdale. Lord Gervase admired his scholarship."

"You were his valet then?"

He nodded. "Since the winter of '84. My uncle served his lordship's godfather, Sir Anthony Stirling, but he retired after Sir Anthony's passing. Lord Gervase inherited the house, and asked me to stay on."

"And you are content in your situation, Mr. Farnsworth?"

"I am. His lordship is a fair and generous master, although more independent in some ways than I had imagined a duke's son to be. But I have no complaint to make of him. I trust you are similarly happy in Lady Bellamy's service?"

"Oh, yes," Tilda replied with alacrity, recalling some of her previous situations. "Her ladyship is by far the easiest mistress I have served. And sweet-natured into the bargain." She smiled fondly. "It is good to see her happier and taking an interest in things again."

"Lord Bellamy's death must have come as a terrible shock to her."

"Oh, it did! I know he was quite a bit older than she, but he wasn't ancient by any means. And he was a fine gentleman, though I did not know him well. He died only a year after I joined the household." And her ladyship had been devastated, wandering white-faced and silent through the early days of her widowhood.

Mr. Farnsworth leaned forward a little, his gaze intent. "Has Lady Bellamy acquired any... admirers since coming out of mourning?"

Tilda shrugged. "A few, I daresay. There have been callers, and some gentlemen have even sent flowers. But I haven't noticed Lady Bellamy offering them any encouragement. When all's said and done, she seems to prefer Lord Gervase's company—"

She broke off, light dawning with almost painful clarity, and regarded her companion with deep suspicion. "Mr. Farnsworth, just *what* are you playing at?"

"Nothing that need alarm you, Miss James," he assured her. "I have just been thinking these past few months that his lordship would be the better for a wife. The *right* wife. And he and Lady Bellamy seem admirably suited. Would you not agree?"

Tilda hesitated. While she would never presume to offer Lady Bellamy unsolicited advice on her private life, she had sometimes thought that it would do her ladyship good to remarry. She was too warm, too affectionate, to remain uncomforted forever. And she could do far worse than Lord Gervase, who was already a friend. Tilda had noticed how her mistress's face would brighten when she received a letter from him or when he came to call on her at Bellamy House. And his lordship was courteous, clever, good-looking, and prosperous enough in his own right that he could not be considered a fortune hunter. And at twenty-eight, much closer in age to Lady Bellamy than her late husband had been.

"I... would not *disagree*," she conceded at last. "They

know each other well, and they do share similar interests. But can you be sure that Lord Gervase is in a position to marry? Or that he feels the inclination to do so?"

"His lordship's firm is doing quite well, Miss James. Indeed, he is becoming one of the most successful solicitors in London. And while he lives comfortably, he has never been one for undue extravagance. As to the latter, I have observed him in the company of other women, but I believe that he esteems Lady Bellamy above them all."

"Ah." Tilda allowed herself to relax; it was reassuring to hear that Lord Gervase was neither a spendthrift nor a roué, and that Lady Bellamy would have no rivals to contend with. The last thing her mistress needed was more heartache. "So you are thinking that we should perhaps encourage our employers to—form a closer attachment?"

"They are to spend the Christmas holidays in Yorkshire, under the same roof. I believe that propinquity might help matters along." He steepled his fingers again, his eyes—rather fine dark eyes, she observed—narrowed in thought. "A gentle nudge in the right direction might be all that's needed. So if the opportunity should present itself..."

"You believe that *we* should provide that nudge."

"Only if we deem it necessary, Miss James," he qualified. "I trust your judgment on Lady Bellamy as I would my own on his lordship. But we might do well to confer now and then on how matters progress between them during the house party."

"Mm." Tilda leaned back in her chair and engaged in some cogitation of her own. There were any number of subtle strategies a lady's maid might employ on her mistress's behalf to attract or encourage a favored suitor. Ensuring that Lady Bellamy always looked her best was the easiest, especially as she'd left off mourning and was starting to purchase clothes in hues more flattering to her rich autumnal coloring. That, and granting her sufficient privacy to spend more time in the gentleman's company. Fortunately, as a widow, Lady Bellamy had far more freedom than an unmarried girl.

Yes, Tilda could certainly help to further this budding romance, if romance it was. And if her efforts brought her into increased proximity with Lord Gervase's decidedly attractive valet... well, that was not a benefit to be dismissed either.

She looked up, ventured a smile into those dark eyes. "I agree, Mr. Farnsworth. We should definitely speak more of this, in Yorkshire."

His answering smile stirred something in her that she had not felt—or allowed herself to feel—in many years. "I shall look forward to your insights, Miss James."

The Story Behind The Story

I was in high school the first time I saw *The Lion in Winter*, staying up late one Saturday night when the local PBS station was broadcasting classic movies. For two hours, I sat spellbound as Peter O'Toole and Katharine Hepburn as warring spouses Henry II and Eleanor of Aquitaine matched wits, traded barbs, and sought to outmaneuver each other on everything from the royal succession to the allegiance of their three competitive sons. The ensemble was among the strongest I've ever seen and included several newcomers who would go on to long, successful acting careers, like Anthony Hopkins, Timothy Dalton, John Castle, and Nigel Terry. Soon after, I hunted up the play—by James Goldman—and various historical references to fill in the blanks about one of the most dysfunctional royal families ever.

While *The Lion in Winter* is very much "The Henry and Eleanor Show," I became increasingly interested in their sons on subsequent viewings, particularly the middle son Geoffrey, of whose existence I had been unaware. I knew about Richard the Lionheart and John Lackland, who both figured prominently in the legend of Robin Hood, another pet interest of mine, and went on to become kings of England. But Geoffrey II, Duke of Brittany, predeceased his parents, dying of injuries suffered in a tournament in 1186, just before his twenty-eighth birthday. To make matters more confusing, Henry II had an illegitimate son, also named Geoffrey, by one of his many mistresses. This Geoffrey was attached to the royal household and eventually maneuvered into the Church by his father for political reasons, though he apparently lacked a true vocation.

Historically, the legitimate Geoffrey was said to be well-spoken, calculating, ambitious, and ripe for any intrigue, a characterization that *The Lion in Winter* adopts. But I was struck by other nuances in Geoffrey: the intelligence, the sardonic humor, the detachment, and the hints of vulnerability under his seemingly impassive political mask. John Castle's ability to suggest pain and pique even when his character appeared most aloof and remote likewise impressed me. So when, years later, my love for *The Lion in Winter* germinated into **The Lyons Pride**, I knew whose story I would be telling first. Lord Gervase Lyons, the hero of *Devices & Desires*, owes something to both Geoffreys, though his personality most closely resembles that of the Duke of Brittany. Unlike his historical counterpart, however, Gervase eventually wins through to a happy ending.

I went further afield for my heroine, however. The historical Geoffrey was married to Constance, Duchess of Brittany, a politically arranged match that resulted in several children, including the ill-fated Prince Arthur. Constance does not appear and receives no mention in *The Lion in Winter*. I decided to go in another direction and explore the possibility of Gervase being in love with someone much more inconvenient—namely, his brother's fiancée.

Just as the Lyons family is based on the Angevin Plantagenets, so are the Carlisles modeled—albeit more loosely—on the Capets, the French ruling dynasty. Never one to overlook the advantages of matrimonial alliance, Henry II betrothed his two eldest sons, Henry the Young King (whose death is the catalyst for much of the action in *The Lion in Winter*) and Richard to French princesses, Marguerite and Alais, who were the daughters of King Louis VII, Eleanor of Aquitaine's ex-husband, by his second wife! Richard and Alais never married, though there is no evidence beyond unsubstantiated rumors to suggest that Alais eventually became his father's mistress (*The Lion in Winter* is brilliant drama but spurious history). Henry the Young King and Marguerite did marry, though they were separated and possibly estranged at the time of his death in 1183. Marguerite later married King Béla III of Hungary.

Little is known about the historical Marguerite's personality, so I could develop her counterpart, Lady Margaret Carlisle, as I chose. I have a particular fondness for sane, sensible, warm-hearted heroines, so that is what she became. A woman uniquely equipped to deal with the Lyons family's particular brand of lunacy and exactly what the hero needs: warm where he is cool, open where he is reserved, impulsive where he is deliberate, but an equal match for him in wit and intellect. A woman who, unbeknownst to her, has held his heart in her hand for the last ten years.

With those characterizations in mind, I could explore a trope that I've always enjoyed but hadn't yet used in my own romances: friends to lovers. Because I'm a firm believer that friendship is an essential component to every lasting love affair. And because the conflict arises naturally from whether or not two people have the courage to venture beyond what they already share into uncharted waters and reach for something *more*. Something that can transform their entire lives.

Steering Gervase and Margaret through the shoals of family strife, long-buried secrets, and their own complicated history to a safe harbor was profoundly satisfying for me. I hope you enjoy their story too. And given the intertwined nature of their family dynamics, expect to see them, their relations, friends, and acquaintances in future installments of **The Lyons Pride**!

Acknowledgments

WHEN YOU'RE WRITING the books of your heart, the support and input of colleagues, family, friends, and readers are invaluable. My deepest thanks to the following:

My beta readers, chief among them Angela, who read my work in smudgy longhand on college-ruled paper long before either of us knew what a beta reader *was*.

Kim Killion, who rose to the challenge of creating another holiday-themed cover that was beautiful and evocative, but dramatically different from its predecessor.

My agent, Stephany Evans, for having faith in this story from the start.

The self-publishing community, which shares its collective wisdom and experience so generously.

My family, for respecting my need to do what I do. Especially my sister, who never passes up a chance to help me spin plots.

Henry II, Eleanor of Aquitaine, and their "Devil's Brood" for leading such complicated, fascinating lives.

Everyone whose immediate response on hearing about my attempted homage to *The Lion in Winter* was "Oh, I love that movie!" You'll never know how much that helped me through the tough spots!

Anyone who's reading this book now.

Also by Pamela Sherwood

The Lyons Pride
The Advent of Lady Madeline
Devices & Desires
Twelfth Night
Epiphany
Intimate Delights (collection)
A Lyons in Winter (box set)
A Bride by Michaelmas (forthcoming)
Women & Wine (forthcoming)

The Heiress Series
Waltz with a Stranger
A Scandal in Newport
A Song at Twilight
A Wedding in Cornwall
The Heiress Brides (collection)

Short Story Collections
Awakened and Other Enchanted Tales